GOODNESS
AT THE DISMAL RIVER

Phyllis,
How bountiful is the
Goodness of God!

Lloyd Warner
2.28.2014

LLOYD WARNER

Goodness at the Dismal River

Published By:
Spizzirri Press Inc.
P.O. Box 9397 Rapid City, South Dakota, 57709
800-325-9819 • www.spizzirri.com

ISBN: 978-0-865459-922-3

CHAPTER 1
LESSONS LEARNED

The first day of summer was an exciting time at the 99 Ranch located in the Sandhills of Nebraska. The early morning sun peeked over the rolling hills, as the occupants of the ranch began to stir. The red rooster strutted out of the hen house and into the fenced enclosure. He was the first to recognize the beginning of the day.

Tag Taggat was pulling on his boots to begin his workday when he heard the rooster crowing to announce to him that the day had begun. Being the owner, he took on the responsibility to get the occupants of the main ranch house out of bed. His wife Laura had first come to the ranch as Tag's bride, but also as the ranch cook almost 25 years ago. She knew what it was like to hit the floor running. It had begun as a marriage of convenience. She had wanted a husband and a father for her son Tylor. Tag had wanted a cook. Laura learned to love Tag, but was never sure that Tag reciprocated his love. She began the morning by braiding her hair, but it wasn't long before she was ready to go to the kitchen to prepare breakfast for her family. Making up the bed, she carefully placed the revolver exactly in the center under her pillow. It was common knowledge that Laura Taggat slept with a revolver under her pillow and that she knew how to use it.

In another part of the house, TJ, the youngest son was struggling to get out of bed. TJ was home from college for the summer. He was blonde, handsome and a born athlete. He was in his last year of college and was headed for a promising career as a baseball pitcher. TJ would be the last one to breakfast.

Sharing the bedroom with TJ was his older brother Tylor. Tylor was a sharp contrast to his brother. He had black hair and dark eyes, but was not as robust as TJ. However, there was a depth to his character, unlike TJ who had a devil-may-care attitude. Laura Taggat had sent this son to the Army at the time that the nation was engaged in the Vietnam War. He had left as a serious minded, unassuming young man that had finished college in three years. He had only an internship to complete before receiving his degree. The only recognizable feature between the lad that left for the Army and the man that returned was that Tylor still stuttered.

The returning Tylor Taggat was a troubled young man. He was a gentle lad who had been troubled by the demand that as a sniper, he had killed other men. The enemy had imprisoned him and an enemy Camp Commander had mutilated his right hand. Following his escape from the prison camp, Tylor had spent almost six months in the jungle in an effort to return to his unit. During that time, he had been listed as Missing in Action.

His childhood sweetheart, Becca Barnes had given up hope of his return and was married to Harry Kurtz a few weeks after Tylor had returned home. Most puzzling to Tylor was the thought that his father did not love him. He didn't know why, but he had sensed it while just a small boy. He was unaware that Tag Taggat was his stepfather.

The last occupant of the house was Katie O'Neal. She was a dark haired, winsome Irish lass. She was making the coffee when Tag came into the kitchen. He remarked, "Morning, Katie. Did you spend the night in the kitchen? You were cleaning up from our late night snack when I went to bed."

"No, Mr. Taggat. It is just too fine of a morning to sleep late. I just love the freshness of the early morning." Katie was glad to be working for Laura this summer, with the promise that she would continue through the school year. She was seventeen and would be a senior this fall at Summit City High School. She had come to the ranch upon the

4

recommendation of Dr. Jessup. She was to help Laura during Laura's time of depression when Tylor was an MIA. She had also accompanied Laura and assisted her in nursing Tylor back to health when he was hospitalized in San Francisco. She had four younger brothers at home, so she was glad for the privacy of her own bedroom.

Laura had an insight that it was not good to have her two sons living under the same roof as Katie. This morning at breakfast, she laid down her fork. She announced, "I have too much to do to see to the welfare of my sons. Therefore, you will move out today and begin living in the bunkhouse with the rest of the men." She paused a moment. She looked to her husband. "No, Tag, I know what you are thinking, but you will remain here in the ranch house. Tylor and TJ will take their meals with the crew, with the exception of supper, which we will share as a family. Each Monday morning you will place in the laundry room the clothes you want washed. Seeing that you have no comment on the matter, it is now settled." Laura picked up her fork and continued with her breakfast. She noted the shock on the face of each of her sons, as well as the scowl on the face of Katie. Laura made a note of Katie's reaction. She thought, Katie is in love with one or both of my sons. Tag was noncommittal in his reaction, except for the fact that he would get more work out of the two, now that they will start the day with the ranch crew.

Laura continued, "Katie and I have a lot of catching up to do around the house and garden. The spring work did not take care of itself while we were away." Having finished with her breakfast, Laura took her plate to the sink. She said, "Katie, when you have finished with the breakfast cleanup, you might want to put on some old clothes. We will be going out to the Teasdale cemetery to keep it looking nice throughout the summer." Laura thought, *that is another thing that I have noticed about that girl. She is dressing each day as*

5

if it was date night!

Laura and Katie loaded one of the ranch pickups with shovels, rakes, hoes and whatever else Laura thought they might need. At about ten o'clock, Laura's face was flush, so flush that Katie thought she might be ill. She asked, "Laura, are you all right? You are extremely red in the face."

Laura wiped her brow. "Yes, but I am feeling a bit warm. Let's stop for a moment." They went back to the truck for water, sitting in the shade of the truck for a while.

Katie asked, "Why is there a cemetery way out here? There is nothing but grass all around it."

Laura replied, "Katie, the first family to live in this area was the Teasdales. There was no town, or even a county. It was probably 80 miles to where they could purchase supplies and provisions. One of the young cowboys that had helped trail the first herd to the ranch, died as a result of drowning in the Dismal River. It was at that time the cemetery was established. Did you notice the sign and the year, 1880? I had only been married to Tag for about a week, when Viola Teasdale and her daughter Claire came to the cemetery on Decoration Day. I showed an interest in the cemetery and we developed a friendship. Later, she gave me the furniture that I have in the house. Much of it was her original furniture. Today, some of those pieces are priceless antiques. She and her husband are buried over there." She pointed toward the two larger headstones that were side by side. She continued, "This cemetery is not a part of the ranch, but has a separate deed. I am the administrator of the cemetery, so I have a vested interest in its upkeep. When Decoration Day occurs, I come out and place flowers on the graves in remembrance of the deceased. That is why we are spending this morning, cleaning away the debris, so that it might always be presentable."

Katie was fascinated with the history of the cemetery. "Laura," she asked, "when you die, are you going to be buried here?"

6

"Yes, Katie, that is my desire. There is something about the Sandhills that enthralls me. This cemetery is a part of that history. This ranch has been so much a part of my life. Yes, I plan to be buried here."

"Is Mr. Taggat going to be buried beside you too, like the Teasdales?"

Laura thought a moment before answering. *Should I go into the details of why Tag will not be buried beside me? Perhaps this is the appropriate time and subject for Katie O'Neal to see the real Laura Taggat.* "No, Katie, he is not, and I will tell you why. Tag and I have a differing philosophy of life and death. Perhaps I shouldn't tell you this, but to better understand the real Laura Taggat, maybe this is what you need to know. I am overly forgiving to a point, but my forgiveness is like a teeter-totter. When it tips to the other side, I can be very judgmental and demanding. You probably have noticed that in my dealing with Tylor at times. It is common knowledge in the community that Laura Taggat sleeps with a loaded gun under her pillow at night. Have you heard that about me?"

Katie nodded, but said nothing.

Laura continued, "And, did you check it out to see if that was true?" Again Katie nodded, but this time she blushed. "The first Decoration Day, or some now call it Memorial Day, that I was on the ranch, I asked Tag if he was going to the cemetery in Madden. He said it was just another day and if the men wanted the day off, it was without pay. I had no family here. All of my ancestors are in Maine. I have maintained this cemetery since first coming here. It was while Tylor was in college, that I came to the cemetery to clean it up, as we are doing here at this time. The tombstones were toppled and cow tracks sunk into the grave sites. Tag had shut a bull in the cemetery and I was devastated! After getting my revolver from under my pillow, I was very close to killing him, but the Lord prevailed and I didn't shoot him. It was so traumatic to me that

7

I did go into a deep depression."

Laura paused, as the desecration of the cemetery flashed before her mind. Once again, she continued. "Fortunately, Jim McCann, TJ and Tylor repaired the damage and put up this sign. The cemetery is better than it has ever been. I have forgiven Tag and made peace with him. However, in my cemetery journal that night, I wrote that Tag Taggat would not be buried here. He would not be buried here because he had not shown remorse in desecrating the cemetery. He can be buried in Madden, but not here." Katie was shaken at the things that she had heard.

Laura stood up, "Well, I guess it is time to get to work. We need to get back to the house to fix Tag his dinner."

After dinner, they worked in the flowerbeds around the house. When they stopped for their afternoon tea, Katie mentioned to Laura, "Have you noticed how Tylor has trouble getting his right hand in the sleeve of his shirt? How is he going to manage when the weather turns cold?"

"Well, Katie, I guess I never paid a whole lot of attention. What is the problem?"

Katie replied, "On the western style shirts with the snaps, the cuffs flare out when they are unsnapped. With a regular shirt, or a jacket for that matter, there is not sufficient give to allow the enlarged fist to work its way through. You know, I feel uncomfortable calling it a hand. Is it appropriate to call it a fist?"

"I suppose so, seeing it resembles a fist more than a hand. Tylor seems to be able to use his thumb to his advantage and his left hand is becoming more limber. What do you suggest for enlarging the sleeve?" Laura was uncertain if there was a solution unless a tailor fitted his shirts.

Katie didn't say anything for a short time. It was as if she was pondering a solution to the problem. Suddenly, she said, "I think if I were to enlarge the cuff and then set the snaps

8

so that the sleeve would fit normally at the wrist it would work. Tylor seems to work the snaps after a fashion. I'm sure that he will certainly become more adept as time goes on."

Laura was puzzled. "What do you mean, if you were to enlarge the cuff? Can you do that?"

"Well, I am thinking I can, but, you don't have a sewing machine. I knew there was something missing. You have an easel in your bedroom, but you don't have a sewing machine. Can you sew at all?" Katie was amazed at her discovery.

Laura was flustered. She had been found out. "Of course I can sew. I sew buttons on and do some patching. Tell me Katie, are you able to sew?"

"I could if I had a sewing machine. Three-fourths of the dresses in my closet I have made myself. The rest are the ones that my mother made me. I have missed sewing since I came here. But, I have been so busy that I didn't realize it has been some time since I did any sewing. Oh well, maybe we can think of some other solution to the problem."

"Katie, if you think you can make it work, I will buy a sewing machine and put it in your room. However, I am not going to replace my easel with a sewing machine."

Katie nodded, "It may take some adjusting, but I'm sure that I can make it work. Should we try it on my mother's machine before you invest in something that you can't operate?"

"No," said Laura. "We will need Tylor here to try each change. I am willing to purchase a sewing machine, whether it works or not. As they say, nothing ventured, nothing gained. After all, if it doesn't work out, I can always use it for a plant stand. Can we buy one in Summit City?"

"Maybe you could find a good used one to get by with for a while."

"Katie, there is no such thing in a sewing machine or a husband as a good used one. Start out with the new. Do we have time to get one this afternoon?" Laura was all excited, as if it had to be done today.

"Laura, I can see that you are enthused about this, but it can wait until tomorrow. Besides, we are to fix supper for the family tonight and we don't want to keep Mr. Taggat waiting while we are sewing machine shopping. Keep in mind too, the bank will be closed by the time we close the deal. Besides sleeping with a loaded revolver under your pillow, is it true that you don't have a checking account? Do you always have to go to the bank to get money out of your safety deposit box when you need it?" Katie laughed, thinking that she had a good one on Laura.

"Katie that is one thing that you have not been able to snoop into to find out if it is true. Tomorrow morning we will go shopping for a sewing machine. Then you will see if this woman has to go to the bank to get the cash. In the meantime, be thinking of what we are going to feed the men of the family, now that we have kicked two of them out."

Tag, Tylor and TJ arrived at the ranch house, eager for their supper. Katie let them know that it would be a few minutes before the meal would be served. She had Tag's slippers ready. When he sat down in his chair in the living room, she pulled his boots off and put his slippers on. She had been to the mailbox, so she had the mail for him to go through before supper.

TJ was the first to complain about the preferential treatment that his father had received. "Katie, why are you doing this for Dad, but not for Tylor or me? Don't you think that we would like to have our boots pulled off as well?"

"Probably the primary reason is the fact that you and Tylor don't change your socks each day. There are times that I do the washing and in counting socks, I know that you two come up short each wash day. I imagine that your mother sees to it that Mr. Taggat has clean socks every morning. Now that you are responsible for seeing that we have your laundry on Monday, it will probably be even worse. When you improve, I will be glad to assist you with your boots. Incidentally, do either of you have slippers to wear? We will not have you walking around in here with your dirty socks."

Laura came to the living room and announced that supper was ready. The men started to fill their plates and pass the food around, their conversation centered on the events of the day. Katie interrupted, "I have been here for several months now, but I never hear you thank God for the food." She stopped. Being embarrassed, she said, "I'm sorry, I shouldn't have said what I did." She lowered her head and a tear started down her cheek. She wiped it with her napkin and was silent.

Silence reigned at the table. Laura was sitting next to Katie. She reached to her right and touched her hand. "Katie, as a part of this family, you have every right to say what you did. We are the ones that should be embarrassed, not you. I pray to God every day, but it is usually asking Him for something and I neglect to thank Him for His goodness, as well as the food at our table. Just because we have 400 cows on this ranch, we think that we are self-sufficient. Katie, would you like to thank God for this food?"

Katie nodded. Suppressing a sniffle, she began, "God is great, God is good, and we ask Him to bless this food. Amen."

"Thank you, Katie. And, I do thank God each day for having you in our home. Have any of us gone a day without food, other than Tylor? I rather doubt that we have even missed a meal, except by choice. Tylor, what was it like, the first time that you experienced hunger?"

"The first t-t-time was when Lionel and I had been c-c-captured. It was almost a d-d-day that we went without any f-f-food. And then, the food in the prison c-c-camp was l-l-lacking, so we were constantly s-s-suffering from hunger. The w-w-worst was when I was t-t-trying to meet up with my unit.

11

My f-f-first meal was the b-b-bird eggs. I r-r-remember after I had eaten, I apologized to God for n-n-not thanking Him for the f-f-food. Here I am, with an abundance of food and still I d-d-do not thank Him. Thank you, Katie, to b-b-bring this to our attention."

Laura spoke up. "Tag, Katie and I will be going to town in the morning. Is there anything that you want us to pick up while we are there?"

Tag abruptly said. "Stop at the veterinary clinic for some vaccine. I ordered it a few days ago, so they will know what to send home with you. We have a few of the late calves to vaccinate." Tag forked up another piece of steak and after placing it on his plate, he asked, "What are you two going to town for anyway?"

"Well, Tag," Laura said, "we really don't know until we see it, but don't worry, we will be home to fix your dinner. Then, at supper time, the three of you can view the purpose of our trip."

After washing the dishes, Laura said, "Katie, it is such a beautiful evening, I am going to see if the Dismal River is still flowing. Would you care to join me?" Katie nodded, not sure what Laura had in mind. Arriving at the river, Laura sat on the edge of the cottonwood stump. "Katie, it is good to have you with me on the ranch. For the rancher's wife, it can be lonely. The people she is in contact with day after day are usually males. We women desire some female companionship. I hope that you are happy here at the ranch."

"Oh, I am, I am," she replied. "You and Mr. Taggat have been good to me."

"Sometimes," related Laura, "I feel so inadequate in my relationship with others. I find myself being too abrasive or too shy. When I come here to this spot, I am most comfortable in the presence of my Lord. But when I am in the presence of others, I am uncomfortable in sharing what the Lord means to me. I guess," it was here that Laura was quiet. She began again, "I guess I don't want to offend them, but God has meant so much to me and the assurance of salvation through His Son, Jesus Christ, that I want them to have the peace that God grants to me. See, even now I am stumbling over what I want to say." Standing up, she hugged Katie. "Oh, Katie, I love you as a daughter that I never had. I love you." Holding Katie for a short time, Laura ran back to the house, saddened and fearful that she may have failed to convey her love to Katie.

The next morning before Tag came to breakfast, Laura and Katie discussed giving thanks for the food. It was decided that Laura would give thanks on the odd days of the month and Katie the even days. However, if one of the men were led to give thanks, then they would supersede the women on their chosen day. When Tag came to breakfast, Laura greeted him. "Tag, each meal we will give thanks to the Lord. Would you like to thank the Lord for the food this morning?"

Tag shook his head and responded, "I don't want you to ask the blessing on any of my food. Let's eat." He sat down and began to eat. Katie looked at Laura and Laura nodded. She began to put food on her plate. Katie was fearful of what Laura might say or do. There was very little conversation during the meal. Tag stood up and was out the door; ready for a day's work.

After Tag left, Katie got up to begin clearing the table. Laura said, "Just a moment, Katie. I would like to say something." Bowing her head, she began to pray. "Father, I thank you for this food which we have just consumcd. Forgive me for not thanking you before we ate, but I will honor my husband's request that we not pray over his food. Amen." Katie smiled.

After the dishes were washed and put away, Laura and Katie were ready to go to Summit City. Laura backed the car out of the garage. Once it was headed down the road, she stopped and turned to face Katie. She asked, "Do you know how to drive a car?"

Shaking her head, Katie answered, "My father has a car, but unless we go out of town, we rarely ride in it. I know very little about driving. Does asking that question mean you are willing to teach me to drive? I would love to learn to drive and then I could help Mr. Taggat on the ranch."

Laura laughed. "Katie, you were doing fine until that last sentence. That was the wrong answer. I am not teaching you to drive so that you can be driving the ranch pickup around these Sandhills. What you want is that power, but I am offering you style. Come and get behind the wheel. We will choose another day to take the pickup and drive out to the cemetery. When I learned to drive, the only vehicle was a ranch pickup, but it was not the better one that Tag drove." Laura was very patient in teaching her. They neared the outskirts of town, and Laura took over.

Driving to the Courthouse, Laura said, "Let's stop in here and see about getting you a learner's permit. Sheriff Morgan is a bit fussy about who he lets drive in his county." Their next stop was to look for a sewing machine. Laura let Katie ask the questions about the machines, while the clerk demonstrated the machines displayed.

After some time, Laura asked Katie, "Well, which one is your choice?"

Katie was uncertain, but she had heard that Laura Taggat was careful with the dollar. Cautiously she said, "The $79.00 machine is quite adequate for what we will be doing. That one is fine."

"Katie O'Neal, is that your choice, or are you trying to make me happy by choosing the lower priced machine? Isn't the $99.00 machine adequate?"

"Oh, Laura," Katie asked, "are you unhappy with me? Yes, the $99.00 machine is adequate, but it is unlikely that you will ever use it, so that is why I said that the other machine is adequate. Why buy a more expensive machine, if you won't be using it?"

"Good thinking, Girl!" Approaching the clerk, Laura said, "We will take the $99.00 machine, but we will have to go to the bank to see if that tight-fisted banker will give us the money. Don't sell it to anyone else. We will be right back." Grabbing Katie by the hand, she said, "Come on, let's go to the bank."

"Why did you say that you will take the more expensive machine if you are not going to use it?" Katie asked.

"I don't want anything cheap. I want the best. Dr. Jessup knows that. That is why he sent you my way. That machine is mine as long as you work for me. Once you leave, the machine goes with you. It is as simple as that. Here is the bank and I want you to meet Todd Holliday."

Entering the bank, they were greeted by a thin, gray haired lady. "Good morning, Mrs. Taggat. What may we help you with today?"

"Is Todd in this morning? I wanted him to meet my friend. Mrs. Stahl, this is Katie. Katie, Mrs. Stahl." Turning to Katie, she said, "This was one of the first ladies that I met when I came to Summit City. It is always a delight to see you." To Mrs. Stahl, she said, "Katie was the young lady that went with me to get Tylor and she was first rate help, too. Tylor treated us to a meal at a Chinese restaurant while we were there. Let me assure you, it was much different than dining at Nick's."

"That sounds like fun. I have never eaten Chinese food, but I hear that it is a lot of rice. Mrs. Taggat, you just missed Todd. He left early this morning to check on some cattle. Is there anything I can help you with? He won't be back until this afternoon?"

"I would like to get into my safety deposit box at this time. We are buying a sewing machine and are a bit short of cash. Katie is our seamstress, so with a new machine, we are expecting great things from her." Laura gave Mrs. Stahl a smile. She knew that Mrs. Stahl so wanted to sign her up with a checking account. It had been more than 20 years since she first tried to get Laura to have a checking account, but to no avail.

Getting the key, she went to open the box for Laura and remarked, "Well, if she is as good a seamstress as her mother, she will do a fine job. I have seen some of the work that Katie's mother has done and it is magnificent." Laura motioned for Katie to follow her.

Opening the lock that held the box for the number that Laura had given her, Mrs. Stahl handed her the box. "Just a minute, Mrs. Stahl," Laura said. "I have a key in this box that I use to open another. Would you wait until I find the key and you can retrieve that box for me as well?" Laura opened a small box located in the corner of the first box. Looking at several keys, she retrieved the one that she wanted and she handed it to Mrs. Stahl. "Number 121 is the box that I need next and that will be the last. Thank you, Mrs. Stahl." Laura placed the box, so that when she raised the lid, Katie could not peer into it. Laura pulled out some currency. After she had counted out what she wanted, she made a notation on a slip of paper. Closing the lid, she put the box back and retrieved that key from the box. She put the key in the first box and replacing that box in its designated slot in the row of boxes, she turned the key. Now that she had completed the process, she replaced the key, along with her currency in her purse. Smiling at Katie, she said, "Now we have our money for the sewing machine. And, maybe a little extra when we stop at Nick's for a morning snack. I presume that you took note of how the safety deposit box system works. Do you have a question, Katie?"

"Yes," Katie replied, "but why do you have so many boxes? Why not one large box? I presumed that you have other boxes, because you sorted through a number of keys. Why not keep those keys with you as well?" Katie was puzzled.

"Katie, dear," answered Laura, "I asked if you had a question and you proceeded to ask me three separate questions. But, I shall try to answer them in the order that you asked. I use the bank vault to protect my important papers, like a filing system. One box is for cash and another for documents. It is neater that way. Also, I need to keep track of only one Master Key."

"You probably think I ask a lot of questions," asked Katie, "but I don't understand why you don't have a checking account. Wouldn't it be simpler to write a check?"

"Oh, I am sure it would, but I like to see how much money it takes to purchase an item. What I am doing is trading my dollars for a piece of merchandise. There is a comparison in the transaction. It is difficult for me to visualize a piece of paper with some numbers on it, as compared to the actual cash. It also prevents me from making any rash decisions. That money is always available, any time the bank is open."

Returning to the store, Laura purchased the $99.00 sewing machine. "Katie," she asked, "is there anything more that you might need while we are here? Go ahead and pick those things out. I will be looking at the dresses. Come and get me when you have finished and I will settle up with the clerk. Then we will go to Nick's."

Leaving the store, Laura had Katie drive to the café. Laura remarked as they were getting out, "Your driving reminds me of the time that I was working for Maude at this very café. There was this eccentric older gentleman, by the name of Homer Crane that was having difficulty learning to drive. Driving to this café, he stepped on the gas instead of the brake and drove into the café. The nose of the car was pushing through the wall. When he realized what he had done, he backed the car to the curb and got out. Looking it over and explaining to the crowd that had gathered, he said, 'well, you

17

will probably read in *The Sentinel* that Homer Crane opened up a café in Summit City.' He got back into his car and later returned with his carpentry tools. By nightfall, he had repaired the damage. The car was skinned up a bit, but the wall was as good as new."

Entering the café, the bell at the door rang to announce their arrival. Laura said, "That is the same bell that greeted me on my first night in Summit City." Seeing Nick, she greeted him. "Good morning, Nick, this is Katie O'Neal. Katie, this is Nick. Nick learned to cook out at the 99 Ranch. He was my favorite among the crew. He always thanked me for the meal and he was always willing to help when I was overwhelmed. I will have cherry pie and coffee. What will you have, Katie?"

"Laura, is it all right if I have a bottle of pop and a doughnut?" Katie asked hesitantly.

"Certainly," affirmed Laura, "just order what you want. It doesn't have to please me."

"Katie has been helping me since that time I ended up in Timmy Holler's cow pasture. Dr. Jessup's orders were that I needed help and I haven't been back to him to have the orders rescinded. I enjoy having her with me."

Nick started to pour the coffee and replied, "Katie, this woman saved my life. When she came to the 99 Ranch, Jim McCann was trying to starve us to death and Tag Taggat was trying to work us to death. The first meal she fed us was spaghetti with a meat sauce, biscuits and fruit cocktail. I do believe that was the best meal that I have ever been served. Not only that, but she was an encourager for me learning to cook and buying this café. Stick with her. You can learn a lot from this lady." Nick finished serving Katie and Laura and then went to the kitchen.

When Nick came back, he asked Laura, "How is Tylor doing? I was sorry about the break-up with the Barnes girl. I'm sure that war is tough enough without coming home to that

18

kind of news."

"He is doing well," answered Laura. "He is learning to do things with his left hand. He is restless, but Tag is trying to keep him busy." She didn't say anything about his occasional outbursts of temper. It didn't need to be known in the community. Getting up to leave, Laura asked, "How much do I owe you for our refreshments?"

Nick reached back into his pie case and brought out a whole pie. Handing it to Laura, he said, "Mrs. Taggat, your money is no good here and take this with you. I know how much Tag likes cherry pie. Thanks for stopping in. Katie, take good care of this special lady."

Laura took the pie and she touched his arm. "Thank you, Nick. It was good visiting with you." When they neared the car, Laura motioned for Katie to drive.

Returning to the ranch, Katie was parking the car when Laura saw the ranch foreman, Jim McCann near the cook shack. He motioned to Laura, as if he wanted to talk with her. After Katie had shut off the ignition, Laura said, "Good job of driving, Katie. If you will set up the sewing machine, I want to talk with Jim a minute. You know what you want to do, so go ahead. I will be back shortly." Laura got out and went to meet Jim.

Jim had walked over by the Dismal River near the cottonwood stump and was waiting for Laura. She sensed that this was important. Jim usually didn't interrupt Laura's day. "Good morning, Jim. Do you mean to tell me you have all the work caught up and can laze around in the shade of these cottonwood trees?" She laughed at her own remarks. "Does Tag know that you have these idle moments?"

"Morning, Laura," Jim replied. His reply triggered a thought in her mind. *Why do the women in greeting say, 'good morning,' but the men use a shortened form of 'morning?' I guess men are not ones to mince words, as they say.*

19

"Is something wrong? You seem rather preoccupied." asked Laura.

"It's Tylor. I don't know if I should be saying anything, but after the crew has gone to bed for the night, he gets up at about 10:30 to 11:00 each night and is gone until 2:00 or 3:00 in the morning. He wears those moccasins, and unless a person is watching for him, he can come and go in a flash. I don't think any of the others know about it. They are so tired that they sleep hard until time to get up in the morning. Sometimes I get up in the night, so I have become aware of his coming and going. I don't know where he goes, but I thought he might be meeting someone."

"What are you saying, Jim?" By Laura's tone in her voice, Jim regretted bringing up the subject. "Do you think that someone is Katie?"

"I don't know, but I'm sorry that I brought it up, but I didn't want to see anyone get hurt."

Laura realized that she was being defensive in the matter. What if it was true? She definitely didn't want anything to happen to Katie. She presumed that Tylor was above such things, but was not certain. If it wasn't Katie, then why was he going out each night? She realized that she had been sharp with Jim in her response. "Jim, I'm sorry that I spoke too soon in this matter. Thank you for forewarning me. I will see what I can find out. I don't think it is Katie, but one never knows. How does Tylor continue to only get four hours of sleep each night and still function? I know that Tag hasn't cut him any slack, just because he is handicapped." Laura went back to the house, uncertain what she should be doing to solve this mystery.

Katie had unpacked the sewing machine and was making plans to begin fitting Tylor with more comfortable clothing. At the table that night, she related to Tag and his sons that she had started her driving lessons and had her learners

20

permit. "Laura says that I am a good driver. Has she ever told her sons that they are good drivers?" questioned Katie, hoping to get an argument started with them.

TJ asked, "She let you drive her car? She never lets Tylor or me drive her car. She doesn't know how good of a driver we might be."

"I know what kind of drivers the two of you have become. I have seen the two of you drive the ranch pickups and that is why I don't let you drive my car. Katie is very careful. She has seen how careful I am with it as well." Laura reached out and touched Katie, as an affirmation of her ability to drive. "Unfortunately, she has a desire to learn to drive the ranch pickups. We will try it someday."

TJ spoke up, "Katie, anytime you want to learn everything about driving a pickup, just let me know. I will gladly teach you."

"Will you?" asked Katie. "That will be great. How about Sunday afternoon?"

"It's a date! Sunday afternoon is good, but be sure to wear jeans. Sometimes the upholstery is worn through and the blanket doesn't always cover the springs." TJ was as excited as was Katie.

That night, while they were doing the dishes, Laura laid the dish cloth on the counter. Turning to Katie, she asked, "Katie, are you aware that Tylor is sneaking out from his bunk each night and not returning until 2:00 in the morning? Has he said anything to you to indicate what and why he is doing this thing?"

"No," she replied, and then she continued. "Are you thinking I should know something about this? Are you accusing me of sneaking out to be with him? It is really me that you want to know about, isn't it?"

"Yes, Katie," Laura said, almost in a whisper. "I didn't think it was, but I had to find out if it was you that he was seeing. I know now that it wasn't, but I needed to know."

Neither one said anything. The silence between the two had become almost unbearable. Finally, Laura said, "Katie, don't think ill of me, but I see myself as your protector and Tylor's as well. Do you have any insight as to why he is doing this?"

"I don't know why, but I do know what he is doing." Laura looked surprised at Katie's statement. "He is running, or at least, I think that he is running. Have you seen the moccasins that I gave him? They are practically worn out. He asked me where I got them and he has ordered another pair. He doesn't say much, but I believe that he is troubled. Troubled about what, I don't know. The day of Becca's wedding, he was very distraught that he had been rejected by Becca. I tried to comfort him. I am ashamed for what I did that day, but at least it may give you comfort in regards to Tylor's character. I asked him if he thought that I was pretty and he nodded his head. Then I asked him to kiss me. He got very angry in his refusal. Don't worry about Tylor. It is me that you need to be concerned about!"

Laura was shocked by what she had been told. "Both of you are in my prayers. There are times when any of us are weak, but I also have confidence in the integrity of each of you."

Katie didn't share everything with Laura that took place the day of Becca's wedding. It was that day she remembered that people would remark that Laura Taggat always had a plan. *I have learned from her, and now, Katie O'Neal has a plan! I have one more year in high school. As I remain here at the 99 Ranch, my plan will be fulfilled! Next year at this time, it will be me walking down the aisle of the Good Hope Church. Becca Barnes had her chance and failed. Now it is my turn!*

Katie worked hard on Tylor's wardrobe. She thought that it would be ready for a fitting in a week. Sunday afternoon was a day of anticipation for Katie. All week she had talked about learning to drive a ranch pickup, along with the shifting of gears and driving the trail roads in the pastures. Katie had insisted on packing an afternoon lunch and some iced tea for TJ and herself. They had been gone for some time, when TJ drove into the yard. Laura looked out and saw that he was by himself. Thinking the worst, Laura ran out and asked, "Where is Katie? Has anything happened to her?"

"She is walking in. She wouldn't ride with me. It is my fault. I apologized, but she wouldn't get into the pickup." TJ threw his hands up in disgust.

"TJ," screamed Laura, "you just don't leave someone out on the prairie. What is the matter with you?"

"I figured if I came in alone, someone else would go back for her, and she would ride in with them." TJ shook his head, "What else was I supposed to do?"

Laura ran back to the house. Entering the house, she hollered for Tag. He had been working on his ranch books when he heard her cry out. "What are you upset about?"

"Katie and TJ had words. She wouldn't ride back with him. She is out there walking. He came in, thinking that someone else could go out and get her. That is, someone that she would be willing to ride with. Can you go get her? I would go, but I'm not sure where she is."

Now, Tag was mad. "I ought to skin that kid alive, leaving her out there by herself." Grabbing his hat, he stormed out the door.

TJ saw his father coming. He said, "She is just west of the east windmill, heading this way."

Tag, in his fury, spun the wheels in the dry sand, creating a cloud of dust. He saw the lone figure, walking the trail road. He pulled alongside and she jumped out of the trail, into the grass. "Get in and we will talk about this on the way back. What did TJ do that made you walk?"

23

"Mr. Taggat, I'm sorry, but it was my fault."

Tag saw that she had been crying. "Okay, so it is your fault, but what did TJ do?"

"I told you, he didn't do anything! It was my fault." Katie just looked straight ahead the rest of the way to the ranch.

Katie was glad to be back at the ranch and headed straight for her room. Laura and Tag were unable to find out what had happened. Neither Katie nor TJ would blame the other. They insisted on assuming the blame solely upon themselves. Two weeks later, Laura took Katie for a driving lesson in a ranch pickup.

CHAPTER 2
BURIAL IN THE TEASDALE CEMETERY

The early days of September were hot and blistering on the 99 Ranch, as the summer drought continued. This year, Tag was not able to brag about the best set of calves that they had ever produced on the ranch. In dry years, there is only so much a manager could do. One of those is that he cannot make the cattle fat and sleek when the grass is short. Not only was the grass short, but so was the temper of Tag Taggat. He berated Laura and Jim for not praying for rain. The ranch cook was feeding the men too good for what little they did. Poor Tylor could do nothing right. But still, he continued to show respect for Tag, trying to please a man that it was impossible to please. Only TJ and Katie seemed to avoid his wrath. TJ didn't let Tag's rages bother him and Katie made sure that she had his slippers and mail when he came in for supper. The one redeeming feature for Katie was that she had started school and she was only around Tag in the evening. By that time, his anger was pretty well spent. TJ counted the days until he would return to college. This was to be his big year in baseball. The pro scouts would be watching him. It was now to the point that his coach had forbidden him from entering any more team roping contests, in order to protect his fingers from injury.

Tag came in at noon and threw his hat on the washing machine. "Laura, Jim will be eating with us tonight. We need to come up with a strategy to keep us out of the poorhouse. Why don't you set in as well, since you keep the books? TJ and Tylor may as well join us. Maybe they will see that they need to put in a little more effort to keep this place going. A good fall rain would start some of the grass and maybe give us some fall grazing to save our hay crop. Plan on eating at about six if you can manage it." That was about the extent of his conversation. He was preoccupied with the problems of the ranch.

Laura was determined to make this a good meal. She spent the afternoon preparing the food for supper. Katie came home from school and Laura put her right to work. "Katie, I will be sitting in on the meeting tonight, so I will count on you to keep the coffee pot full. I won't be able to help with the dishes. I would appreciate you doing what you can. How much homework do you have?"

"Don't worry, Laura," she replied. "I can finish after I am through with the dishes."

Laura had things ready and had a bit of extra time, so she walked down to the Dismal River and her cherished spot at the cottonwood stump. She saw that the Dismal River was at its shallowest since she had first seen it that wintry morning in January 1951. She prayed for rain and for her neighbors that were also suffering from the drought. She especially prayed for Tag. First she prayed for his salvation and that he might experience God's peace. Also, she prayed that he might exhibit gentleness toward others. She prayed for the others that would be at the meeting tonight and that they might contribute to the affairs of the ranch.

Laura had prepared an excellent supper, but she might as well have served cold porridge. The men were on edge. Laura encouraged them to retire to the living room. She and Katie had continued to pray at the table after each meal, rotating each day as to who was responsible. Laura was encouraged. Katie was becoming more specific in her prayers and it was creating even a closer bond between the two women. She especially wanted to pray with Katie tonight. They had established previously to thank God for the food that had been provided, even though it had already been consumed. After praying, she went into the living room where the men were finishing their coffee. Tag started the meeting. "I have called all of you here tonight to see if anyone has any thought how we can come out of this drought and still remain solvent. Our calves are light in weight, probably the lightest bunch of calves in years. Because of the widespread drought, there will be a lot of cattle on the market and they will hit the market two or three weeks early. Our hay crop was down as well. I'm not sure that we can handle the cowherd we've had in the past if we have a tough winter. Are there any ideas?"

Jim was the first to speak. "What about culling the older cows and reducing the cowherd to the level that we can handle through the winter. If you sold 50 cows, that would still leave you 350 head. Those older cows are the ones that will have the lighter calves next year if you kept them. It would also give you some cash to make up for the smaller check on the sale of the calves."

Laura spoke up, "That is fine for this year, but eventually the loss will hit. Next year the gross from the cattle will be less because of fewer numbers. Or, if the grass is good next spring, you will be buying back to bring the herd back to size."

Tylor was the next to speak. "Will the b-b-bank permit you to p-p-put the l-l-light calves in the feedlot until they have g-g-grown some more? They w-w-won't show the effects of the drought and should b-b-bring more per p-p-pound."

Tag vetoed that right away. "We can't put any more money into those calves. I would rather sell them now and avoid the risk. That won't work!" Tylor blushed. He saw that Tag did not like his suggestion. This was one of the things that he had learned at the university when they studied the effects of the drought on a cattle market.

They talked back and forth. It was decided to follow Jim's suggestion of reducing the cowherd. Tag said, "The first of next week we will start sorting cows. We might have that done before TJ leaves for college."

TJ, Tylor and Jim left the meeting. They stepped out

into the front yard with Tag and Laura following them. They could smell the freshness in the air. TJ remarked, "There is lightning off to the west. Maybe we will have a good rain out of this." They continued on down the path to the bunkhouse. Later, Tag and Laura returned to the ranch house.

When Laura got up the next morning, she was aware that it had not rained. She went to the Dismal River and saw that the river was up. The water was higher along the bank. It was flowing more water this morning than it had the evening before. Evidently, someone along the river had received rain in the night. Laura thanked the Lord for the rain that had fallen on the neighbors, whoever it might have been.

Katie was off to school. Laura was busy harvesting the last of the garden vegetables before the end of the growing season. She had already prepared the dinner for Tag. She had some time before he came in, so she went for the mail. *The Sentinel* was the only item of mail. She tucked it under her arm, and her thoughts turned to the editor, David Riggs. *He had become a dear friend and an avid suitor. It seemed strange to her that he had never married. When she first heard about him, the lady described him as the town's most eligible bachelor.*

Laura waited for Tag. In the meantime, she thought she would see what news was in *The Sentinel*. The front-page headline caught her eye. "Barton County Pioneer Dies at Age of 92." The article went on to say that Metta Taggat, age 92 had died at the Barton County Nursing Home. Laura continued to read. It stated that her husband, Hiram Taggat, had preceded her in death in 1956. Her son, Tylor George Taggat also preceded her in death when he was killed in action in Korea, September 30, 1951. There were no living survivors. Services will be Thursday at the Catholic Church at 10:00 a.m. The rest of the article gave an account of her life, having lived in Barton County since her birth.

Tag came in for dinner and that was the news that Laura

28

greeted him with. The first thing that Tag asked, "I wonder who is going to get all that money that she has been hoarding all these years?"

"Why darling," Laura purred, "undoubtedly she will be leaving it to her nephews. You being her favorite, she will probably leave it all to you. Then you will have two ranches that will be drying up and twice as many hungry cows. Now isn't that a pleasant thought?" After Laura said that, she wished that she hadn't tried to be funny. She remembered what happened when Tag's father had died. Tag's stepmother had inherited everything and when she died, she left it to her nieces and nephews on her side of the family.

Laura asked, "Tag, will you be going to the funeral?"

"Laura," replied Tag, "she was a miserable woman and I am not going to spend my time going to her funeral. I doubt if there will be many Taggats going there. Besides, I have too much to do."

"If there won't be many going, all the more reason for you to attend." Laura knew that Tag wasn't much for funerals. Her New England culture deemed it necessary to go to community funerals, regardless of how well you knew the individual, or what you might have thought of them.

"Laura, if you think that the Summit County Taggats should attend the funeral, then I hereby appoint you as our personal representative, but I am not going. Now, let's eat. I have a lot of work to get done today." Laura knew by the tone of his voice not to press the matter any further.

At breakfast Thursday morning, Laura asked, "Tag, I feel it necessary that I go to Metta Taggat's funeral, but I have a bit of a headache. Would you be so kind to let Tylor off this morning, so that he could drive me to the funeral? We won't tarry and I will have him back here as soon as possible."

"I suppose so. I don't know what it is, but I seem to get less and less work out of that boy each day. He acts like he is tired all the time. I thought he would have his strength back by now. Considering all he went through, I guess it is understandable." Tag got up from the breakfast table. Before going out the door, he turned to Laura and said, "I will tell him to come to the house. Just be sure that he is dressed halfway decent. He never wears anything but those moccasins on his feet."

Tylor came to the house and he did look 'decent,' as Tag had requested. However, he was wearing his moccasins. Laura asked, "Tylor do you have any shoes or boots that you could wear this morning? Your moccasins are looking a bit worn."

Tylor looked down at his feet and replied, "M-M-Mama, I can't g-g-get my shoes or m-m-my boots on. They are too t-t-tight. I know these d-d-don't look the b-b-best, but they are all I have."

"Then they will have to do." Laura paused a moment, as if she was coming up with some solution. "Tylor, we have some time, so let us stop in Madden at the boot shop and see if we can have you fitted for a pair of custom made boots. That is where your father has his made. Going barefooted for five months spread your feet out and the moccasins have not helped any. I know they are comfortable, but if you continue to wear them, we must keep an extra pair on hand for dress or at least until you get accustomed to the boots."

"But, M-M-Mama," Tylor pleaded, "we are in a d-d-drought and we don't have m-m-money for new boots. The m-m-moccasins are fine, except when the horses s-s-step on my feet. I think they see who isn't being a c-c-cowboy for the d-d-day, so they choose me to w-w-walk on."

Laura spoke up, "Tylor, you are now receiving a disability check each month from the government for the injuries you received during the war. You haven't cashed any of them. Use that money!"

"I don't feel right t-t-taking that money. The war and what h-h-happened is p-p-part of being a citizen. I have v-v-very little need of m-m-money."

"Because of that war, your feet are in the condition they are right now. You are entitled to a new pair of boots. We will stop at the bank and cash the checks that you have accumulated. Part of that is for back pay when you were a prisoner. The government doesn't like it when they send you money and you don't cash the checks. Consider that you are doing them a favor by cashing the checks." Laura stopped. *Here I am talking to him as if he was a child. Sometimes his thinking is at the seven year old level. He has no interest in girls, nor the ranch and not even the church. I encouraged him to go to church with me. He refused, because that was where Becca was married. His main interest seems to be running at night. Why, I have no idea!*

Tylor drove, not because he wanted to, but because Laura insisted that he drive. He seemed to have a sense of inadequacy when it came to doing any task, as if he couldn't do it well enough. Arriving at the bank, Laura went through the process of setting up a safety deposit box for his money. She feared that people might dupe him out of his money in a checking account, or even worse, to overdraw the account. For the time being, it would be cash only for Tylor.

Arriving early in Madden, mother and son stopped at the boot maker. Tag would go no place else when it came to boots. Harley, the boot maker greeted them. When Laura said that she was Mrs. Tag Taggat, he was most gracious. "Mrs. Taggat, what can I do for you?"

She answered, "My son Tylor has need of a pair of boots. What do you suggest?"

"Oh, my," said the man, "the moccasins are not good for the feet. There is no support and no class that you will find in a pair of my boots." Reaching down to remove the

31

moccasin, he felt the foot. "The moccasins are made of good leather and workmanship, but all the time of going barefoot will make it difficult to fit you with a pair of boots. However, you have come to the right place. The boots that I make will not be cheap, but they will be good. I guarantee." The man had an accent that made it difficult for Laura to understand. She had heard that he had come from Hungary after WWII and set up his shop in Madden.

Harley took note of the deformed hand and the fact that the mother did all of the talking. "With the thickness of your feet, I will need to make a special last. A pair of boots will run about $130.00, unless you want some fancy stitching."

Tylor jerked his foot from the boot maker's hand and started to put on his moccasin. He was so anxious, that he was unable to speak. His stuttering could not get him past the first syllable. "N-No. N-N-No. There is a d-d-drought. That is t-t-too much m-m-money!" Fitting his moccasin back on his foot, he fled out the door and to the car.

Laura stood up and apologized. She said, "I am sorry, Mr. Mazak. My son was in a prison camp and he spent five months in the jungle, barefoot and without clothes. That is why his feet are this way. We have been talking about the drought around the dinner table, so he is concerned about money. He has money. He needs the boots so I will try to get him back here for a fitting."

"Oh, yes. I read about him in *The Sentinel*. He has never come in here with Mr. Tag, so I do not recognize him. Mrs. Taggat, for a veteran, there is no charge. The boots are free! I will go tell him." He went outside to the car and approaching Tylor he said, "Tylor, I was in the war like you and I was taken prisoner like you. This country means much to me. Because you fought for this country, the boots are free. But, only the first pair. After the first pair it is full price. Come back in and let me measure your feet. You will see, these boots will be as comfortable as the moccasins. Come back inside." Harley went back inside and he gave Laura a wink. He sat back on his stool, giving the indication that he was ready to start measuring. Tylor came back and sat down, observing all that Harley was doing.

When Harley finished, he said, "They will be ready in three weeks. Now, Mrs. Taggat, did you come for the boots for your son, TJ? They are ready, if you want to take them with you."

Laura was surprised. She didn't know that TJ had ordered new boots. She paid the $100.00 for the boots and she and Tylor left the boot maker's shop. It was now 9:30 and Laura was anxious to get to the church for Metta Taggat's funeral. Laura was going early, having no desire to come into a funeral late. Arriving at the church, she saw that they were evidently plenty early. The last time that she had been in this church, it was a bitter cold day. It was the day that Tylor George Taggat had been buried, Tylor's father.

The funeral was short, perhaps in respect of the few mourners that were present, a total of twenty. This was unlike the funeral of Metta's son, when about 100 family members were present, besides the others in the community to pay their respect. There was no one that Laura recognized. Metta Taggat was buried beside her husband and son in the cemetery adjacent to the church. When Laura viewed the body, Metta Taggat was just as she remembered her the last time that she had seen her on that cold wintry day in January 1951. After the graveside service closed, Tylor looked up at the adjacent tombstone and remarked to his mother. "Mama, look, there is a T-T-Tylor T-T-Taggat, except his m-m-middle name is George." Looking more closely, he remarked, "He d-d-died the same d-d-day I was born."

"Yes, he is your father's cousin. He was killed in the Korean War. Wars are such a waste of youth. Will it ever end,

Tylor, will it ever end?"

Laura and Tylor returned home in time for dinner. Tag asked, "How was the funeral, or should I even ask such a question? They certainly aren't a joyous occasion?"

"It was well that we went. There were only about 20 people at the service. It was short, so we stayed for the graveside service. Also, we stopped at Harley's Boot Shop to fit Tylor for a pair of boots." Before Laura said anything more, Tag interrupted her.

"I thought we talked about being in tough times and you are getting Tylor a pair of handmade boots?" Tag was furious. He continued, "Do you know what he charges for a pair of boots?"

"Yes," Laura calmly answered. "Yes I do. It is $100.00, or at least that is what I had to pay for TJ's boots that he sent home with me. I paid that out of my money, so who is going to reimburse me for that amount? Incidentally, because of the shape of Tylor's feet, his boots are $130.00, unless we wanted fancy stitching; that would cost more. Inasmuch as you don't give Tylor any money for his labors, I thought that he needed a pair of boots."

"Well, he could have got a pair off the shelf, or else keep wearing those scruffy moccasins."

"No, Tag," insisted Laura, "he deserves boots as much as TJ or you for that matter. As I said, he has money, but I have found Mr. Mazak more benevolent than you. Because Tylor is a veteran, he has promised these boots to him free of charge."

"How well he should," exclaimed Tag. "That old Hungarian immigrant has been overcharging me for years."

"Then," asked Laura, "why do you go back year after year for your boots if he is overcharging?"

"Well," countered Tag, "he does make a good boot."

"Dinner is ready, such as it is," said Laura. She put out the sandwiches that she had made before leaving for town. She had potato salad and Tag insisted he have coffee at noon, no matter if the weather was hot or cold.

"Seeing that you wasted the morning, what else did you learn?" queried Tag.

Laura replied, "We stopped at the bank for Tylor to cash all of his disability checks."

"And, what else?" Tag asked. "That gossipy Mrs. Stahl always has some kind of news to relate to you. What did she tell you that would interest me?"

"Just that Todd was out of the bank, checking some cattle, and, oh yes, you know that rain that missed us the other evening? Carl Barnes had a heavy rain at their ranch. I knew that someone had received a good rain. The Dismal River had a lot more water flowing by."

"Evidently the Barnes people know how to pray for rain. We got nothing. I rode over the whole ranch, and there was nothing, absolutely nothing! If you and Jim McCann don't get me some rain from your prayers, I am going to get some reservation Indians to hold a Rain Dance!"

"Tag, I prayed for rain and I also prayed for rain for our neighbors, so my prayers were not a total loss." Laura continued. "I imagine that the Barnes family was also praying for rain for their neighbors as well. Keep in mind, the Lord sends rain upon the just and the unjust. It is not that we merit rain, for if it were based solely upon our merit, we would receive no rain at all. It is through His grace and goodness that we receive His blessings."

Tag had finished his dinner and gulping down the last of his coffee. He gave one big 'Humpf,' and left the house.

Laura was saddened, as her thoughts turned to Tag. *Why can't I be more loving towards my husband? Do I delight in antagonizing him with bad news? Lord, help me to watch what I say, that it might be more uplifting to Tag. I love him and I must not let his remarks about my relationship with you irritate me. Forgive me, Father.* Laura wiped the tears from her eyes and began to clear the dinner dishes from the table.

For early September, the days were hot. After cleaning the kitchen, Laura sought the shade of the cottonwood trees near the Dismal River. While Laura sat on the cottonwood stump, she began to meditate about the blessings of the Lord. *It was a year ago that she had bid Tylor goodbye at the railroad station. Now he is home. He is not whole, but he is home.*

That night after supper, TJ took possession of his new boots. He pranced around the house and said, "Won't the girls at school admire me with my new boots?"

Katie said, "It may take more than new boots for you to get the admiration of the girls. I think that you need to improve your pitching skills as well." Ever since the problems at the time of the driving in the pasture, they had been at odds with one another.

TJ laughed, and said, "Katie, did you know that Tylor is getting new boots? Now tell him what he needs to improve to have the girls look at him." TJ continued to laugh. Tylor blushed with embarrassment.

Laura interrupted, "Tomorrow, I want all of you to eat dinner here at the house. It is Saturday, so Katie and I will have fried chicken for dinner. With TJ going to college on Tuesday, it will be the last time we will be together for a while."

Tag said, "That would work well with my plans for tomorrow. After dinner, you two boys can load up ten bags of salt and take it to the East pasture. Tylor, you can get the tanks cleaned out and put oil in the windmill while TJ puts out the salt at the two salt stations. I will ride out and bring two horses with me. Jim can follow along with the pickup and check all the gates. Then, you two can help me start to move some of the sorted cows and calves. We will put them on the fresh grass. Maybe they will fatten up some by the time to sell them."

It was then that Katie spoke up. "Guess what I saw

36

today when I came home on the bus?" As no one responded, she said, "A tornado! It passed right in front of the bus and swirled dirt and dried grass into a big funnel!"

TJ laughed. "Katie, you are exaggerating things. That was a 'dust devil.' Maybe you could call it a miniature tornado, but it is a long way from an actual tornado."

Katie was embarrassed. She looked to Tag for assurance. It was then that he said, "Katie, he is right, but I know that you meant no harm in calling it a tornado. They mostly occur when it is hot and dry. We have them frequently in the summer time when it is weather like we are having now. Unless they cross your path and stir up a bit of dirt, they go unnoticed. When I was a small boy, we had one come through the yard and it upset a small chicken house. I was terrified and I still don't like it when I get caught in one. It fills your ears and nose full of dust and dry grass."

Laura added, "Evidently they are more frequent now that it is so dry. I think it was Tuesday afternoon that one went through the garden and skipped around through the corrals. When I looked at the garden, the cucumber and tomato vines were twisted around one another. I hate it when you have washing on the line and one passes through. It means that you have to start over again with the washing."

Katie said, "I would like to be in the middle of one. I think it would be fun, as long as you didn't get hurt. Tylor, wouldn't you like to be in one?"

Tylor shook his head. "I d-d-don't think so. It might just s-s-suck the b-b-breath right out of you. No, I w-w-will just w-w-watch it go by."

Katie laughed, "Tylor, you are no fun! If you see one coming, let me know so that I can jump in the middle of it."

After supper, the men went out into the yard to look at the clouds to see if there was the possibility of rain.

Laura and Katie continued their evening ritual of

thanking God for the food, even though it had already been consumed. Katie prayed, "Thank you God for the food and for this family. I love them and give TJ a good year at college this year. I know that I will miss him. And we continue to ask for rain. Mr. Taggat needs it for his cows. Amen." Katie turned to Laura and hugged her. "What special dessert can we make for TJ? This will be his last weekend with us for a while?"

"Katie," Laura asked, "what would you think if we made a pineapple upside down cake? I do believe that it is his favorite. A maraschino cherry in each ring and topped with some nice thick whipped cream is what makes it so special."

"Teach me how to make it," begged Katie. "I want this to be special, just for TJ."

The next day, after the breakfast dishes were done, Katie and Laura began the preparations for dinner. When the men came in at noon, they were surprised at the aroma that came from the kitchen. When it came time for the dessert, Katie brought out a dessert plate and served TJ first. "Oh, Momma, you remembered that this is my favorite. When I marry, that is the first thing you must teach my new bride. Teach her how to make pineapple upside down cake."

Katie piped up, "I already know how to make it. Your mother taught me this morning." It was then that she realized what she had said and left the room, blushing. Still blushing, she returned with dessert for Tag and Tylor, who continued laughing at what they had heard.

After dinner, the men went out and Tag, TJ and Tylor each saddled the horses that they planned to ride that afternoon. Tylor and Tag loaded the salt in the older ranch pickup. Picking up a quart of oil for the windmill they left for the East pasture. TJ insisted that he drive the truck. Tylor complained, "Why d-d-don't I get to d-d-drive once in a while? I am the one that always h-h-has to get out and open and c-c-close the gates."

"Tylor, you wouldn't want me to get my new boots

all dusty and besides, I might cut my pitching hand on some barbed wire when I open the gate. Let me assure you that once I get a pitching contract, Dad won't have to worry about grass for these cows. That is when this family will see the big bucks." TJ laughed. "I might even buy you a truck of your own and then you and Katie can drive around looking for 'dust devils' in the summer time." Then he laughed again and reached over and punched Tylor in the arm.

When they got to the first gate, Tylor tried to get out, but the door handle inside the cab fell off and dropped beside the seat. Tylor was disgusted. What was cumbersome was that he had to reach across with his good hand through the open window to unlatch the door. He said, "I sure h-h-hope that you h-h-hurry and get that ball c-c-contract so we can have a g-g-good truck. The p-p-prairie has shaken this truck to pieces." He reached down into the dirt and retrieved the handle that had fallen to the ground when he opened the door. He tossed it up on the dash of the cab.

After going through another gate and repeating the process of getting the door open, they drove to the windmill. TJ turned off the ignition, stopping the motor. He turned to Tylor and said, "There has been a change of plans. I will climb up the tower and check the oil in the windmill head and you can clean out the tanks. Don't forget to put the plugs in the tanks. Then we both will go to put out the salt."

Tylor started to complain, "But Father s-s-said that I was to climb the t-t-tower and clean the tanks while you p-p-put out the s-s-salt." Tylor started to get out of the truck, but because of the faulty door handle, TJ was out and half way up the tower before Tylor could get out.

TJ was almost to the top. He turned and laughed. "Sorry, Tylor, but you are too slow." He then scrambled up the rest of the rungs of the ladder and pulled himself onto the platform.

Tylor got out and with the wrench and shovel in hand, he started toward the tank. Looking up, he saw a 'dust devil' making its way across the prairie. Throwing the tools down, he waved his arms and hollered, "G-G-Get d-d-down, g-g-get d-d-down!" Tylor then pointed to the 'dust devil' as it drew nearer. At times it was barely distinguishable, unless it crossed some bare ground where it could pick up the dust.

Once again, TJ laughed. "Don't get so upset. Just clean out the tanks. I am up here now."

While this was going on, a quarter of a mile away, Jim was in the truck. Tag was riding his horse and leading the other two horses, heading toward the windmill. Then they saw the 'dust devil' crossing the prairie. They saw the wheel and fan whip around as the 'dust devil' went right by the windmill. The next thing they saw was a man falling from the tower. Tag spurred his horse into a run and the other horses followed him. Jim tried to keep up, but the road was too rough.

Arriving at the windmill, Tag saw Tylor cradling his brother. "He is d-d-dead, F-F-Father, he is d-d-dead." Tylor started to get up.

Tag dismounted and as he was getting off, he grabbed his lariat. Screaming at Tylor, he said, "It was you that was supposed to be on the tower. You disobeyed me and now your brother is dead." He started to flail Tylor with his lariat. Tylor stumbled and grabbing a leg of the windmill tower, he steadied himself as Tag continued to beat him.

When Jim arrived, he saw that TJ was not moving and Tag was beating Tylor. He jumped from the truck and grabbing Tag from behind, he yelled, "Don't Tag. Don't hurt the boy!" Tag flung his arm around and knocked Jim to the ground.

Jim knew that he was not big enough or strong enough to stop Tag, especially when he was angry. He ran to the pickup that he had driven. Reaching inside the cab, he pulled a rifle from the gun rack that hung by the rear window. While he

40

levered a cartridge into the chamber, he yelled again for Tag to stop. When he saw that he would not stop, he pointed the gun in the air and fired, but Tag continued to beat on Tylor. This time, after he had worked the lever and another cartridge was in the chamber, he placed the muzzle to the back of Tag's head and said, "If you don't stop, I will blow your head off. The first shot was to warn you." Jim remembered back 25 years ago. Tag in his anger had almost beaten a young woman to death. Jim was not going to let it happen today.

Tag went to TJ and falling beside him, he began to weep. Tylor could barely hold himself up, still clinging to the post. His shirt was in shreds and he was bleeding from the head and across his back. Jim got him into the truck. He went to Tag. "I will have Laura come out and I will call the undertaker. I'm sorry, Tag, I'm real sorry." He then got into the truck and started back toward the ranch. The horses were grazing nearby after scattering at the sound of the rifle.

Arriving at the ranch house, Jim ran to the kitchen door as fast as he could. Upon entering, he saw that Katie was at the table, working on her schoolwork. Gasping, he shouted, "Where is Laura? Where is Laura?" Before Katie could answer, Laura came from the bedroom.

"What's wrong Jim? Where is Tag?" It was then that she saw the blood on his shirt. "Are you hurt? Say something!"

Still gasping, he said, "There was an accident at the windmill. Laura, TJ is dead, and Tylor is hurt. I have him in the pickup truck. Go to Tag. He needs you at this time. He is at the East mill. I will call the sheriff to send the undertaker. One of the men can show him the way. I will tell them, as they are at the shop working on a gate. I'm sorry, Laura, but I need to get Tylor to the hospital." He repeated, "Go to Tag, Laura. He needs you."

"I want to see Tylor," Laura said as she ran for the door.

Jim grabbed her. "No, Laura, he will be all right. He

is bloodied, but he will be all right. Go to Tag. He is the one that needs you." Turning to Katie, he said, "Get some towels and you can help me with Tylor." Katie's face was white after hearing all the information. She ran to the linen closet to get an armload of towels.

Laura went to get in her car, but before she did, she looked in at Tylor. He heard her gasp when she opened the door. "I'm s-s-sorry, M-M-Mama. It should have b-b-been me." He said nothing more. He had passed out from the pain. Laura closed the door and went for her car, the torn shirt, bloody head and back etched in her mind.

Jim and Katie positioned Tylor so that they could use the towels to cover his wounds to prevent him from sticking to the seat of the truck. Katie cradled his head in her arms. Jim drove to the shop and explained to the men what they were supposed to do. One was to wait for the undertaker and to take him to the windmill site. The other man was to saddle a horse and ride out for the horses still at the windmill. Leaving the ranch, Katie asked, "Jim, what happened out there? Is TJ really dead? We had such a good time at dinner. Everyone was looking forward for him to return to college, and now this."

Jim shook his head. "He was on the platform of the windmill, when a 'dust devil' came sweeping through and whipped the wheel and tail around. It knocked him off. It looked like he struck his head. Tag and I were about a quarter mile away. We saw him falling. Katie, it was what you might call a freak accident."

"What about Tylor? How did he get so bloodied?" Katie looked down at him to see how he was doing.

"Katie," Jim said, "it is best if we don't even speculate as to his injuries. Sheriff Morgan will conduct an inquiry into the accident." Jim didn't say anything more. It appeared to Katie that Jim didn't want to talk any further about the accident.

They crossed the Dismal River on the south edge of town and made their way to the hospital. Katie and Jim got out of the truck. The nurses were ready to take care of Tylor.

Jim looked at Katie. "Why don't I take you to your parent's house and you can get cleaned up. I didn't realize that he would bleed on you."

Katie replied, "If I go, will you come for me? I want to be near him." She wiped her eyes. She had seen how bruised he was when she was holding him. "I can't believe how bad he was hurt."

Jim assured her, "I will be back for you, in say thirty minutes. I need to stop at the store and buy a clean shirt for myself." They got into the truck and Jim took Katie to her parents' home.

Later, when Jim had returned to the hospital, Dr. Jessup came out. "Jim," he said, "I need to talk with you for a few minutes. Come into my office." Jim went into the small office. The doctor motioned for him to sit down. Taking a chair, Jim sat down. With his hat in his hand, he continued to move his hat around and around through his fingers. "Tell me, Jim, how did Tylor manage to get so many bruises on his back and head?" Jim said nothing, just shook his head, acknowledging the question, but not willing to provide an answer. "It looks to me that he took a severe beating with a stiff rope. Do you think that TJ inflicted those wounds to Tylor's back before he fell off the windmill?" Jim shrugged. The doctor continued, "You were there. Surely there is something that you can add to my speculation."

Jim continued to move his hat around and around through his fingers. Finally, he looked up, and said, "Doc, I am presuming that Tylor will recover. There has been enough hurt in that family. I am thinking there is no need for any more questions." Jim got up and putting on his hat, he went out the door, down the hall and left the hospital to go get Katie.

While these events were taking place in Summit City, Laura had driven out to the East pasture. At first she spotted the old ranch pickup and the horses grazing nearby. When she got out, she saw Tag by the water tank, kneeling by TJ. He was a broken man, weeping over his son. Laura knelt beside him, weeping together over their son. Laura was the strong one. She had experienced the death of family and those that she had loved and cared for over the years. However, death never comes easy, especially one as young as TJ. He was one who loved life and lived it to the fullest.

The hearse came about the time that the young rider came for the horses. After the hearse left, Laura and Tag followed in Laura's car. The two ranch hands remained at the windmill, checking the oil level in the head of the windmill, cleaning the tanks and picking up the scattered tools. They released the brake on the wheel and it began pumping water. Removing the bridles from the horses, they started back to the ranch. The horses waited at each closed gate to continue their journey home.

Jim picked up Katie at her home and they stopped back at the hospital. Tylor was awake, but was not saying anything about the accident. He did bid Katie and Jim goodbye. As they were leaving the room, he said, "Thank y-y-you, thank y-y-you for g-g-getting me here." He then dropped off to sleep, the result of the sedatives that he had been given.

Jim and Katie arrived at the ranch. It was starting to get dark and they both went into the kitchen. Katie ran to Laura and hugged her, neither one saying a word. Tag came to Jim, and said, "Jim, can I see you outside?" Jim nodded and followed Tag outside. Tag handed a check to him. "Jim, here is your pay. You are through at the 99 Ranch. No man puts a gun to my head and continues to work for me. I want you off of here by noon tomorrow. Get one of the men to take you to Summit City and don't ever come back. Remember! Noon

44

tomorrow!"

"I'm sorry about TJ, Tag." Jim continued, "There is nothing I can do to bring him back, but I had within my power to save Tylor. I don't regret that. Forty years ago, your grandfather, George Taggat asked me to look after you. He asked that I might keep you from doing harm to yourself and others. Today, I had that opportunity. By your actions just now, I am now relieved of that pledge to George Taggat. Good night, Tag."

Before going to the bunkhouse, Jim stopped by the cottonwood stump by the Dismal River. He put one foot on the stump. He said, "Well, old stump; you have provided me a place to sit all these years, while I read the Bible and prayed. Once again, I am an orphan as I was when George Taggat took me in when I was twelve years old. I surely am thankful that God doesn't kick me out of His family. I am anxious to see what God has for me in the days to come." Jim thought, tomorrow is Sunday. I will have one of the men take me to Summit City early in the morning. No one need know that Tag and I had a parting of the way.

Tag returned to the house. Katie came to him and hugged him. "I'm sorry, Mr. Taggat. I don't know what more to say. Have you two eaten anything?" When they each shook their head, Katie said, "Let me heat some coffee and make some sandwiches. Then you may want some dessert." She suddenly stopped talking. *Definitely not the pineapple upside down cake. There are too many memories with that for right now.* "Tylor was resting when we left him, but they had sedated him. He needs time to get over the shock as well." Katie thought, *please Laura don't ask me anything about his injuries.* "Here, I will look in the freezer to see if we have any cookies to go with your coffee." Katie was intent on keeping busy to avoid any questions. After they had eaten, little as it was, Katie cleaned up the kitchen and went to her room.

45

Laura went to her husband. "Hold me, Tag, hold me. I need the comfort of your arms. I have never been as drained as I am now." Tag took her in his arms and held her. She was comforted. She laid her head against his chest and wept.

The next morning, while the others were at breakfast, Jim gathered his clothing. Putting them in an army surplus duffel bag, he threw it in the back of the older ranch pickup. Earlier, he had carried his saddle and laid it in the back. When the men came from breakfast, he asked the one that he deemed the least inquisitive to take him to Summit City. Stopping at the only hotel in town, Jim took his belongings and bid the fellow goodbye. After checking in, he went to see Tylor at the hospital. Tylor was asleep, so Jim drew up a chair and took a nap of his own. That is where Dr. Jessup found him when he came in to check on Tylor.

Jim awakened and stepped outside of the room. Dr. Jessup closed the door and Jim asked, "How is he doing?"

"Fortunately, he is strong, but he did take quite a beating. I talked a bit with him last night and he seems to think that TJ's death is his fault. What can you tell me, or will tell me?" Dr. Jessup was referring to Jim's earlier plea to let it go.

"Tylor is blaming himself, because Tag said it was his fault. When Tag gave the boys orders, Tylor was to put oil in the gear head of the windmill. I have a hunch that TJ took it upon himself to do that and let Tylor clean out the tank. When the 'dust devil' blew through, it whipped the tail and fan around, knocking him off. There isn't much room on that platform up there. It was one of the taller towers, so he fell quite a ways. Tag rode up, expecting that it was Tylor that had fallen. We could see him go off from where we were. When I got there, Tag was shouting that Tylor was supposed to have been on the tower. It doesn't make any difference now. Tag fired me last night. I came to town this morning with my belongings. I just came down here to see how he is doing. May

I make a suggestion?" Jim paused for a moment. Dr. Jessup nodded and Jim continued. "Don't let him out until after the funeral. I'm not sure what Tag might do." Jim turned from Dr. Jessup and started walking down the hall, a beaten man.

Dr. Jessup called after him, "Jim, have you had breakfast?" Jim just shook his head and continued down the hall. "Wait up! Come with me to the cafeteria and I will buy your breakfast. It won't be anything like the 99 Ranch breakfast, but I'm not sure anything else is open this time of the morning." Jim waited until he came near.

"I will go with you on one condition. There will be no more questions about what happened last night." Dr. Jessup nodded his head and pointed the way to the cafeteria.

Laura was up early, making a list of people to call, as well as what to do in regard to the funeral arrangements. She had already called Pastor Roth to let him know of their loss. She was getting ready to call Hannah, when Tag came out from the bedroom. He reached for the coffeepot. He poured his own coffee and indicated to Laura if he was to fill her mug as well. She held it out. While he was pouring, she responded, "Thank you, Tag. I am making a list of the people to call. Also, what is a good day for the funeral?"

Tag replied sharply! "Laura, how can you ask, what is a good day for the funeral? There is no good day for a funeral!"

Tears crept into her eyes and she apologized. "I'm sorry, Tag. It was a poor choice of words. What day do you want the funeral held?" Tag sat down and cradled his coffee mug in his hands as thcy rested on the kitchen table.

"Just pick a day. You make the arrangements. I will be there." He continued to cradle the mug. He looked down into it, saying nothing more.

Katie came into the kitchen. Passing Tag, she caressed his shoulders and continued on to Laura. She touched her arm and asked, "Can I fix some breakfast for the two of you? There isn't much sustenance in just coffee." Katie sensed that she had come at a bad time, but was determined not to let that bother her. She got out the waffle iron and started mixing the batter. While the iron was heating, she started bacon cooking in a skillet. In a matter of minutes, she had breakfast on the table and was surprised that they seemed to enjoy it. However, very little was said between Tag and Laura.

By the second cup of coffee, Laura asked, "Tag, can we go to the mortuary and make the funeral arrangements? Then we can pick out the casket and—."

Tag interrupted, "Laura, I told you to just do it! How many times do I have to tell you?" Laura started sobbing at Tag's outburst. Tag jumped to his feet and started to leave.

Katie rushed to Tag, putting her arms around him, she pleaded, "Please, Mr. Taggat. I know you are saddened at TJ's death, but you break my heart when you talk to Laura that way. You need to be involved, too. I can't stand it to hear the two of you fight. Don't leave it all up to her." Now Katie was weeping as well, as she clung to Tag.

Tag put his arms around Katie and kissed her forehead. "I'm sorry. You are right. I think that when the undertaker was at the windmill, he said that things would be ready at ten this morning. We will go in at that time. Katie, will you go with us? I would like it if you did." Tag released Katie and went to Laura. He held her, until she stopped sobbing.

While driving to Summit City, Laura said, "Tag, I would like TJ buried in the Teasdale Cemetery."

That statement jolted Tag. He quickly responded. "Laura, that is too close to home. It is too easy to go there to mourn. That is not a good idea."

"Tag," she countered. "Elmer Teasdale purposely put it where it is rather than near the buildings, so that those mourning would have to go a distance to mourn. TJ worked hard in the rebuilding of the cemetery. It is only fitting that he be buried there. I will go this afternoon to lay out where the grave is to be dug. I will get the exact dimensions from the undertaker and you can have Jim get the crew to dig it on Tuesday." Tag didn't tell her that Jim was no longer employed at the 99 Ranch.

Tag asked, "Laura, is that where you wish to be buried?" He anticipated her answer before she replied.

"Yes," she answered, "and how about you Tag? Where would you care to be buried?"

"It doesn't make that much difference to me. I figure that once you are dead, you are dead." Tag purposely made that remark, knowing that it would irritate Laura.

Knowing his intent, she ignored his statement.

After getting out, Laura walked behind the car and said to Tag, "There is one other thing. I want the horse drawn hearse to take TJ's body from the church to the cemetery."

Tag jerked as if he had been slapped. He grabbed her by the upper arms and shouted. "What is the matter with you? Do you want to make a mockery of this funeral? It is totally out of the question! Besides, I don't have any buggy horses to pull it. Forget it Laura, just forget it!"

With tears in her eyes, she stumbled when she stepped up on the curb and fell to the sidewalk. Tag tried to help her up, but she shook her head and said, "Just give me a minute to catch my breath. I'll be all right, Tag. I didn't mean to upset you, but Elmer Teasdale saw that it was fitting for his men to be buried with dignity. Why not TJ? He has worked hard on that ranch." Katie knelt down to Laura and handed her a handkerchief to dry her eyes. She used her hands to straighten Laura's hair.

"Why can't you let it go? I told you I don't have any horses to pull the hearse. Now get up so that we can go inside!"

Katie stood up and went to Tag. She touched his arm and said, "Mr. Taggat, I have seen Grant Holler drive a buggy in the parade each year. Let me call him to see if he will drive the hearse with his horses. This would mean a lot to Laura. If he will do it, I will clean the glass and put a shine on the wheels and the metal."

Tag put his hand on her shoulder. He replied, "All right. You and Laura are just alike, always wanting your own way."

She answered, "Mr. Taggat, I never thought of it that way, but I guess we do if we can attain harmony with dignity."

By now, Laura had got up from the sidewalk, with no more damage than having a bruised knee. After entering the mortuary, they made the arrangements for the funeral. When it came time to view the body, Katie declined. Leaving the mortuary, Laura said, "We need to go see Tylor. I think that I will walk from here. Katie, do you care to walk with me, while Tag brings the car?" Katie nodded. They walked by the City Park and came to the schoolhouse. It was here that they met Dr. Jessup, walking his dog.

"Good morning, Doctor. We are on our way to see Tylor. Is he doing well enough to be released for the funeral on Wednesday?" Laura waited for his answer, which seemed to be slow in coming. Doctor Jessup reached down and adjusted the collar on his dog. The little beagle tugged at the leash, wanting to return home.

Giving the dog a determined jerk of the leash, Dr. Jessup said, "I'm not sure at this moment. I expected him to be anxious to get out, but when I checked him this morning, he appeared to be rather lethargic. He has experienced so much death as of late. I would prefer to watch him a bit more closely before releasing him." *He remembered the request of Jim McCann. Though Jim was a bachelor much like himself, he deemed Jim to be wise in this particular instance. The father/ son relationship was not healthy in this family.* "Go visit him. Maybe a visit from a pretty young lady might be just the thing to put a spark in his life." The doctor laughed. He observed the blush on Katie's face. He pulled on the dog leash and the dog and master continued down the street.

They neared the hospital and saw that Tag had already arrived. He was waiting for them at the entrance. Katie said, "I will wait for you here. You may want to visit him without me being present." She grabbed up a magazine and sat down in the waiting room.

Tylor was partially sitting up, staring at the ceiling. When he saw his mother, he said, "Mama, I'm s-s-sorry, I'm sorry, M-M-Mama." When he saw Tag following Laura into the room, he was quiet and ceased talking.

Laura asked, "Tylor, are you feeling all right?" He nodded and looked out the window. "When did the doctor say that you could come home?" It was then that he shrugged and started to straighten the sheet by smoothing it, over and over.

Tag spoke up, asking, "Is there anything that we can get you, like coffee or a bottle of pop?" Again Tylor shrugged and then shook his head. Tag said, "Laura, I could use a cup of coffee from the cafeteria? Get some for yourself while I visit with Tylor." Laura left and as soon as she was down the hall, Tag said, "Tylor, when you get out of here, I don't want you back at the ranch. You disobeyed my order about putting oil in the windmill gearbox and now your brother is dead. I will not tolerate such actions. You have your own money from your government pension, so you can be on your own from now on. Don't go whining to your mother, or the both of you will be out on the street. Remember! Don't come back to the ranch!" Tag got up and started to leave. Laura returned with the coffee. He said to her, "I will go on down to where Katie is sitting. Go ahead and visit as long as you want."

Laura pulled up a chair near the bed. "Tylor, do you want to tell me what happened yesterday afternoon?" He looked at his mother. Placing his good hand and the stub hand to the sides of his face, he shook his head. He then lay on his

51

side, facing the wall. Laura touched his arm and rubbing it, she said. "Tylor, I love you. I don't believe that any of this was your fault. It was a freak accident that the 'dust devil' caused. I will leave now. Is there anything I can get you?"

Without turning to face her, he said, "Katie, I w-w-want to s-s-see Katie."

Before Laura left the room, she said, "I will tell her that you want to see her. Goodbye, my son."

When Katie came into the room, Tylor asked, "C-C-Can they hear me?"

"Do you mean your parents?" He nodded. "No," she replied. "Why do you ask?"

"D-D-Don't say anything, but I w-w-want you to do something for me." She nodded. "I want you to p-p-pack up all of my clothes, along with my s-s-saddle and bring them h-h-here to me at the hospital."

"But why?" She grabbed his arm, as if he was mad.

"I am not g-g-going back to the ranch. Ever! Get Jim McCann, or one of the m-m-men to bring my stuff here and d-d-don't tell anyone else." Katie saw that he was serious.

"Don't do this to your mother, Tylor. She has already lost one son. She can't stand to lose another." Katie saw that her plea was being ignored, when he shook his head.

"Will you d-d-do this, or do I have to go there in the m-m-middle of the n-n-night and steal my own clothes?" Katie nodded. After touching Tylor's arm, she ran from the room.

Tag, Laura and Katie returned to the ranch. After dinner, Katie walked down to the cook shack and the bunkhouse. Spotting one of the ranch hands sitting on an old wooden chair on the sunny side of the bunkhouse, she asked if Jim McCann was in the bunkhouse. He stopped his whittling on a tree branch and looked up. "Didn't you hear? Jim doesn't work here anymore. I took him and his gear to town early this morning. He didn't say where he was going, but I dropped him off at the hotel."

Katie looked surprised at the news. She then asked, "Did he say why he was leaving?"

The man shook his head. "We never said one word to each other, until he told me to go to the hotel. I knew he didn't want to talk, so I said nothing to him."

"You appear to be a quiet sort," said Katie, "so I will ask a favor of you. I need to get Tylor's clothes and his saddle. Is it so that I can go into the bunkhouse and get his clothes, while you put his saddle in the older ranch pickup?"

Laying the tree branch aside, he said, "There is no one inside. I will show you where he keeps his clothes. Then I will go get his saddle. He mostly keeps his clothes in an old suitcase. Is he fixing to leave the ranch as well?"

"I don't know. He asked me to get his clothes and his saddle. That is why I am here." Katie smiled at the man. "I said you appear to be a quiet sort, so let's keep it that way." She started for the bunkhouse to begin gathering Tylor's clothes. After completing her task, she walked to the ranch house.

Tag and Laura came out and started for the car. Laura said, "We are going to see Pastor Roth to go over some of the details for Wednesday. We shouldn't be gone very long, unless you want to come with us?"

Katie shook her head. "No, but I was wondering if I could take the older pickup and go into town to see my family? I need to tell them what is going on. I had stopped there when we took Tylor to the hospital to change clothes. Momma was making me a new dress, so she may want me to try it on. I shouldn't be gone too long, that is, if you don't mind, Mr. Taggat?"

Tag was quick to respond. "That will be fine. Take your time, but try to be home before dark."

"Oh, I will," replied Katie. "And, thanks a lot. I should be home by suppertime. I will take care of the chickens and

the feeding of the cows, so don't worry about those chores."
As soon as she saw them cross the Dismal River, Katie hurried
into the house and gathered what clothes Tylor had there. She
remembered that she had finished tailoring a shirt for him to
get his club fist through the sleeve, so she grabbed it. Digging
into the dirty clothes hamper, she found some more clothes.
Carrying all of these to the pickup, she drove to Summit City.
The hospital was her first stop. Carrying the suitcase and one
box into the lobby, she asked at the front desk, "These are
things that Tylor Taggat requested. Is there somewhere that
they can be stored, so that they can be available upon his
release? I have another box and a saddle."

The receptionist came from behind the desk. "We have
a small storeroom here. Then tomorrow, the custodian can
put them in a safe place. Here, let me help you." Katie set the
suitcase and the one box down and returned to the truck for the
last box and the saddle.

After she brought the last load, she said to the
receptionist, "Thank you, you have been a great help. Now, I
have one last request. May I see him for a few minutes to let
him know that they are here?"

"Go on down the hall. Mr. McCann is with him now,
but that should be no problem."

When Katie entered the room, she went to the bedside
of Tylor. Weeping she said, "Tylor, please don't do this to
your mother. She needs you now more than ever. I brought
your clothes and saddle. They are in a storage area near the
front desk." Turning to Jim, she said, "You are a part of this! I
learned this afternoon that you have left the ranch. Are you the
one taking Tylor with you?" She waited for Jim's answer.

Jim was uneasy at Katie's accusations. "I am not taking
him, but he is going with me. Katie, there are some things that
you don't understand and it is just as well that you don't. I will
see that no harm comes to him. He is safe with me. I hope to

54

be finding a place to stay and maybe find some work. If so, then we will have a place of our own. I have money saved up and Tylor has his own money as well. I'm sorry that you have become involved in all this, but I do appreciate your getting Tylor's belongings to him."

Katie looked back at Tylor. "I feel like a traitor to your mother, but I see that your mind is made up in this matter. If you need anything, get in touch with me. I'm sure that you will be able to find a way. Incidentally, your new boots will be ready in a week. Harley the boot maker would be disappointed if you fail to pick them up as soon as they are ready." All the time Katie was in the room, Tylor said nothing. She bent down and kissed his club hand before rushing out of the room. She continued down the hall, trying to control her weeping for Tylor.

Katie visited momentarily with her parents, so that she might say that she had stopped.

CHAPTER 3
A DOG NAMED 'DOG'

Jim McCann was having breakfast at Nick's Café. It was the Monday morning after he had been fired by Tag as foreman of the 99 Ranch. He was rehashing in his mind the episode with Katie the night before in Tylor's hospital room. His big concern at the time, would Katie reveal to Tag and Laura his plan for Tylor not to return to the 99 Ranch? Bill Dolan, who had the insurance agency two doors down from the café stopped in for breakfast. Sitting down next to Jim, he asked, "What are you doing? I see you are having breakfast with the town crowd this morning."

Jim was reluctant to say much. "Oh, I just happened to be in town. I saw that it was time to eat, so thought that I would give Nick a little of my business."

Jim continued to eat his breakfast in silence. He got up to leave and Bill touched his arm and said, "Jim, have another cup of coffee. I am about done, but I would like you to stop by the office. I want to talk with you. That is, unless you are in a hurry."

"Well," said Jim, "I think I have had enough coffee. I will mosey around outside for a bit and watch for you when you are finished." Jim went outside and walked toward the Dismal River. Yesterday he had sat quite a bit with Tylor, so he was glad for the opportunity to stretch his legs. When he figured that Bill had finished his breakfast, he went back to Main Street until he came to the office of the Dolan Insurance Agency.

Jim entered the office. It had that peculiar smell of having been closed up over the weekend. Bill was sitting at his desk to the back of the large office. The other desk nearer the door was as yet unoccupied. Jim presumed that Bill had someone coming in later to sit at that desk. Jim, in his many years, had very few dealings with insurance people.

Bill got up and motioned to Jim. "Come on back and have a seat." Bill sat down as he began the conversation. "Jim, news travels fast in a small town. I was surprised to hear that you are no longer with Tag. I was sorry to hear that this came at the time of TJ's death. What a tragedy!" Bill had not heard of the reason of Jim leaving, but he thought Jim might open up to him. Then he would be in the know and would have news to pass along to others in Summit City.

Jim was cautious in his answer. "Well, sometimes change comes quickly and sometimes it takes decades. But, change happens eventually."

Bill nodded. Then he asked, "Jim, what are your plans?"

Jim was rolling his hat in his hand, just as he had done when Dr. Jessup was querying him yesterday. He looked up at Bill. He was deliberate in his answer. "Bill, I have no plans. I haven't had a plan in fifty years. The last plan I had was when I was about twelve years old. Every morning I planned how I was going to find something to eat that day. When George Taggat took me under his wing, I had no need of a plan. So, I have no plan this morning. However, I sense that perhaps you have a plan for me. If so, Bill, give it to me."

Bill chuckled. "Jim, you amaze me. Had you been born 2000 years earlier, you might have been a counterpart of that Greek philosopher, Socrates. You have an amazing view of life!"

"Now you are funning me," said Jim. "I have never heard of an Irish philosopher; especially, one named Jim. I would need a fancier name than Jim. Just give me your plan."

"Alright, here it is. As you know, about 15 years ago I inherited Dad's ranch. It isn't big enough to make a living by itself, but I don't want to part with it. I am getting tired of fixing fence on weekends and looking after what cows I do run. I like the horses. I enjoy some team roping now and then, but Marilyn and I have purchased a house here in town. She is cleaning the ranch house this morning after moving. I don't want to drive back and forth, checking cows. What would it take for you to move out to the ranch and look after things?"

Jim eased back in his chair. Crossing his legs, he set his hat on his knee. He was being cautious before he spoke. "Bill, you have had time to think this thing through. I have admitted that I haven't formulated a plan in 50 years, you tell me what you would consider as fair for both parties."

Jim immediately knew that he had made a wise decision in letting Bill declare his plan. Bill started right in with the plan. He said, "We are now running 75 cows. We keep back 10 to 15 replacement heifers each year. There are three horses on the place. We raise enough hay for the cattle, but I hire it put up. If I was to give you one-third of the calf crop and pay all expenses of running the operation, would that be satisfactory? Keep in mind, I would want you to live on the place and do the necessary repairs. I would want the horses rode, so that if I am to do any team roping, I don't want any buck in them."

Jim leaned back. He picked up his hat and straightened his legs. "It sounds fair to me. I do want you to know that I want to bring another person to live with me. I will need to buy some furniture to get started."

Bill smiled. He pondered what Jim had told him. "Marilyn bought quite a bit of new furniture when we moved into town. You are welcome to use what we left, but if your lady friend would have something different, just store the old in the shop."

Jim blushed. "No, no, nothing like that. You see, I kind have taken Tylor Taggat under my wing for the time being. Will this be a problem?"

"Jim," he said. "I am the insurance agent for the 99 Ranch. It is a good account. Do you see this as a problem? I like Laura. She is all business. However, if she thinks that something isn't just right, she can be kind of feisty. Is this boy okay? I have heard some weird things about him." Bill stood up and shook Jim's hand. "You haven't said anything about the death of TJ, nor has anyone else. What about that?"

Jim quickly replied. "It was a freak accident. It was a case of being at the wrong place, at the wrong time. As for Tylor, he will be all right with me. He has been through a lot. With the death of his brother on top of everything else has not helped. He is like his mother. They are both survivors." Jim started for the door. "I'm going to look for a used pickup. I wouldn't feel right using your truck for my own personal use. When I'm ready to go out, I will stop by and let you know." He left the office and while he walked along, he thanked God for providing for his livelihood as well as a sanctuary for Tylor.

Jim found a good used pickup. It wasn't one that had been a ranch pickup, but had been owned by a local schoolteacher. The man had married and had learned after becoming a family man that he needed a car instead of a truck. Jim stopped back at the insurance agency and the secretary had the keys to the ranch house ready for him.

Jim drove to the Dolan Ranch and a dog came to greet him. Bill hadn't mentioned anything about a dog. He was a rather small dog and Jim identified him as being a 'heeler.' A number of the ranchers were starting to use a dog in working the cattle. Most of them were 'blue heelers,' but this one was red. Jim neared the house and the dog beat him to the door, turned and growled. Jim stopped in his tracks. This was not any ordinary growl. Jim had not been around many dogs, but he knew that this was one that he didn't want to mess with. He slowly backed off. The dog lay down in front of the door, allowing Jim to leave. The 99 Ranch was unusual, because Tag had never permitted a dog on the place. A dog had mauled Tag when he was quite young, so he had developed a fear of dogs.

As far as Jim knew, dogs and guns were the only things that Tag had ever feared.

While Jim drove back to town, he pondered about the first impression that he had of the ranch. He noted that this was one ranch that needed a bit of tender care. He had sensed that Bill was not one to spend much time fixing things around the place. Especially, if there was a team-roping contest in the neighborhood. Bill would be one to throw down the hammer and saddle the horse. Arriving back at the insurance office, he went in and noted that Bill was alone. He went back to his desk. Bill looked up from his work and began to laugh. "Alice said that you stopped by for the keys. I see by the look on your face that you have met 'Dog.' I meant to tell her to have you wait. I will go out with you and introduce the two of you."

"Oh, we met," said Jim, "but it wasn't a very friendly meeting."

"I have a few minutes, so let's go out and get you acquainted. It will give you a chance to look things over without the fear of being bitten. I won't promise that he won't nip your heels. That is his way of showing his affection." Bill wrote a note and placed it on the front desk. Bill got into his pickup. After seeing Bill's pickup truck, Jim was glad that he had parked his further up the street. Bill's truck was big and black, and did have a shine to it.

Arriving at the ranch, Dog came running to the familiar truck. Jim stepped out and Dog came and sniffed him. Dog then sat down and looked up at Jim. Jim was a bit apprehensive as he reached down to pet the dog. The animal wagged his tail and went over to lay in the shade of the truck. Bill said, "Well, Jim, it looks like you are in. Let's go take a look at the house."

After Jim's assessment of the house, he determined that all he needed was groceries to set up housekeeping. Bill and Marilyn had left enough furniture, bedding and kitchenware in the house to make it livable. They had anticipated that Bill might need those things left to be comfortable, should he need to stay overnight to look after the livestock.

Jim ate dinner at Nick's and then went to see Tylor at the hospital. Tylor had just finished eating when Jim arrived. Tylor greeted him with a wave of his good hand. Since the death of TJ, it seemed that Tylor spoke less and less. He had confided in Jim that he felt responsible for TJ's death because of his inadequacy to warn TJ about the dust devil's approach. He had told Jim that all he could do was stutter. Jim pulled up a chair and sat down near the bed. Speaking in a low voice so that anyone out in the hall might not hear him, he said, "Tylor, I have a place for us." He quickly took note of the smile that Tylor exhibited. It was the first smile that Jim had seen on his face since the accident. "Maybe I should rephrase that statement. The Lord has a place for us. I was eating breakfast at Nick's this morning and Bill Dolan sat down beside me. He approached me with a plan to look after his ranch and cattle. In return, I am to receive a share of the cattle. He has agreed that you can be with me. All we need are our groceries. I even bought a used pickup that is green." Jim paused a moment to let the news sink in. He continued, "The place is five miles east of town on Little Woman creek. Are you willing to live with me? Before you answer, keep in mind, I don't cook like the women of the 99 Ranch. It will be plain, but there will be plenty of it." Jim laughed, awaiting Tylor's answer.

"It sounds g-g-good to me. Now, when do I g-g-get out of here?"

"Whoa now," said Jim. "Dr. Jessup said the earliest that you get out will be Wednesday afternoon or Thursday morning. I don't want an invalid on my hands. When you get out of here, you had better be able to keep up your end of the bargain. That ranch needs a lot of work. Bill Dolan is a nice guy, but he certainly is no handyman." Jim stood up, getting ready to leave. "I am going to leave now and go get some groceries. I may need to practice some, as I haven't cooked since the time I starved the crew so bad that they refused to work. That is another story that I will have to tell you when we are hunkered around the stove this winter." Making his way to the door, he turned and waved good bye.

Tylor was excited about the news that Jim had given him. Now, if he could keep this from his mother until he was out of here. Each evening Laura came, but Katie had not accompanied her, begging off that she had homework to finish. Evidently, Tag had been able to keep the departure of Jim from Laura as well.

CHAPTER 4
THE BURIAL

It was a lovely fall day for the people of the community to pay their last respects to a popular young man. The funeral began at 10:00 a.m. in the Good Hope Community Church. There was an overflow crowd of people that filled the sanctuary and the church basement as well. Six members of the university baseball team served as pallbearers for their teammate that was being laid to rest that day. Following the service, Pastor Roth spoke to the mourners. "Burial will be at the Teasdale Cemetery. Today, you will observe a custom that was begun a number of years ago involving those that have played an active part in the history of this great ranch. The deceased will be taken to the cemetery in the ranch's horse drawn hearse. For those of you that wish to attend the graveside burial, you may follow along in your vehicles and park on the county road. We will proceed on foot for about one hundred yards to the cemetery. If you don't care to attend the burial service, you may remain at the church where a community dinner will be served upon our return."

The pallbearers carried the casket out of the church and placed it into the hearse. Grant Holler dressed in a black suit, complete with a black top hat, was driving the team of matched black geldings that pulled the hearse. True to her word, Katie had the hearse gleaming in the bright sunshine of the day. After pulling into the ranch property, about fifty people accompanied the hearse. The pastor walked directly behind, followed by the pall bearers. Following them was Laura and Tag. Hannah walked beside Laura and Katie was beside Tag. The rest of the mourners followed behind. Though he was at the funeral service, Jim McCann did not go to the cemetery, but observed the burial service from the hillside away from the property line of the 99 Ranch. Neither did he stay for the dinner.

During the time that the people gathered at the church for the community dinner, Laura was a very gracious hostess. She greeted the people and thanked them for coming to her son's service.

Returning home, Laura changed her clothes and sat down for a cup of tea with Hannah. Katie was busy in the kitchen, when Laura and Hannah got into Laura's car and left the ranch, headed for Summit City. At the time that they crossed the bridge south of town, Laura exclaimed, "I forgot to bring clean clothes for Tylor. I'm hoping they will dismiss him today. If not, I wanted you to see him. Hannah, he has regained his strength, but sometimes he seems rather distant. It was difficult for him to learn that Becca was marrying someone else. Oh well, if he is dismissed, I can always buy him some new clothes. I am anxious for you to see him and to see if you denote much change in him" Laura parked the car. No one was at the front desk, so they went down the hall to Tylor's hospital room. Laura was the first one through the door. She abruptly stopped. The room was empty and the bed had been made!

Returning to the front desk that was now occupied, she confronted the receptionist. "Where is Tylor Taggat? He is not in his room!"

"Why, Mrs. Taggat," she replied, while she checked her records, "he checked out at 2:00 p.m. this afternoon. Didn't you know?"

"Who checked him out and where did he get clothes to wear? The ones that he wore in here were nothing but shreds." Laura positioned herself directly in front of the receptionist.

"There was a pretty black haired girl that brought a suitcase and several boxes in here Sunday evening. She even had a saddle that she left. You know her. She is the one that was with you Sunday morning." The receptionist, sensing the hostility of Laura was glad that she had remembered the girl.

"Did you let him out without paying his bill?" Laura

66

was visibly upset that Tylor was gone.

"Mrs. Taggat, when he checked out, he said that he had to go to the bank for the money to pay his bill. He was back in about fifteen minutes and paid in cash. I'm sorry that you missed him, but we presumed that it was alright to dismiss him. Dr. Jessup had signed off on his dismissal. After all, he is an adult."

"I am well aware of that. Thank you for the information." Laura retained her composure until she reached her car. It was then that she leaned back against the fender. "Hannah, I need to take a moment before I get under the wheel. I fear that the mood I am in right now, I might be a menace to society." They got into the car and continued on their way home. Laura said, "I don't understand how Katie could do this to me. She waited until Tag and I left to see Pastor Roth and then she brought Tylor's clothes and saddle to him. That little schemer!"

After they arrived at the ranch, Hannah got out of the car and cautioned Laura. "You are still upset. I don't want to be a witness to any part of this. I already know too much. I'm going down to the river. I will be back in about one-half hour. By that time, I hope that things have been settled. One-half hour."

Laura entered the house and could smell supper cooking. Tag was in his comfortable chair and was reading the newspaper. Katie was busy setting the table when Laura entered the kitchen. Slamming her purse down on the counter top, she said in a loud voice, "Katie, when were you going to tell me that Tylor was not coming home?" Fear was written all over Katie's face. She said nothing and the only noise was the squeak of Tag's chair. He got up to see what had angered Laura. "Are your bags packed so that you can run off with him? If they aren't packed, then you better go pack them, because I am taking you home right now."

Tag came to the kitchen. He leaned against the opening of the door and asked, "What is all the noise about?"

Laura spoke up first. "While we were at Pastor Roth's, this little schemer gathered up all of Tylor's clothes and his saddle. She left them off at the hospital. He checked out this afternoon, paid the hospital bill and is gone." Turning to Katie, she asked, "When were you going to tell me?"

"I'm sorry, Laura," began Katie. "I pleaded with Tylor to return home. He said if I didn't bring him his clothes, then he would come here and steal them. I don't know where he is, but I'm not running away with him. I know that I did wrong. I will go pack my clothes like you asked. I know that I have disappointed you, and for that I am sorry." Katie started to remove her apron. Taking the edge, she wiped the tears from her eyes.

"Hurry it up," said Laura. "I will have me a cup of coffee and then I will take you home." She reached for a cup and started to pour her coffee.

"No," said Tag.

Laura stopped pouring. She turned to him. "What do you mean, no?"

"I mean no! Katie is not leaving. Katie is a part of this family. In the past six months, she has gone through more with this family than most kids do during a lifetime. Laura, this is one time that you are not getting your way. I will not allow you to run this girl off because of something that your son coerced her into doing. Katie stays!"

"Mr. Taggat," whispered Katie through the tears. "I don't want to cause problems between the people the two I love. It is best that I leave."

"Katie," Tag continued, "It isn't just about you. This is about Tylor and his irresponsible behavior. Laura can't see it, nor will she admit it. Katie, I don't want you caught in the middle, but I would prefer that you stay. You are the only sane one here in a time of crisis."

"That's fine," shouted Laura. "Make your choice, Tag. It is either Katie or me."

"Laura, I have learned long ago, not to give a person an ultimatum." Tag paused. After a moment, he continued. "Generally, pride overrules logic or common sense. You are counting on me to choose you, but are you willing to risk all these years of marriage because of your pride? I'm not going to choose. I want both of you in this family. I'm going to leave the choice up to the two of you. If either of you think that you cannot live with the other, then you are free to go, but I will not choose."

Katie rushed to Laura and embraced her. She cried out, "Please don't go, Laura, please don't go. I'm sorry for the hurt that I have caused. There has been too much hurt."

Laura hugged Katie. "I'm not going. I'm sorry for being selfish and not trusting you."

Hannah came in, and when she saw the two women embracing, she knew that things were well. That reminded her of the song that was sung at the funeral this morning. It was, When Peace Like a River, by H. G. Spafford/P. P. Bliss.

When Peace, like a river, attendeth my way,
When sorrows like sea billows roll;
Whatever my lot,
Thou hast taught me to say,
It is well, it is well with my soul.
It is well, it is well
With my soul, with my soul, it is well, it is well, with my soul.

****

Wednesday afternoon, following the funeral, Jim stopped by the hospital. Tylor had checked out of the hospital and was waiting for him. Tylor appreciated his mother's help with his finances. He was now independent from the 99

Ranch and Tag Taggat. He had paid his hospital bill and still had money in the bank. When they drove up to the house at the Dolan ranch, Jim remarked. "Well, Tylor, this is it. I have brought you here, but what you do with your life from here on out is up to you. Keep in mind, I am not your mother."

When Tylor got out of the truck, he was greeted by 'Dog.' Tylor was excited! "You have a d-d-dog. I can't believe after all these years, you have a d-d-dog." He reached down and petted the red heeler, who was eagerly wagging his tale. "What's his n-n-name?" asked Tylor.

"His name is Dog," replied Jim, "and don't get excited about him just yet. He is part of the package of 75 cows, three horses and a lot of work. Bring your gear inside for now."

Upon entering the house, Jim pointed and said, "That is your room at the end of the hall. How about if we take turns cooking and cleaning? It will be one week at a time, starting Monday morning. I have already started, so next Monday morning, I expect to see you in the kitchen."

Jim started each day with breakfast at 6:00 a.m. and they were at work by 7:00. Jim saw what work was needed and he began to prioritize the tasks to get the small ranch ready for winter. They began by working on the cattle corrals, but that was delayed, when they found 40 head of Johnny Collins' yearlings in with the cows. They spent two days fixing fence and another day of sorting cattle. Jim was disappointed in the horses on the ranch, but he didn't think he would spend his share of the cattle money on a horse of his own. With the fences fixed, he anticipated there would be little need for a good ranch horse. He would use the horses that they had to check the cattle, so that they would remain gentle for Bill to ride.

The first time they went to Summit City for groceries and supplies, Tylor stopped at the hardware store and ordered a bow, along with arrows for hunting. On the return home, Tylor asked, "Jim, if I were to b-b-butcher a deer, w-w-would you object?"

Jim turned off the main road and started up the trail road to the house. "I'm not sure what you are trying to tell me. Are you going to buy a permit to shoot a deer, or are you going to just shoot the deer because it is running on the ranch? You realize, if you shoot a deer out of season, the game warden may hear the rifle shot and come to investigate. That would be illegal."

Tylor thought a moment before explaining what he meant. "I didn't say that I w-w-would shoot the deer. I was t-t-talking about b-b-butchering a deer. I don't own a r-r-rifle anyway. We need some way to c-c-cut our costs of living. Do you r-r-realize that Bill Dolan is not g-g-going to give you any c-c-cattle money until next fall? Right now, we are w-w-working for our board and boarding ourselves. I have ordered a b-b-bow and some h-h-hunting arrows. I can keep us in meat if you don't mind eating v-v-venison. My way of thinking is, the d-d-deer are eating our grass, so therefore we are entitled to h-h-harvest a few now and then. Would that bother you?"

"I understand about them eating the grass on the ranch. For me to take a deer out of season would be wrong. Maybe it isn't for you, but for me it is." Jim anticipated that this would be the end of the conversation, but it wasn't.

"Let me p-p-present an analogy," began Tylor. "In the book of First C-C-Corinthians, the Apostle Paul c-c-covered the eating of m-m-meat offered to idols. Now if I understand that r-r-right, what if the Christians were invited to eat at a f-f-friend's house? But, they suspected that the m-m-meat they were about to eat had b-b-been from animals sacrificed to idols. If they d-d-didn't ask, then it was all r-r-right to eat the meat. But, if they asked and they were told that it had been s-s-sacrificed to idols, they shouldn't eat it. Therefore, if you d-d-don't ask, and I d-d-don't tell, then you can eat my v-v-venison."

Jim laughed and shaking his head, he said, "I am thinking that it will be a long winter in the same house with a theologian. Bill Dolan accused me of being a philosopher, comparable to Socrates that lived 2000 years ago. Maybe it is a good thing that we don't have a gun."

CHAPTER 5
THE READING OF THE WILL

Katie got off the school bus at the corner near the bridge that crossed the Dismal River. She looked in the mailbox and retrieving the mail, she continued the walk to the ranch house. It occurred to her that this was the third day in a row that Laura had not picked up the mail. This may be no big deal, but Laura was a great one for getting the mail as soon as it had arrived. Entering the house, she went to the kitchen, placing her schoolbooks on the kitchen table. This was to be her last year in high school, so she was looking forward to leaving Summit City. Since the death of TJ, and the departure of Tylor, life at the 99 Ranch was not the same. She called out, "Anybody home?" She detected a muffled sound from the spare bedroom. Opening the door, she was startled at what she saw. Laura was at her easel, brush in hand. She was still in her nightgown with a flimsy robe that did little to cover her. She was barefoot and her hair had not been combed.

Flinging her palette at Katie, she screamed, "Why didn't you tell me, why didn't you tell me?" She began sobbing, as she slumped down on her stool.

Katie rushed to her and taking Laura in her arms, she asked, "Tell you what? What was I supposed to tell you?" It was then that she saw what Laura had been painting. The canvas was entirely black, with four large red animals, one at each corner. Rather hideously painted, their focus was drawn to a young girl in the center of the canvas. Katie had never seen Laura paint anything like this before. All these things were troubling to her. Not only the painting, but also how unkempt Laura appeared. She knew that Laura was sleeping later each day and not fixing Tag's breakfast. When Katie saw this, she began to get up earlier to prepare Tag's breakfast. Tag never said much, but Katie could see that the absence of Laura at breakfast disturbed him.

"Jim," she cried out. "Jim is gone, and I don't know where he is. But you know where he is. Katie knows everything. Why didn't you tell me that he had left? I want to know if Tylor is with him?"

"Why blame me for his leaving," answered Katie. "I would have thought that Tag would have told you. I am presuming that Tylor is with him. I accused Jim of taking Tylor with him. He refuted my allegation, but he said that Tylor was going with him. I would be surprised if they would have gone very far. I can find them, but tell me Laura, do you really want me to find them?"

"Of course I do," Laura fired back. "What kind of a mother do you think I am?"

Taking Laura by the arm, Katie pulled her until she was standing in front of the dresser mirror. "Why don't you tell me what kind of a mother you are! Take a good look at yourself and tell me what kind of a wife you are as well. You haven't fixed Tag his breakfast this past week, because that is what I have been doing. The same goes for his supper. You aren't the only one to have lost someone. We all have. Now, let me start braiding your hair and I will tell you what I will do." Katie began to comb and braid Laura's hair, all the time, carefully massaging her scalp and shoulders. When she was finished, Katie had Laura go to her bedroom, where Katie began to apply make-up to Laura's face. Soon she restored the radiance in her countenance. While all this was going on, Katie was talking to Laura. "Tomorrow, with your permission, I will drive one of the ranch vehicles to Summit City. I believe that I can find Tylor. If I find Tylor, I will also have found Jim. I have a hunch that they have not gone far, as neither one is comfortable in strange surroundings. I sense that they are within a ten mile radius of town, probably in some rundown abandoned shack." Katie began to lotion Laura's arms and hands. She followed up with a manicure. "Now, I want you to find one of your better dresses and then we will stop for tea. Tonight I will fix supper so that you can entertain Tag during that time. Try to reminisce about the good times. Tonight I will permit you to remove his boots and fetch his slippers. If you want to be loved, you need to show love. There is one other thing that I would ask of you Laura. I would like to have the picture that is on your easel. May I have it?"

Laura answered, "But why would you want that ugly thing? I have better pictures than that one."

"Why, you ask? Because it is ugly and depressing, that is why! It is totally out of character of the artist and I want to destroy it. I want you to know what I plan on doing with it. I will burn it! That is what I will do, I will burn it!" The very thought of the hideous animals made Katie shudder.

"Take it, Katie, take it and burn it," Laura exclaimed. "I had so much hatred in my heart, that I revealed it on the canvas. I have never painted anything so revolting. Oh Katie, my Katie. How fortunate I am to have such a discerning friend as you. I guess that I am ready for my tea."

After they had their tea, Katie took the canvas to the burning barrel. She cleaned up the paint from the palette that had been thrown at her earlier that afternoon.

Tag came into the house, bearing the look of a defeated man. The drought still continued. With the absence of Jim and Tylor, and of course the death of TJ, the ranch was greatly undermanned. Laura met him at the door. "Oh, Tag," said Laura, "you look exhausted. Katic is preparing supper for us. In the meantime, I have some coffee by your chair. Here, let me get your boots off and put on your slippers. The mail is here also. I see you have a letter from a Mr. Adkins in Madden. Do you know him?" Laura kneeled down to remove his boots.

Tag looked down at Laura. He remarked, "Laura, it is good to see you looking so beautiful tonight. You must have had a good afternoon." He picked up the letter and took out his jack knife to slit it open. "It is from a lawyer. Who is suing me now? This is just what I need on top of everything else. Here, Laura, read it to me and explain the big words to me as you read along."

Laura took the letter and began to read; "So much for the usual salutations. The contents of the letter states: The reading of the will of Metta Taggat, deceased, will take place at the office of Mr. Thomas Adkins, Attorney at Law, on Tuesday, October 23rd, at 2:00 p.m. The office is located at 208 Main St., in Madden, Nebraska. As your name is mentioned in the will, it will be of your interest to be present at this time. I apologize for the time lapse between the demise of Mrs. Metta Taggat and the reading of the will. However, her last will and testament was discovered as a result of going through Mrs. Taggat's personal items. Sincerely, Mr. Thomas Adkins." Laura set the letter down. "Well, Tag, what do you think of that?"

"I think that it would be a wasted afternoon, that is what I think. If you think that woman would leave anything to me, you don't know Metta Taggat." Tag settled in his chair and picked up *The Sentinel* to catch up on the latest news. Now that the paper came twice a week, he enjoyed looking through it.

Laura was behind his chair and glancing at the paper over his shoulder. She started rubbing his shoulders with her hands. She began running her fingers through his hair. As Tag aged, his hair continued to remain thick. She sensed that he was enjoying this attention. "Tag," she said, "let us make an afternoon of it. We can eat dinner at Nick's in Summit City and then drive over to Madden. The reading of the will shouldn't take long. You need to get away for a short time." Tag didn't say anything. He continued to read the paper. Laura stopped caressing him and went around to the front of Tag. Peeking over the top of the paper, she continued her plea. "Tag Taggat, aren't you the least bit curious as to what the will says? It will be just like Christmas. You never know what you are going to get until the wrapping comes off."

Katie came to the living room and told them that supper was ready. After they sat down, Laura said, "Guess what? Tag has been named in Metta Taggat's will, so we will be going to Madden on Tuesday afternoon for the reading of the will. Tag and I will eat dinner at Nick's and then drive over. I can hardly wait. Tag, do you have a will?" Laura paused a moment before continuing. "Do you realize that if you don't have a will, the state appoints an executor? Then, your estate is divided up according to the laws of the state. At that point, you have nothing to say about your estate. Well, Tag, do you have a will?" Finally, Tag shook his head. "Well, I think that you should contact that attorney of yours. What is his name?" Tag didn't say anything, nor did he supply the name of his attorney. "Karl Larson! That is his name! A bit pompous, but I am sure that he is a fine lawyer. I have a little money in the bank and I have continued to own my milk cows. Perhaps I should have Leon Kelly prepare my will. I could give out a dollar here and a dollar there. It would be like a shopping spree, as I hand out my money and assets to those I find worthy."

Katie reached out to Laura. "Don't you think that we should eat before the food gets cold and you give away all of your estate?" Katie was amazed at the change in Laura's demeanor in such a short time. And, Tag was apparently encouraged at Laura's gaiety, charm and beauty.

The next morning Katie came out to the kitchen to begin preparing breakfast for Tag. Prior to entering the kitchen from the dining room, she saw Laura at the stove. Tag came up behind her, putting his arms around her. He asked, "Does the lovely cook need help preparing breakfast?" It was then that Katie returned to her room, tiptoeing down the hall.

"No," she answered, "but perhaps my handsome husband could set the table. Where is that Katie? I thought she would be up by now."

"Oh, let her sleep. She is so busy matchmaking that I am sure it is taxing on such a one as young as she." Tag grinned at the thought.

Laura replied at his insinuation that Katie was a matchmaker. "She does no such thing! Just because I happened to bring you your slippers last night---." Laura stopped in mid sentence.

Tag asked, "And, what were you going to say? Katie has always brought me my slippers, almost from the beginning. I remember the first time that she removed my boots. It was one of those days that the horse had stepped on my foot and getting that boot off felt good. And then I remembered all the filth and dirt that boot had stepped in that day and she gripped and tugged until the boot came off. She never commented about the smell or filth. Tell me, Laura, why didn't she bring my slippers to me last night?"

"You are right, Tag. It was she that made last night so special. It was like the honeymoon that we never had. I'm sorry Tag, that I have failed you as a wife. In my own self-pity, I drove us further and further apart. Yesterday, Katie came home from school and I lashed out at her, but it was she that made me see myself as I really was. I was still in my nightgown and my hair was uncombed and in tangles. When she forced me to look at myself in the mirror, it was then that I realized how far I had gone. Katie was the one that encouraged me to put on one of my better dresses and to greet you as you came in the door. And to think, I was willing to send her home because of my anger. It was you, Tag, and your wisdom that prevented me from sending her out of our lives. Thank you."

While they ate their breakfast, Tag thought, *if only someone such as Laura or Katie had been available to prevent me from forcing Jim McCann to leave the ranch.* After breakfast, Tag kissed Laura and went to his truck to begin the day on the ranch.

After Tag had left, Katie came to the kitchen. She opened the refrigerator door and as she pulled a jar of milk from the top shelf, she said, "I guess that I must have overslept. I need to hurry if I am going to find Jim and Tylor as I promised."

"Thank you, Katie," Laura said. "I saw you in the kitchen doorway when I turned to Tag after he gave me a hug this morning. I know that you tiptoed back to your room. You have shown me how I need to put romance back into my marriage. It seems that I need to continually thank God for your coming into my life. What disappoints me most is that from time to time, in my own selfishness, I forget what a blessing you are."

"Laura," responded Katie softly. "You have taught me many things about life in the time that I have been here. I see that in the community, you and Tag have great wealth. Yet, in all this you are not immune from heartache and despair. But, you continue to praise God. When I marry, I hope that I will remember the things that I have learned here to help me be a wife and mother like Laura Taggat." She hugged Laura, while trying to suppress a sob. Laura hugged her in return. They clung to one another for a short time.

"What vehicle do you want me to take this morning?" asked Katie.

"I failed to check with Tag, so it would probably be best that you take my car. I will take the morning to go through TJ's clothing and things. I think that it is best that I do this alone." Laura took a moment to gaze out the kitchen window.

Katie drove Laura's blue sedan to Summit City. Stopping at the County Court House, she went directly to the sheriff's office.

"Sheriff Morgan," she began, "I imagine that you keep tabs on about everyone in your county. So, perhaps you can tell me where I might find Jim McCann."

"How can I be sure that you are looking for Jim McCann?" The sheriff tipped his white hat back on his head and leaned back in his chair. "Or, perhaps you are really looking for young Tylor Taggat?"

"Actually," she replied, "it is both of them, but I figured that if I found one, I would find the other. Where are they?"

"I will tell you, but I might give you a word of warning as well. Feel free to pass it along to those two. I'm keeping my eye on young Taggat. I get reports that he is running the countryside at all hours of the night. He and a dog have been caught in the headlights of people late at night. I don't like it, but I guess there is no law that he has broken. You might pass this information along to Jim, that I will be watching Tylor and his activities. This will save me a trip. Now, take this road that goes by the Courthouse and go five miles east. As soon as you cross Little Woman Creek, turn right. It is where Bill Dolan lived before he and Marilyn moved into town. It is a white stucco house. Jim bought a green Ford pickup and it will be parked under the cottonwood tree east of the house unless he has cleaned out the garage. Have you got all that?" he asked.

"Yes, sir," answered Katie. "It appears that someone from your office has been rather thorough in their reporting. Thank you for your information, Sheriff." Katie left the Courthouse, troubled by what the sheriff had told her. The directions were precise and Katie arrived at the ranch house a few minutes after ten o'clock. Parking alongside the green pickup, she got out and was met by a small dog. The coloring was similar to some of the cows that Laura had, which she had described as being roan, a mixture of red and white hairs. Katie saw that Tylor and Jim were near the barn, apparently working on the corral. Katie chose to ignore the dog and proceeded to walk by him. As she passed by, the dog touched his nose to her bare heel. She jumped and screamed. Tylor heard her and came running. Katie was yelling, "That dog bit me. That dog bit me."

Tylor came around the barn and saw that it was Katie. "What h-h-happened? I h-h-heard you screaming?"

"That dog, that miserable creature bit me. Besides that, he scared me half to death." Katie felt down on her ankle, but found no blood.

Jim came around the corner. "Morning, Katie. I see that you have met 'Dog.' Yes, that is his name. It is not very original, but he answers to that and it is easy to remember. He is what you might call a red heeler. He enjoys nipping at heels, whether it is beast or human. Not to change the subject, but what brings you out to our abode?"

Katie was still miffed by the greeting from Dog. "You two could have told us where you were living. You both took off like a couple of thieves. I stopped at the sheriff's office, figuring he would know where all the low-life was hanging out."

Jim replied, "I'm sorry if we worried you. It took us a while to get settled and I guess we figured that we wouldn't be missed. So, we just kind of let it stay that way. Now that you have come to visit us, we will need to remember to send you a Christmas card."

Katie was upset. "Jim McCann, this is no joking matter. You two sure remembered whom to call on when Tylor wanted his clothes and saddle. Laura doesn't know why you left. She had already suffered enough grief in the loss of TJ and then for the two of you to disappear, it was too much."

"I had no intention to hurt her, but I couldn't face her and tell her why I left. I am sure the same goes for Tylor. We will just leave it that way. Please tell her we are sorry that things turned out the way they did."

Tylor spoke up. "Katie, we t-t-take turns c-c-cooking and this is my w-w-week. Will you stay for d-d-dinner, so you can tell Mama what k-k-kind of a cook I am?"

81

"Sure," said Katie, "I will stay for dinner. Jim can show me around the place while you fix it."

When Tylor neared the ranch house, Jim hollered to him. "Be sure to wash your hands and use the clean plates now that we are having company." Tylor waved his good arm and disappeared around the corner of the house.

Katie came right to the point. "Jim, the sheriff sent a message with me this morning. He has had reports of people seeing Tylor and the dog running around the countryside late at night. He said that he was keeping an eye on young Taggat and his late night runs. Why is he out late at night?"

Jim shook his head. "I don't know and he won't tell me. I was first aware of him leaving when I heard something outside at about eleven o'clock one night. I got up and Dog was nowhere around. I thought that strange, so I went to Tylor's room and he was gone. I stayed up and it was three in the morning before the two of them showed up. The next night I stayed up to determine when he would leave and it was about ten that night. I work him hard through the day, thinking I can wear him out, but each night he is out running. He is only getting five or six hours of sleep, except for Sunday when he sleeps much of the day. However, Dog sleeps most of the day so that he can run with him at night. Maybe Tylor will tell you. I will try to get him alone with you to see if he will." Changing the subject, Jim said, "Tell Laura, I'm sorry to cause her worry. Katie, between you and me, it was impossible for Tylor to remain in the home any longer. He had to get out!" It saddened Katie to hear Jim say that. She didn't understand why Tylor had to leave. Dinnertime was drawing near, so she and Jim started for the house.

Upon entering, Katie could smell dinner cooking and already she was impressed. Jim showed her through the house. She noticed how well kept the home was for being inhabited by two bachelors. When they sat down, Jim asked the blessing on the food and they began to eat. After two bites of the meat, Katie asked, "What kind of meat is this? It's different than beef."

Jim and Tylor exchanged glances and Jim nodded. Tylor said, "It is v-v-venison." He gave no further explanation.

Not thinking, Katie said, "But, deer season doesn't open for another two weeks!" She then realized what she had said. Then trying to recover, she said, "I don't know how you do it, but in cooking your beef, you certainly have given it a different flavor. I like it!"

After they finished their dinner, Katie thanked Tylor for the meal. "Now I can go home and tell your mother that you and Jim are not going to starve to death. You are doing well. Now, let me help you with the dishes."

Jim got up and started for the door. "Katie, I will go and finish repairing the corral gate. Thanks for coming out and I will see that Tylor keeps in touch with his mother. We have a phone now." Tipping his hat, he said, "Bye."

That was his indication that Tylor was all hers. Tylor started washing the dishes and Katie blurted right out, "Tylor, why are you running the countryside late at night? Sheriff Morgan has had reports of others seeing you and Dog roaming well into the night. He is disturbed by this and he is waiting for you to make one misstep."

Tylor slumped down on a chair. "It is the d-d-demons, Katie. It is the d-d-demons. They won't let me sleep. It is that they k-k-keep going through my head all n-n-night long. If I r-r-run, I can escape them. Finally, I'm so t-t-tired that I can s-s-sleep until morning."

"What demons?" she asked. "What are they like?"

"Faces! They are f-f-faces! They are the faces of m-m-men that I have k-k-killed in the name of war. When I put that riflescope on those m-m-men, once I p-p-pulled the trigger, it was l-l-like taking their picture. Unfortunately, my m-m-mind

83

is the film." Tylor slapped the side of his head. "It is here, it is all r-r-right here!"

Laura stood up and held his head to her breast. "I'm sorry, Tylor, I'm sorry. Do you remember that you asked for God's forgiveness? Do you remember that it was the shed blood of Jesus Christ that paid the penalty for your actions in killing those men? You were under orders by the Army. Had you disobeyed, you would have faced the firing squad. Does it help to pray?" She released him and turning her back to the sink she leaned against the counter.

Tylor nodded. "I p-p-ray and then I fall asleep while p-p-praying. Then I dream and the demons come b-b-back in my dreams, but they won't l-l-leave. That is when I run." Tylor continued to sit on the chair.

Katie saw how tormented he appeared and was perplexed as how she might help him. "Tylor, perhaps you could talk with Dr. Jessup about this and he could get you some help."

It was then that he jumped up from his chair. Reaching out and taking Katie by the wrist, he shouted, "No, no, no! They would l-l-lock me up for being c-c-crazy. I can't be l-l-locked up! I have to run from the d-d-demons! And don't you t-t-tell anyone. Not even J-J-Jim knows about the d-d-demons!"

Katie tried to pull his fingers of the left hand from around her wrist. "Stop, Tylor, stop. You are hurting me!"

He released his grip and tried to apologize to her, but she was out the door before his stammering words could leave his lips. He looked out the door and saw that she was talking to Jim, while they stood by Laura's car. He couldn't hear what they were talking about, but Tylor saw that she was angry. She was rubbing her wrist where he had held her.

Jim asked, "What happened in there?"

"Nothing," answered Katie, "it got a little heated, but nothing serious."

Jim took her hand, and turned it over. He noticed that her wrist was red. "Then why are you rubbing your wrist?"

"He didn't realize that he was holding me so tight. He does have a tremendous grip." Trying to defuse the matter, lest Jim get angry with Tylor, she asked. "Does he have a gun?"

"No. Why do you ask?" Jim thought, *does she think Tylor is dangerous to others?*

"How does he kill the deer?" asked Katie.

Jim laughed, "What deer? He has a bow and arrow. He rigged it so that he could shoot it and he is good with it, but no deer. He just has a different way of preparing beef."

Katie started to get into the car. She said, "I will leave now. Tell Tylor that I'm all right." Reaching out to touch him, she said, "Jim, thanks for taking him under your wing. You two stay busy and out of trouble."

Katie returned to the 99 Ranch in time for her afternoon tea with Laura. Laura was anxious to hear if she had located Tylor or Jim. Laura asked, "Well, did you find them? Tell me. I want to know if they are all right."

Setting her cup down, Katie said, "Yes, I found them. They are looking after the cattle for Bill Dolan. Apparently he and his wife have moved into town and he needed someone to live on the property. They have been busy fixing fences and corrals. The house was neat and clean. Tylor prepared a tasty dinner for Jim and me. They trade household tasks each week and it was Tylor's week to cook. The family dog, appropriately named 'Dog' stayed at the ranch. While I was walking by, the nasty little creature nipped me on the heel. Incidentally, Sheriff Morgan knew where they were and gave me excellent directions to the ranch." Katie reached out and took Laura's hand. "I think that now you know where they are located, it is a good time to let them make the next move."

"Thank you, Katie. The next move is theirs to make. I will interfere no further."

Tuesday morning arrived as scheduled with the sun coming up later each day during this late fall season. Should you have been a visitor at the 99 Ranch, one would have thought it to be Christmas morning, except for the absence of the Christmas decorations. Laura was absolutely euphoric when she came out to prepare breakfast. The moment that Tag and Katie came into the kitchen, she proclaimed, "Today is the day of the reading of Metta Taggat's will!" Tag nodded, and headed for the coffeepot for an early morning cup. Laura waltzed around the kitchen, proclaiming her message.

Katie spoke up, "This sounds like a holiday. Does that mean that I don't have to go school, so that I can attend the reading of Metta Taggat's will?"

"No, Katie," stated Laura, "it means that you have to go to school, so that you might get some smarts to make enough in your lifetime in order to have a will. No holiday for Katie O'Neal."

Tag set his coffee cup on the counter. "Katie, you can go in my place. I have work to do and I imagine the extent of my inheritance will fit into a paper sack."

"Tag Taggat! We talked about this the other evening. We will have dinner at Nick's and then go to Madden for the reading of the will. I think it is quite exciting." Laura continued. "How often is a person included in a will?" After Laura said that, she wished she could take those words back. At the reading of his father's will, everything was left to Tag's stepmother, Mavis. She in turn left her estate to her nieces and nephews. Tag had received nothing. Laura said, "I'm sorry Tag, to have brought up old wounds. In my gaiety, I was thoughtless. But, I do want to make it a day away from the cares of the ranch for us. Besides, I have no plans for dinner other than Nick's."

"Nick's is a good place to eat, so we have a date. I will be ready at 11:30, and yes, I will clean up and wear my good boots." Tag noticed the smile of triumph on Laura's face.

After a good meal at Nick's, they had a leisurely drive to Madden. It was interesting to see how the summer and fall rains had a hit and miss pattern over the landscape. Those ranches that had received the fall rains were pleasant to view. Those that were missed by the rains were somewhat depressing. Tag could sympathize with those ranchers. He was also experiencing the same drought conditions at the 99 Ranch.

The town of Madden was comparable in size to many of the Sandhills county seats. Each county seat was self sufficient to a point, offering law and order, educational opportunities and medical services. It was easy to find the attorney's office. His name was on the large window facing Main Street.

Tag and Laura remained in the truck until just a few minutes before two o'clock. They went into the office, and Tag identified himself. He and Laura were ushered into a conference room, occupied by a priest, two nuns and the attorney. The attorney introduced himself as Mr. Thomas Adkins. He then acknowledged Father Peroni, Sister Jacoby and Sister Reilly. They were seated on one side of the table. He turned and acknowledged Mr. and Mrs. Taylor George Taggat.

The attorney opened a document and began to read and define. "This is pretty much a forthright will, with the usual terminology. Let me begin with the crux of the will, but I may interrupt at various times. Metta Taggat included some explanations as to her reasoning in her decision making. Keep in mind, they have not been notarized, so they are not official, but I am sure you might find them interesting as I did. Shall we begin?"

"To my late husband Hiram's nephew, Taylor George Taggat, I bequeath cemetery plot 11A in the Madden Catholic Cemetery."

"What the ---," Tag started to blurt out when he received a sharp kick under the table from Laura.

Mr. Adkins looked up. "Mr. Taggat, I know this seems unusual, but please bear with me, as I read what Metta Taggat had to say. In her letter she says, 'Tag, you are the only Taggat for which I had any compassion. Your mother died at the time of your birth. Hiram and I were childless for a number of years. We pleaded with your father to give you to us that we might raise you. He refused and later he remarried, and another raised you. This plot is next to where I will be buried and if I could not have you in life, perhaps I could have you in death.' A bit unusual, but we are here to honor her wishes nevertheless."

Laura would not look at Tag for fear that she would break out in laughter. To think that I brought him all this way to inherit a cemetery plot.

"There is one other item that pertains to you, Mr. Taggat," said the attorney. "Well, actually two, but they are somewhat linked together in her correspondence. To Taylor George Taggat, I bequeath the sum of Ten Thousand Dollars and the contents of the attached envelope." Mr. Adkins handed the envelope to Tag. "Please note that it has not been opened, so you may open it if you desire."

Tag opened the envelope and in tipping it on end, a like new gold wedding band rolled into the palm of his hand. Looking in, he saw a slip of paper. Tag read it to the group. "See, I wasn't so bad after all." He looked up at the others to see if these words meant anything to them, but there was no sign of recognizable significance. Had he looked to his wife, he would have seen by the flush of her face that she recognized the wedding band that Metta Taggat had requested Laura return on the day of her annulment.

Laura asked, "Is there a date on these correspondence items?"

Mr. Adkins responded, "Why yes, yes there is, let me see." Looking up, Mr. Adkins said, "September 30, 1972. Keep in mind, that even though these things are rather unusual,

I certainly believe that Metta Taggat was cognizant of what she did and wrote. Mr. Taggat that is the extent of what Metta Taggat had for you. However, you are certainly welcome to remain for the balance of the reading of the will."

Tag looked at Laura and she looked at him and they each nodded to one another. Tag spoke up, "Mr. Adkins, we will stay, if nothing more than to see what other surprises are in store. Knowing Aunt Metta, I'm sure we haven't heard the last." The others nodded in agreement.

Mr. Adkins continued, "To the Sisters of St Elisabeth, I bequeath the balance of my estate for the continued operation of their orphanage." Mr. Adkins paused while he pulled a letter from an envelope. He continued, "There is a note as well and it reads as follows: Hiram and I dearly sought to have children and when it became evident that we could have no children of our own, we looked to adoption. All state and private adoption agencies refused us because of our age, except for the Sisters of St. Elisabeth. They found us a son, and we called him Tylor George Taggat. He was a blessing to our heart and a devoted son. Unfortunately, he was taken from us all too soon. Because of the devotion of the Sisters of St. Elisabeth, I wish to reward them for their gift of loving-kindness. Her signature appears at the bottom of the letter."

"That concludes the reading of the will. Are there any questions?"

Father Peroni asked, "Is there any estimate of the value of the estate? And, do you expect any contesting of the will?"

"Apparently there are no blood relatives and this is rather a forthright will. I don't foresee any problem, but you never can be sure." Mr. Adkins seemed reluctant to disclose the value of the estate. However, he did say, "The estate is rather large and could be in excess of three million dollars. The Taggats were a frugal people." Sister Reilly had not heard that the Taggats were frugal. She had fainted at the three million-dollar mark.

Tag and Laura didn't stay for Sister Reilly to be revived. When they got to the street, they both burst with laughter. Tag stood with his hand on the hood of his truck and laughed until he was crying. Laura had her hand on the door handle of the truck and was laughing so hard that her side ached.

After they left Madden, Tag started to laugh. "Now I remember you saying it was just like Christmas. You don't know what you are getting until the wrapping comes off. That was true today. Had I known that she was giving me a wedding band, I could have waited until today to marry you. Just think, I could have saved twenty dollars. Did you see that ring? It was like new."

"With a remark like that, you may use that cemetery plot quicker than you think. Do you realize that had your father given you up, that entire ranch would have been yours? Life certainly has some strange twists." Laura thought that Metta certainly had a strange sense of humor. The ten thousand dollars is what Metta received at the time of her son's death. Evidently she realized that she was paying Tag for raising her grandson. As to the ring, she knew that Laura would recognize it immediately.

Supper that night was just as much fun. Tag and Laura each tried to tell Katie about the reading of the will. Each story brought fits of laughter.

That night, Laura lay in her bed and the thought came to her; *all that was rightfully Tylor's, but she determined that a court battle over money could only bring heartache. It would reveal to Tag the biological father of Tylor. Metta gave Tag and Laura what she wanted, and she gave the Sisters of St. Elisabeth what they needed. There is no place for greed.* That night, Laura had a peaceful sleep.

90

CHAPTER 6
A DRINK NOW AND THEN

The days following the reading of the will brought
about some interesting revelations to the inhabitants of the 99
Ranch. Laura chose a warm afternoon in late October to go
to the Dismal River to pray and thank God for His goodness
and grace. She now knew where Tylor and Jim were and that
they were safe. She pondered about going to see them, but
had decided to wait until her heart could stand no more before
her visit. Perhaps Tylor would contact her. She trusted that
she had not caused anything for Tylor to reject her, but she
was uncertain. Laura tried to remember if there was anything
in TJ's accident report that would give her a clue of Tylor's
failure to return to the 99 Ranch. She had requested that Sheriff
Morgan give her a copy of his finalized report, but to date she
had received nothing.

Laura walked along the Dismal River, watching
the stream as she tossed bits of sticks into the water. How
interesting she thought; *the river is like life and we are like*
the sticks. We go along through life, never to return to retrace
our steps. Laura thought back to Metta Taggat and the will.
Metta Taggat had the opportunity to establish contact with
her grandson Tylor shortly after his birth. Each year, Laura
afforded her that opportunity, and yet she rejected, year after
year. It is amazing. God affords us the same opportunity to
establish a relationship with His Son, and yet, people reject
Him, year after year. One year, it will be too late, as it was with
Metta Taggat.

Laura returned to the familiar cottonwood stump. Tag
had given Laura the wedding band that Metta Taggat had
bequeathed to Tag. *I shall put the ring into my safety deposit*
box until such time that Tylor has use for a wedding band. Tag
was encouraged with the ten thousand dollars that he would

soon receive. He intended to use the money to hire additional help on the ranch. Yes, it is always about the ranch with Tag. We always seem to have our own priorities. Laura was jolted back to reality. She saw the school bus turn the corner and Katie was crossing the bridge that spanned the Dismal River. Katie will be expecting me to have her tea ready. If I hurry, I can be to the house before she realizes that I am late. When Katie saw that Laura was trying to get to the house first, she started to run. Waiting at the gate, Katie teased Laura and called her 'slowpoke.'

Katie said, "I had thought I might ride home with Mr. Taggat, but I wasn't sure how long he was going to stay in town. I knew if I didn't come home on the bus, you would be worried."

"I didn't know that he was going to town," said Laura. "I was down by the river, but I never saw him leave. I do admit to daydreaming, but surely I would have heard him. That is strange, unless he went out the back way."

Laura and Katie waited supper until after dark. Finally at 7:30, Laura said, "Katie, we just as well eat. I have no idea what could be keeping him this late. I thought that he would at least call to let us know that he was going to be late. Surely, he didn't have an accident on the way home. I will wait until 9:00 before I go looking for him, but sure as I do, he will show up and wonder what all the fuss was about." Laura looked out the window, thinking that he would show up at anytime. Katie was working on her homework, but she was troubled as well.

It was almost nine o'clock when Katie came to Laura. "Laura," she said, "I didn't want to say anything, but I don't know if you should go looking for him. He might be awful mad. I know my dad gets mad when Momma goes looking for him when he is in the bar. Mr. Taggat's truck was parked at the Corner Bar when the school bus went by on the route."

"That is unbelievable! Are you sure that it was Tag's

truck?" Laura was dumbfounded.

"I know what I saw. It had the dent in the right rear fender, where Tag slid into the tree. It was daylight, so there is no mistake. That was his truck!" Laura saw that there was no further need of questioning Katie about what she had seen.

"Oh, Katie, what should I do now? This has never happened before," said Laura.

"I think we should go get him. If he has been there since three o'clock, he might not be able to drive home. Laura, I think that I should go with you."

"Katie," said Laura, "this is not a good situation for you. I don't want you involved in our family affairs. I will see what I can do on my own."

"I am involved. I was involved the minute I told you where his truck was parked. I sense that we will need two drivers. That is, two sober drivers. Let's go!" Katie got up from her homework and grabbing a jacket, she had her hand on the doorknob.

Taking Laura's car, they drove to Summit City. Katie pointed out Tag's truck. Laura parked alongside and they got out of the car. Laura whispered, "What do we do now? I don't want to go in there and tell him to come home. It will be embarrassing for him and me."

Katie said, "Leave it to me. Move your car, so that when he comes out, he won't recognize your vehicle. I will wait until you have it moved and then you wait in the shadow of the building." Laura moved her car and came back. They waited a short time and a man came out of the bar. Katie approached him and said, "Mister, do you know Tag Taggat?"

He replied, "Sure, sure, I know Tag, but who are you?"

Katie answered, "I'm his daughter Katie and I have been waiting out here a long time. Would you tell him that I need to get home, because tomorrow is a school day? I'm getting cold, but I don't want to go inside. Please get him out here." Katie had used a whiny, little girl voice in her plea.

He turned to go back inside. "Sure, sure, I'll get him. Did you say the name was Katie?" Katie nodded and shivered to show the man how cold she was getting.

A few minutes later, the man came out and Tag stumbled after him. Katie asked, "Can you help me get him into the truck, but first I need the keys? Pappa, give me the keys and I will drive."

Katie opened the door on the passenger side and she spotted the keys still in the ignition. She and the man tugged and prodded until they got Tag inside. With slurred speech, Tag said, "I can drive. Don't worry Katie, I'll get you home. I'm sorry. I thought you took the bus." After getting Tag in the truck, Katie locked his door. Getting behind the wheel, she eased the truck back into the street. Pulling ahead, she saw that Laura was following her. Before they got to the bridge over the Dismal River at the edge of town, Tag was asleep or passed out, but he certainly knew nothing about the ride home. Katie drove carefully and after about ten minutes on the road, she pulled up in front of the ranch house. She removed the keys and carefully closed her door. She walked to the house and Laura came up alongside of her.

"Katie," she said, "we can't just leave him there."

"Laura," she replied, "we can't get him to the house. Even if we could, we wouldn't want him inside. If he gets sick, it would be better in his truck than in your bed. He may get a little cold, but he won't die. By tomorrow morning, he may wish that he had died. It has been a long evening and I am going to bed." By now she had reached the door.

"Wait, Katie," said Laura, as she caught up with her. "Thank you. I had no idea of how to get him out of there, or how to get him home. I'm sorry to put you through this and I hope that this is the last time that this occurs. Good night."

"Good night, Laura. It will be interesting to see how he

feels in the morning. I'll see you then."

Laura and Katie were eating breakfast when Tag came into the house. He looked bad. The first thing he said, was, "Coffee, I want coffee."

"You will get coffee when you have showered and put on clean clothes. And, be sure to shave. I can't stand the smell of you long enough to have you drink coffee." Laura was slicing bacon with a butcher knife while she talked with Tag. He remembered another time that she had threatened him with a knife and he took her threats seriously. Tag lumbered off to the bedroom, mumbling as he went. Laura winked at Katie.

By the time that Tag came to the kitchen, Katie had already left for school. Laura had a cup of coffee waiting for Tag. Laura asked, "Do you care for any breakfast? There is still some bacon left and I can fry you some eggs."

Tag shook his head. "Just coffee for me. My stomach can't handle any food" He sat at the table, holding his head and occasionally taking a drink of his coffee.

Laura poured herself another cup of coffee and her elbows braced on the tabletop. She held her cup in both hands. Staring at him, she asked, "What do you have to say for yourself and your little escapade of last night?"

"Laura, this is no concern of yours. I am a grown man and if I want a drink now and then, that is what I will have. I see no harm in that. It is none of your business if I decide to stop at the bar for a drink." Laura saw his reasoning in what he was doing. *Tag was taking the initiative and striking out at me before I strike out at him.*

"Tag, when you were a bachelor, you could party all you wanted and it was no concern of mine. But now that we are husband and wife, it is a concern of mine. Tell me Tag, how did you get home last night and at what time did you get home?"

Tag spoke up. "I drove myself, but I don't remember the time. The house was dark, so I just slept in the truck so that

95

I didn't wake you up when I came into the house. How else do you think I got home?"

Laura asked, "Tag, how do you explain that I have the keys to your truck? Do you remember a man at the bar telling you that your daughter wanted a ride home, and that she had been waiting a long time for you? Does anything like that sound familiar? When you endanger your life and the lives of this family, then yes, it does become my business. Katie and I went for you last night. Katie drove the truck and you had passed out before she left town. Are things so bad that you have to resort to alcohol to function?"

Tag looked up at Laura. "You really don't understand, do you? In your grief, you have that old cottonwood stump like some Aztec idol that you go to. You go to mourn and pray. I go to the bottle to forget! To forget that it was my son that was knocked off that windmill that day! But no, your son Tylor had to disobey. So, now he is living and running free, but TJ is in the grave! Laura, you knew that I was this way, wild and free, so why did you marry me? Had we not married, I would not be hurting like I am now."

Laura was shocked at the accusation he hurled at her. She determined to remain calm in order to come to an understanding. "Tag, there is nothing magical about the cottonwood stump as a place to pray. It is comfortable and quiet there among the trees and along the Dismal River. I could be sitting on a milk stool in the cow barn and find solace and peace with my Lord, but I have chosen the cottonwood stump. I go there, not to forget, but to remember; to remember that we had TJ for twenty years to love and to cherish. I don't blame anyone and I certainly don't put the blame on Tylor. Only he knows what happened minutes before the accident and as far as I know, he has said nothing about the accident." Laura paused as she tried to control her emotions.

She continued, because she had more to say to respond

96

to Tag's accusations. "Tylor is a follower, not a leader. As a mother, I remember the jeers of the other students as he went off the basketball court, yelling at him, 'T-T-Tagalong.' So, if TJ chose to go to the top, Tylor would have let him. Likewise, if Tylor refused to go to the top, TJ could have refused. Tag, you need to let it go! Let it go about your son, my son. I always considered us a family. You asked, why did I marry Tag Taggat when I knew that he was wild and free? You have every reason to question my integrity. I married you, that as a single mother, I would be called Mrs. Taggat. Also, I married you that my son would have a name as well. I wanted a father for my son. Though Tylor has respected you and honored you as his father, but you have never been a father to him. When I married you, I didn't love you, but I have come to love you and I love you now. It is a love that is deeper than you can ever understand, as only a woman can give. Tag, no matter what happens, I will not leave you. I will only leave if you no longer want me to stay. I told Tylor as a small boy, 'you can't make people love you, but they can't stop you from loving them.' I will always love you, Tag."

Laura got up from the table and putting on her coat, she left the house. She walked to the Dismal River, the river of promise. She remembered God's promise that he would never leave her or forsake her. She recalled what she had said to Tag, but she knew that she had purposely refused to ask him for what reason he had married her. She didn't want to hear that he had not loved her, but that he was in need of a ranch cook. One other time, she had given him the option of having her stay or leave. Tag chose to have her stay, but at that time she was carrying his son in her womb. *Now I am barren and old and the son that we cherished, lies in the grave. Does Tag hate my son Tylor and me so much that he wants us out of his life? Oh, Lord, I pray that you will heal his hurt.*

The morning air had not warmed up yet, so Laura

97

returned to the house. Tag was not in the house and Laura began to clear away the breakfast dishes. The phone rang and Laura answered it. It was Todd Holliday of the Cattleman's Bank in Summit City. "Good morning, Todd. What can I do for you today?" Laura remembered Todd as a young man in the Holliday home when she had cared for his mother.

Todd was rather hesitant, but asked, "Is Tag available? I wanted to come out to the ranch, but I wanted his permission before I came out." Laura thought, *that is rather odd to ask for Tag's permission. Most people make an appointment and show up.*

"Tag is not here right now," answered Laura, "but, is anything wrong?"

Todd replied, "Yes, there is. Tag was in the bank yesterday and we had words. I was in the wrong. I want to come out to the ranch to apologize. After Tag left, I thought, if only you had been here, you would have seen that peace prevailed."

Laura said, "Todd, I am not sure that always happens. However, I appreciate your call and I am sure that Tag will receive you. When can we expect you?"

"So that I don't take up any more of Tag's time, I will be out a little before one. That is, if that is satisfactory?"

"Absolutely," said Laura. "We will be expecting you. Todd, thank you for calling. Goodbye."

Laura replaced the receiver and leaned against the kitchen counter. Her first thought was, *so that is why Tag was in such a tizzy and went on his drinking binge. Usually I am with Tag when he goes to the bank. Why did he leave me out in his meeting with Todd? I have sensed that Tag has harbored some animosity toward Todd, but I attributed that to Todd's youth. Todd had helped out on the ranch one summer when he had been in high school. While Todd's father Ken was at the bank, Tag got along fine with him. Now he was at the bank in*

Lincoln. Todd took over the local bank when his father moved. Well, I guess I will find out this afternoon.

Tag came in for dinner and he had little to say, but he certainly exhibited no remorse for his actions earlier that morning. Midway through dinner, Laura looked up from eating, and casually remarked, "Oh, I almost forgot. Todd Holliday called this morning and wanted to come out to the ranch after dinner. I didn't know where you were, so I told him that it would be all right. It is all right, isn't it?"

Tag's face turned red and he burst forth, "What does that snot nosed kid want now?"

Laura remained calm. "Tag, he is my friend and he is also a grown man. I would prefer that you not refer to a friend of mine in that manner. What took place between the two of you? He said that he was coming out to apologize? It might be well that if you two are going to have words when you meet, that I be included in the meeting. That way I would know why he wants to apologize."

Tag's face was still red. He tried to explain. "Those bankers know everything. He got wind of my inheritance and he wanted me to apply the money on the note at the bank. I wanted to use it toward additional help on the ranch. We had some hot words and that is when I left the bank. Consequently, I ended up at the bar. You certainly know the rest of that story."

Laura looked at Tag. She began, "Did either of you consider a compromise? Suppose that when you get the ten thousand, you give it to him to apply to the note. Provided that when you are in need of additional help, he agrees to loan you up to the amount of ten thousand dollars. In reality, because the money was not earned through the ranch production, the bank has no claim upon the ten thousand. Because of the drought, we will probably come up short of paying out. If you show good faith, the bank will be more likely to help you through another year. Tag, does that sound feasible to you?"

Tag nodded. "I guess so, but what does feasible mean?" Laura said, "I'm sorry, but I guess I'm still a schoolteacher. Feasible means reasonable enough to be accepted. Do you think that Todd would accept such a plan?"

"I would think so," said Tag. "After all, he would have his ten thousand dollars for a while anyway."

"Good," said Laura, "and do you think that you can treat him civil when he comes this afternoon?"

Tag nodded. "Laura, next time I will take you with me."

Todd came at his appointed time. Tag greeted him, and Todd said, "Tag, I'm sorry for pressing you for the inheritance money. I should have realized that you are a good steward of your assets and you had need of the money." He reached out and shook Tag's hand. "I will go now, but I wanted to apologize to you face to face."

He started to leave, but Tag stopped him. "Wait a minute. Laura and I have come up with a plan that should make everyone happy in this situation." Tag turned to Laura, and said, "Tell him what we can do as soon as we get the inheritance money." Laura went over what she and Tag had discussed. From time to time, Todd nodded. When Laura finished, Tag asked, "Well, Todd, does that sound feasible to you?" Laura gritted her teeth to keep from laughing at Tag's use of the word 'feasible.'

Todd nodded, "It sounds reasonable to me and it sure ought to pass the bank examiners. Why didn't we think of that yesterday instead of losing our tempers? Thanks for letting me come by to apologize. I will go now. I know you have a lot of work to get done." Todd shook hands again and started toward his vehicle.

Tag and Laura returned to the house. Tag put his arm around Laura. "Did you notice how I used that big word you taught me?" Laura laughed. Tag continued, "Laura, you are a manipulator. Yesterday, we almost came to blows and today, everyone is happy. Thank you, Laura Taggat."

Laura always enjoyed when her husband called her 'Laura Taggat.' It indicated to her that she was still part of the family. She knew that it was a small thing, but she cherished his use of her name.

CHAPTER 7
WINTER IN THE SANDHILLS

Tag had sold his calves the first week of November. He had spent the next three days sorting and culling his cowherd to reduce the numbers for the ranch to winter. The calves brought a good price per pound because of their lighter weight. However, the total dollars was less than what they had brought in prior years. The hay crop had been short because of the drought, consequently the need of selling the older cows.

Saturday morning, Tag and Laura were eating breakfast. Tag set his coffee mug down. Without another word, he got up and went to the telephone. Evidently, as he dialed, it was someone familiar. He didn't have need to refer to the directory. "Harvey," he said, "can you get me two semis here tomorrow morning? I want to take my cows to the auction barn to the western part of the state. I hear that those irrigated farmers are buying these cull cows to put on beet tops and corn stalks." There was a pause. "All right, eight o'clock tomorrow morning. Goodbye." Tag hung up the phone and returned to his coffee. "Laura, you heard the conversation. Can you have me a suitcase packed? I will be gone for a couple of days. I should be back late Tuesday night, or early Wednesday morning."

Laura was excited, as she mulled over the possibilities. "Tell me, Mr. Taggat, would you like some company on your trip?"

Tag was quick to answer. In fact, he was much too quick with his answer. "No, no," he replied, "this will be a fast trip and strictly business. I don't think you want to spend your time at a cattle auction. They are dirty and noisy. Perhaps another time would be better. Besides, Katie shouldn't be left alone." Tag took his mug to the kitchen sink and put on his jacket and hat to begin his workday.

Laura was disappointed. It was easy to figure out that

Tag didn't want her to make the trip. She was staring into her coffee mug when Katie came into the kitchen. "Laura, I'm here." This startled Laura. Apparently she was deep in thought.

"Good morning, Miss Katie O'Neal. Are you always in the habit of interrupting a person's thoughts?"

Katie replied, "No, but I feared that Mrs. Laura Taggat had turned into a pillar of salt. I wasn't sure how I would get her out of the kitchen. Do you want me to go back out and come in again? This isn't working."

Laura said, "No, no. I was thinking that it is almost two weeks until Thanksgiving. Usually I shoot a turkey at the Holler Ranch, but this year, I'm not into hunting. Yet, a turkey is traditional. Katie, what do you think?"

Katie thought a moment. "Laura, we never had a turkey at home on Thanksgiving. If I can find you a turkey, would you teach me how to cook a real Thanksgiving dinner?"

Laura nodded. "Katie, do you know how hard it is to buy a turkey in the Sandhills? However, if you have me a turkey a day before Thanksgiving, I will teach you how to cook a turkey."

"Oh, Laura." Katie laughed as she envisioned what the turkey might look like. "Could I invite my parents and brothers? I have told them so much about the ranch and everything, or is that too much to ask?"

"What an excellent idea," said Laura. "I'm glad that you came up with the idea of having your family. My friend Hannah Williams usually comes from Washington, so she will be here. Do you think you could encourage Jim and Tylor to come as well? Let's make it a festive occasion."

Katie was quiet. Finally, she said, "Laura, I will ask Jim and Tylor, but don't count too heavily on them coming to the ranch. I don't know what has happened between the men of this family. No one will say anything against one another, but I would be surprised if they would commit to coming for dinner.

I will ask, if you will pray. It will take something mighty big to bring about reconciliation." Katie shook her head, "Yes, something mighty big."

Laura nodded her head and said, "Katie, I have been praying and I will continue to pray for these men."

Sunday morning, Tag was up well before daylight. He and the ranch crew gathered the cows that were to be shipped. The bawling of the cows awakened Laura. She saw the trucks come in and cross the river bridge. It wasn't long before the cattle were loaded and the trucks were on their way. Tag came in and ate a quick breakfast. Gulping down the last of his coffee, he grabbed his suitcase and made his way toward the door. Laura blocked his way, and said, "Don't I get a kiss? It won't hurt if the cows get there before you arrive at the sale barn." Tag kissed her rather hurriedly and was in his truck and leaving the ranch in a matter of minutes. She remembered the last thing that he had told her; 'I will see you late Tuesday night, or first thing Wednesday morning.'

Laura went to church that morning at the Good Hope Community Church. Each time that she went, she anticipated that Jim would be there. From the time that he had first moved into the community, he had been such an integral part of the church. It was strange not to see him sitting near the front of the church. Katie had reported to Laura that Jim was now attending church in Summit City. Unfortunately, Tylor didn't go with him.

While Laura was at church, Katie called Tylor on the phone. Immediately when she identified herself, he hung up. She then decided to wait until Jim was home. Later in the afternoon, Laura was taking a nap and Katie tried again. This time, Jim answered the phone.

Katie said, "Jim, I'm glad to get you. I called earlier and Tylor answered, but then he hung up. I wasn't certain if it was me, or if he didn't want to talk."

Jim said, "Tylor is quite self conscious about talking on the phone. Sometimes he will take a message. He did tell me that you had called, so I was expecting your call. What can I do for you?"

Katie decided that she would be direct with him. "We, meaning Laura and I, would like you and Tylor to join us for Thanksgiving dinner. There is one catch, and that is if you will furnish the turkey. We do need it at least a day ahead of time. Laura has promised to teach me how to cook a turkey. I am inviting my parents and my four brothers. Laura is expecting that Hannah will be here as well. So, with us here at the ranch, there should be about twelve of us to get together. What do you say, can we expect you and Tylor?"

Jim quickly answered, "I'm sorry, but Tylor and I have other plans. But, we would still be able to furnish you with a turkey. I promise to have it there the day before. Is that a deal?"

Katie thought, *this is what I feared, but I understand.* Responding to Jim's offer, she said, "Jim, I would rather have you and Tylor here, but I will settle for the turkey. Tell Tylor hello for me. And thank you for the turkey, in case I miss you. Goodbye." She hung up the phone, uncertain of how to tell Laura that the two of them would not be coming on Thanksgiving.

Tuesday night, Laura stayed up late, waiting for Tag. Finally at midnight, she went to bed, but didn't sleep well. Each little sound would awaken her. When Tag didn't come home on Wednesday, Laura drove her car to Summit City on Thursday morning. She arrived at the County Courthouse as soon as they opened. Sheriff Morgan was sitting at his desk, looking over some papers and having his morning coffee. Looking up, he saw Laura coming through the door. He got up from his desk and greeted her. "Good morning, Mrs. Taggat. You are certainly out and about early this morning. What can I do for you?"

"I'm sorry to bother you, but it is Tag. He left home Sunday morning. He was selling cows in the western part of the state on Monday. He was to be home late Tuesday, or early Wednesday. He still hasn't showed up, nor has he called. I don't know how to go about finding him, or even if he is all right. Is there anything you can do to help me?"

Sheriff Morgan grabbed a pad and pencil, and asked, "Exactly where was he going?"

"I'm not sure, but he did say that he was consigning the cattle to The North Platte Valley Auction. It is in the western part of the state and it is an irrigated region. That is all I know, but he is driving his red Ford pickup truck. It has a dent in the right rear fender. Here is the license number." She handed the sheriff a slip of paper. He looked at it and wrote the number down.

"Did anybody else go with him?" Laura shook her head. Then the sheriff asked, "Why didn't you go with him? It would appear to me to have been a good opportunity for the two of you to get away."

"He didn't want me to go. He said that we shouldn't leave Katie alone. Are you insinuating that he took someone else with him and left me home? That is ridiculous! He wouldn't do that to me!" Laura was getting upset.

Sheriff Morgan said, "Mrs. Taggat, I have been sheriff of Summit County for 30 years. Nothing surprises me anymore. Your husband is wound as tight as an Ingersoll pocket watch. His drinking at the Corner Bar two weeks ago was just a tip of the iceberg. I have a cousin out in that county that is a deputy sheriff. I will have him find him. My money says that he sold his cattle and went on one big bender. Once he sobers up, he will come home. Most husbands usually do. Let me know when he shows up, so that I can call off the dogs. Now if you will excuse me, I will get started on the search for this errant husband. You do want me to find him, don't you?"

"Of course I do," said Laura. "Tell me sheriff, if you knew that Tag was in the Corner Bar, why didn't you get him out of there before he was almost lifeless?"

"Mrs. Taggat," said Sheriff Morgan, "the county pays me to know just about everything that goes on in this county. And what I don't know, I have enough information to fill in the blanks. I didn't get him out of the bar that night, because you needed to know what you are facing. Mrs. Taggat, if your husband doesn't get some help, you are going to have a perpetual drunk on your hands. If you think your life is miserable now, you haven't seen anything yet. Jim McCann was the shield that kept Tag from destroying himself. Jim is gone, and now there is only you to keep Tag from harm. Good day, Mrs. Taggat."

Laura turned and hurried down the Courthouse steps. She fled to her car and leaning against the side she sobbed. Not for herself, but for her husband and the harsh words of the sheriff that pierced her very soul. Her tears were not unnoticed. The sheriff was looking out of his window high above the street. He sensed that her tears were for her husband. How long before she would be shedding tears for the son that ran night after night throughout the county? The sheriff wanted to tell her, but there is a limit to the burden one woman can bear.

Just as the sheriff predicted, Tag returned to the ranch. It was a bit after dinnertime on Thursday. Laura was putting the dishes away when he came through the door. She ran to Tag, and hugged him. "Well, darling, welcome home!" She looked over at the wall calendar. "My goodness, no wonder I was worried about you. I must have pulled three pages off that daily calendar instead of one. Is it Tuesday, or is it Thursday? That was careless of me. And, to think that I went to the sheriff to ask for help finding you. He assured me that most husbands do return. I will call him right now and tell him he was right, and to call off the dogs. My husband has returned!" She started for the wall phone and he blocked her path.

"Don't bother. He knows already. I stopped at Nick's to eat and he was there. He was very pleasant, but he had that little smirk on his face. He asked about the cattle market at the North Platte Valley Auction. The first time I met him, he had that same smirk on his face, as if he knew about everything there was to know about me. Before he left the café, he used that same remark. He said that he had to go call off the dogs." Laura saw that Tag was furious. He continued, "Laura, I don't want you to call that man again. I am a big boy and I don't need him checking up on me. And, that goes for you too!"

Laura took a deep breath. She quietly said, "I'm sorry for my snide remarks. Let me start over again. Welcome home, darling. How was your trip and did the cattle sell well? Did you leave the cattle check with the bank, or do we need to clean up and take it into the bank this afternoon? The earlier we take it to the bank, the more interest we will save. Would you like a cup of coffee now, or after you have had a chance to freshen up? I have some good news! Katie is cooking the Thanksgiving dinner and has invited her family to share with us. She is excited about learning how to cook a turkey. My goodness, I'm so excited to have you back, I need to quit rambling on with my news. I haven't given you an opportunity to tell me about your trip."

Tag reached into his shirt pocket. Pulling out a large check, he threw it on the table. "You don't fool me, Laura. What you really want to know if I blew the whole check, or just a portion? Well, it is all there, so we can take it in this afternoon and give the banker his pound of flesh." Tag stomped off. Later she could hear him showering. That is good. He certainly needed it in order to make himself a bit more compatible. Especially, if we are to meet with Todd Holliday!

While Tag was busy cleaning up, Laura called Sheriff Morgan. "Thank you, Sheriff, and I'm sorry to have caused you extra work. You were right, my husband has returned, as you are aware of at this time. Tag said that he had seen you at Nick's. Have a good Thanksgiving."

Laura had the coffee hot when Tag returned to the kitchen. "Do you care for some coffee before we go to the bank? I also have a cherry pie that I will share with you, if you will tell me about the cattle auction."

"Pie and coffee sounds good to me." Tag picked up the check from the table. He said, "Laura, the cattle sold quite well. I was surprised. I would say that the market was hot. We got in there early enough on Sunday, so that the cows had a chance to fill up. It cost a little more for the trucking, but we made about $2500.00 more for the extra work. This is a fine pie and I believe I told you once that you do make good coffee." Laura laughed. She remembered the occasion. *It was when she thought that there was no pleasing Tag, so she challenged him to name one thing that she did that pleased him. After a long silence, he had said, 'you do make good coffee.' That was the icebreaker that had turned a tense situation into a time of laughter.*

As always, Laura enjoyed when she could accompany Tag anytime that they left the ranch. She decided that the next time he wants his suitcase packed, it would also include some of her own garments as well. No more of this being gone overnight without her.

When they arrived at the bank, Todd was with a bank customer, so Tag and Laura had to wait. Laura visited with Mrs. Stahl and deciding that she had some extra money in her purse, she added this to her funds in her safety deposit box.

When they met with Todd, he was pleased with Tag's cattle sales. "Tag, I will be out of the bank the week of Thanksgiving, so if you will need any funds, we can set it up today if you would like."

"No," said Tag, "I think that Laura has us set up until

after the first of the year. The drought has made us look long and hard before we spend any money. We are doing fine, but it has been a difficult year."

"I understand. I will be going to Lincoln to visit Dad and Mother Natalie. Laura, every time I see my grandmother, she asks about you. She thought a lot of you because of the care you gave mother, as well as our household."

"Tell everyone hello for me. Your grandmother made quite an impression on me. She was one to tell it like it is, pulling no punches whatsoever. It is good that you can get away now and then. Katie's family is having Thanksgiving dinner with us this year and I am expecting Hannah to make her annual appearance. Katie wants to show off the ranch to her family. This will be a different holiday this year, yes, a different holiday." It was difficult for Laura to think how people and situations had changed in such a short time.

The Tuesday morning before Thanksgiving, Laura awakened to see the landscape covered with snow. It was still snowing with large flakes, laden with moisture. It was one of those mornings that one wanted to be out, catching snowflakes on the tongue. Laura prepared to go out to look at the snow, when she saw the oven-ready turkey that had been placed on the freezer. It was a beautiful bird, as clean and white as it could be. She noted a few small puddles on the tile, indicating that it had been delivered after it had started to snow. She looked outside and saw one footprint near the door. Laura recognized that it was the imprint of a moccasin. Tylor had been here!

Katie came to the back porch and saw the turkey. She exclaimed, "What a beautiful turkey! When did they bring this turkey? Did I miss Tylor and Jim? Laura, I miss them so, that it hurts. Tell me Laura, why are men so stubborn? Do they actually realize how much hurt they bring upon you and me because of their stubbornness? I just know that this will be a great Thanksgiving, but it would be even greater if we had our men at the table." Katie's thoughts returned to Thanksgiving. "Oh, Laura, when may I start making the pies?"

"There will be ten of us, so you will need to determine how many pies you want to make."

Laura went to look into the pantry. "After determining the number of pies it will take, the next step is to consider what kind of pies that you wish to serve. Keep in mind that pumpkin is the traditional pie for Thanksgiving." Katie wrinkled her nose when Laura mentioned pumpkin. "Katie, I saw you wrinkle your nose when I said pumpkin. What is wrong with pumpkin?"

"But, Mr. Taggat is partial to cherry, so I will make two cherry pies and one pumpkin."

Laura was starting to get upset. "Katie O'Neal, why is it that you always cater to Tag? There are other people to consider besides Tag!"

"Oh," said Katie, "would those other people by chance include Laura Taggat? What is wrong with considering what Tag likes or dislikes?"

Laura was surprised by each of their outbursts. "Katie, I'm sorry that it has come to this over the choice of pies. Let us consider that Wednesday afternoon I will meet you after school. Then, we will go shopping for the ingredients for our dinner that will include two cherry pies and two pumpkin pies. We can make them up before supper if we have time. Otherwise, we will make them later in the evening. Can I assume that for now, we have buried the hatchet?"

Katie laughed. She asked, "Laura, why do you say something like buried the hatchet, instead of saying that we made peace with one another?"

Laura responded to her question. "That is a euphemism, and is another way of making a statement. In this case, the hatchet indicates divisiveness. But, by burying the hatchet, it means that next time it is more difficult to find cause to be divisive, just as it is harder to find the hatchet if it is buried."

Katie shook her head and muttered, "Hannah Williams told me that you would spring odd words on her from time to time. Evidently, you haven't changed much over the years."

The next day was a flurry of activity, while the two women prepared for their company. Hannah came early Thursday morning and was helping in the kitchen. At about eleven, Katie's family showed up. Katie was busy in the kitchen, so Laura went to greet them. She had met the parents earlier, Darla and Derk, as well as the boys; Dan, David, Donald and Daryl when she had taken Katie to the house. "Happy Thanksgiving to the O'Neals! Welcome to the Taggat Ranch! Let me take your coats."

The youngest boy, Daryl spoke up. "We aren't O'Neals, we are Donnellys!"

Laura was shocked. She looked to the boy's mother for some explanation. Darla blushed, and whispered to Laura, "I will explain later." She continued to help the boys out of their coats.

Laura had games and toys out for the boys. She hurried to get coffee for the father and to make him comfortable. She explained, "My husband Tag will be in shortly. He is caring for the cattle."

When everyone was settled, Darla got Laura aside. "I guess no one told you, so it was a natural mistake. I was married before and this is my second marriage. I married Derk when Katie was four years old. It was the stipulation of the divorce decree that Katie retain the O'Neal name."

Laura said, "Now I see. For a moment there, I thought that I had invited the wrong family. Come and meet Hannah Williams. She is here from Washington, D.C. Hannah is the U.S. Congresswoman from this district and a lifelong friend. She was an eighth grade student when I taught at Good Hope

School."

Laura ushered Darla into the kitchen. Katie saw her mother and said, "Momma, I am having so much fun. I am glad that you decided to come. Momma, this is Hannah Williams. This is my mother, Darla."

Hannah was cutting up carrots, so she nodded her head, and said, "I am so glad to meet you, Mrs. O'----."

"Donnelly, Mrs. Donnelly," interrupted Laura. Laura's next thought is, I need to catch Tag before he greets anyone in the house. She heard Tag come in the back porch and she rushed back to explain the introductions before he had the opportunity to greet anyone. Laura placed a cup of coffee in his hand and escorted him into the living room where he and Derk could get acquainted.

Katie called everyone to the table. Since she knew the family situation, she arranged the seating. She brought the turkey in and asked, "Mr. Taggat, would you please carve the turkey?"

Tag blushed. It was his first carving of a turkey, but he had seen enough carved over the years, that he did a commendable job.

Little Daryl was sitting by his mother and he spoke up. "Aren't we going to hurry up and say the blessing? I am hungry." His mother blushed and tried to quiet him.

Laura smiled, "Daryl, here at the ranch, we have men just like you. They come in from working hard and they are anxious to eat. Katie and I tried something different. We wait until after we have eaten, so that we can properly thank God for the food. We are no longer hungry and the men are not so anxious to return to their work. If the food was not good, or there wasn't enough for everyone, then we don't bother thanking God for a poor meal. Do you know, since your sister Katie has been helping in the kitchen, we haven't had a poor meal!"

Tag interrupted, "Amen to that!" Katie blushed and the others laughed.

Laura continued. "Shall we try that here today? And then Daryl, if you think it was a good meal, you may be the first to thank God for the food."

Daryl nodded his head, and said, "Please pass the olives."

Laura smiled and said, "Let us start this meal with the passing of the olives. Help yourself everyone, the meal has begun."

After it appeared that everyone had their fill, Laura said, "Normally we have dessert after the main course here at the ranch. But on Thanksgiving, we usually eat so much that we wait until the middle of the afternoon for our dessert. Incidentally, today it happens to be pumpkin pie and cherry pie, baked by our ranch chef, none other than Katie O'Neal! Next, we will thank God for the meal. After that, the women will clean up the kitchen, while the men entertain themselves in the living room. With all of this fine snow, Katie had you boys bring your winter clothes and we will go sledding. Katie and I have been at every ranch in the neighborhood, borrowing sleds, so that everyone will have their own sled. Back of the ranch house is an ideal hill for sledding, which will take you almost to the schoolhouse." Hannah interrupted her with her giggling. It got so bad that Laura stopped talking. "Hannah, what is so funny?"

Hannah was gasping for breath from her laughing. She said, "I had a flashback to the day that you hit Tag's horse alongside of the head when the horse tried to bite you. Tag's horse knocked Jim's horse to the ground and both cowboys were on the ground. You and all of us school kids ran for the schoolhouse, scared to death of Tag. I'm sorry, Tag, but as a spectator, it was funny. That black horse was running one way and kids and teacher running another."

Tag laughed. "That was quite a day. Fortunate for all of us today, had I not got tangled up in the barbed wire, we wouldn't be eating turkey here today. Or at least one of us wouldn't." He looked at Laura and gave her a wink.

Laura blushed. "All right. Should we thank God for the food?" Everyone nodded. "Then Daryl, you may be first, but I do need to know how old you are, in case you are too young." Daryl held up five fingers. "Good, that is the right age, so you may begin."

Daryl folded his hands and closed his eyes. "Dear God; I want thank you for the olives and thank you for the turkey and thank you God for all the food, because it was real good. But, mostly I thank you for the olives. Amen."

"Thank you, Daryl. You did a fine job of thanking God. Who will be next?" When no one volunteered, Laura gave Katie a quizzical look, but Katie shook her head. Laura bowed her head and began to pray. "Our God and our Father, we thank you for this food; its abundance and its taste. But thanksgiving is more than food. It is people, made up of family and friends, as we gather today. Some are friends of years past and some are just recent. But, friends and family have an impact upon our lives each day. I am thankful that Hannah could be with us today. She is one of my first friends in this community. It is amazing that she is so much like my latest friend, Katie. Every day I thank you God for sending Katie into my life. We have shared many sorrows, but we have also shared victories as well in the past six months. Some people do not experience in a lifetime the sorrows and victories which we have shared in these few months. I thank you God for Katie's family that has permitted her to be in our home. And, last, but certainly not least, I thank you for my husband Tag, the love of my life. By his generosity, what we are sharing today, Tag has made possible through his hard work. I thank you in the name of Jesus. Amen"

After they got up from the table, the Donnelly boys came to Laura and thanked her for the meal. They each picked up their plate and utensils and took them to the kitchen, leaving them on the counter before going into the living room. Katie came to Laura and hugged her. With tears in her eyes, she asked, "Do I really mean that much to you?"

"Of course you do!" Laura replied. "Don't I tell you that you do?"

Katie nodded. "But, when you tell God, it makes it extra special."

"Katie," Laura said, as she returned Katie's hug. "You are extra special!"

The women neared the end of the cleanup of the kitchen, and Laura said, "Hannah and I can finish up here, if Darla and Katie want to help the boys into their coats and such. Everyone is welcome to play in the snow. We have lots of sleds and plenty of snow."

After a time, Katie came into the kitchen. "Laura, I can't find my old shoes, you know, the ones that I wear when I am working in the yard. I wanted to wear them in my overshoes, because they fit better. What did you do with my old shoes?"

"Why would I have your old shoes? But, perhaps I put them in my closet, thinking they were mine. Look in my closet and see if they are there. If not, you can take my yard shoes and wear them." Laura dried her hands, and went to the back porch, thinking the shoes might be there. She returned, but found no shoes.

Katie returned, almost in tears. "They weren't there and neither were your old shoes. I think that you threw all of them away in your constant house cleaning. Now I can't go sledding, or play in the snow."

"Oh, Katie, let's not blame each other for the loss of a couple pair of old shoes. I know now what happened to them."

117

Katie perked up at the thought of finding the shoes. "It is the 'glove bandit' that has our shoes! He is becoming bolder in his theft. Notice that I said 'he.' Only a male would do such a thing. He started stealing one glove at a time; never a pair. But now, he is taking old shoes. Watch your old purse and expect to have him take at least one sock every wash day. Be vigilant, but keep in mind that you will never catch him."

Katie smiled, "Laura, you are funny. Just when I thought I was going to be overcome with gloom, you come to the rescue. I will wear my school shoes and when they become scuffed and worn, they can be my yard shoes."

"That's a good attitude. Let's go have some fun!"

Tag saddled one of the gentler ranch horses and used the horse to pull the sleds of the smaller boys to the top of the hill. He let Daryl ride the horse with him. When they tired of sledding, everyone was engaged in building a snow family in the front yard, comparable to the three bears. Tag returned his horse to the barn and came to the house. He put his arm around Laura. "Laura, you certainly know how to entertain. Everyone enjoyed the day."

"Thank you, Tag. It was good of you to provide the horse. Isn't God so good and gracious? He sent the snow, just the thing to keep four young boys entertained. I think the adults had as much fun as the children. Sometimes I think we are all children, some of us are bigger than others."

"There you go, Laura," said Tag. "I give you a compliment and you give the glory to God. Can't you just take a compliment, without spiritualizing everything?"

Laura said, "I can't make it snow, but God can give me the snow and tell me, there it is Laura Taggat, do something with it that shows you are glad." Laura reached down, and forming the snow into a ball, she threw it, hitting Tag near his ear. She laughed, "That is one of the things that I can do with the snow!"

Tag grabbed her and wrestled her to the snow covered ground. He kissed her cold lips. "And that, Laura Taggat, is what I can do in the snow!"

The back porch was littered with wet clothes, mittens and overshoes. It was a perfect haven for the 'glove bandit.' It was now time to warm cold fingers, feet and faces. Katie and Laura started to take orders for pie, hot chocolate, coffee and tea. Everyone gathered around the table once again. They relived the afternoon in stories of their deeds.

The Donnelly family left, laden down with leftover turkey, pumpkin pie, and a partial jar of olives for Daryl.

After the Donnelly family was on their way, Katie came to Laura. "Thank you, Laura, for being so kind to my family. I am happy that they could be here."

"You're welcome. I enjoyed having them. You can be proud of such a fine family."

CHAPTER 8
THE SOFT SLIPPER

Sheriff Morgan stood at his office window in the Summit County Courthouse. Holding a cup of cold coffee in his hand, he gazed out at the falling snow. The first day of December and already the Sandhills have received more than the seasonal snowfall accumulation. It still wasn't enough to keep that Taggat kid from running the countryside. I don't know if four feet of snow would keep him snowbound on the Dolan Ranch. People were keeping the sheriff posted of sightings throughout the county. Most vocal was an order cattle buyer, Tubro Turner, referred to as Tub Turner by all who knew him. Tub was an appropriate nickname. He was a rather large man with an even larger protruding stomach. Tub drove a luxury Cadillac and he drove it fast, all the time smoking his cigar. It was he that brought about the sheriff keeping a file on Tylor Taggat.

No one saw the file other than the sheriff. He kept it locked in his desk drawer. It included a map of the county and a record of each spotting with location, date and time of spotting, as well as the person that spotted Tylor. The sheriff was trying to find out if there was any evidence of false reporting of Tylor being spotted. Neither was there any evidence of Tylor breaking any laws, unless someone cared to report him trespassing on their land. No one had sighted him near any of the ranch buildings in the county. The furthermost sighting from the Dolan ranch was about 15 miles. Most of the times, Tylor was carrying a bow and usually accompanied by that red heeler dog that belonged to Bill Dolan. Sheriff Morgan surmised that Tylor was poaching deer, but no need of going very far. There were plenty of deer on Little Woman Creek. No need of carrying a deer 15 miles when you could kill them from the front porch. If he is poaching deer, the sheriff had decided that to be a problem for the Game and Fish Department.

Monday morning was the favorite time for Tub to report his weekend sighting. First he reported to the sheriff and then on to the coffee shop. It would be there that Tub would give a detailed account of seeing Tylor Taggat and his dog caught in his headlights when they crossed the road.

With the winter weather, things had been rather peaceful throughout the county. Tag Taggat had been staying home, so Laura Taggat had not bothered him. There was one thing that the sheriff had learned in 30 years of law enforcement, peaceful was not the norm.

The week before Christmas, Laura and Tag were still at the supper table, drinking the last of their coffee. Katie was clearing the table and putting the food away. Turning to Katie, Tag said, "Katie, now that we have married men working on the ranch, we give them an option of a Christmas gift. You have been especially faithful in helping Laura, so we will give you the same option, but I am sure I know which you will choose. Think carefully before you make your choice. You can have your choice of a quarter of beef, wrapped and frozen at the local meat locker plant, or one hundred dollars."

Katie spoke up, "That's easy, I will take the beef." Tag looked shocked! Katie didn't realize that he expected her to take the money. "I tell my family how great it is to have all this beef. Now they will be able to find out for themselves. Oh, thank you, Mr. Taggat and Laura." She gave each of them a hug.

That night, Katie was getting ready for bed, when Laura knocked on the door. She went in and sitting down on the edge of the bed, she said, "That was a very thoughtful thing you did for your family. I know that you have been helping them as much as you can, but you have needs of your own. So that you will have your own gift, here is one hundred dollars to spend on yourself." Laura handed her five twenty-dollar bills.

Katie looked at the money and handed it back. She said, "But, I can't take that. It wouldn't be right."

"Why not, it is a gift. That is all right to have this and the beef. You have helped me so much this year."

"But, Laura. Mr. Taggat gave me one hundred dollars after supper, while you were in the bathroom. He made me promise not to tell, but I knew it wasn't right to take money from both of you. I'm sorry, but don't let on that you know."

Laura handed the money back to Katie. "Here, take the money. This can be money toward your education. If you don't take this, then I will tell him that you told of his gift. How is that for blackmail? Remember, not a word to him."

Katie laughed as she took the money. "How can I refuse, now that it has come to blackmail? Thank you, Laura."

Laura was leaving the room and Katie asked, "When do we put up the Christmas tree?"

Laura started to weep. She tried to answer Katie. "You know, this year I don't feel like decorating. Every year before, there was activity, and we had guests---." Laura stopped and could say no more until she dried her eyes. She continued, "But, this year is different. I am tired, just like this year, as it comes to an end. TJ is gone and Tylor might as well be in the grave. I have lost my sons. I'm sorry Katie, but no tree this year. Likewise, I am forbidding the giving of gifts this year. You have received your end of the year bonus and that is sufficient. I have no desire to receive a gift from you in exchange." Laura left the room, leaving a young lady shocked at what she had heard.

Katie could not sleep, rehearsing the words of despondency that Laura had uttered. When sleep did overtake her, it was riddled with dreams. She dreamt of decorating a tree in the living room, but despite her efforts, it always fell over when she stepped back to admire her work.

Katie awakened when she heard Tag in the kitchen. She hurriedly grabbed her robe and putting on her slippers, she went into the kitchen. Tag was trying to make coffee, but with his large calloused fingers, he was having trouble separating the coffee filters. "I'm sorry, Mr. Taggat, I slept so poorly last night, that I failed to hear my alarm that I forgot to set. Next time, if I'm not in the kitchen, come and rap on my door. There is no need of you fixing your own breakfast." Katie busied herself with breakfast, starting with the coffee first.

"Katie, I don't think that you are a morning person. I don't understand what you mean, when you said that you failed to hear your alarm that you forgot to set. Of course you won't hear an alarm that isn't set."

"Oh, but I do, Mr. Taggat. If I don't set my alarm, it gives a little click at the time it should go off, if it were set. It may not make much sense to you, but it does to me."

Tag finished his breakfast. He dressed in his warm garments. Thanking Katie for fixing his breakfast, he stepped out the back door and let out a holler. Katie heard him fall to the ground and rushing to the door, she looked out. The morning was beginning to lighten up and there was Tag sprawled in among the branches of a Christmas tree.

Katie let out a squeal. "Mr. Taggat, Mr. Taggat, my prayers have been answered. God sent me a Christmas tree!"

Tag rolled off to the side and began to stand up. "That is fine, but God didn't need to put it where I would fall into the thing."

Laura joined them at the back door after being awakened by the commotion. She asked, "What is taking place?" She saw Tag struggling to get up. "Tag, are you hurt?"

"Laura, Laura, look. It is a Christmas tree. God sent me a Christmas tree. Look, there is a note attached to the trunk." Katie was so excited, that she was starting to shiver from the morning cold.

Laura reached out and pulled the note from the trunk. Stepping inside the back porch where the light was better, she read, "No tree, no presents."

Katie grabbed the note. "Is that all? They didn't even sign their name."

The last words from Tag, as he walked around the tree, were, "God doesn't need to sign his name."

Katie looked at the note again. "Look, Laura, do you recognize that printing? It was Tylor! He brought us that tree! Laura, do you believe in signs? Tylor saw that we didn't have a tree, so he brought us a tree. Today we decorate the tree. Yes, today we decorate our tree."

When Laura saw the enthusiasm of Katie, she knew that there was no denying her. The tree would be trimmed. It was almost perfect and the right height for placing in the living room in front of the picture window. They had the tree trimmed by mid-afternoon. They were having their afternoon tea, when Katie said, "Something is missing and I know what it is that we need. We need some Christmas cookies. I will make some as soon as we finish our tea."

Darla Donnelly called Laura and invited the Taggats to eat Christmas dinner with them. It was a welcome invitation. Laura was uncertain how they would be celebrating Christmas. Katie decided that she would spend Christmas Eve at the ranch and go to her parents on Christmas Day.

Christmas Eve was quiet. They drank eggnog and Laura played a number of Christmas songs on the piano, while Tag and Katie sang along.

The next morning, Katie got up early to fix Tag his breakfast. He had cattle to feed before going to the Donnellys for dinner. Katie thought it strange that the lights on the tree were lit. Laura was insistent that they not remain lit overnight. It was then that Katie saw the gifts under the tree. She decided that she would wait until the others came for breakfast, so that they might share in the opening of the gifts.

Katie had the coffee going when Tag and Laura came into the kitchen. Katie said, "Did you see that we have gifts under the tree? I waited until you sleepy heads showed up for the occasion of opening gifts. May we open the gifts before breakfast?"

Laura said, "Let me get a cup of coffee first. It smells so good. Tag, I have a cup for you as well. Now, let us see what we have here this morning."

Laura looked at the packages. "Here is one with the name of Katie O'Neal." She handed it to Katie.

Katie opened the package. She saw the leather slippers that were lined with sheepskin. She was enthralled with the softness of the leather. "Who gave these to me? They are so soft. Did you give these to me?"

Tag said, "Katie, let me see them." Tag examined them and handed them back to Katie. "I don't know who gave them to you, but I do know that they were made by Harley, the boot maker. Here is his mark at the heel. These slippers are custom made. Try them on and see how they fit."

Katie sat down and put her feet into the slippers. Standing up she exclaimed, "Oh, they fit perfectly. They are so soft and warm, but whom do I thank? Laura, open your gift!"

Laura opened her gift. She saw that she had the same, but the leather was a shade darker. But, the workmanship and comfort was equal to those of Katie's slippers. Laura paraded around the living room in her new slippers. The others in the room could see the glow return to Laura's face.

Katie reached down for the next package, though the Christmas tree lights were inadequate, she saw scrolled on the paper, 'Father.' Handing the gift package to Tag, she knew the identity of the giver. It was Tylor!

Tag opened the gift, and he saw a larger version of the earlier gifts. He tried them on, and settled back into his chair. "Now, if I had a silk robe and a pipe, I could set back in my chair and read the paper in style. Forget feeding those old cows." Katie laughed, as if he would ever forget his cows.

There was still another package with the name, Katie O'Neal scribbled on the paper. Katie opened the package. Looking in, she said, "Look, my old shoes that I first missed on Thanksgiving Day. But why would I get them now?"

"Katie," Tag said, "remember that I said the slippers were custom made by Harley, the boot maker. He took your old shoes, so that he might have a pattern for the slippers. I imagine that other gift is Laura's old shoes as well. The boot maker has my measurements on file from my previous boot orders. It was pretty clever of the gift giver."

Laura opened her package and held up her old shoes. She said, "See, Katie, I didn't throw your shoes away as you thought I had." Laura sat on the sofa and said, "Would the maid please bring me another cup of coffee, along with my toast and orange marmalade."

Katie settled herself in another chair and extending her legs out in front of herself, she admired her slippers. "Yes, I do think that you must hire a maid. I am too refined to be waiting on either of you." They all laughed while they admired their slippers.

Tag got up and said, "Until such time that we hire additional help, I guess I should get some breakfast and go feed the cows." Katie and Laura got out of their chairs and went to fix his breakfast.

After Tag left to fced the cattle, Katie said, "Laura, do you know who gave us the slippers?"

Laura nodded, "It was Tylor. It was his way to show each of us that he doesn't hate us." Laura took a moment to compose herself. "I feared that we had lost him. I really did, but I didn't know why. The tree had given me hope, but the slippers has given me assurance."

127

Christmas dinner at the Donnellys was an adventure. Daryl had insisted that Laura sit beside him. Darla had cooked a beef roast, which was a portion of Katie's year-end bonus.

During the meal, Daryl confided in Laura. "You know what, Mrs. Taggat? When we were at your house, we played in the snow, but here we are going to play on the ice. Do you know how to skate on the ice?"

"Hmmm," Laura thought a moment, "I knew how to skate when I was the age of your sister. Do you think that it is possible to forget how to skate?"

"I don't think so," he said. "I learned to skate last winter and when I started to skate a week ago, the ice was frozen, but I could still skate real good. I am a good skater, you know. Will you skate today?"

"Yes, I think that I will try. But, if I fall, will you laugh at me?"

"No, but I will help you up and brush you off."

"Thank you, Daryl. I do believe that you are a gentleman."

Katie found a pair of skates for Laura and despite a few bad falls, Laura was happy with her performance. Afterward, they returned back to the Donnellys for dessert. Derk had blended Irish coffee for Tag and himself, while the rest of the group had cocoa. Laura noticed that Tag had taken a liking to the Irish coffee.

Katie remained with her family. She thought that it would be fun to have Christmas vacation in Summit City. Laura was in agreement and confided in Katie that she would probably begin painting again, now that she was somewhat housebound because of the weather.

The day after Christmas, Katie asked Derk, "May I take the car to visit a friend tomorrow afternoon? It is about five miles outside of town and I want to thank him for the slippers. I promise that I will be back before dark."

"Yes," said Derk, "but, don't you think that your mother should go along?"

"She could, but I would rather go by myself. It is up to you, however." Katie did want to see Tylor alone. Otherwise, she would have arranged to take Laura with her.

Katie thought it would be great to surprise Tylor with some cookies and perhaps even a cake as well. However, before seeing Tylor, Katie decided that she would visit with Sheriff Morgan. Right after breakfast, Katie went to see the sheriff, bearing a plate of cookies. She entered his office and he remarked, "I see you are driving a different vehicle than the last time you were here. It is your father's car no doubt." Noticing that she was carrying a plate covered with a small dish towel, he continued, "And, what have we here, a bribe no less? I can spot a bribe from across the room. Therefore, it is my responsibility to seize and confiscate all bribes. Unfortunately, most of the bribes such as this have been lost before the day is over. Tell me, are you seeking information on a certain young man?"

"I confess, but surely you have some information for me." Katie saw that the sheriff had lifted a corner of the towel and was making ready to destroy the evidence.

After tasting the cookie, he said. "These are good. The only thing I have to offer you is coffee, but I will share what I know about Tylor, along with a cookie or two." He sat down at his desk, not certain that he should show Katie the file he had on Tylor.

"Sheriff," she asked, "has he caused any problems since I last talked with you?" The sheriff shook his head.

"If you mean, has he broken any laws? No, but he certainly has a lot of people nervous over his late night activities. Some people are locking their doors at night that have never locked their doors before." Taking out his keys, he chose a key and unlocked the bottom drawer on the left side of his desk. Pulling out a file, Sheriff Morgan said, "Katie, I am going to show you something that no one else is aware that it even exists. I want this kept confidential. But, when you look at this, you will know what I am up against and why I am concerned."

He opened the file and Katie saw the map and the numerous dots on the map, along with some sort of data with dates and times. "These are sightings that have been reported to me. Fortunately, none of the sightings are near a residence. Have you seen him at the 99 Ranch?"

Katie shook her head. "No," she answered, "but I know of three occasions that he was at the ranch. It was twice this last week when he brought a Christmas tree and then Christmas Eve when he left gifts for us. The other time was before Thanksgiving when he stole two pair of shoes." Katie told the sheriff about him using their old shoes for a pattern.

"Are you on your way to see him?" asked the sheriff. "If you have the opportunity, see if he will tell you when he was at the 99 Ranch and if anyone was in the house at the time. I cannot determine any pattern to his late night runs." The sheriff did add, "That is, other than his reason for being at the 99 Ranch." The sheriff got up out of his chair and refilling his coffee mug, he picked up two more cookies and returned to his chair. "Katie, I have been forthright with you. Now it is your turn. Why is Tylor running?" Katie didn't answer him, but that did not stop his questioning. "Is he capable of murder? I know that he has been through a lot and this being rejected by Becca Barnes has always bothered me. I live in fear of the day when I get a call that she and her husband have their throat slit. If it is not that, then it is to learn that he has done something to himself. Katie, you know something that you are not telling me. What is it?"

Katie was quick to answer. "He is not homicidal! He loved Becca too much, but he was not jealous of Harry Kurtz.

At one time I thought he might be suicidal, but he realizes the hurt it would cause Laura. I can't reveal why he does what he is doing, but I am positive that he will endure what he has to, rather than hurt anyone else." Katie got up to leave. She stopped at the door. "Keep him safe sheriff, keep him safe." Katie left the room and her footsteps echoed down the hall. The thought went through the sheriff's mind, *'yes, he and the other 1200 residents of Summit County.'*

Katie arrived at the Dolan ranch and except for the smoke coming from the chimney, it appeared deserted. Evidently, the green truck was in the garage. When she got out, Dog greeted her with a sharp bark. At that point, she began to yell, "Anybody home? Is anybody home?" Tylor came to the door and she shouted, "Get this dog away from me, or I will feed him the cake I brought you."

Tylor shouted, "D-D-Dog, heel!" Dog left Katie and came to Tylor. Tylor held the door open and greeted her. "Are you l-l-lost? I had g-g-given up hope of s-s-seeing you again."

Jim laid a book aside and got up from his chair. Taking the cake, he said, "Take off your coat. I will heat up the coffee and sample this cake. If you prefer, I will heat water for tea. How have you been?"

"Tea will be fine. The fire feels good. I borrowed Father's car and the heater is not the best, so I am a bit chilled. I don't know about you, but I am ready for spring." Katie removed her coat and laid it on the sofa. Tylor was busy getting the cups and plates and setting out the silverware. After a short time, Jim had the water boiling and they were ready to eat.

Tylor said, "Thank you for the c-c-cake. We haven't d-d-done much pastry b-b-baking." After taking his first bite he sighed, "Ah, German Chocolate; my f-f-favorite c-c-cake. Did you know that it is m-m-my favorite?" Katie nodded.

Jim asked, "What is new at the 99 Ranch? We get *The Sentinel,* but you folks aren't making the headlines."

Katie began to laugh. "Tylor, you went to Metta Taggat's funeral. Well, about two months after that, Tag received a letter from an attorney in Madden that they were to read the will and he was in it. Tag didn't want to go, but Laura insisted that they be there for the reading. Tag was listed first and she willed him a burial plot in the Catholic cemetery, right next to her."

Jim and Tylor started laughing. Jim said, "I would have liked to have been there. I can imagine what Tag might have said."

Katie continued, "Tag wanted to leave, but Laura insisted that he stay. The attorney said there was more. I guess with each bequeath, she had some comment. Because Tag was her favorite nephew, she left him $10,000.00 and an almost new gold wedding band. No one knew the significance of the wedding band. The balance of the estate was left to the Sisters of St. Elisabeth for the continued operation of their orphanage. It seems that she and Hiram were unable to have children. The Sisters found them a son to adopt in their advanced years."

Jim said, "I remember them getting a son. Isn't it strange, these things coming back after all these years. I had only been with George and Mrs. Taggat a few years."

"When the attorney announced the estimated balance of the estate to be near three million dollars, one of the nuns fainted." Katie added, "The attorney remarked that the Taggats were very frugal people."

Jim said, "That is putting it mildly. Metta Taggat was interested in more cows and more land. To accomplish that, they lived like paupers. Metta was the driving force behind the whole operation. I don't think that woman ever cracked a smile."

Jim got up from his chair. "I will go fetch more wood for the fire. I see it is getting low." He gave Katie a wink when he went by, as if to say, 'alright Katie, he is all yours.'

Katie quickly gathered up the dishes and took them to the sink. She returned to the sofa where Tylor was still sitting. She sat beside him and touched his arm. In a low voice, she said, "Thank you for everything Tylor, especially for the turkey, the tree and those precious slippers. My family came for Thanksgiving dinner and we had so much fun playing in the snow. Tell me Tylor, when did you get our shoes out of the closets? Were we at home at the time?"

Tylor nodded, "I got the shoes when I b-b-brought the t-t-turkey. You looked p-p-peaceful as you slept."

"And, when you brought the gifts, did you see me sleeping then?"

"No, K-K-Katie, no," denied Tylor. "Not when you were s-s-sleeping. I wanted to s-s-see you, but no, not then."

"Are you sleeping any better at night?" she asked.

Tylor shook his head. "Maybe it is even w-w-worse. The long n-n-nights afford them darkness. It seems that they l-l-love darkness."

"Who do you mean by them?" asked Katie.

Tylor appeared agitated. "You know, the d-d-demons, the d-d-demons. I told you about the demons. They continue to r-r-run through my h-h-head when I sleep."

"When you run at night, where do you run?" Katie was trying to determine if there was a pattern to his actions. Tylor looked at her as if he didn't understand the question. "Do you run down the road, or across pastures? Is there any purpose to where you run?"

"Down the r-r-road, but on moonlit nights, I run in the p-p-pastures. When I ran to the 99 Ranch, I cut across a lot of p-p-pastures." Tylor paused, and then laughed. "I like to run in f-f-front of cars. There is this one b-b-big black Cadillac that tries to r-r-run over me. He w-w-will speed up when I am on the r-r-road. I think that he cruises around after m-m-midnight to see if he can get close to me. It breaks up the b-b-boredom of just r-r-running. One day, Jim and I were in Summit City and I spotted the car. It b-b-belongs to Tub Turner, a c-c-cattle buyer, but he never saw me. He knows who I am. The p-p-people have r-r-recognized Dog, as Bill Dolan's dog. Don't worry, Katie, I'm not c-c-crazy. I may be weird and I m-m-may be eerie, but I'm not crazy. People want to think that I'm c-c-crazy so they can l-l-lock me up."

Once again, Katie reached out to him. "Tylor, the people are scared of you. Don't do anything foolish and do keep a low profile. I have seen Tub Turner. He is full of hot air, but he doesn't like to be made a fool of by the likes of a crazy man. He is dangerous!"

Tylor reached down and taking her hand, he kissed it. "All right, K-K-Katie. I will b-b-be careful." He got up from the sofa and walked toward the door. "I w-w-will holler at Jim. He can c-c-come in now. We have d-d-discussed this long enough. I s-s-saw the wink he gave you."

Katie returned home, uncertain of how much she should or would share with Sheriff Morgan.

CHAPTER 9
THE NIGHT VISITOR

The hardy souls of the Nebraska Sandhills survived the January cold by remembering that it is followed by the warmer days of February. An occasional chinook blows through to announce that March is close behind. March, the month that brings out the love/hate relationship the Sandhills rancher has with the calendar. Marked on that calendar is the anticipated calving date of the herd of cows that he has been feeding all winter long. The new calves bring a smile to his face, but until this phase of the ranching operation is concluded, there are long days and sleepless nights to be endured.

After Katie's visit to the Dolan Ranch, Tylor didn't run the road as often as he had previously, but he still continued to run most nights. So that Tub Turner wasn't disappointed in his quest to run Tylor down, Tylor watched for his headlights. At least once a week, he made it a point for Tub to see him close enough to be able to tell the men at the Café that he had seen Tylor. Of course, this would be after Sheriff Morgan had been informed of the time and place of the sighting.

Now that the ranchers were checking the cows in the pasture from late at night until the predawn hours, there were more sightings of Tylor running the pastures. More disturbing to Sheriff Morgan was the report of a young calf that had been killed under unusual circumstances. The rancher that had reported the killing was sure that it wasn't from the coyotes in the area. After the second report of a calf being killed, the sheriff called the Game and Fish Department to investigate. The absence of snow and the continued dry weather didn't provide any tracks for the Game Warden to determine the culprit. However, Tub Turner had the answer he shared with the listeners at Nick's Café. "It is blood! He has finally developed a thirst for blood. The Army created a mad dog killer and now

135

they have released him in this county. Also, Sheriff Morgan won't do anything until he has killed someone. He tells me he can't arrest him until he breaks the law. Then it will be too late!"

Tylor knew nothing about the first calf that had died, but he and Dog had witnessed the death of the second calf. They were running on the road where Nearly Dry Creek flowed under the bridge. Tylor heard a calf bawl out in the night, as if experiencing pain. Its mother came rushing up from the creek bed where she had gone for a late night drink. When the cow came to the aid of her mangled calf, a startled animal burst from the brush that bordered the creek. The animal appeared to be a large cat, possibly a young mountain lion. It ran across a small clearing, disappearing into the brush once again. It was difficult for Tylor to believe what he had seen. However, he was certain that he had seen a mountain lion, a rarity in the Sandhills!

The following night, Tylor saw the black Cadillac speed by where he and Dog were hiding alongside of the road. It was past midnight and Tylor noticed that the car was weaving as it sped down the dirt road. When Tylor thought that the taillights should have disappeared around the curve ahead, they remained fixed in the night. Tylor and his companion ran ahead to where the car had stopped. The car had missed the curve and went through the barbed wire fence and crashed into a cedar tree. Tylor saw that Tub Turner was unconscious and was slumped over the steering wheel. The smoldering of the engine and the smell of gasoline alerted Tylor to the possibility of fire. He pulled Tub from the car. He struggled with the huge man, but he got him over his shoulder and carried him across Nearly Dry Creek. Tylor had to wade through about two feet of water. Laying Tub on the grass, he placed him into a comfortable position, away from any harm that a fire might cause.

A rancher, Chuck Messner, was checking his cows that

night. Spotting a fire in the distance, he called the rural fire department. Chuck drove to the fire. While waiting for the fire truck, he started searching for Tub when he saw that he was not in the car. The men with the rescue unit aided in the search and one of them saw that Tub was on the other side of Nearly Dry Creek. He was sitting up and holding his head. After wading across the stream, they observed that he was stunned. One of them asked, "Tub, what happened here?"

Tub spat out, "That Taggat kid and his dog darted in front of me and I swerved to miss them. That is what caused me to crash and knock me out. Now, maybe that lazy sheriff will lock him up."

The two men looked at one another. They detected the heavy odor of alcohol on his breath. One asked, "But, Tub, how did you get over here? Your feet aren't even wet." That was one of the few times that Tub was at a loss for words.

It wasn't until a week later that Tylor saw the mountain lion once again, feeding on a turkey near the Grant Holler ranch. After the incident of killing the calf, Tylor was prepared to kill the lion with his bow and arrow. Upon seeing the young cat eating the turkey, he decided that perhaps she wasn't so bad after all, presuming that she was a female. Tylor had a distaste for the wild turkeys, so if she was willing to live on turkeys, he was willing to let her live. Each had eyed the other rather closely for a few moments before Tylor decided to let her eat in peace. He backed up slowly until it was safe for him and Dog to make their exit. What puzzled Tylor was that the second time he had seen the lion was about eight miles from where she had killed the calf.

Now it was a game for Tylor to determine how long it would be, before he saw her again. Was it possible that she would appear in the headlights of Tub Turner's car as he too roamed the back roads of Summit County? And then too, there was the possibility that someone from the sheriff's office might see her, when they patrolled the county at night. How long before she would go undetected? Keep in mind, the ranchers were out all hours of the night, checking to see if there were cows needing help with the birthing process. Eventually, someone would report seeing a mountain lion. Could she have migrated from the Black Hills of western South Dakota?

The days were lengthening, but the demons continued to run through Tylor's head, causing him to find refuge in his run each night. Some nights he would run, not knowing where he was going, only to retrace his steps back to the ranch. This night he had run further than he intended, when he realized that he was near the Barnes Ranch. It was in that portion of the ranch where Carl Barnes kept his small band of brood mares. Tylor sensed uneasiness among the horses. It was then that he spotted the young mountain lion bring down the youngest colt of the herd, dragging it into the brush. Notching an arrow into the string of the bow, he cautiously pursued the young mountain lion when it ran up a dry gulch. Seeing that it was going to get out of range, he released the arrow. He saw it strike a tree about six inches above the head of the mountain lion. By now his quarry had made her way up the dry gulch and would soon be gone. Only then did he realize that he was being pursued as well. He heard the noise of a vehicle and the glint of a spotlight as it searched the blackness of the night. Looking down, he saw his own shadow on the ground, as the light reflected off the trees around him. He made a few fast steps to reach the dry gulch that the lion had entered earlier. This would provide him cover until he was well out of the range of the spotlight. He was not concerned about meeting the mountain lion. She would well outdistance him in her escape. Dog stayed close to him and they reached the Dolan ranch at three in the morning. Sleep would not come to Tylor. He realized how close he came to his kill. Then too, how close he was to being caught himself!

At breakfast the next morning, Tylor asked, "Jim, could I t-t-take the truck to t-t-town this morning? We need s-s-some groceries and I want to c-c-cash my check from the g-g-government. Also, I am thinking that the w-w-winter is over and I will have the b-b-barber cut my hair and shave my beard." Tylor laughed, "Do you r-r-realize that it was H-H-Halloween when I had my last hair cut?"

"It looks it," said Jim. "I don't see how you manage to get your hat on your head with all that hair. I hope that I recognize you when you come back. Pick up five pounds of staples at the hardware store and charge to Bill. The heavy snow popped a lot of staples out of the posts this winter. I will ride out and check the cows." Jim got up and putting on his hat, he told Tylor, "Just be sure to be back here to fix dinner."

At the same time that Tylor was cleaning up the breakfast dishes at the Bill Dolan Ranch, the 99 Ranch owners were finishing their breakfast. There was a knock at their door and Tag got up to answer it. Opening the door, he saw that it was Carl Barnes. "Come in, Carl. We still have some coffee left."

Carl shook his head, "No, I need to talk with you outside."

Tag said, "Carl, this must be pretty serious. What is it?"

"It is serious," said Carl. "It's about Tylor. I didn't want to say anything in front of Laura, but I thought you need--."

Tag interrupted him. "If it is about Tylor, she needs to hear it! Come on in, and there is no need of being apologetic."

Tag brought him into the kitchen and nodded toward a chair. Carl sat down and began to roll his hat from hand to hand. Finally he spoke, "Laura, I almost shot your son earlier this morning. I went out at about two to check the mares to see if any of them were about to foal and if they needed any help. Something had them stirred up. I moved the spotlight around, and it shone on Tylor. I had thought something was after the mares, so I was ready to shoot. I had him within my sights when I realized that it was Tylor. As soon as it was light, I got Harry to help me. Harry has been staying close to the house. Becca hasn't been feeling real well now that she is pregnant. Anyway, we started looking around and we found this colt that had been killed. He was the youngest of the bunch. By the time we found him, the coyotes had eaten on him. But, we found an arrow embedded in a tree with the initials TT on the shaft. I'm sorry to tell you this, but he has been causing a lot of havoc in this county. I don't believe he ever sleeps. He is here and there most every night. I'm sorry, Laura, I'm real sorry."

Laura sat at the table, saying nothing. She looked at Carl. "The two calves that were killed previously; do you think he was responsible?" Carl nodded.

Laura looked at Katie and saw that she was shaking as if she was chilled. "Katie, what do you know about all this regarding Tylor?" Katie said nothing, but ran from the room. Entering her bedroom she slammed the door.

Laura said, "Apparently, I have one question answered. Tag, what do you know about Tylor?"

"Laura," he replied, "I have heard nothing. According to the paper, it appears that the sheriff has nothing to go on at this time. However, Sheriff Morgan usually knows much more than he is willing to reveal."

Laura walked across the kitchen and positioned herself with her back to the sink. She leaned against the counter. With her arms folded, she looked at Carl. "I might ask, Carl, what do you plan to do with this information? Or rather, what do you think we should do? Do you want restitution for the loss of the colt? I want to be fair and open about this, but I need to hear from you in this matter."

Carl asked, "Laura, how stable is he? What worries me is that he has come close to our ranch and Becca in particular. Was he seeking some form of revenge upon her jilting him?

140

I'm not going to report what has happened to the sheriff at this time, but I think it best if you go talk with Sheriff Morgan. That is all that I ask." Carl got up from his chair and putting on his hat, he went out to his truck and drove home. Neither Tag nor Laura said anything to him.

Katie came out to the kitchen. "Tylor would not be involved in a senseless killing. Never!"

Shortly after the time of Carl Barnes' visit to the 99 Ranch, Tylor Taggat had entered the bank and cashed his check. He stepped out the door to the sidewalk. He heard a commotion to his right. He looked and saw a young woman kneeling on the sidewalk. Tylor stopped to help her and asked, "Did you f-f-fall? Here, let m-m-me help you."

A young man appeared between the two trucks and quickly said, "She doesn't need any help from the likes of you." Tylor turned to see who had spoken to him. He recognized that it was the upper classman that always picked on him when he was in high school. His name was Gordon Collier and his mother was a cousin of Tag. "Well, well, if it isn't T-T-Tag-a-long. Just keep your hands off my wife, or you will get what she got!"

"Did you knock h-h-her to the g-g-ground?" asked Tylor. "She deserves b-b-better treatment than being knocked to the g-g-ground." Gordon gave Tylor a shove. "I don't want any t-t-trouble. Just let me g-g-get into my truck and I will b-b-be gone," begged Tylor.

It was then that Gordon crowded Tylor into the front of his truck and punched him in the stomach. Tylor bent over from the blow and brought his club fist forward, striking Gordon in the middle of his forehead. Gordon Collier's knees gave out and immediately he began to fall. Tylor caught him and gently laid him out on the sidewalk. Mrs. Stahl was coming out of the bank. Tylor said, "Mrs. Stahl, c-c-call the r-r-rescue unit!"

Gordon Collier's wife knelt at his side. Looking up at

141

Tylor, she screamed, "You killed him! You killed him!" It was then that he recognized her. She was a girl that had been two grades behind him in school. At that time her name had been Jenny Morgan, the sheriff's granddaughter!

CHAPTER 10
INCARCERATION!

Tylor knew that he had hit Gordon Collier a severe blow. It was not intentional, but more of a reflex from being hit in the stomach. While he waited for the rescue unit to arrive, his stomach still hurt, but he was not going to run. The rescue unit arrived and after checking Gordon, they were preparing to load him in the ambulance. Sheriff Morgan and his deputy drove up alongside of the ambulance. The sheriff went to talk to those that were putting Gordon in the ambulance. After the ambulance left, Jenny Collier ran up to Sheriff Morgan. Pointing to Tylor, she shouted, "Grandpa, there is the man that tried to kill Gordon! That is Tylor Taggat! He is the one that hit Gordon. Arrest him, Grandpa, arrest him!"

Taking her by the arm, he said, "Jenny, I will handle this, so take your truck and go to the hospital. I will see you when I finish here."

Approaching Tylor, the sheriff was amazed at how different he looked since the last time he had seen him. He remembered visiting him at the hospital after the death of his brother TJ, to determine what had happened at the windmill on that fateful day. Today, his hair was long, almost to his shoulders and as black as midnight. His beard was just as black, but had apparently been trimmed from time to time, as it was well shaped. He noted the leanness of the body, undoubtedly from the constant running. But it was the stub hand that intrigued him. He remembered when questioning Tylor at the hospital that he had kept the stub under the covers.

The sheriff began, "Tell me, Tylor, what happened here today?"

Awaiting Tylor's response, he saw Tylor lift his head and stuttering he said, "N-N-No excuse, sir."

Sheriff Morgan was puzzled. He knew that Gordon was

a hothead and probably perpetrated the fight. He asked again, "What happened and who started the fight?"

Tylor shook his head. "I really d-d-don't know what s-s-started the fight. I c-c-can't help you."

"Tylor, this is serious. I have never seen anyone out cold like Gordon is today. I am going to have to arrest you. Do you understand?" Sheriff Morgan wanted to be as direct as he could.

Tylor nodded and stuck out his hands. It was then that he said, "I n-n-need to get b-b-back to Jim with his t-t-truck. Tomorrow is S-S-Sunday and he will want to g-g-go to church."

The sheriff said, "That is thoughtful of you. Give us the keys and I will see that Jim gets his truck today. Is that what you want?"

Tylor nodded. "The k-k-keys are inside, but he w-w-wanted me to f-f-fix his dinner. Will I be out in t-t-time to fix his dinner?"

"No, Tylor," replied the sheriff, "but I will let Jim know that you won't be fixing his dinner."

Tylor shook his head, and said, "But, Jim won't l-l-like that. It is my week to d-d-do the cooking. He thinks that I am the b-b-best cook."

The sheriff prepared to handcuff Tylor, but he had remorse at what he was doing. He thought, *this young man went to college and had such great potential. And yet, now his thought and verbal skills are at the third grade level. He is so naïve, that he has no idea of the seriousness of the situation.* Placing the handcuff on the wrist of the club hand, he pulled it behind Tylor's back and placed the second handcuff on the left wrist. He purposely pushed his thumbnail into the club portion of the hand. *There was no evidence of flinching. The flesh was as a mass of steel!*

The sheriff and his deputy went to the courthouse and

144

placed Tylor in a cell. He was their only prisoner, but Saturday night usually resulted in one or two additional inhabitants as a result of disturbing the peace. The deputy was sent out to the Bill Dolan Ranch to bring Jim in to get his truck. The deputy had informed Jim that he preferred that he not visit Tylor for a few days.

Tylor didn't want to call anyone after given the opportunity. Sheriff Morgan called the 99 Ranch and Laura answered the phone. Sheriff Morgan came right to the point. "Laura, I have Tylor in jail and I wanted to let you know. He has refused to call anyone, but you might want to seek legal counsel in his behalf."

"Well," said Laura in a caustic tone of voice, "I see Carl Barnes didn't waste any time."

The sheriff was puzzled. He replied. "I don't know what you mean. Carl Barnes has nothing to do about Tylor being in jail. This involves a fight on Main Street this morning with Gordon Collier. I don't have all the details, but I will find out. Tylor won't tell me much and Gordon is in the hospital. He was still out cold when they put him in the ambulance. Laura, Tylor needs help with this one. It could be serious."

"Thank you, Sheriff," responded Laura, "Tag and I will be in after dinner. Sheriff, please don't feed him eggs while he is in jail."

Laura called Leon Kelly, her attorney. She arranged to meet him at the jail at 1:30 p.m. Laura had a few minutes before preparing dinner. She went to the cottonwood stump to pray. She prayed for Tylor that he meant no harm to Gordon Collier and for Gordon and his recovery. The news that she had received from Carl Barnes and the sheriff had completely unnerved her. She was spent with grief, weeping for her son. She felt a hand on her shoulder and Katie asked, "Why are you grieving?"

"It's Tylor, it is always Tylor."

"What is it? Has he been shot?" Katie had shouted out her questions, as one in fear.

Laura shook her head from side to side in unbelief. "No, he is in jail. He had a fight with Cordon Collier and now he is in jail."

"What! He had a fight with Gordon Collier? He is a troublemaker. Father says he is a part of the Taggat clan and they are mean!" Bringing her hand to her mouth, she said, "Whoops, I'm sorry Laura, I shouldn't have said that, but it sort of slipped out by mistake." Katie felt bad about what she had said about the Taggats.

Laura laughed at Katie's embarrassment. "That's all right. I am aware of some of the Taggats and their meanness. Gordon didn't fare so well. He is in the hospital while Tylor is in jail. I have made arrangements to meet with my attorney this afternoon. I will try to get Tag to go with me. I would appreciate it if you would come along as well."

Katie was happy that she had been invited. "Yes, I will go with you, but I'm not certain how much good I will be. Oh, look, Mr. Taggat is going to the house for dinner. Come, let's hurry!"

Laura entered the house and saw Tag in the living room. Running to him, she put her arms around him and sobbing said, "Oh, Tag, Tylor is in jail. What am I going to do? I have been a terrible mother. And, I don't have your dinner ready for you. I am a terrible wife as well. I can't seem to do anything right." She sank down on the sofa and continued to sob.

Once again, Katie was there. "You are not a bad mother or a bad wife. Let me fix dinner, but it might be a bit late. Talk with Mr. Taggat about what you want to do. I will call you when it is ready."Laura nodded her head and reached up to pat Katie's hand.

Tag sat beside her on the sofa. He hugged her and asked, "What do you think we should do? I have never known Laura Taggat not to have a plan."

Laura sat up and said, "Well, I have called Leon Kelly and he has arranged to meet us at the jail at 1:30 this afternoon."

"See, Laura," Tag encouraged her, "don't berate yourself. You have started to put your plan in action. Evidently, Carl Barnes has chosen to file charges against Tylor. I thought that he was going to give us a little time on this problem, but apparently not."

"It's not that," Laura whispered. "He was in Summit City and had a fight with Gordon Collier. Gordon is in the hospital and Tylor is in jail."

"Gordon Collier!" Tag was amazed. "Cousin Carol's son is the bully of the town. Tylor must have had a club to put him in the hospital. Good for Tylor!"

"I don't like him fighting. There are better ways to settle grievances than fighting. I thought I taught him better than to engage in such things."

Tag said, "Gordon Collier doesn't understand other ways. He is mean."

Katie came into the living room. "I have dinner, such as it is. I'm not sure how much of an appetite you might have. You two go ahead and eat. We are running a bit behind schedule. I will fix something for Tylor to eat in case Sheriff Morgan didn't feed him at noon. I was thinking some sandwiches and a slice of pie might go well."

"Thanks, Katie," said Laura. She got up from the sofa. "That was thoughtful of you. I think one of the cafes furnishes the meals for the inmates." Laura started to cry again. "Here I am, referring to my son as an inmate."

"Don't worry so, Laura." Tag was trying to comfort her. "We will talk with the sheriff and Tylor should be released this afternoon. They have fights in town every Saturday night. With Gordon Collier in the hospital, they will have fewer fights this Saturday night."

With his coffee mug in his hand, Sheriff Morgan looked out the window, down to the street. He saw the familiar red truck of Tag Taggat pull into the curb. He recognized Tag and

Laura, accompanied by Katie O'Neal. He went into his back office and picking up the phone, he dialed the hospital. After a moment, he said, "This is Sheriff Morgan. I need to talk to Dr. Jessup regarding the condition of Gordon Collier. Just get him. I will wait, but I need to speak to him now!"

"Good afternoon, Sheriff. This is Dr. Jessup. Gordon Collier has not regained consciousness. I have never seen anything like it. Usually, a blow to the head will result being out for a few minutes. I cannot see where he might have struck his head when he fell. Your granddaughter Jenny said that Tylor caught him as he was falling and laid him out gently on the sidewalk. I will keep an eye on him and if there is any change, I will let you know. Goodbye."

The sheriff hung up the phone and returned to the front desk, as people began to file into the room. He noticed that Leon Kelly was with the Taggats.

"Sheriff," Leon said, "Mrs.Taggat has retained me to represent Tylor Taggat. I would like to know on what charges you are holding Tylor and what are your plans for releasing him."

"Mr. Kelly, your client has been a bad boy." The sheriff sat down in his chair and tilting it back, he continued. "I just talked with Dr. Jessup. Gordon Collier has not yet regained consciousness. At what point he considers that Gordon is in a coma, is up to him. However, I am holding Tylor on assault and battery as a result of Gordon's injuries. Then Carl Barnes' name was brought up and I checked with him. I am thinking that I could possibly get him to file a complaint of destruction of property as a result of a dead colt. There is certainly a trespassing charge because of an arrow marked TT. So, Mr. Kelly, I will be conferring with the county attorney to determine what charges might be filed. There is also the question of the suspicious death of two calves in the county to consider. I have a call into the county attorney regarding bringing Tylor Taggat before a judge to determine if he should be released on bond. I know that his parents are respected citizens of this county, but I for one will sleep better tonight, knowing that Tylor Taggat is in my jail. He won't be running about in my county tonight!" Easing his chair forward, he continued his show of authority. "Now, if you would like, I will let you see your client, if you desire."

Leon Kelly nodded, "Yes, we would like to see Tylor. The Taggats have assured me that they have brought nothing with them to aid Tylor to escape custody. Miss O'Neal has brought food for Tylor in the event that he has not been fed. I realize that much has happened in the last few hours and we are only looking after his welfare."

The sheriff replied, "That's fine. After I have given you access to the prisoner, I will be back to examine the food. My deputy has driven Jim McCann's truck back to the ranch. Tylor was concerned that he would be without transportation. Normally I would have picked up food at a local café, but with the deputy gone, I am running late. I appreciate your bringing Tylor his lunch. Come with me." Katie remained behind while the others went to see Tylor.

The sheriff brought Tylor into the room and Laura gave a gasp. She could not believe her eyes. Her son was in jailhouse clothing, with his legs shackled and cuffs on his wrists. His hair was long and he had grown a beard. It appeared that he had neither shaved nor had a haircut since he left home at the time of TJ's death, six months earlier. Sitting Tylor on a chair across the table from his visitors, the sheriff said, "You may touch his hands, but nothing more."

Laura reached out and touching Tylor's hands, she said, "Tylor, how could it possibly come to this? This is Leon Kelly, my attorney. He has some questions to ask of you, as do Tag and I. Tylor, Carl Barnes came early this morning and said you were at his ranch last night. Is that right?" Tylor nodded. "He also said that you killed one of his colts and they found your arrow stuck in a tree trunk. Is that true?"

Tylor vigorously shook his head. "No, I did not k-k-kill a colt. It was a m-m-mountain lion. I tried to k-k-kill it with my bow and arrow, but I m-m-missed. Someone p-p-put a light on me and I ran."

Tag slammed his fist on the table. "Don't lie to your mother. There are no mountain lions in Summit County! What about the two calves that were killed earlier? Did a mountain lion kill them as well?"

Tylor jumped when Tag hit the table. "I was there r-r-right after one was k-k-killed along Nearly Dry Creek. I heard the calf b-b-bawl out in p-p-pain. It was a young mountain l-l-lion that killed the calf. And, there was a t-t-turkey that was killed and eaten."

Tag was furious. "Was it a mountain lion that attacked Gordon Collier?"

Tylor said, "No, but neither d-d-did I. He pushed me into m-m-my truck and hit me in the stomach. That is when I h-h-hit him. I didn't mean to hit him with my b-b-bad hand, but the reflex brought my fist d-d-down. Is he g-g-going to die? Did you know that I once k-k-killed a man with that f-f-fist?"

Leon Kelly had let Tag do the talking until now. "Tylor, don't tell anyone that you killed a man with that fist. Do you understand?" Tylor nodded. "Tell no one."

Tylor reached out to Laura and touching her hand, he said, "Mama, I'm sorry. I d-d-don't like it here. They haven't f-f-fed me. Mama, can I g-g-go home with you? Please, M-M-Mama, please."

Laura held his hand and wept for her son. Except for his beard and long hair, she would have thought he was at that age when he asked his mother why Tag hated him. He was seven then. "Tylor, Katie has some sandwiches and pie. She will bring it to you. Goodbye, my son."

"Katie is nice to m-m-me, but I don't want her to s-s-see me l-l-like this, all chained and cuffed. It isn't r-r-right. G-G-Goodbye, Mama. Goodbye, Father. G-G-Goodbye, Mr. Kelly."

They returned to the front office and Katie asked, "Can I see him now?"

Laura replied, "No, Katie, he didn't want you to see him in his handcuffs and shackles. He appreciated your fixing something to eat."

Leon Kelly told his clients, "I think that we should return to my office and discuss the situation. I have several thoughts to go over with you, regarding Tylor."

Mr. Kelly's office was close by, so they left their vehicle at the courthouse and walked to his office. Upon entering, Leon apologized, "Normally I would have coffee for you, but as this is Saturday afternoon, I don't have any made. However, this should not take long." After they were seated in his conference room, he began. "Mrs. Taggat, how did Tylor appear to you today?"

"How did he appear? Well, he certainly needed a haircut and a shave!"

"No," interrupted Leon, "I mean, I was referring to his demeanor. Was there anything unusual in his state of mind? That is, did he appear as being juvenile?"

"Did you pick up on that as well? At one point, except for the beard and long hair, I remembered him being seven years old. What has happened to him?" Laura shook her head in disbelief.

Tag spoke up, "And this ridiculous notion about a mountain lion. How does he account for being clear over to the Barnes Ranch at two in the morning, shooting off arrows?"

Katie was irritated by these accusations, but said nothing.

"With Tylor in jail," Leon shared, "if the livestock

killings continue, then we will know that there was something other than Tylor doing the killing. The assault charge may be a different matter, depending on young Collier's recovery. You need to know that I am not a defense attorney in criminal matters. Karl Larson is the prosecuting attorney and he is tough. He may recuse himself. I believe that he is Tag's personal attorney. Is that correct?"

"I wouldn't say that," answered Tag. "It has been over twenty years since I used him at my father's insistence, but that is long past."

Leon continued, "Sheriff Morgan is going to fight bond being set. I have the feeling that the sheriff feels a lot safer with Tylor in jail. Normally he is not as cautious as he was today. This is the first prisoner that I have talked with in that jail that has been cuffed and shackled when conferring with their attorney. Are you aware that ever since he moved in with Jim McCann, Tylor has been running at night from one end of this county to the other? People have spotted him and the red heeler dog of Bill Dolan's all hours of the night. Sheriff Morgan wants it stopped, but until these livestock killings and the assault charge, his hands were tied."

Katie turned pale. She saw that Laura and Tag were ignorant of Tylor's midnight runs.

"But," Laura exclaimed in unbelief, "why would a grown man do these things? Is he trying to establish himself as some kind of a legend in the county? It doesn't make sense!"

"It didn't until the livestock killings began," said Leon. "Tub Turner has seen him more than even the deputies that patrol the country side. He maintains that Tylor and the dog are blood thirsty and he fears that some local resident will be the next victim."

"Oh, good heavens, what will people think up next?" said Laura. "With that kind of thinking, maybe jail is the safest place for Tylor."

Leon Kelly said, "If Tylor is innocent of the livestock killings as he says he is, and they continue while he is in jail, then he is exonerated of that charge."

Laura was indignant. "He said he didn't kill any of the livestock. That should be good enough!"

Leon quietly said, "Mrs. Taggat, I am his attorney, not his mother. I am presuming him to be guilty, so that I may prove him innocent. The next thing is to have young Collier regain consciousness and have him not press charges. Considering his reputation, that might be possible. Unfortunately, apparently the only witness was his wife. There may be others that we don't know about. Let's see what takes place next."

****

That night, the female mountain lion decided that her short foray into the Sandhills must come to a close. The man and his dog had marked their territory over a wide expanse of the region. It was now becoming impossible not to have their paths cross in the night. Besides, as the days were lengthening, she was encountering the yearning to find a mate. She would go back to the land where the four faces of man *(Mount Rushmore)* were on the rock. These men didn't mark their territory, as did the man with the dog. Tonight, she would make her last kill. Then she would make her way south to the big river and follow it to the setting sun. There was food along the big river and the deer were plentiful. From the big river, she would go north to the land of the four men. This is where she was born and this is where she would find her mate. She planned to make her kill early in the evening so that she might be filled as she made her way through the breaks. These breaks would provide her cover through the night until she reached the great river. She found a hen turkey, sitting on her nest. It was not what she desired. She had prepared to make her last kill the succulent flesh of a young colt. But, in her haste to leave

153

the Sandhills, this would do, even though she did not like the feathers of a turkey that tickled her nose.

****

That night, while the mountain lion was making her kill, a young man lay in a hospital bed clinging to life. His wife at his side was rehearsing the events of the morning that resulted in his hospitalization. Meanwhile, another young man lay on a hard cot in the county jail, questioning his fate. Only Sheriff Morgan was experiencing peaceful sleep.

CHAPTER 11
THE NAME IS LAURA, LAURA TAGGAT

Sunday morning, Laura anticipated that Sheriff Morgan would purposely serve Tylor eggs. Or, completely forego breakfast because the cafes in town didn't open on Sunday. With this in mind, she had fixed biscuits and gravy to take to Tylor. Arriving at the jail, she was greeted by the deputy in charge. "I will take these to your son this morning, but the sheriff wanted me to inform you that he would no longer accept food for any prisoner."

"Very well. When may I see my son?" asked Laura.

"Visiting hours are two to three in the afternoon on Sunday, Wednesday and Friday. The sheriff will be here this afternoon, so if you have any further questions, you can take it up with him at that time." He picked up the food and left the office.

Laura stepped out of the courthouse and decided to go to the hospital. She stopped at the front desk and asked, "Has there been any change in the condition of Gordon Collier?"

The nurse on duty shook her head. "He is about the same. Dr. Jessup will be in at eight if you want to talk to him."

"No," said Laura, "that will be fine. Is there anyone with him now?"

"Why yes, there is. His wife has been with him all night. Poor thing. He is in room 106, if you care to speak with her."

"Thank you. I will just slip in for a moment."

Laura went down the hall and looked into the room. She saw a young girl sitting at a chair near the side of the bed, holding the hand of the patient. She smiled when Laura stepped into the room. Laura asked, "Have you been with him all night?" The girl nodded. Laura put her hand on her shoulder. "You must be tired out. Would you like to go with me for some

155

breakfast? I think the cafeteria is open now and we can get a bite to eat."

"Oh," she said, "I don't want to leave him. He might wake up and see that I am not here."

"I will stay if you want. And then, if he awakens, I will come and get you." Reaching in her purse, Laura found three dollars that she handed to the girl. "Here, get yourself some breakfast. Do you mind if I pray for your husband while I sit here?"

"Oh, no, that would be real kind of you. I would like that. I will hurry right back."

Laura began to pray, "Father, I ask that you would heal Gordon and that he will be all right. I don't understand a lot of things, but I don't want to see neither this boy suffering, nor his wife as she grieves for her husband. I pray for Tylor that he might be remorseful for what he has done to Gordon. I pray for Tylor's release from jail and that he can be restored to his family again. Lord, there are times that I feel as a withered vine, not able to reach out to those that I love. Help me to be a compassionate person in all this turmoil. I ask this in Your Name, Amen."

Laura took hold of Gordon's hand. She noticed how rough it felt. She found a bottle of lotion in the small cabinet and began to massage the fingers and the back of each hand. She was doing this when Jenny Collier returned to the room. She asked, "What are you doing?"

Laura said, "I was massaging his hands. I noticed how rough and cracked they were. He must work real hard to have hands that rough. Did I do anything wrong?"

Jenny shook her head, "No, that was nice of you to do that for Gordon."

Laura said, "Do I need to stay a while longer for you to rest? If not, then I will go."

"No, I will be fine. I dozed some last night. Thank you

for the breakfast." Laura started to leave the room when Jenny asked, "What is your name? I don't believe that I know you."

Preparing to leave the room, she turned and said, "The name is Laura, Laura Taggat; Tylor's mother."

When Laura returned home, she looked through her writing desk. She had scrutinized every scrap of paper in three of the drawers before she found what she was seeking. Going to the phone, she dialed a number and waited for an answer. "Is this Miriam Whitman? Oh, good. I thought I might have lost your phone number. This is Laura Taggat. I need to get in touch with Lionel. Oh, he is there. Then, may I speak with him. Thank you, Miriam." There was a pause, as Lionel came to the phone. "Lionel, I need your help. Tylor is in jail, accused of assaulting the town bully. The bully is in the hospital in an apparent coma. They are trying to bring other charges against him, such as killing calves and a colt. Lionel, he has regressed to the point that he is thinking and talking like a seven year old. My attorney admits that it is more than he is capable of and suggested that we need help. I will be glad to pay you for your assistance, but we are at a loss as what to do at this time." There was a pause while Lionel checked his calendar. "Thank you Lionel. Then we will see you on Wednesday. Goodbye."

Lionel arrived at the ranch midmorning on Wednesday as promised. A very attractive black lady that he introduced as his wife accompanied him. Marsha was doing the driving. Lionel still experienced difficulty walking, a result of his imprisonment in Vietnam.

Laura was happy that he had come, but it was difficult for her to express herself, as the tears streamed down her cheeks. "Oh, Lionel, I don't know what to do. It is as if I have lost him. I thought I was bringing him back to the family and to my bosom as his health was restored from his imprisonment. But, when TJ died, he turned from his family and now he is a renegade and a stranger to me."

"What about Jim McCann, does he have any influence with him? I knew that he often referred to him as Uncle Jim." Lionel asked the question and remembered that Jim was a gentle man, a man of strength.

Laura shook her head. "Lionel, at the time of TJ's accident, everything seemed to fall apart. Jim left the ranch. I don't know if he and Tag had words. No one will say. Jim had been with the Taggat family for more than fifty years. Tylor was hospitalized for injuries as well at the time of the accident. When he was dismissed, he went to live with Jim on a small ranch east of Summit City." Laura stopped and putting her hands to her face, she said, "Here I am, telling you all of my problems. Come into the house and we will have some refreshments. Then I will show you your room. Tell me, how long have the two of you been married?"

"Three months and four days," said Marsha. "We met the first day in kindergarten and I knew that he was the one for me." Marsha laughed, giving Lionel's arm a squeeze. Laura saw there was no doubting their love for one another.

Always eager to put her plan to work, Laura said, "Lionel, I thought that we might meet with my attorney after dinner and then I will take you to see Tylor. Does that sound all right?"

Lionel seemed a bit reluctant, "Well, I suppose, but I was hoping to see Tylor this afternoon."

Laura laughed. She said, "I'm sorry. See how we fail to communicate, living in two different cultures. Dinner to the people in the Sandhills is at noon. The only time we have lunch is when we carry the meal in a bucket and it is eaten away from the house. We will see Tylor this afternoon after we have eaten our noon meal."

Lionel said, "I should have remembered that. Mother so enjoyed eating dinner with the ranch hands when she and I visited."

After dinner, Laura said to Marsha, "If you want, you may

158

go with us, or stay here at the house. Feel free to roam around. Katie, our high school girl that helps me, will be home about four. She will keep you entertained."

"I believe that I will stay and rest up a bit. I do all the driving, but I did enjoy the relaxing drive through the Sandhills. We saw so many cows and calves in the pastures and met a vehicle every thirty minutes or so. When Katie comes home, I may have her show me around here before you and Lionel return."

Before they arrived at the attorney's office, Laura said, "Perhaps it is best if I don't sit in with you and Leon. Tag insists that I am too determined to have my way, so you two experts can come to a consensus. I will leave it up to you. Is that fair enough?"

"It is indeed, fair enough!" declared Lionel.

After the meeting with Leon, Lionel wanted to see his friend Tylor. Lionel asked, "Mrs. Taggat, does Tylor know that you called me for assistance?"

"No," she replied, "I haven't told him. He has regressed so, that I am not sure that he will remember you, so don't be too disappointed. After the judge denied bail, the sheriff has become such a stinker about letting anyone see Tylor. Unless he is cuffed and shackled, we have been meeting in his cell. He is the only prisoner, so we do have an element of privacy."

"Don't tell him that I am here, or that you have anyone with you. I can hardly wait to see him, but I want to test him. I will stay back and to the edge of the corridor. We will surprise him."

They entered the sheriff's office and found that Sheriff Morgan was on duty. Laura approached the desk, and smiling at the sheriff, she said, "Sheriff Morgan, I want you to meet an Army buddy of Tylor's, Lionel Whitman. Lionel, this is Sheriff Morgan." The two men shook hands. Sheriff Morgan took note of the unsteadiness of the man's walk, as well as the refinement of his body structure.

"So, you two were in the Army together. Did you serve overseas?" Sheriff Morgan was a master at sizing up people by his questioning them.

"Yes," Lionel said, "we were in the same unit overseas and consequently were in the same prison compound. I was more fortunate than Tylor. I was rescued, while he endured the agony of finding his way back alone to our own line. It was a remarkable feat to say the least. Wouldn't you agree?"

"Oh, yes, yes. No doubt about it." The sheriff was caught off guard by Lionel's praise of Tylor.

"Sheriff Morgan, after I have visited Tylor, might I have a moment of your time?" He handed the sheriff his card. "I may be assisting Mr. Kelly in his defense of Tylor. Now, may we go see my friend? I have asked Mrs. Taggat to not reveal my presence. I want to surprise him"

Upon entering the corridor, Lionel could hear Tylor calling out, "Mama, Mama is c-c-coming to see her b-b-bad b-b-boy."

When she entered the cell he hugged her. Holding her at arm's length, he said, "M-M-Mama, you have a surprise f-f-for Tylor. I know it! I know it! Whiteman! Whiteman! C-C-Come here. Lionel, come here. I can s-s-smell you. No matter how m-m-much you scrub, you can never get r-r-rid of that Vietnam s-s-stench."

The sheriff had a look of amazement as the two friends hugged. He locked the cell door, uncertain of how Tylor knew that his friend was in the corridor.

Lionel took another look at Tylor and said, "Redneck, you look like a typical redneck now; beard, long hair, scruffy clothes, but wait, there is hope. I don't see any tattoos. The first things are easy to fix, but tattoos, no. Tylor, if we are going to get you out of this, Leon and I have agreed that there are certain things that you must do. These things are nonnegotiable. Beginning with the hair and the beard, they both need to go. We will arrange with the sheriff to allow a barber to shave you and give you a haircut. The frontiersman look is out! No moccasins or leather attire. Western wear is fine. Your mother says you have a fine pair of handmade boots. Get used to wearing them. I'm going to visit with the sheriff to see what it will take to get you out of here. What do you have to say for yourself?"

"It sounds l-l-like you have said it all. But, I have s-s-something to s-s-say for you. Go back to Kansas City. I don't n-n-need you to tell me how to d-d-dress and how to act. I g-g-got myself into this m-m-mess and I will g-g-get myself out! If I can't get m-m-myself out, then I will s-s-suffer the consequences." Tylor put his face to the bars and hollered. "Sheriff! Sheriff! Get these d-d-do-gooders out of my cell!"

When the sheriff got to the cell, he saw that the reunion that started out so well had quickly deteriorated. Laura was in tears and Lionel had a blank look on his face. When they got to the front office, Lionel said, "I told the sheriff that I wanted to visit with him. Do you want to stay?"

Laura said, "No, I want to go to the hospital. I won't be gone long and I will come back to the car, or you can come to the hospital and wait for me in the lobby."

"I will meet you at the hospital," said Lionel, "if that is all right with you?" Laura nodded and left the courthouse.

The sheriff waited until Lionel had finished his conversation with Laura. "You said that you wanted to visit with me, what did you have in mind? It didn't sound like your reception went real well."

"No," Lionel replied, "it didn't. He is like a lion in a cage. Tell me sheriff, at the bond hearing, why were you so opposed for the setting of a bond so that he might be released?"

"Mr. Whitman, I am getting to be an old man and I like to sleep at night. When Tylor Taggat is in my jail, I sleep like a baby. Maybe some lawmen like the excitement of cops and robbers. I like it when I am in control. I know who the troublemakers are in this county and I am right there among them. Tylor Taggat was a good kid, but the Army ruined him. I don't know if he is blood thirsty, or just baiting me. He complains that the food we serve him is overcooked, particularly the meat. The beef he wants raw! Raw mind you! I told him that I would give it to him rare, but not raw. You are right. He is like a caged lion. I have watched him as he paces back and forth for hours. There have been two calves killed and one colt. The number one suspect is Tylor Taggat. The last animal killed was a colt, early Saturday morning. Tylor was jailed Saturday noon. Here it is Wednesday and I have no report of any young stock being slain. He has run the county at night for six months with nothing happening. That is, other than a very nervous sheriff. Let me put it this way, Mr. Whitman. I consider that Tylor Taggat is in the Summit County jail under protective custody. Every truck in this county has a rifle in the rear window, hanging on a rack. Because of the mood of this county, if I were to release Tylor, he would be out running along the creeks and through the breaks. If a rancher spotted him, they would shoot him, just as if he were a coyote. At this point, they are not only fearful of the life of their livestock, but the lives of their families as well."

"Why," asked Lionel, "is he running? You say that he runs every night and has run for six months. Then, all of a sudden there is the loss of young livestock. Are you sure he is responsible?"

"It might partially be circumstantial. Now is the time that the cows are calving and foals are being born. Carl Barnes had a spotlight on him at two in the morning and had him in the sights of his rifle when he identified it was Tylor. He also recognized that red heeler that runs with him. When he started running, there were no young calves or colts. I talked with Jim McCann where Tylor lives. He has no clue. But, I have a hunch, but only a hunch." Sheriff Morgan stopped and unlocking a desk drawer, he pulled out his file on Tylor. "I sense that you are here to help a friend, so I will share what I have put together." He showed Lionel the file. He tried to explain the sightings and the reliability of the person that reported them. Sheriff Morgan continued, "About every year at Christmas time, the merchants of Summit City have a Christmas Extravaganza. They have a treasure chest with $200.00 of merchant money to be spent in Summit City. They send out a thousand keys to the people in this county, but only one key fits the lock. Many try, but only one fits the lock. That is how it is with Tylor Taggat. Many people think they have the key to the reason for his actions, but only one person is the key! And, as of now, there is only one person that knows who is that key, or at least thinks he knows. That person is me! Yes, it is me!"

Lionel asked, "Are you going to tell me who is the key? Why haven't you used the key, if you know who it is?"

"Oh, I have tried and tried, but to no avail." The sheriff stopped to wipe his brow. The things that he had shared with Lionel were exhausting. "Katie O'Neal. I do believe that Katie O'Neal is the key. She knows what drives him to run night, after night, after night! To get her to tell is another matter." The sheriff got up from his chair and declared, "End of interview. Good day, Mr. Whitman." He returned the file to his desk and left, going to a back room.

While Lionel was talking with the sheriff, Laura went to the hospital. She went to room 106. Jenny Collier was still there, keeping watch over her husband. She almost appeared frightened when Laura entered the room. "Hello, Jenny. Is Gordon any better today?"

Shaking her head, she said, "No, he just lies there."

"Jenny," asked Laura, "would you care for a cup

163

of coffee or tea?" Reaching into her purse, she found some money. "I could go with you, or I could stay as I did the other day."

"Would you mind staying with Gordon? It might be good if I walk around a bit. When is he going to wake up? It has been four days, and still no sign of coming around."

Laura handed her some money. "Here, get something to eat if you like. There is no hurry. I have a friend that will meet me here. May I pray for your husband? I see his hands are much better. Have you been applying the lotion and rubbing them? Would it be all right if I put lotion on his feet as well? The nurses should be doing this, but sometimes they are overwhelmed with other responsibilities."

Jenny managed a smile, and said, "Yes, I have been using the lotion on his hands. I think that he likes it, but I'm not sure. Please pray for him. Nobody else has come to pray for him. I never thought about putting lotion on his feet, but if you want, I am sure he would like it. I don't know if I could lotion a stranger's feet. People's feet are kind of ugly." Jenny left the room, gripping the money that Laura had given her.

Laura found the lotion bottle and pouring some in the palm of her hand, she began to lotion Gordon's feet. While she massaged his feet and ankles, she started to pray. "Father, as I minister to Gordon, I would ask for his recovery and the strengthening of his body. Bring him out of this coma and restore his health. Might he see in all this, the folly of the use of violence to accomplish one's goals? I would pray for Tylor that he might have remorse for his part in this violence. Thank you for Jenny and her faithfulness in staying with her husband, day after day." Laura was so overwhelmed with her grief that she began to weep. She wept for this young man in the bed and she wept for her son in the jail. All the time, she continued to massage the feet and ankles. Now she was unable to pray audibly while she wept, but she began to hum the hymn, 'Rock of Ages,' while she massaged the feet of Gordon.

The feet began to move. Laura looked up, and saw that Gordon's eyes were open. He gripped his head and asked, "Who are you?" Laura stopped rubbing. He said, "Don't stop. That feels good. And continue to hum that song."

Laura continued to hum and rub until Jenny came in and saw that Gordon had regained consciousness. "Oh, Gordon, you are awake. I was afraid you were never going to wake up." Laura dried her hands on a towel and prepared to leave the room.

Gordon said, "Wait, lady, you never told me your name."

Laura turned to leave the room. She said, "The name is Laura, Laura Taggat, Tylor's mother."

Lionel was waiting in the hospital lobby. Laura came running down the hall. He saw that she had been crying. He asked, "Mrs. Taggat, is something wrong?" She shook her head.

"No," she said, "something is right. Gordon Collier has come out of his coma."

On the ride home, Lionel cleared his throat. "Mrs. Taggat, I'm sorry. There in Tylor's cell, I did it all wrong. At least we know that he hasn't regressed. I will go back tomorrow and apologize. I learned one thing. Sheriff Morgan is not being obstinate. He is being careful. He says that if Tylor were released, he would be out running. He says that he cannot stop running. Because of the threat to the livestock, people also feel threatened for their own lives as well. He is protecting Tylor from being shot. I sense that tempers might be running high in this county. Do you know why he runs at night?"

Laura shook her head. "No, as far as I know, it didn't start until after TJ's death and he moved in with Jim McCann. Perhaps Jim might know."

"No, no," said Lionel. "Sheriff Morgan has visited with

165

him and Jim has no clue. Tylor wouldn't tell him when Jim asked."

When they arrived at the ranch, Katie was home. She instantly began to prepare some refreshments for them, now that they had arrived. Lionel excused himself for a few minutes. He wanted to confer with his office. Later he returned to the kitchen. Katie poured him coffee and offered him some cookies. She asked, "Well, Lionel, how did the reunion go? Was Tylor surprised to see you?"

Lionel looked at Laura. "Mrs. Taggat, you were there, suppose you answer Katie's question."

Laura moved her coffee cup around before answering. "Katie, you know that you don't surprise Tylor. Lionel remained out of sight, but Tylor knew he was near. To answer your question about how the reunion went," Laura paused as if searching for the right word. She continued, "Well, Tylor was belligerent! He actually called for the sheriff to open the door and remove us from his cell." Katie was shocked at the news.

Lionel spoke up. "He was justified in his actions. I overstepped my authority. I was making demands of what he was to do and the cell was his territory. I am going back tomorrow and try to renew our friendship."

Laura got up from the table. She turned to the group, and said, "It is such a beautiful afternoon that I am going down to the Dismal River. Does anyone care to join me?"

Lionel tapped his wife's foot under the table. Miriam said, "That is a good idea. I will leave Lionel here to help Katie with the clean up. Thank you Katie, for the refreshments." She got up from the table and reached across and gave her husband's cheek a pinch.

After the two women left the house, Katie started to pick up the dirty china and silverware. After setting these in the sink, she came back to the table and sat down. Lionel had not yet stood up to leave. Katie said, "Is there something you want

THE NAME IS LAURA, LAURA TAGGAT

to ask me?"

Lionel was surprised by her directness. "Well, yes there is." Lionel was beginning to think that this family is certainly gifted. Tylor with an unusual ability to detect odors and this girl with ESP! "How did you know?"

Katie smiled and answered, "I saw the signal of the tapping of the foot and the eye movement. And then too, I do have ESP." Katie laughed as she wiggled on her chair. "Go ahead and ask, but there is no guarantee that I will answer."

"My," said Lionel, "you certainly are direct. The question is, 'why is Tylor running night after night?' Even in the jail cell he is pacing most of the night."

"And you think I have the answer to that question?" asked Katie.

"I don't know," said Lionel, "but there is a man that thinks you and only you know why he is running, and running and running! Sheriff Morgan says that you know. Will you tell me?"

Katie shook her head. "Lionel, I gave my word to Tylor that I would tell no one. You will have to get that information from him." Katie got up from the table. Lionel reached out and touched her arm.

"Wait, Katie," he said. "There is more. Please sit down." Katie sat down, but did not sit back. "Sheriff Morgan is not a mean sheriff, but a compassionate man that wants peace in his county. He will do whatever he deems necessary to have that peace, even if it means putting Tylor in jail or prison as long as it takes to preserve that peace. Tylor has created a situation in which he is at risk of being killed. Many of the people in this county do not know Tylor as we do, but see him as a threat to their property, or their life. He has become a legend as a renegade, bloodthirsty animal killer, also capable of killing other people. The Tylor I know is none of these things. At this point however, I am content to let him be imprisoned in order to preserve his life"

"But, that is what he feared!" shouted Katie. "If anyone learned why he was running, they would think him crazy and put him away. He said, to be locked up would kill him!"

"Katie, he is in a pattern that is almost like a rut and he cannot escape. I know how he thinks and I know what he fears in his mind. The death of those that he killed has returned to plague him. There are times that he has victory over his thoughts and other times he succumbs to the past. You two must be quite close if he confided in you." Lionel paused for a few moments before asking the next question. "Katie, do you love him?"

Katie blushed and was taken aback at Lionel's question. "I don't know. He is a man, and I am a mere schoolgirl. I have never been in love, so I wouldn't know if I am in love or not."

Lionel continued to question Katie. "How did Tylor describe his torment and why did the running help?"

"He called them demons that came to him in his dreams. He would fall asleep and that is when he would see those that he had killed. If he ran they would not bother him. After four hours of running he would be so exhausted that he could sleep for a few hours. I wanted him to see Dr. Jessup, but that is when he said they would think that he was crazy. What is strange in all this, he was all right until after the death of his brother." Katie could only shake her head in wonderment.

Lionel got up and strolled to the back door. "Thank you, Katie. You have helped to give me some possible solutions to our problem. Sheriff Morgan knows his people. He was sure that you were the key to what was bothering Tylor. Katie, I think in all this, we forgot to tell you that Gordon regained consciousness this afternoon. That is a big obstacle removed in getting Tylor released from jail. Now, we must insure his safety."

The next morning, Lionel was on the phone for about

an hour with his office in Kansas City. He was writing much of the time. At dinner, Lionel said, "I am going back to visit Tylor once again and to try to make amends for my actions yesterday. Does anyone care to drive me into Summit City?"

Laura spoke up, "I will take you in, but it is probably best for the two of you to work this out, without a meddlesome mother to interfere. Miriam, would you care to join me and we can look over the city together?"

"I would like that," Miriam responded. "Rural America is so different and serene. It is difficult for me to imagine living in such a place. Maybe if I see it up close, it will be more real to me."

That afternoon, they arrived in Summit City. Leaving Lionel off at the courthouse, Laura and Miriam had made arrangements to meet him back at the hospital after two hours. If either party was early or late, the lobby was a good place to wait.

Entering the sheriff's office, he said, "I am back to try and mend the friendship that Tylor and I once had, providing that he will see me."

"Oh, I think he will," the sheriff said. "Yes, I think he will."

When Lionel looked into the cell, he had difficulty in recognizing Tylor. Tylor said, "I'm sorry the w-w-way I treated you yesterday. I f-f-figured if you c-c-care enough about my welfare, then I should t-t-take your advice." Tylor was clean-shaven and had a haircut. Gone was the woodsman look. He was dressed in blue jeans and a snap button shirt. Lionel looked down and saw that the moccasins were gone and a new pair of boots was on his feet.

"How did you manage all this? Did they forget to lock the cell and you sneaked out after dark?"

Tylor laughed, "Sheriff Morgan r-r-runs a tighter j-j-jail than the Viet Cong. He did l-l-let me get a b-b-barber to come

169

in and g-g-give me a haircut and shave. I did c-c-call Uncle Jim to bring m-m-my clothes to me. Now that you are here, m-m-maybe he will r-r-release me into your custody."

"That is highly unlikely, unless you are willing to live in Kansas City." After Lionel said that, Tylor looked at him as if he had lost his mind. "Tylor, your days of running free in Summit County are over. In visiting with the sheriff, he has been protecting you by keeping you in jail. As long as you are in Summit County, the demons will be after you."

"What d-d-demons?" he shouted. "Katie told you! She p-p-promised not to t-t-tell, but she told you!" Tylor turned to his bunk and kicked out with a vicious blow.

"No," Lionel said, "I surmised that is what was bothering you. Remember that I was with you during those perilous times. I know what has troubled you since the very beginning of your sniper days. God has forgiven you. He knows that you cannot bear the burden alone. I want you to consider a new start in a new place." Lionel handed Tylor a folder. "I have outlined a proposal for you to consider. Read it over and pray about it. It isn't perfect, but I believe it is the best that we can expect at this time. I want you to tell me what you think of it tomorrow. I will see if you, Leon Kelly and I can meet with the sheriff, the county attorney and possibly the county judge. Gordon Collier is conscious now, so that should be no problem. I would like to meet with the others tomorrow afternoon. I will see you tomorrow forenoon." He hugged Tylor. "Now you look like someone from the Sandhills. That is a good start. Goodbye."

Lionel stopped to talk with Sheriff Morgan regarding his plan for Tylor. The sheriff agreed to alert the others involved so that they could meet tomorrow afternoon.

Lionel left the courthouse and went to the hospital to wait for Laura and Miriam. When he arrived at the hospital, he found Laura in tears. Miriam was trying to console her, but to no avail. Lionel inquired, "What are all the tears about?"

Miriam answered for Laura, who was unable to compose herself. "It is Gordon Collier down in room 106. Laura went to visit him and he started in on her, threatening to sue the Taggats. Laura tried to reason with him about paying the hospital bill instead. He insisted that if he didn't get any money, then he would demand that criminal charges be filed for assault. He claimed that Tylor made a pass at his wife, Jenny. When he confronted Tylor about making the pass, it was then that Tylor hit him in the head." Miriam reached out to Lionel. "This has completely unnerved her. Is there anything that you can do?"

Returning the touch, he said, "Miriam, wait here." He walked over to the reception desk and asked the nurse on duty, "May I visit the young man in room 106?"

"Certainly," she said. "It is down the hall and on the right."

"Would you be so good as to accompany me? It will only take a moment."

The nurse nodded. "I guess I can. I need to stretch my legs anyway. Just follow me." Lionel struggled to keep pace with her. Fortunately, it was not a long walk.

They entered the room and Lionel asked the nurse, "Would you please wait? I need a witness to what I have to say." Turning his attention to Gordon, he said, "I am Lionel Whitman, a friend of Tylor Taggat. I understand that you wish to sue Tylor. Unfortunately, he has no assets and his income is comprised of a disability payment that he receives from the Army. His parents have no responsibility now that he is considered an adult. Interested parties are meeting tomorrow afternoon at 2:00 p.m. at the courthouse to determine the fate of Tylor Taggat. Perhaps you would like to be there at that time. If you wish to have an attorney to represent you, he is welcome as well. Good day, Mr. Collier." Lionel nodded to the nurse and they left the room. They continued down the hall. He said to the nurse, "Thank you for your time. I appreciate you accommodating me."

Lionel struggled to return to the reception area where he found that Miriam had managed to restore some calm to Laura. Lionel sat down on a chair and said, "Let me rest a moment. If you ladies have seen enough of Summit City, I suggest that we return to the ranch. I have a little more work to do on my proposal before I present it tomorrow afternoon. After our supper tonight, I want to relate to you what I will be presenting to the interested parties tomorrow afternoon. I would like Tag and Katie to be present tonight as well."

The trio returned to the 99 Ranch. After dinner, Lionel rested for about thirty minutes before he began compiling his proposal. That night, he laid out his proposal, which read as follows:

1. Regarding the death of two calves in Summit County, for lack of evidence, Tylor Taggat will be absolved of any responsibility.

2. Regarding the death of one colt owned by Carl Barnes, Tylor Taggat has not admitted any guilt, but is ordered to make restitution to Carl Barnes for the loss of this colt. Carl Barnes will establish the value of the colt. It is deemed that Carl Barnes will be just in establishing the value of the animal.

3. For the safety of Tylor Taggat, he is forbidden to reside in the State of Nebraska for a period of five years. Neither will he visit, or pass through the state for this period of time.

4. During this five-year period, Tylor Taggat agrees not to own or possess any firearms.

5. Tylor Taggat agrees to seek gainful employment so that he might not be dependent on any local, state or federal government.

6. Tylor Taggat agrees to register his place of

residence with the county sheriff in which county he is residing within fifteen days of his establishment of residence. That sheriff will notify the Sheriff of Summit County of the establishment of residence.

After Lionel read the proposal, the residents of the 99 Ranch were silent. Laura began to weep and Katie went to Laura, her eyes were brimmed with tears as well. They were shocked to think that Tylor would be leaving them. Tag said nothing, nor did he show any emotion as the proposal was read.

Lionel spoke up, "I sense by your silence that you are stunned at what has been prepared. The reality is that Tylor cannot remain in this county. There are too many memories and too much history. Tylor is not a bad person, nor have I indicated as such. By his unusual behavior, he has amassed a reputation that is not fitting for this county. The law firm that I work for has arranged employment for Tylor with a feedlot in Kraemer County, Oklahoma. The owner, Bill Boyle is a reputable man. He has offered employment to Tylor. Also, Tylor will be able to complete his internship that is required for getting his degree from the University of Nebraska. I am sorry if you expected more, but this is what I considered best for the benefit of my friend."

Laura got up from her chair, and going to Lionel, she put her hand on his shoulder. All she said was, "Thanks, Lionel, thanks." She went out the door and those who knew her, realized that she was going to the cottonwood stump beside the Dismal River. Once again, the stump would soak up the tears of a mother for her son.

Katie handled it differently. She rushed from the room. Those that had remained in the living room heard the bedroom door slam. That answered the question that Lionel had asked Katie previously, 'are you in love with Tylor?'

The next morning, Katie asked Lionel, "May I be present at the hearing? I want to show Tylor that I am in support of him. I promise that I will not say anything, but I will not promise that I won't shed a tear for him."

"I think that it would be good if you were there. You have been involved in this, in a good way, as much as anyone else." Lionel put his hand on her shoulder. "I'm not sure that I can keep from shedding some tears for my friend as well." Katie nodded at him and a smile came upon her face. She now realized the kinship of the two men.

After dinner at the ranch, it was a somber group that made their way to Summit City that cloudy afternoon. Even the weather had an eerie feeling to it that early spring day.

At 2:00 p.m., the meeting was convened in the small courtroom at the Summit County Courthouse. Those present were Judge Coy Burns and his court reporter, attorneys Leon Kelly, Lionel Whitman and county attorney Karl Larson. Also present were Laura and Tag Taggat, Katie O'Neal and Miriam Whitman, as well as Gordon and Jenny Collier, accompanied by their attorney, who had entered the courtroom after the others.

Katie looked over her shoulder. She saw Sheriff Morgan bring Tylor into the room. She was shocked to see that Tylor was shackled and handcuffed. While Tylor shuffled in, Katie also saw two others in the courtroom. Back in a far corner, Jim McCann was seated by himself; moving his hat around and around on his lap. In an opposite corner, another man had come in later and sat down. Katie did not know his name, but she had seen him on the train when they had returned from San Francisco. He had boarded the train at Madden.

When Laura saw that Tylor was shackled and cuffed, she leaned forward and said something to Leon Kelly. Leon stood up and said, "Your Honor, I object to having my client appear in court in shackles and handcuffs."

Judge Burns questioned the sheriff. "Sheriff Morgan, this is an informal hearing. Is it necessary to have Tylor Taggat in such restraints?"

"Yes, Your Honor. I have a policy that states, anytime a prisoner is removed from his cell, they will be handcuffed and shackled. To date, I have not had anyone escape my custody."

"Very well. Objection is overruled. Shall we proceed? Each of you has a copy of the proposal submitted by the attorneys for Tylor Taggat. Are there any questions regarding this proposal?" The judge looked out over the courtroom.

Gordon Collier's attorney stood up. "Your Honor, I am Porter Thomas, an attorney representing Gordon Collier who was assaulted by Tylor Taggat and hospitalized for almost a week. There is no provision in this proposal for the arrest on assault charges. Also, by refusing him access to the State of Nebraska, we may not be able to bring him back to sue for damages, or at least for five years."

"Mr. Larson," said the judge. "You are the county attorney. Is there any reason that assault charges were not filed against Tylor Taggat?"

Karl Larson started to rise, when a lady broke into the courtroom, crying out. She was a rather attractive woman in her early forties, but quite distraught. She sought out Sheriff Morgan. "Sheriff, Sheriff, it is Johnny! He didn't come home from school and we can't find him anywhere! Do something, please! We have looked everywhere. He wasn't in school this afternoon."

The judge rapped his gavel. "This hearing is recessed for one hour to give the sheriff time to deal with this situation. We will reconvene in one hour." He got up to leave when he heard the prisoner speak.

"I-I-I c-c-can f-f-find J-J-Johnny."

The judge turned, and asked, "Did someone say something?"

Tylor nodded, but as he opened his mouth, he was unable to utter a sound.

Lionel stood up. "Your Honor. The accused has a speech impediment, but he said that he could find Johnny. He is quite capable at tracking and smelling out individuals. I think that he is offering his services to locate the missing boy. I served with him in the Army and I can attest to his ability. He can find the boy!"

The judge looked to the sheriff. "Sheriff Morgan, do you know the missing boy?"

The sheriff nodded. "Your Honor, he is my grandson. He is ten years old, and somewhat troubled. There has been a divorce in the family. I have no idea where he might be."

"Very well, Sheriff Morgan, use your discretion in the matter and we will reconvene this hearing when I am notified that all parties are available. Dismissed."

Lionel went to Tylor. "Do you think that you can pull this off?" Tylor nodded.

Sheriff Morgan said, "I am taking you back to your cell while I look for my grandson."

Lionel said, "Wait, Sheriff, you saw how Tylor knew it was me when I came to the jail. It had been over a year since I had seen him, but he remembered my scent. I have seen him work. It is uncanny. At least, give him a chance."

"All right," said the sheriff, "I will give him twenty four hours, but I am going with him!"

"Good choice, sheriff," said Lionel. He turned to Tylor. "What do you need, and we will get it for you?"

Tylor picked up a pencil from the table and began to write on a tablet. 'I have taken a vow of silence until the boy is found. I need sixteen hours to find him. We will meet you at Nick's Café for breakfast. No shackles or cuffs. I want my moccasins, knife, bow and arrows, and Dog. I need to see the boy's room and I want to take a package of wieners with me. We need to hurry. An afternoon rain shower is approaching. Nobody is to go with me.'

When Lionel saw the list, he called Katie over. "Katie, I see Jim is here. Whatever Jim has that is on this list, have him bring it in. I will take Tylor to look over the boy's room and meet you back here. We need to hurry."

Tylor observed Johnny Morgan's room and he was encouraged. There were the pajamas still on the bed and a dirty T-shirt on the floor. Tylor kept the T-shirt. When they returned to the courthouse, Jim and Katie had everything else for Tylor. Dog was excited to be reunited with Tylor. Tylor let him sniff the T-shirt and then placed it in his knapsack. The dog and the young man returned to Johnny's home. After a few minutes, they were headed in a southeasterly direction at a fast pace. Tylor saw that he was being followed. He knew that Sheriff Morgan didn't want to be left out of the hunt. He also knew that the sheriff should have saddled his horse. There was no way that he could keep up with Tylor and Dog on foot. At the first cover of cedar trees, Tylor moved to a northeasterly direction in order to throw the sheriff off the trail. An hour later, Tylor saw the sheriff break through an open area, still moving in a southeasterly direction.

It was getting dusk when Tylor and Dog found Johnny. He was two miles from home, and trying to start a fire with matches that he had brought with him. Tylor approached and broke his vow of silence. "Johnny, Johnny M-M-Morgan. I'm a friend of your g-g-grandfather. M-M-May I approach the c-c-camp? I have my d-d-dog with me and we are hungry." When Tylor spoke, he was within twenty feet of the camp and startled Johnny.

"Who are you?" he cried out.

Tylor answered, "I'm T-T-Tylor Taggat and this is my d-d-dog, called Dog." Tylor moved closer. "I can help you get that fire g-g-going, if you will l-l-let me." It didn't take Tylor long before he had the fire going. The air was starting to cool off. The clouds rolled in and some large drops of rain began to

177

fall.

The camp was sheltered among the large cedar trees and Tylor knew that Johnny had been here before. He had passed this camp on several occasions, but each time it had been unoccupied. Tylor said, "This is a g-g-good camp site. You made a g-g-good choice." Johnny was evidently pleased with Tylor's praise. "Now, what d-d-do you have for s-s-supper?"

"I brought a can of beans and a pot to cook the beans in and two spoons. But I forgot to bring a can opener. I don't know why I would bring two spoons and no can opener?" A few tears started to well up in this frightened boy's eyes.

"Johnny," said Tylor, "sometimes G-G-God works things out that we d-d-don't understand. I have come to your c-c-camp this evening and I have a knife to o-o-open that can of b-b-beans. But, the only thing I have to eat is a p-p-package of wieners. Now, if we were to share and I open your b-b-beans with my knife and slice the w-w-wieners into your b-b-beans, we would have supper with two spoons. We might g-g-give Dog a wiener or two, s-s-seeing that we might have m-m-more than we could eat." Tylor began to open the can of beans and slice bits of wiener into the pot. Then he poured the can of beans over the wieners and set the pot among the coals.

While they were eating, Tylor handed Dog one of the wieners. He said, "If I was h-h-hungry, I would m-m-make Dog catch a r-r-rabbit, or I might even shoot one with my b-b-bow and arrow. He likes the w-w-wieners, because he can gulp them d-d-down. He is a glutton."

They finished off the beans and wieners and Tylor asked, "Johnny, are you g-g-going to stay here all n-n-night?"

Johnny didn't say anything, just nodded.

"Won't your m-m-mother be w-w-worried about you?" Before he could reply, Tylor asked a second question. "How o-o-old are you?"

"Nobody worries about me. I am twelve years old. I can take care of myself."

Tylor said, "Now, wait a m-m-minute. Here we are sitting around this f-f-fire and sharing our f-f-food with one another. We n-n-need to be honest with one another. I know f-f-for a fact that you are only t-t-ten years old. Your grandfather t-t-told me that when I was in his j-j-jail. You can't take care of yourself. You didn't b-b-bring anything to open your c-c-can of beans and besides that, I had to get your f-f-fire going."

"You were in jail? What did you do?"

"Do you know G-G-Gordon Collier?" asked Tylor. "I hit h-h-him with this and he was in the hospital for five d-d-days." Tylor showed Johnny his stub hand. "Here, f-f-feel it." Johnny touched it as if it was a hot rock.

Johnny said, "Gordon is married to my sister Jenny. He is mean to her and to me if I get too close."

"Johnny, your m-m-mother is worried about you." Tylor got up and added a few branches to the fire. "She cc-came to the j-j-jail and said that you were gone. I went to your r-r-room so that I could g-g-get something for Dog to smell, so that we c-c-could track you down. Kid, your room was a mess! Your b-b-bed wasn't made and I f-f-found this dirty T-shirt on the floor." Tylor pulled out the T-shirt and handed it to Johnny. "Here, p-p-put this on. It will help k-k-keep you warm. Tomorrow morning we are g-g-going back to t-t-town. We d-d-don't have enough food for b-b-breakfast, so we will eat at Nick's Café."

Tylor kept the fire going through the night, but not too high. He wanted Johnny to be cold in the morning after his night away from home. At early light, he awakened Johnny and they walked the two miles into town. They were the second and third customers of the day at Nick's Café. Sheriff Morgan was the first. He was sitting at the counter, drinking his first cup of coffee of the day. When the sheriff slid off the stool at the counter, he moved slowly. He appeared to be stiff and sore. He didn't say anything, but he hugged his grandson.

Tylor grinned, and said, "Sheriff Morgan, how f-f-far did you go b-b-before you g-g-gave up and came back to t-t-town? I told you that I didn't w-w-want anyone to f-f-follow Dog and me."

The sheriff crawled back on the stool and said, "I suppose it was about four miles. I believe that you may have purposely misled me, but I'm not sure. Now, order your breakfast. If the county doesn't pay for it, then I will have to wash dishes to settle the bill."

Johnny got up on the stool beside his grandfather. He said, "Grandpa, I'm sorry that I ran away. I didn't think anyone cared about me. Tylor said that Momma was worried about me. I'm sorry that you had to walk so far. It was cold last night. I won't run away anymore."

"Maybe we can go camping when you get out of school. We can get sleeping bags and plenty of food." The sheriff gave his grandson another hug. "Now, order your breakfast."

Before Johnny had an opportunity to order, they were joined by Lionel, Miriam, Laura and Katie. Lionel struggled as he came in the door. Laura saw her son and went to him and gave him a hug. "Tylor, it is good to see you out of that awful jail and those shackles. I'm saddened that you will be leaving, but maybe it is for the best as of now." Tylor kissed his mother on the cheek, but said nothing.

Laura went to Nick. "We haven't had breakfast, so I will take care of the bill. Maybe we could put several tables together, so that we might all sit as a group."

Tylor motioned to Johnny, "Let's g-g-go wash up b-b-before we eat."

After Johnny and Tylor came out of the restroom, Katie was there to greet Tylor. "I'm glad that you will be out of jail, once the judge signs the order. But, I don't want to see you leave. It isn't right for this to happen."

Tylor touched her arm. "Thanks, K-K-Katie. But, it isn't a l-l-lifetime. Maybe by leaving, I will find p-p-peace at last." Katie nodded her head and returned to sit at the table.

When it came time to order, Johnny was first. "I want wieners chopped up with heated beans, a glass of milk and a doughnut. Also, I want two whole wieners for Dog. I will take them outside to him when you bring them."

Tylor ordered next. "Those b-b-beans sound good, so I will have a s-s-side order. I want three pancakes and a l-l-large steak, cooked m-m-medium well. Also, c-c-coffee with cream."

Sheriff Morgan jumped to his feet and threw his napkin on the table. He shouted, "Tylor, what is with you? All the time you were in my jail, you wanted your steak raw! When I refused, you accepted your steak rare. Now, you can order what you want and you order it medium well. I don't understand!"

Tylor remained calm. He replied to the sheriff's accusations. "Sheriff, I was j-j-just trying to please the p-p-people of Summit County. What the people s-s-saw was a b-b-bloodthirsty animal killer; seeking r-r-raw flesh to eat. So, I ordered my m-m-meat raw, knowing that you w-w-would insist upon no l-l-less than rare. I saw no harm in t-t-trying to please the people. If you insist, tell Nick how to c-c-cook my steak this morning." Lionel muffled his laughter in his napkin.

The sheriff sat down, but he wasn't through with Tylor just yet. "I suppose this finding Johnny was another one of your hoaxes. You knew where he was all the time. You really can't sniff out people as you have Lionel and the others believing."

"Sheriff," said Tylor, "you n-n-never know which is the real me. You n-n-never know."

Everyone finished their breakfast. The hearing was to continue at eight o'clock that morning before the regular court docket was to begin. Johnny went home to be with his mother, while the rest of the group went to the courthouse. Tylor made Dog sit outside at the entry to the courthouse.

All of those except for Jim McCann that had been present the afternoon before were in the courtroom. Even the stranger that had been in the courtroom the day before had returned, taking the same seat. Jenny, Sheriff Morgan's granddaughter whispered something to her grandfather.

Judge Coy Burns called the meeting to order. He began, "Yesterday, we were about to hear from the county attorney, when our meeting was interrupted due to a lost boy. I understand that Mr. Taggat was successful in finding the lad and that he is now safe at home. Thank you! Now, Mr. Larson, you were going to enlighten us as to why no charges were filed against Tylor Taggat for assault."

Jenny Collier stood up. "Judge, it was my entire fault. I smarted off to my husband and he knocked me to the ground. Tylor tried to help me, but that is when Gordon hit him in the stomach. When Tylor was bent over, he hit Gordon in the forehead. I'm sorry, but it was my fault. And now, Tylor was good enough to find my brother, Johnny."

Thomas Porter, Gordon Collier's attorney, jumped to his feet. "You can't accept the testimony of a wife against her husband."

The judge responded, "Mr. Thomas, this is an informal hearing, but keep in mind that should you press the issue in a civil case, it might be difficult to convince a jury. Incidentally, if Mr. Collier continues to hit his wife, he might not have a wife to hide behind."

Thomas Porter had one more item. He stated, "Mr. Collier asks that Mr. Tylor Taggat be held responsible for the medical bills as a result of his coma." Tylor whispered to Lionel.

Lionel stood. "Your Honor, we will agree to one-half of the liability. Mr. Taggat will offer a private apology to Mr.

Collier as well at this time."

The judge was pleased with the counter proposal. "Very well, Mr. Tylor Taggat will pay for one-half of the medical care up to the time of Mr. Collier's dismissal from the hospital. Mr. Taggat, you may present your apology."

Tylor got up and went to Gordon, where he was sitting in his chair. Tylor put his left hand on Gordon's shoulder. He whispered to him, while his stub hand rested in the center of Gordon's chest. Gordon turned pale, which was surprising, as Tylor had a smile on his face. Before he left, he tapped Gordon on the shoulder with the left hand and with a nod, he returned to his chair.

"Very well," said Judge Burns, "if there is nothing further, I will sign off on this agreement. Tylor Taggat, you have seventy two hours to get your affairs in order. Please stay out of trouble during this time frame. Dismissed."

Tylor shook Lionel's hand, using his left hand. "Thank you, L-L-Lionel. You are a true friend."

"Tylor," asked Lionel, "what did you say to Gordon? He turned as white as a sheet."

"I just s-s-said, if I ever heard of him m-m-mistreating Jenny or Johnny, I w-w-would slip across the state line one n-n-night and p-p-punch him in the heart. It would be h-h-hard enough to stop it and he would die! Then, I would m-m-marry his widow." Tylor smiled and nodded his head.

Sheriff Morgan nodded to Tylor. "Remember, seventy two hours. Then I can sleep again." The sheriff turned and went to his office, where he would watch from his window to see Tylor Taggat leaving Summit City for the day.

The Stockgrowers Association had taken an interest in the reported mutilation of the two calves and the one colt in Summit County. They had sent Chase Adams to Summit City to confer with Sheriff Morgan and offer any assistance in his investigation. For lack of any concrete evidence, he was satisfied with the decisions of the Sheriff, County Attorney and Judge Burns in the matter. He had been present both days of the court proceedings. He watched Laura Taggat to see how she was taking the drama being played out in the courtroom. He remembered observing the unpredictability of Tylor on the train during that brief train ride between Madden and Summit City. That night, he wrote in his journal:

A dove of peace hid among the thorn
Protecting her chick since he was born
She pushed him out, now that he is grown
She nurtured him; now he's on his own
Suddenly, she flew away, she flew away
Will she return another day?
Will she return another day?

CHAPTER 12
BANISHED!!

Katie had brought the ranch pickup into town in anticipation of Tylor's release. After the hearing came to a close, Katie handed the keys to Tylor. "Your mother said that you might want to gather your things that you have at Jim's and bring them out to the ranch. You do have Dog to return, unless you plan to take him with you."

"Thank you for r-r-reminding me about Dog. Would you c-c-care to ride along? Katie, while I am gone, w-w-would you check on Jim from t-t-time to time? He has been a g-g-good uncle to me and I will m-m-miss him."

Katie was enthused by Tylor's invitation. "Sure, I will go with you. Since I have been entrusted with this vehicle, I should see that it is returned. Unless of course, you intend to steal away with this truck while I am still an occupant. That I will sanction. Tylor, take me with you to Oklahoma!" She gripped his arm. He looked at her in disbelief.

He jerked his arm free. He replied to her request in a scolding tone of voice. "Katie, I can't take you with m-m-me. I can't even take c-c-care of myself. Look at the m-m-mess I have made of my life and there is no n-n-need of me m-m-messing up your life as well. Besides, you have six m-m-more weeks of school b-b-before you graduate. Let it g-g-go! Find someone that is decent. You d-d-deserve someone better than me!"

Katie got out of the truck and slammed the door! Through the open window, she shouted at Tylor, "Go ahead and take this old truck. This is the last time that I will throw myself at you! I love you, Tylor Taggat, I love you! You may not love me, but you can't stop me from loving you!" She turned, and stepped to the sidewalk. Tylor sat in the truck and watched her leave. She was soon out of sight when she turned the corner. He shook his head. He backed the truck from the curb and headed to the Bill Dolan ranch to bid Jim McCann goodbye.

When Tylor reached the ranch, he parked the truck near the house. He saw that Jim was on horseback and checking the cows that were feeding near the creek. Dog jumped out of the back of the truck and ran to be with Jim, expecting there were cows to be chased. Tylor gathered up his clothes and crammed them into his suitcase. He went out to the barn to pick up his saddle. Jim had ridden to the barn and was putting his horse into his stall. "Tylor," he said, "I certainly hate to see you leave, but I presume that you will return by the time the five years have gone by. Come up to the house and we will share a last cup of coffee." Tylor nodded and followed Jim to the house. Neither one said anything while they drank their coffee.

Tylor got up to leave and Jim went to the back porch and brought a denim jacket with him. "Tylor, don't forget your jacket. This is the one that Katie remade so that you could get your club hand through the sleeve. It does get cold in Oklahoma." Jim shook his hand and gave him a hug. "Write when you get a chance. I will continue to pray for you."

Tylor hugged him back. "Thank you f-f-for everything. I will be b-b-back. Take c-c-care of Dog." Tylor got in the truck and not looking back, he headed for Summit City.

Tylor's first stop was at the bank where he emptied out his safety deposit box. He gave the key to Mrs. Stahl. He had no further need for the box and key. His next stop was at the hospital. He had agreed to pay half of the medical bills of Gordon Collier and this had depleted most of his funds. Tylor counted his remaining cash. His funds were now down to $40.00, and one more stop to make at the Carl Barnes ranch.

Arriving at the Barnes ranch, Tylor saw that Carl was getting out of his truck that was parked in front of the house. His wife, Peggy, was working in a flowerbed near the front gate. When Tylor greeted Carl, Carl said, "I came to the house for a midmorning snack. Would you care to join us?" Before

Tylor could answer, Carl said, "Peggy, I think it is time for something cool to drink. Come on Tylor, and we will find some shade."

Evidently, Peggy was expecting Carl. She had iced tea made and the cookies on a platter. She was bringing them out when Tylor spoke up. "Mr. B-B-Barnes, I will be l-l-leaving in the morning and I stopped by to m-m-make restitution for the c-c-colt that was k-k-killed. How much do I o-o-owe you?" Tylor expected Carl would ask more than he had with him. He didn't want to ask for a loan from his mother, but he wanted to have everything clear before he left the state.

Carl took a long drink of his iced tea and motioned for Tylor to help himself to the cookies. "Tylor, did you kill the colt?" Carl was looking hard at Tylor.

"No, sir," Tylor said. "I didn't k-k-kill your colt. However, I have agreed with the c-c-court that I am to p-p-pay what you d-d-deem as fair value for the colt. I was p-p-present when the colt was k-k-killed."

Peggy spoke up. "Carl, I believe Tylor is telling the truth. Laura taught him as a small boy to tell the truth. If he said he didn't kill the colt, then he didn't kill the colt."

"But, you do know how the colt died," said Carl.

"Yes, s-s-sir," answered Tylor, "but this may s-s-seem more incredulous to you and h-h-harder to believe. It was a m-m-mountain lion. I was nearby when the second c-c-calf was killed. The arrow in the t-t-tree on your ranch was meant for the b-b-big cat. When you p-p-put the spotlight on me, I ran. I will p-p-pay you for the c-c-colt, but you are to s-s-say nothing about the mountain l-l-lion. Father didn't b-b-believe me either, but I know what I s-s-saw. Where the m-m-mountain lion is now, I have no idea, but there was a mountain l-l-lion."

"I believe you, Tylor," said Carl. "I can't ask you to pay for something that you didn't do. Your secret is safe with us. Thanks for stopping by and we wish you success in Oklahoma." Carl reached out and shook Tylor's hand. Tylor extended his left hand and it was then that Carl saw how gruesome the stub was, enlarged and a deep purple.

Tylor asked, "How is B-B-Becca? I hear that she is s-s-soon to have a b-b-baby."

"Yes," said Peggy. "She is doing fine, and it will be another month before the baby is born."

"I loved B-B-Becca, you know," said Tylor. "I did l-l-love her."

"Yes, Tylor, and she loved you," said Peggy, "but things just didn't work out with the war and everything. These things come into our lives and we just need to start over again. Goodbye, Tylor."

"Goodbye, Mr. and Mrs. B-B-Barnes." Tylor walked slowly to his vehicle and drove off. He was unaware of the man and his wife, standing by the front gate while they held one another, weeping for the son-in-law that they never had.

Tylor had passed the Good Hope School when he saw Katie was about to cross the bridge that spanned the Dismal River on the 99 Ranch. He pulled up alongside and he saw that her face was red and the perspiration had made her hair wet, causing ringlets to hang over her ears. He asked, "D-D-Do you want a r-r-ride?" Katie continued to walk, looking straight ahead, her eyes never acknowledging that she had heard him.

At her refusal, Tylor stepped down on the gas, causing the truck to spin dirt and gravel. He drove the truck the last hundred yards to the ranch house. Tylor took his saddle and suitcase out of the back of the truck and carried them to the back porch. He was planning to make his departure tomorrow morning. Katie came through the back door and walked past him. Tylor started to apologize, but as he was stammering with the beginning word, Katie was already slamming the door to her bedroom.

Fifteen minutes later, Katie came out to the kitchen and started dinner. Lionel and Miriam had made it known that they would be leaving after dinner. Dinner was a rather quiet affair.

188

The Taggat family had already expressed their gratitude of Lionel coming to defend his friend Tylor. Tylor had indicated that he would leave early the next morning, so was saying his good-byes today. He didn't share the news of his lack of funds with the family. He had said earlier that he would purchase a vehicle for his journey to Oklahoma.

The next morning, Tylor got out of bed and after pulling the covers up, he straightened up the pillows. He knew that his mother would change the sheets, but he wanted it to look neat until that time. Picking up his boots, he tiptoed out into the living room when he saw that the lights were on in the kitchen. Katie was setting out two plates and the silverware when he entered the room. She looked up and said, "Good morning. The coffee is ready and if you will give me a few minutes, the steak and pancakes will be ready as well. How would you like your steak this morning?"

"Why d-d-did you g-g-get up so early?" asked Tylor. "I was g-g-going to l-l-leave before anyone awakened."

Katie had her hands on her hips. "Don't change the subject. I asked about the steak."

"M-M-Medium, yes, m-m-medium will be fine."

"Now that we have the status of the steak settled, I have packed you a lunch to take with you. Incidentally, I looked out this morning and I didn't see any form of transportation. I presume that you will be hitchhiking your way to Oklahoma, now that they are no longer running passenger trains. After breakfast, I will take you to Summit City and perhaps you will get someone to give you a ride. I learned yesterday, there is very little traffic from the Good Hope School to Summit City." Katie put two pancakes and the steak on his plate. "Go ahead and eat. I learned long ago that the Taggats don't pray over the food until they are assured that it was fit to eat." Katie fixed her plate and sat down to eat. Evidently, they had done their talking before breakfast, and they ate in silence.

Katie gathered up the dishes and put them in the sink.

She picked up the brown paper sack that contained Tylor's lunch and asked, "Ready?" Tylor nodded his head. He picked up his saddle and suitcase from the back porch. Katie got behind the wheel of the truck, while Tylor tossed his gear in the box of the truck.

The only conversation they had was Katie asking, "Tylor, why didn't you ask your mother for a loan to buy a vehicle? She would have given it to you, or I imagine even Todd Holliday at the bank would have loaned you the money. I sense that you used most of your funds to pay Gordon's medical bill and Carl Barnes for the colt. But no, you are so independently stubborn, you wouldn't ask."

Tylor chuckled, "Carl B-B-Barnes wouldn't take any m-m-money for the c-c-colt. Speaking of stubborn, you s-s-should meet this girl I know at the 99 Ranch. Now, she is s-s-stubborn!" Katie blushed and smiled at his remark.

After they crossed the bridge, they entered Summit City. Katie asked, "Where do you want me to drop you, Tylor?"

He replied, "There is the g-g-gas station on the east edge of t-t-town. The livestock truckers stop there and I m-m-may get a r-r-ride from one of them."

Arriving at the station, Katie pulled up near one of the trucks in the lot. Tylor opened the door. He turned to Katie and kissed her. It wasn't a quick peck, but it was deliberate. Tylor grabbed his gear and the sack containing his lunch. After talking to a driver briefly, he tossed his gear into the truck. He turned and gave a wave. The truck pulled out onto the highway.

Katie had not moved after the kiss, but had her arms draped over the steering wheel as she wept. "Tylor, oh, Tylor. How I wish I could hate you!"

She watched the truck disappear down the highway. She then reflected, *there goes my plan of walking down the aisle of the Good Hope Church. Becca Barnes had her chance and failed. So have I, so have I.*

190

CHAPTER 13
B & B--A NEW BEGINNING

Tylor's first ride was with a trucker pulling an empty livestock trailer that was going as far as the Kansas-Nebraska border. He was to leave the trailer at the weigh station. There was the possibility that he could ride with the next trucker when he picked up the trailer later in the day.

It was noon when they arrived at the weigh station. Tylor entered to purchase a soda from the vending machine to drink with his lunch. He approached the scale master, "Sir, is it all r-r-right if I eat my l-l-lunch here in the w-w-waiting area?"

"Sure," said the man, as he looked Tylor over. "Tell me, are you waiting for someone?"

Tylor nodded. "Yes sir, I c-c-caught a ride from S-S-Summit County up in the S-S-Sandhills and I am wanting to g-g-get to Kramer, Oklahoma. I have a j-j-job waiting for me at the B & B Feedlot."

"If I remember right, that is in the Oklahoma Panhandle. That is good feedlot country." The scale master took note of Tylor's club hand. "I might be able to find you a ride, if you are willing to wait. Just eat your lunch and relax."

"Thank you. I am a b-b-bit short of cash. I had hoped to b-b-buy a pickup t-t-truck to get me to Kramer, but n-n-now I am hitchhiking m-m-my way." Tylor bought his soda from the vending machine and sat down in a chair nearby. He opened the paper sack that contained his lunch, which Katie had made up for him. Inside were two steak sandwiches, each wrapped in their own package of wax paper. Between the sandwiches was a small envelope. Tylor opened the envelope and found that Katie had inserted $50.00, with a note in her handwriting. 'Dear Tylor, Just a little something to tide you over until you get on your feet. This is a gift, so don't try to repay me. Love, Katie.' The thought went through Tylor's mind. *Katie, Katie,*

Katie, why do you do these things when I continue to rebuff your love?

It was almost five o'clock in the evening before the scale master shook Tylor awake. Tylor had dozed off in his chair and he was dreaming of home when he was awakened. The scale master said, "Talk about good fortune, this fellow that we checked through the port of entry has a load of feeder cattle on his truck. Would you believe it? They are consigned to the B & B Feedlot. When the sun comes up in Oklahoma tomorrow morning, you will be at your job!"

"Thank you, s-s-sir," said Tylor. "Thank you for l-l-looking out for m-m-me." Tylor grabbed his saddle and suitcase and was bound for the Oklahoma Panhandle. Tylor knew it was not just good fortune, but the hand of God. He was reminded of that verse in Jeremiah 10: 23 'O Lord, I know that the way of man is not in himself: it is not in man that walketh to direct his steps.' *That was one of Mama's favorite verses in the Bible. I don't know why I am headed for the Panhandle, but I know that you know, God.*

The truck driver wasn't much of a conversationalist, but enjoyed playing his country music. Tylor sat back and took in the scenery of the Kansas countryside. After a time, Tylor began to realize that each mile was taking him further and further from home. It felt like a spike being driven into his soul. *Banished! Banished! Would he ever see his beloved Sandhills and the cleansing waters of the Dismal River again? Oh! Mama, Mama, how could I disappoint you again and so soon!* It was then that Tylor realized that earlier he had been praising God for leading him and now was bemoaning God's leading. *'Oh Lord, I am weak. Help me in the days to come.'*

After a few stops through the night, they pulled up to the scale house at the B & B Feedlot. The night was turning to dawn. The driver said, "I won't be able to weigh until seven o'clock, so I will catch a few winks while I wait."

Tylor stepped out and drug his gear out of the truck. "Thanks for the r-r-ride. I will g-g-get out and walk around a b-b-bit. Take c-c-care."

Tylor parked his gear near the door of the scale house and began his walk. It was good to stretch his legs. He had been riding since yesterday morning at this time. He noticed the activity began to pick up as the early morning sun was heating the atmosphere. A grain truck had pulled up behind the cattle truck, just as a small blue pickup drove up to the scale house. The activities of the day were soon to begin.

By the time that Tylor had reached the scale house, the cattle had been weighed and the grain truck as well. Tylor had seen the scale master probe the grain in several locations and return to the scale house. A red Peterbilt tractor, pulling a flatbed trailer loaded with hay, was driving on the scales as Tylor was walking up the five steps of the scale house. When he opened the screendoor, a voice from the darkened interior shouted gruffly, "Don't slam the screen door." Tylor was careful not to let it slam shut.

Tylor waited until the scale master had locked down the scale and punched the scale ticket before greeting him. A nod of the head and a simple 'morning,' had the short thin man's attention. Peering over his half-rimmed glasses, he eyed Tylor cautiously. He asked, "What can I do for you, stranger?"

Tylor chuckled, "Well, you have me p-p-pegged right. I am a s-s-stranger and m-m-most people would say that I am s-s-stranger than most. I'm l-l-looking for B-B-Bill Boyle and thought you might t-t-tell me where I could f-f-find him?"

"That depends," said the man. "If you have grain and feed-stuffs to sell, then I am your man. If it is feed for the horses, Buck Draper, the head cowboy is the one to see. If you are looking for work, you will find Bill in that two-story frame building about 100 yards south of here. Now if you should be a jealous husband, I don't expect him back until sometime next month." With that last remark, he gave a shy grin and introduced himself. "Hi, I'm 'Shortie' Pounds."

"You've got to be k-k-kidding me, a scale master c-c-called 'Shortie' Pounds?"

"That's right. Kind of strange isn't it?" he replied.

"I r-r-reckon. I am Tylor Taggat. I n-n-need work, so I will see if I can c-c-catch up with Mr. Boyle before any j-j-jealous husbands. Thanks." Tylor extended his left hand and Shortie gave him his right hand in a clumsy handshake.

"He is a great gent. You will like him and I hope you get the job, whatever it might be." Tylor went out, being careful not to let the screen door slam.

Once outside, Tylor picked up his saddle and suitcase and started walking toward the feedlot office.

Leaving his gear outside, he entered the office. Seated at a desk was a petite blonde woman in her early twenties. Tylor thought her to be the prettiest woman he had ever seen. It was then that he saw a man in his mid forties seated on a corner of her desk, visiting with her. On second glance, it appeared that he was attempting to charm her. Tylor noted that the man didn't like the intrusion of Tylor.

"Good morning," greeted the lady. "May I help you?"

Tylor removed his hat, "Yes, ma'am," he said. "I am Tylor T-T Taggat and I was w-w-wanting to see Mr. B-B-Boyle, regarding employment."

The man that had been sitting on the receptionist's desk stood up. Tylor had been so enamored with the beauty of the young lady, that he had failed to see how big the man was until he stood up. Looking down at Tylor, he said, "I'm Buck Draper, the head cowboy and feedlot foreman. We aren't hiring any help right now. You might try the Kraemer County Feeders east of town." He turned to the young lady. "Janice, give them a call and ask if they are hiring. Don't tell them we have a cowboy here with no car or horse. They might get the idea that he is a drifter." Buck shifted his attention back to Tylor. "I saw your gear setting outside of the scale house when I came in this morning."

Tylor stammered, "Ma'am, d-d-don't call just yet. I will w-w-wait for Mr. Boyle. I was specifically told to see Mr. B-B-Boyle." Tylor didn't want a confrontation with Buck Draper, so he went across the room and found a chair to sit in while waiting.

After Tylor was seated, two other women came through the door and greeted Janice. They went to their desks and began their work. Buck Draper left the office in somewhat of a huff. Janice picked up the phone and began dialing. After a brief conversation, she came to Tylor. "Mr. Taggat, Mr. Boyle will see you. Take the stairs by the door where you came into the office. I'm sorry about Buck trying to send you on your way, but that is Buck's way."

When Tylor got to the top of the stairs, he was greeted by Bill Boyle; a small man in his early fifties. The first thing that Tylor noticed was his warm smile. He reached out to shake Tylor's hand. Tylor offered his left hand and Bill's eyes sought out Tylor's stub of a right hand. "Good morning, I'm Bill Boyle. Glad to meet you, Tylor. I know very little about you, except for the letter from Lionel Whitman. He did say that you two were friends and that I would need to make my own decision in regard to hiring you. Have a seat," as he gestured with his right hand. "I noticed your right hand. Do you consider yourself handicapped? Was this a result of a farm or ranch accident?"

Tylor brought up his right hand. "Here, t-t-touch it. I don't c-c-consider that I am handicapped, but rather l-l-limited. I can still milk a c-c-cow, or play a m-m-musical instrument, but it takes me l-l-longer to accomplish some t-t-tasks. It was not an accident, but the p-p-purpose was intentional. I was a p-p-prisoner in a Viet Cong p-p-prison camp when the camp commander severed my f-f-fingers. I have l-l-life, which I

195

cherish. This other is an inconvenience."

Bill Boyle put his head in his hands. "I'm sorry, I shouldn't have asked. My oldest son was killed in Vietnam a year ago." He shook his head. He continued, "War is such a terrible waste, a terrible waste."

Tylor stood, preparing to leave. "I'm s-s-sorry, sir. I was unaware. I f-f-fear I have given you too m-m-much information. I will l-l-leave now."

"No, no. Please stay. Tell me a little more about yourself and then I might ask more questions later." Tylor sat back down.

Tylor began, "Sir, I was r-r-raised on a ranch in the S-S-Sandhills of Nebraska. During my high school years I established a s-s-small herd of Hereford c-c-cattle, which I sold to help p-p-pay for my college training. I went s-s-summers and worked on c-c-campus, so that I w-w-was able to complete my Agricultural B-B-Business classes in three years. I had p-p-planned to work at a f-f-feedlot to complete my internship to obtain my d-d-degree. I was d-d-drafted before I was able to c-c-complete the internship. I want to learn the f-f-feedlot business from the ground up. I am s-s-single, and I have no b-b-bills, but neither do I have m-m-much money. That is why it was necessary for m-m-me to hitchhike d-d-down here. Lionel Whitman is a g-g-good friend and he is the one to d-d-direct me to come to you."

Bill leaned forward as he spoke. "Tylor, I would be glad to teach you the feedlot business. I will pay you $150.00 per week. You will work from 7:00 a.m. to 6:00 p.m. six days a week. Your schedule will rotate so that you are not working every weekend. We pay Saturday noon. You may have one horse of your own if you care to have a horse here. If you can start tomorrow morning, that will be fine. I am going into Kramer in a few minutes. You can go with me and I will take you to the bank to vouch for your employment. They will loan

196

you money for a vehicle, or to rent a room. Any questions?"

Tylor stuttered, "Mr. B-B-Boyle, I thank you, but I met B-B-Buck Draper earlier and he said that you weren't hiring. Will this be a p-p-problem?"

Bill looked at him, "No, no problem. Buck is jealous and doesn't like good-looking fellows like you. He likes himself to be the only charmer. There is one other thing Tylor. Would you mind if I called you Ty? My son's name was Tyler. When I hear your name, it brings forth too many memories."

Tylor nodded, "Ty it is sir. I have always w-w-wondered why it wasn't shortened. My f-f-father goes by Tag and my b-b-brother was TJ. He is d-d-dead now. I am the only child left."

Tylor went downstairs and began giving information to Janice to get on the payroll. By the time she had finished, Bill Boyle came down the steps and asked, "Ty, are you ready to see the town of Kramer?" Bill drove by a stable and corral and said, "This is our horse barn, so be here by seven tomorrow morning. Buck will put you to work. When I get back, I will leave your saddle at the barn, so you won't have to drag it around today."

Their first stop was at the bank. Bill said, "The bank hasn't opened yet, but Larry Harris comes in early. He will let us in if I bring him donuts. He will have the coffeepot going, so it is an even trade." Bill pulled a box of donuts from back of the seat and going to the door, he began to pound on the glass.

A man about the same age of Bill, but somewhat heavier, came to the door. He unlocked the door and grumbled at Bill. "You are late. I thought that you had forgotten about me." He saw Tylor and introduced himself. "Good morning, I am Larry Harris." He stuck out his hand.

Tylor gave him his left hand and stammered, "M-M-Morning. I am Ty T-T-Taggat."

"Larry," said Bill, "Ty is my new hire. He has come

down from the Sandhills of Nebraska to learn the feedlot business. He will need a little financial help until he gets on his feet. He starts tomorrow morning, so he will spend the day finding a place to stay, as well as a vehicle. I will vouch for him, but treat him right." Bill went to a counter behind a desk and set the box of donuts down. Reaching for the coffeepot, he began to pour the coffee. Sharing the coffee and donuts with Larry and Ty, Bill asked Larry, "Where is a good place for Ty to stay?"

"Mrs. Wayne has some small units with a kitchenette that she rents at a reasonable rate." Larry took a sip of coffee. He continued, "She makes sure that they are clean, as well. You might try there for a start." Tylor listened, taking a bite out of his donut. He was hungry, not having eaten since the two steak sandwiches he had at noon the day before.

Bill and Ty drove to the address that Larry had given for Mrs. Wayne's. Ty was impressed by the neatness and he told Bill, "Let m-m-me off here. You have things to d-d-do and this looks good. If it isn't, I will f-f-find something. You will l-l-learn that I am a survivor. I w-w-will see you tomorrow. Thanks for g-g-getting me situated."

Ty got out of Bill's truck. Grabbing up his suitcase, he knocked on the door marked 'Office.' A white-haired lady opened the door, and Ty asked, "Do you h-h-have s-s-something for rent?"

She looked him over closely, taking note that he needed a shave, but his clothes were clean. She asked, "How long do you plan to stay and do you have a job? Also, how many will be staying?"

Ty removed his hat. He said, "Ma'am, I have j-j-just h-h-hired on with the B & B Feedlot. I plan to stay to l-l-learn the feedlot business. I am alone. I just c-c-came d-d-down from the Sandhills of N-N-Nebraska." Ty added, "Until I get p-p-paid on Saturday, I c-c-could only afford to r-r-rent for a week."

"Let me show you the unit. It is $100.00 per month, with a $100.00 deposit. If you are a smoker, the deposit is $500.00." She snickered, as she continued. "Normally, I don't get any smokers. I pay all the utilities, unless you decide to burn the lights day and night. If you party and are noisy, I will boot you out faster than you came into the unit." She looked at his club hand and asked, "Can you hold down a job being handicapped?"

Ty blushed and answered the lady. "I am p-p-presuming that you are r-r-referring to my stuttering. My first words were stuttered and n-n-nothing seems to change. I am close to completing my c-c-college courses. I was also in the Army and l-l-later a POW. None of those c-c-considered it a handicap and Mr. Boyle has heard me s-s-stutter. I am sure that I c-c-can hold a job, but thank you for asking."

The lady was so flustered by Ty's remarks, that she waived the damage deposit provided he pay her the monthly rent the following week.

Ty rented the unit and carried in his suitcase. He placed it on the bed and began to pull the clothes out and hang them in the closet. The jacket that Jim had encouraged him to take was on top. He pulled it out and noticed a small envelope stuffed in the pocket. He had been looking for a piece of paper to jot down what he needed to set up housekeeping, so he pulled the envelope out of the pocket. On closer examination, he opened it to find a note from Jim and $100.00 in cash. He sat on the edge of the bed. He thought about Jim and his faithfulness.

Using the envelope as a scratch pad, Ty began to determine what he needed for kitchenware, as well as food. Having completed his list, he returned to putting away his clothes. Pushed down along the edge, he found another envelope from his mother. Held in place by a rubber band were five, twenty dollar bills and a note that read, 'I love you,

Mother.' Ty wept as he thought of his mother. The people that he had to leave behind are what made him yearn for the Sandhills of Nebraska.

In his search for a vehicle, Tylor had a philosophy. 'Used will do, when you can't buy new.' Consequently, he found an older model sedan with low mileage. However, the original color was red, but replacement doors were blue and the hood was white. The first owner had replaced those items, but had bought a new car and still had this car in his driveway. His intent was to repaint it, but had never found the time. Tylor had bought it at a bargain. Later, his fellow employees referred to it as the 'CCC Vehicle,' or the Cornhusker Circus Car. Tylor was happy. Because of his gifts, he didn't have to borrow from the bank. He started a 'new car fund' the day that he received his first paycheck.

CHAPTER 14
THE LETTERS

The first day of work and Ty was up and ready, well before the appointed time. He was eager to start his learning process. After making his breakfast, he also put together a lunch, not sure what the rest of the crew might do for their lunch break.

Some of the cowboys were already at the barn. Ty was introducing himself when Buck Draper drove up. The first thing he said, "Well, I see you didn't take my advice and check with Kraemer County Feeders. Before the day is over, you will wish that you had. Take that last horse in the stall. That will be your horse for the morning. Get saddled up!" Ty went back to claim his horse and saw that the palomino gelding was standing lazily in the stall. After getting the saddle on the horse, he led him outside. He was ready to mount, when he stopped and looked the horse over again.

Ty remarked, "B-B-Buck, this horse is s-s-sick. His b-b-breath is something awful."

"I didn't expect you to kiss him. Get on, and let's go," said Buck. Before Ty could do anything more, the horse lowered his head and gave a wheezy cough. Ty looked at Buck, as if to say I told you so. Buck said, "Go put him away. You have got him to thinking that he is sick. Take that little black across the alley from where you found this one."

Tylor went back and putting the palomino in his stall, he saddled the black. When he came back, Buck was fumbling with his tally book and it fell at Ty's feet. Buck said, "Whoops! Would you hand me my tally book?" Ty reached to retrieve the book. Just as he bent over, the black horse bit him in the side below the rib cage. Ty let out a yelp and swung his club fist around, hitting the horse in the head between the ear and the eye. The horse immediately dropped to his knees and had a glazed look to his eyes, his chin resting on the ground. The horse remained there as the rest of the pen riders stared in amazement.

Ty picked up the tally book and handing it to Buck, he remarked, "You m-m-might want to take better c-c-care of your t-t-tally book." Ty pulled up on the reins and the horse got to his feet, but was unsteady. "Do you h-h-have any other h-h-horses available? This horse s-s-seems to have a bit of t-t-trouble standing. He m-m-might also be complaining of a h-h-headache as well."

Buck turned his horse to leave, and said to Ty, "Put him back in his stall and report to the processing barn. You can work with the doctoring crew. You seem to be an authority on the ills of livestock."

The rest of the pen riders followed Buck. The last one to leave gave Ty a thumb up. Riding by he said, "The horse's name is 'Nipper.' He needed a good thumping."

Ty put 'Nipper' in his stall. He pulled his saddle off the horse and brushed him down while observing if the horse was going to be all right. At no time did he offer to bite Ty while he worked with him. After finishing with the horse, he checked the palomino, observing that the hay he had been fed was moldy. Pulling it out, he added fresh hay to the bunk and gave the horse a pat on the rump before he left to go to the processing barn.

Ty entered the processing barn and saw that it was another world. The odors were different than those of the rest of the feedlot. The smell of burnt hair and blood brought memories as a youth of Branding Day on the 99 Ranch.

Each day at the processing barn was different. They were busy first thing in the morning with the doctoring of the animals that had been brought in sick the previous days. When new cattle were brought into the lot, it was necessary to process them with preventive medicine, along with the branding and

202

in some cases dehorning an animal. Muggs Lewis was in charge and he was good to work with as an instructor of animal medicine. Bill Boyle kept tabs on Ty's progress. He informed him that every three months he would be moved to a different department. Bill was to inform the University of Ty's progress in feedlot management.

Tylor became accustomed to his little apartment. It was well lit and clean. Mrs. Wayne didn't bother him much, but he knew that she was keeping a close eye on him. He made sure that she had no reason to complain. After he was settled, he wrote his mother:

Dear Mother,

Thank you for the precious gift. You, along with two other benefactors enabled me to get settled here in Kramer, Oklahoma. I was able to pay my first month's rent with the money. The lady I am renting from was gracious enough to forgo a damage deposit, so that saved me a $100.00. Mama, you have an uncanny ability to stow money away in my luggage so that I don't find it until I am in desperate need of funds. I certainly thank you for the help.

The feedlot has a coed softball team. I wish I had inherited your skills as a pitcher. I am getting better using my left hand to throw, but I do lack some accuracy. As far as batting, I am definitely not a power hitter, but I usually get a hit each time I am at bat.

Bill Boyle, the feedlot owner is a swell fellow. He reminds me so much of Uncle Jim. He is patient and kind. I am to work three months in each department and I am now working in the processing and overseeing the cattle in the sick pen. Every day is like branding day with the smell of burnt hair and blood. Other than my clothes smelling bad, I do enjoy it immensely.

Write when you can. I probably won't get a phone. I am saving my money for a new truck.

203

Love, Tylor

Tylor addressed the envelope and placed it by the door to take to the feedlot to go out with their mail.

Laura received the letter a few days later. She was happy with the letter and shared it with Katie and Tag. That is, except for the first paragraph telling about her gift to him. Katie was disappointed that Tylor hadn't written her, but she was aware of the closeness of mother and son. Every day she expected a letter and every day she was disappointed with the absence of even one word from Tylor. She tried to forget him, but found that it was impossible. One Saturday afternoon, she had determined that if she didn't hear from him today, she would erase the memory of his name forever.

She walked across the bridge that spanned the Dismal River and opened up the mailbox. Sorting through the mail, it was as she expected. He hadn't written. The tears began to flow. Her heart could no longer bear the sorrow. Katie started across the bridge when she heard a car horn behind her. She turned and saw the mailman pull up beside her. He rolled down the window and said, "I stopped at the Good Hope School to leave their mail and found this letter in with theirs. I thought you might be expecting it, so I came back. Sorry about the inconvenience." He turned his vehicle around and went back. Wiping the tears from her eyes, she tore open the envelope and began to read.

Dear Katie,

Please forgive the delay in writing you. I haven't forgotten you. Who could forget the one that has ministered so often in my behalf? I sensed that you and Mother would share your letters from me, or at least in part, so I delayed a week before writing to you. Thank you for your generous gift. I discovered it when I decided to eat my lunch that you had packed for me. I was at the port of entry at the Kansas-Nebraska border. I was already feeling a touch of homesickness

204

when I read your note. Thank you so much for your thoughtfulness. It was an encouragement for me to go on with my journey.

I am settled in a routine and the money that you sent me, along with other benefactors has made it possible for me to buy a car. It isn't pretty, but it was cheap! Do you remember that red headed kid from Idaho that worked at the feed store? He had a pickup that was mismatched as far as colors. I think that the fenders and the tailgate were different colors than the body. After seeing his truck, whenever we saw a vehicle that was mismatched, we would call it an Idaho vehicle. Now I am paying the penalty for making fun of his pickup. My car has a red body, with blue doors and a white hood. My coworkers call it a 'Cornhusker Circus Car.'

What are your plans following graduation? I know that at one time you wanted to be a schoolteacher. I know how costly schooling can be, so I want to send you $25.00 every month to help you with your expenses. I know it isn't a great deal, but I want you to consider it as a gift as long as you are in school. Then, when you have your education, perhaps you can help someone else along the way. Let me know what your plans are for the future.

Oh, before I forget, here I am called Ty. Bill Boyle, the feedlot owner, said that his son was named Tyler. He was killed in Vietnam and to hear me called Tylor brought sad memories. He asked if I would go by the name of Ty, which I agreed.

Sincerely, Ty

P.S. I have been sleeping well, with no unpleasant dreams.

Katie read and reread the letter as she returned to the ranch house. She in turn shared portions of her letter with Laura and together they wept over the absence of the one that each loved in their separate way.

While they were sharing Katie's letter, a lonely man

205

was reading his letter from Tylor. Jim McCann was sitting on a step of the front porch on the Bill Dolan Ranch when he opened his letter. He realized that the words were too faint for him to see, so he stood up slowly and went into the house, looking for his reading glasses at the kitchen table. He began to read:

Dear Uncle Jim,

Greetings from the Sooner State! I am getting settled into a routine and enjoying my work here at the B & B Feedlot. The owner, Bill Boyle, is a real gentleman who has promised to teach me the feedlot business. The first three months I will be in the sick barn, doctoring cattle and processing the incoming cattle.

Thank you for your generous gift. It enabled me to buy a vehicle to drive to work. The feedlot is rather isolated, as it is six miles from Kramer, a town of about 3000 people.

I miss you and the ranch, but I plan to return when I have completed my period of rehabilitation. Give Dog a pat on the head.

Sincerely, Tylor

Jim folded the letter and put it back into the envelope. He anticipated that he might read it again. He took time to pray for Tylor, a man from his youth that had endured difficulty.

The summer days were beginning to inflict their heat upon the inhabitants of the Oklahoma Panhandle. Laura was the first to answer Tylor's letter:

Dear Tylor,

It was so good to hear from you. You cannot imagine how happy I was to hear that you have settled into your job. Katie and I share your letters, so whenever you write, it is a double blessing. We don't let the other one read the letter, so by reading the letter to the other person we are able to censor the material on a need to know basis.

The calf crop here at the ranch is doing well this year.

We have been getting ample spring rains. Last Saturday we branded. Oh, Tylor, I shouldn't write this, but it was a sad day. TJ so loved the branding, and he was so good with a rope. Jim was not here and you are gone to Oklahoma. Needless to say, the days have warmed up. I have cherished sitting on the cottonwood stump by the Dismal River to pray and rejoice in the Lord.

I sense that Katie will soon be leaving to begin preparing for her vocation in life. It is my prayer that I will have her this summer. She has been going to church with me. Katie is very discerning regarding the message and the order of worship. One Sunday, she asked me about a song that we had sung. She said, 'in the song you sang, I lift up my hands to you, and some of the congregation lifted their hands. In the next verse you sang, I bow down before you, but nobody bowed down. I would think that they should be consistent.' And, when we take communion, Katie doesn't take part, but she always has a myriad of questions to ask me on the way home.

Tylor, at any time you wish to talk with me, feel free to call collect. I would love to hear your voice.

Incidentally, I have finished the portrait of Katie that I started some time back. I will have it framed, ready to give to her the night that she graduates. I have wanted to begin painting a portrait of TJ, but I am not sure that I am up to it just yet. His high school graduation picture is probably the best to paint from. The Teasdale cemetery is looking beautiful after all of the spring rains that we have been having of late.

Love, Mother

Tylor read the letter from his mother. He envisioned her as she was writing the letter. She was now, almost fifty years of age, but she was as beautiful as the day that he first became cognizant of her beauty. She still had her hair in a single braid, but now it was beginning to have a touch of gray, particularly at the temples. Most unique were her hands, which possessed a softness that was difficult to explain. Tylor so wanted to hear her voice, but he knew that if he called her, she would be able to detect the homesickness in his stuttering speech.

Three days after Tylor had received the letter from his mother, there had been an accident at the processing barn. A metal bar on the squeeze chute used to restrain an animal broke loose, injuring one of the employees. Bud Banner received a broken arm and some cracked ribs. It had taken the crew about two hours to get the steer untangled as well. Now that they were short handed, the men had to work every day. It was wheat harvest in the Panhandle, so it was difficult to find additional help.

A week after the accident, Tylor came home and saw that he had a letter from Katie. After supper he opened it and as he began to read the letter, he fell asleep. Later, he woke up in the dark. He stumbled into bed and slept soundly until his alarm awakened him the next morning. It wasn't until the next night that he realized that he had not finished reading her letter. When he arrived at home, he read the letter before he began his supper.

Dear Ty,

How about that? I remembered your new name and I like it. It seems more informal and personal. The news here is, I have graduated! Your parents gave me a portrait of myself, which your mother had painted. I was totally taken by surprise.

The other news is that I have decided to go to nursing school at Lincoln. I will be leaving in a week. The next session will be starting in ten days. Your mother has promised to take all of my belongings and to help me move into an apartment. I will be living off campus and will have a roommate. I am excited to get started. Yes, earlier I was interested in elementary education, but when I look back, I think that nursing you back to health was what made me change my mind.

Ty, I will be sending you my new address. I appreciate

your offer of financial assistance, but don't think that you need to do that for me. It sounds like you need to save your money for a new vehicle.

Pastor Roth had a Decoration Day service at the Teasdale cemetery. Your mother and I had the cemetery cleaned up and a light rain the night before certainly freshened up things. Tag and Laura hosted a dinner for about twenty friends that came for the service. Pastor Roth had a fine service. I don't know if your mother told you, but I have been attending church with her each Sunday. It certainly has been a new experience for me, but I do enjoy it.

Ty, I look forward to hearing from you and knowing what you are doing at the feedlot.

Love, Katie

Ty read and reread the letter and he began to pray. He prayed for his mother. He knew that she would miss Katie tremendously. Perhaps Dr. Jessup can find another young girl for Mother to mentor. Ty prayed for Katie, knowing that she was about to enter the world of adulthood. Exhausted from the labors of the day, Tylor went to bed early that night. He was awakened at three in the morning, drenched in perspiration. The demons had found him! Ty got up and turned on all the lights in his apartment. Taking his Bible, he began searching through the New Testament. He was looking for a verse about fear, but was unable to find the verse or remember exactly what it said. After about an hour, he dropped off to sleep, the lights still burning. He was awakened at 5:30 when his alarm went off. Throughout the morning, the verse kept escaping him.

After eating his lunch, Ty went to the feedlot office. He knew that Janice took the incoming calls during the noon hour and he remembered seeing a Bible on her desk. That was the first day in which he was hired. He waited until noon, as he sensed that Buck Draper made her desk the first place to stop at in the morning. He didn't want to encounter Buck Draper.

Approaching Janice at her desk, he removed his hat. He said, "Excuse me Janice. You p-p-probably don't remember m-m-me, but I am T-T-Ty Taggat. I have a question t-t-to ask of you, that is if you aren't too b-b-busy."

"Sure, Ty," she replied, "I remember you. You are the fellow from Nebraska that drives that multi-colored car. What can I do for you?"

"W-W-Well," he stuttered, "the first d-d-day that I was here, I n-n-noticed that you had a Bible on your d-d-desk. Early this morning, there was a v-v-verse that I was trying to r-r-remember, but I couldn't quite r-r-remember all of it and I thought you m-m-might recognize it. It s-s-said something about God d-d-didn't give us the spirit of f-f-fear, but he g-g-gave us, and I can't remember what he g-g-gave us. Do you know that v-v-verse?"

"Yes, yes I do." Janice said, "That is an excellent verse, and a good one to commit to memory. It is II Timothy 1:17; For God hath not given us the spirit of fear; but of power, and of love, and of a sound mind." Janice wrote it on a slip of paper and handed it to Ty. She asked, "Were you fearful? Is that the reason of trying to remember the verse?"

Ty nodded his head and she thought he mumbled something about 'demons.' He thanked her and left the office.

That evening after Ty had finished his supper, he walked from his apartment to the downtown area of Kramer. The trucks were hauling wheat to the elevators and many nights, he could hear them going by on the nearby road until midnight. From all reports, it was a bumper crop. Ty rehearsed the verse that Janice had written on the slip of paper. When he returned home, the sun was bidding the day goodbye and the moon was beginning to edge over the horizon to the east. That night, Ty slept well. He realized that it had been sometime since he had written his mother, so he would take time to write on Friday night.

Dear Mother,

Today I started a new phase of my internship. I will work in the feed mill and later drive a feed truck used to auger feed into the feed bunks. It is a bit dusty, but the aroma of the ingredients is pleasant. One cannot help running their hand through the mixed feed. It is almost like playing in a sandbox. Because many of the levers have a ball end, a little smaller than a gear shift lever, I am drawing up a plan to take to the saddle shop. I want to be fitted with a leather sleeve to fit around my club fist with a cup on the end. In the feed truck, the levers are worked with the right hand while the left is used for steering.

I was sorry to hear that Katie was leaving you for school, but happy for her as she begins her nursing school. I just know that she will be an excellent nurse. She did say that she had been going to church with you and that she enjoyed it. However, she also said that it was a new experience for her as well.

I am beginning to see that Katie and I have lived a sheltered life on the ranch. It was a much slower pace than the life I am now living. I am sure that once Katie starts nursing school, she will experience the same. On the ranch, if you didn't get the fence fixed today, in all likelihood, the cows would stay in the pasture. Here, it must be fixed immediately. The same way with everything else, whether it is machinery or a waterline, it must be fixed now!

I will close for now. I love you, Mama.

Tylor

Ty had asked for time off to go to the saddle shop to see about fixing his sleeve with the cup feature. After some measuring, the man told Ty to come back in a week and they would see how it might fit.

About two weeks after the last letter from Katie, Ty checked his mailbox and was excited to see that she had written. The day had been hot and Ty decided to celebrate the day by eating at his favorite café, where it would be cool. He anticipated that his apartment would be stifling hot and he could read her letter in the coolness of the café.

Dear Ty,

I am now in Lincoln and busy, busy, busy. I have put my address on the enclosed card so that you might keep it handy. I do enjoy hearing from you and the accounts of the feedlot. This first semester is classroom work and a lot of reading. I have a part-time job, working the dinner shift at a nearby café. For your information, this is in the evening and not at noon. I have a roommate, but she is from close by, so she goes home every weekend. Usually I don't see her from the last class on Friday, until the first class Monday morning.

I enjoy Lincoln. It is relatively quiet. There is nothing similar to the hustle and bustle of San Francisco, when your mother and I were there for you.

I have a lot of reading tonight, so will close. I did want to give my new address to you in hopes that you will write. I fear that despite letters from you, Laura and my mother, I am experiencing a bit of homesickness. Perhaps, in one of my textbooks, I will learn the cure for homesickness.

Love, Katie

Ty stuffed the letter in his shirt pocket. He finished his supper and after paying for his meal, Ty made his way to the door. He saw Janice, the receptionist from the feedlot. She was with two other young ladies. Ty tipped his hat in recognition and said, "G-G-Good evening, J-J-Janice."

Janice replied, "Hello, Ty." Ty continued toward the door. He could hear the girls giggling in the background. Embarrassed, Ty left the café.

The hot days of summer gradually faded into the hot days of fall. The only difference was that the mornings were cool, but by mid-afternoon the days were quite warm. Laura wrote Tylor more often than he wrote her, but she realized that he was much busier. A letter arrived on his birthday, September 30th. For the occasion he treated himself to a steak dinner at the café, taking his mother's letter with him. He opened the envelope and started to read the letter while waiting for his meal to be served.

Dear Tylor,

Happy Birthday! My goodness, the years do move along. Enclosed is a little something for you to use in buying yourself a gift for your birthday. ($50.00 in cash) I have no idea what you might want or need.

Earlier this summer, Tag was elected as a director of the Stock Growers Assn. This has taken some of his time, but it does give him an opportunity to get away for a weekend now and then. With the change of Governor in the state, Tag is now in favor with the party that is in office and the Governor appointed him to the Brand Board. Consequently, he is gone about once a month. He can drive to one of the other members close by and they can share the travel costs. It is good that he can have some free time. I have offered to accompany him, but he is afraid that I might be bored. I sense that this gives him the opportunity to party in excess, but I'm not sure. I don't hear much from Katie, other than that she is busy. I think that Tag misses her as much as I do. She kind of babied him by pulling off his boots and fitting his slippers to his feet. She always had the paper and mail on the stand beside his chair. He will chide me if I don't have the mail where it is handy for him.

I don't remember if I told you that Becca had a baby boy the middle of June. He is real cute and Carl is happy that there is a boy in the family, even if they had to skip one generation.

Have a good birthday.

Love, Mother

Ty had wished that his mother had not written about Becca. It brought about so many memories, some good and some bad. He thought, *despite the reality that she is a mother and married to another man, I still have feelings for her. He questioned if he would ever be able to get her out of his heart. Evidently, she had no problem in this matter.*

The other part of his mother's letter that bothered him was Tag being gone from the ranch so often. He was aware of his mother's fear of an intruder. It had been over twenty years since Charles Williams supposedly had entered her bedroom. As far as he knew, she still slept with a loaded revolver under her pillow.

Bill Boyle called Ty to his office soon after Ty had stopped to pick up his paycheck. He said, "Ty, I have good reports of your work here at the feedlot. Fall is our busiest time of the year, so I would like you to start riding the pens in the morning and processing in the afternoon. I have been able to hire a man to work as a feed truck operator. Thornton Marsh is quitting as a pen rider, so Buck will need more help. If you are looking for a horse, Thornton wants to sell his. But he wants someone to own him, other than a feedlot. I tried to buy him to have in our string of horses, but he said, no. I have two requests of you. The first is, try to get along with Buck. He is the only one to write a negative comment about your work. The second is, leave the horse called Nipper alone. He hasn't bit anyone since he bit you. However, he hasn't acted real normal either. Report to Buck on Monday morning."

Ty replied, "Yes, sir. Monday m-m-morning I will r-r-report to Buck as ordered."

Ty wrote to Katie that night, enclosing the $25.00 that he sent her each month.

Dear Katie,

I wanted to send you your money and tell you about my latest purchase. I bought an Appaloosa horse that is black with small white circles on his rump. I call him Domino.

Sincerely, Ty

The letter to his mother was a bit more informative, as he had more time to write.

Dear Mother,

Thank you for your birthday gift. I have gone off the deep end and added money with your gift and purchased a horse of my own. Monday I will start as a pen rider, working in the mornings. Then, in the afternoon I will be helping with the processing. We are getting a large number of yearlings in because the fat cattle market looks good for the future.

Let me tell you about my horse. His name is Domino and he is six years old. He is a black Appaloosa with small white spots on his rump. This breed of horse was developed by the Nez Perce` Indians of the Northwest. He is gentle. One of the men was leaving, so I bought him to ride as one of the horses that I will use.

I am keeping extremely busy, which is good. It makes the time go faster.

Mama, I am concerned that you are being left alone so much of the time. Perhaps you should have someone stay with you on those weekends that Tag is gone. I am amazed that they have so much to do each month.

Love, Tylor

November and December were busy months and Ty worked Thanksgiving and Christmas, which allowed the men with families to have a day off. Spring came with the warm weather and the rains, which turned the red clay to mud. Ty did miss the spring calving, but part of the spring he was in the office. He was buying commodities and learning how things ran in the office. He had dated Janice twice, but thought it not good to be too familiar with the fellow employees.

Ty had completed his internship and was invited to go to the University of Nebraska to be honored with twenty others from the School of Agriculture. Ty had contacted the Judge of Summit County for permission to attend. He had been granted permission, but was cautioned to enter the State using the shortest route to the University. It was to be held on a Saturday evening. Ty was excited at the prospect of seeing Katie. He wanted it to be a surprise, so he had planned not to let her know until he had arrived in Lincoln.

Ty left after work on Friday night and drove all night, arriving in Lincoln in time for breakfast. He planned to see Katie at her apartment shortly after eight on Saturday morning. Studying a city map, he arrived at her apartment and entering into a hallway, he knocked on the door. He heard footsteps and Katie came to the door. She had a towel wrapped around her head and was in a bathrobe with fluffy slippers on her feet. Her face turned a bright red at the sight of Ty. Hurriedly, she stepped out into the hallway. "Let us talk out here. My roommate is still sleeping. What are you doing here?" she whispered.

"I have c-c-completed my internship, and I w-w-will be one of the honorees at a b-b-banquet tonight. I wanted to s-s-see if you w-w-would go with me. I will stop by for you, if you like."

Before Katie could answer, the door opened. There stood his father, dressed in his jeans and a white tee shirt. He stepped out into the hallway. Ty saw that his hair was uncombed and he was bare footed. Tag held a mug of coffee in his right hand. He put his left hand around Katie and rested it on her shoulder. Tag said, "I thought I recognized the voice." Lifting up the coffee mug, he asked, "Would you care for a cup of coffee?" As soon as Tag had opened the door, the color had drained from Katie's face. In contrast, Ty's face became bright red.

Ty hurriedly turned for the outside door and mumbled, "N-N-No thanks." Once outside, he ran to his car, stopping long enough to vomit in the bushes. Once inside of his car, Ty drove until he came to the highway that would take him back to Kramer. With the tears rolling down his cheeks, he prayed to God. 'Thank you God for stopping me. I wanted to kill Father, but only you prevented me from doing that to him. Thank you, God.' Ty drove back to Kramer, only stopping long enough to refill his car with gas. The next morning, he was back at the feedlot.

CHAPTER 15
MANEUVER AND MANIPULATE

It was a long drive back to Kramer for Ty. The scene back at Katie's apartment played over and over in his mind, but it always came back to his mother. *Mother was the one that had been betrayed when it appeared that the marriage vows had been broken by his father. And certainly, the trust that Mother had placed in Katie had been breached as well. Had Katie been so desperate for love that she sought out Father, or was it a collusion of each of them? Certainly, Katie exhibited shame, but with Father, there was an evidence of brashness at what he had done. Had Father stayed behind the door, I would have been none the wiser. But no, he didn't even care enough for Katie to shield her from shame. He had misused Katie to belittle me.*

Mile after mile, the scene back at Katie's apartment dogged him. Ty tried to downplay Katie's affection for Tag. *Katie has now entered the adult world and she has made her choice. Katie and I have no allegiance to one another.* Ty paused in his thoughts. *Then, why am I so angry? Am I angry because Katie is so vulnerable, or is it because of my love for Katie? Perhaps I am angry with myself for being so smug. I thought that I could drop in on Katie and whisk her off to the banquet without any notice!* Ty slammed his hand on the steering wheel of his car. He realized that all this could have been prevented, except for his own stupidity!

He continued on his way, when Jeremiah 10: 23 came to his mind. 'O Lord, I know that the way of man is not in himself: it is not in man that walketh to direct his steps.' *Is this what God wanted me to know? I don't know why, but God wanted me to know about Father and Katie!*

Agonizing as the trip home was for Ty, the situation in the little bedroom apartment in Lincoln was not going well.

Katie was in tears. She verbally attacked Tag. "Why did you do that? Why did you have to flaunt your being here to Ty? Don't you care anything for my feelings?"

Tag gripped her arms at the shoulder and replied. "Katie, Katie, don't get so upset. I did it for you. Don't you see? You mean nothing to him. The quicker you get him out of your life, the better it is for you. He is still mooning over that Becca Barnes."

Katie struggled loose from his grip. "What about Laura when she finds out? He will go back to Oklahoma and either call her or write her as to what he saw here today. That will be the end of your weekend visits."

"Don't be so sure," answered Tag. "Ty won't say anything to upset his mother and Laura won't cause any fuss if he did tell her. Laura has lived on the edge of poverty early in her life and now she is living in prosperity. Let me assure you, Laura Taggat likes prosperity much better. It is not easy for a woman of her age to start over in life. Now that we have that settled and the tears are gone, how about some breakfast?"

She began to get the eggs out of the refrigerator. "All right, but tomorrow morning, I want you to leave right after breakfast. Also, be sure to take your liquor bottles with you. Last month you left one in the trash. Fortunately, it was my turn to take out the trash, so I took it out and put it in my book bag. I got rid of it on my way to school."

"But, I don't want to leave so early," begged Tag. "Why can't I leave early Monday morning?"

Katie replied, "I need to spend time cleaning this place, so my roommate Amy won't see any evidence of a man being here over the weekend. Just make sure that you are sober enough to make the trip home." Katie took the eggs out of the skillet and put them on his plate, along with the toast and bacon. She filled his coffee mug before sitting down to her own breakfast.

Tag replied, "Katie, don't nag me. I could stay at home and be nagged. Besides, why do I have to leave so early tomorrow morning? Couldn't I leave after dinner?"

"No, Tag, you can't." The tears were beginning to well up in Katie's eyes. "I plan on going to church tomorrow morning. After this morning, I feel the need to go to church."

Tag was quick to respond. "To church? You aren't getting religious on me, are you? I have one of those at home, too!" Katie got up and went to her bedroom, trying to dry her tears.

After a few minutes, she returned. "I'm sorry, Tag. I don't mean to upset you, but I do need to have time tomorrow to clean. Just as you will need a drink of liquor tomorrow, I will need to be in church. Maybe we both have an addiction." She said nothing more while she finished her breakfast.

Tag also knew that Tylor was on probation and was not to return to Nebraska for five years. Should he cause any problems, Tag would let the authorities in Nebraska know that Tylor had been seen in Nebraska. He was unaware that Tylor had cleared his visit with the county judge.

At the same time that all this was going on in Lincoln, a similar scene was unfolding at the 99 Ranch. Laura was fixing her own breakfast. She had not slept well. Neither did she like to be alone at night. Even though she locked the doors and kept her loaded revolver under her pillow, she missed the presence of Tag beside her. Sitting at the table alone, Laura slammed her coffee mug down on the table, slopping coffee on the table and the floor. She thought, *people are always saying, 'Laura Taggat has a plan. Laura is never without a plan.'* Laura began to mop up her spilled coffee and the more she mopped the bigger the plan became.

Laura began on the premise that Tag was untruthful and in all probability, unfaithful as well. I shall portray myself as the sweet little wife that is understanding and willing to

221

stay home. No longer will I ask to go with him, or question his coming and going. However, I will read the odometer on his truck to see how far he goes on his monthly trips. Better yet, on his next trip, I will follow him. He will recognize my blue sedan, but I will rent a vehicle and follow him. I will find out where he goes and who he is seeing. Now, Laura has a plan!

As he usually did on the first of each month, Ty would write a note to Katie and enclose the $25.00 for her schooling. This month, after their encounter in Lincoln, he sent the $25.00 without any note.

Katie received the monthly money from Ty and promptly returned it with a note, which read; 'Dear Ty, I am sorry for what happened between us, therefore, I am returning the $25.00 to you.'

Ty received Katie's note and returned the money with a note. 'Katie, I made a promise to send you $25.00 each month. I intend to keep my word on this promise.'

Upon receipt of Ty's note, Katie stuffed the money in an envelope and mailed it back to Ty with no message whatsoever.

When Ty got the money back from Katie, he was prepared to handle it a bit differently. He knew that Katie had a checking account in the bank at Summit City. He purchased a money order for the amount, made payable to the bank at Summit City. He informed them to deposit it to the account of Katie O'Neal. It took three months for Katie to determine why she had more money in the bank than she had recorded in her checkbook. She gave up, realizing how determined Ty was to keep his promise. Besides, she had no time for frivolous mind games. She was now spending more time with clinical work.

Ty survived his period of pen riding, despite the constant ridicule of Buck Draper. Fortunately, he was able to ride Domino most of the time and not depend on the unreliable feedlot owned horses. With each segment of the internship, Ty began to formulate a plan as how to improve the process. Some of the improvements would be to replace certain personnel that were not a fit for the job. Other improvements included a change of procedures or the purchase of equipment. All in all, Ty was enjoying his tenure at the feedlot.

With Laura, this was to be the weekend that would give her some answers where Tag went each month. Friday morning at breakfast, Tag said, "Laura, could you pack my suitcase for the weekend? I will be leaving after dinner and will be back late Sunday evening or Monday morning. We have a meeting in the western part of the state. I may take a little time to look at some bulls while I am there."

Laura replied, "That will be fine. I will have your suitcase in your truck. Is there anything I need to pack special for you?"

"No, no," he said. He hugged her shoulder. "You do a fine job, as always."

After breakfast, Laura packed his suitcase and placed it in the cab of the red truck that Tag considered his. She read the odometer, writing it on a slip of paper. She packed an overnight bag of her own and placed it in her car.

After dinner, Tag kissed her goodbye and went to his truck. Seeing that everything was in order, he left the ranch. Laura hurried and followed Tag at a reasonable distance. Arriving in Summit City, she saw that he entered the main highway and turned to go east. Laura parked her car at the dealership and started up the rental car. She noticed that the gas gauge was a little over one-fourth full. She hurried to a gas station and filled the car. She knew that Tag was a fast driver, so she hurried to catch up. She then feared that she might be picked up for speeding. Traffic was light and after thirty minutes, Laura observed Tag's red truck ahead about one-fourth mile. She slowed to match his speed. Following him for another thirty minutes, he pulled off the highway and drove about ten miles. He pulled into a ranch near the road.

Laura slowed up and driving by slowly, she observed Tag get out of the truck. But, it wasn't Tag! It wasn't even a Ford truck. She had been following the wrong truck! Disheartened, she drove to the next crossroad and turned around and went back to Summit City. Next month she would try again. But, she would take note of the odometer reading when Tag returned.

Ty realized it had been two months since he had written his mother, despite her faithfulness of writing him every two weeks. *I probably should write, or she will be calling Lionel Whitman to find out what has happened to me.* Ty had a day off, the first since he had gone to Lincoln, so he took advantage of the day to write his mother.

Dear Mother,

I am sorry for not writing, so I will offer no excuse. I do enjoy the letters that you are so faithful in writing. I have completed my internship and my degree is official. My intentions are to stay here until my probation is fulfilled with the Summit County court system. I have learned so much that seemed immaterial in the classroom. We are adding more pens and Bill Boyle has given me the responsibility as foreman, working with the engineers and coordinating the construction process. Things are a bit slower right now, so we will utilize our workers in the construction of the pens. Each pen we add boosts our revenue. I have spent the last few months in the office, learning about our billing process. The feedlot owns no cattle, which I see has its advantages.

I have been studying some of the history of the area. It is rather unique. The county is called Kraemer and the county seat is Kramer. Jacob Kraemer married Martha Kramer and they had twin sons; Claude and Clyde. Martha continued to use her maiden name of Kramer, and after a time, Jacob also started going by the name of Kramer. Never underestimate the power of a woman! The sons came out to this part of the country and settled here, and became quite wealthy. Because of the similarity of the first names, Claude, being the favorite son of his father, reclaimed the Kraemer name and succeeded in having the county named after him. Clyde, the favorite son of his mother, retained the Kramer name. Clyde was a businessman and the founder of the town of Kramer, being its first mayor. He also succeeded in having the town named as the county seat of Kraemer County. Incidentally they are pronounced differently.

Mama, my horse Domino is a jewel. Without your birthday money, I probably would not have purchased him. Because this is the first day off in months, early this morning, I took him out and we rode one of the nearby pastures. Sometimes it is difficult to determine a horse's worth by riding in the pen all day. At first it was as if I was on one of the pony rides at the county fair. The fat cattle move rather slowly. I like it when we work the yearlings that have a bit more life.

Can you imagine, I have been here more than two years? I have less than three more years until I return to Nebraska. When I return, perhaps I will find a feedlot in Nebraska that will hire me. During football season, you can't imagine how much guff this Cornhusker has to take from these Oklahoma Sooners.

Love, Tylor

While Laura read her son's letter, she too reminisced of the passing of time. It has been almost three years since the death of TJ. Still, it seems that Tag has not reconciled to his death. Laura was of the notion that these monthly visits were somehow as a result of TJ's death. Tomorrow, after breakfast, Tag will tell me he is leaving for the weekend. Tomorrow, the rental car will be full of gas and ready to move.

True to form, after breakfast, Tag said, "I have a Stock grower's meeting tomorrow and Sunday morning. Can you have my suitcase packed and ready to go after dinner?"

Laura said, "Yes, I will have it in your truck. Where is

225

the meeting?"

"Oh, it is down on the Interstate, I think at Seger. Sam Thompson is going and I will go with him."

Laura said, "Tag, sometime when you have a meeting at Lincoln, I might just go along and visit Katie for a day or two. I haven't seen her since she started down there. She writes every now and then and I know that she keeps busy, but surely we could find some time to be together. I do miss her, and I am sure that she misses the both of us as well."

Tag said, "Yes, yes, that would be a good idea. I am never sure of the schedule, as they move the meetings around. I am hoping that sometime they might have one here at Summit City."

"You might suggest that to the committee. I am sure that if Seger can accommodate the few of you, surely Summit City could as well." Laura felt real proud of herself for making that suggestion.

After they finished their dinner, Laura put the dishes in the sink and kissed Tag while he was still sitting at the table. She said, "Tag, I must leave now. I have an appointment to have the oil changed in my car. Then, I want to see Cindy Holler in the hospital." It was then that she remembered that she hadn't read the odometer. Going to their bedroom, she grabbed three handkerchiefs. Passing Tag still at the table, she said, "I forgot to put your handkerchiefs in your suitcase. I will slip them in on my way out. Goodbye." Tag had started to say that he would take them, but she was gone before he had an opportunity.

Laura hurried out and putting the handkerchiefs in her pocket, she looked at the odometer and tried to memorize the number. She hurried to her car and wrote the number on a pad. She started her car and was ahead of Tag. Laura waved at him when he went by the service station in Summit City. She got into the gray sedan by the time that Tag was turning east on the

226

main highway. It was a pleasant drive, so she followed well back. Sometimes she would extend the gap if it was a long stretch of road. Tag never stopped and after several hours, it became evident that Lincoln could be his destination. Who could he be seeing in Lincoln? Probably someone connected with the Brand Board. Laura was getting weary with so much travel. *I wonder, why doesn't he take a break?* Tag exited the main highway and was driving in the business district. Suddenly he pulled into a parking spot. Fortunately there was an empty place to park five cars down. She stopped her car and saw Tag enter a package liquor store. After a time, he came out carrying a bag with several bottles sticking out of the top.

Laura scrunched down in the seat while he backed out and proceeded down the street. After a time, he was driving in an area that was a mix of apartments and businesses. Half way down the block, Tag pulled into an apartment complex and parked his truck. Laura parked on the street and waited to see if Tag got out. He got out, carrying his luggage and hugging the bag that held the bottles of liquor. He went up the steps and turned to look around. Laura ducked down until it was safe to look out again. She saw the door closing behind him. Laura had seen enough, as she recognized the apartment. *This is where I brought Katie two years ago to begin her nurses' training!* Laura rested her head on the steering wheel. She asked herself, *have I seen enough? Maybe Tag has befriended Katie's roommate. I can't believe that Katie would betray my trust. Yet, Tag can be quite charming.*

Laura leaned back and rested her head on the back of the seat. *I need to think, but first, I need to find a restroom and get something to drink.* She spotted a fast food restaurant a half block down the street. Getting out of the car, she locked it, glancing over her shoulder one last time at the apartment. After using the restroom, Laura got herself a cup of coffee. She could still see the apartment from here, but she needed to move her car off the street. There was no parking on that street from 2:00 a.m. to 6:00 a.m. After drinking her coffee, Laura surveyed the apartment complex once again. She found the perfect place for her to park. She moved her car from the street and positioned her car so that the apartment was in view, but the car would be inconspicuous to most residents of the complex. It was now 6:00 p.m. and there had been no activity, coming or going.

After a time, Laura was startled when a young man rapped on her window. She rolled the window down and he said, "Lady, you are parked in my spot. You will have to move your car."

Laura said, "I'm sorry. I have a person under surveillance at this time. Would ten dollars buy this spot for 24 hours?"

"Make it twenty dollars," said the man, "and it is yours. But for only 24 hours."

"Provided I get some information along with the parking spot," said Laura.

"What do you need to know? I am full of information and facts." The young man grinned at his cleverness.

"That red truck over there; does he come here often?" asked Laura.

"He comes once a month, every month. Just like clockwork. I don't think he has missed once in the last two years." Still grinning, the young man asked, "Now can I have my twenty bucks?"

"Not so fast," replied Laura. "For twenty bucks, I need more information. What does he look like and who is he visiting?"

"Well, I would say that he is six foot two and weighs about 225 pounds. He is in his late fifties and in his earlier days a true blonde. As far as who he is visiting, I would say that it is that sweet little Irish gal. Now to answer your next question, is it his daughter or his girl friend? I'm not sure, but most men

228

don't treat their daughters that way. Oh, and he drinks a lot."

Laura reached into her purse and gave the man a twenty-dollar bill. "You are thorough. Thanks a lot. Keep this just between the two of us."

"Don't worry lady! I wouldn't want him to find out that I had talked to you. He is mean. I hope you lock him up and out of our complex." The young man stuffed the twenty into his pocket and moved his vehicle to another spot.

Laura waited a while longer. She was starting to get hungry, so she went back to the restaurant and ordered. She was where she could see the apartment, when a car pulled to the curb. Katie got out and entered the apartment and the car pulled back into traffic. In a few minutes Katie and Tag came out and crossed the street, headed for the place where Laura was eating her supper. Laura grabbed her purse and rushed into the restroom. She remembered there were two stalls. The first one was occupied, so Laura took the second and latched it closed. Laura heard someone come into the restroom and after a few minutes there was a rap on the door. A lady's voice said, "Are you about through in there?" It was Katie!

Laura was tempted to throw open the door and surprise her. Instead she mimicked someone vomiting and Katie left her alone. Laura stayed in there for an hour, fearful that Tag and Katie might still be in the restaurant. While she was sitting on the stool, she wept. Laura thought, *what is the matter with me? I am acting like I am the one that is trying to hide my misdeeds. If I confront Tag with this, then it is up to me to do something and I don't want to do anything about it. As long as he doesn't say anything and no one knows that I know, then everyone is safe. If I could be assured of Tag's love, then my marriage would be worth saving. After the death of TJ, there has been nothing to hold our marriage together. I don't have enough love for both of us. Evidently he has found someone else. I could tolerate his lack of love for me, but now he is able*

229

to love Katie, so there is nothing left. Unfortunately, outside of the ranch, I have no future. I am dependent upon the ranch and Tag knows it.

Laura left the restroom and got herself another sandwich and a cup of coffee and returned to her car. *It then came to her that Tylor must not find out. I sense that Tylor is becoming fonder of Katie. It would crush him to know that Katie was involved with Tag, and yet, how do I discourage his interest in her. Is Katie so devious to keep Tylor interested in her, while she is having an affair with Tag? There, I said it! Katie and Tag are having an affair and I hate that they are destroying this family!*

Laura stayed in her car, but she scarcely slept during the night. The next morning, Tag left in his truck, but he didn't have his luggage, so Laura knew that he would be returning. He had trouble walking to his truck. Evidently he had too much to drink the night before. When he returned, he was carrying another paper bag with a bottle showing at the top.

Laura had seen enough. She left the parking lot and drove about five blocks. She found a nice restaurant where she likely wouldn't have to hide in the restroom. She had her breakfast and took her time to return to Summit City. *She was satisfied. Now she knew, but she really didn't know why.*

Tag returned on Sunday afternoon and Laura didn't ask him about his trip. She filled her conversation with local happenings and things of the ranch. She was through with his games.

Tag's infidelity was not only affecting his marriage, but it was evident also in what was happening at the 99 Ranch. Laura saw it little by little, day by day. It was costing more and more to fund the ranch. Laura could see that the cattle were not doing as well as they had in prior years. The ranch had lost its bloom.

Laura continued to correspond with Katie and from

time to time she sent her gifts of money to help with her schooling. Katie was to graduate from nursing school on the first of August and she indicated that she wanted to remain in Lincoln.

Though the passenger trains no longer ran to Summit City, the railroad continued to send freight trains over the same tracks. Katie's stepfather, Derk Donnelly was the section foreman for the track crew. The family lived in the company house in Summit City. On the 15th of July, the section crew was riding the motor car when it struck a piece of metal that was lying on the track, flipping the motor car, severely injuring Derk. By the time he got out of the hospital, it was determined that he had suffered a disabling injury and was placed on permanent disability. After Katie graduated from nursing school, she was planning to move back to Summit City to help her mother care for Derk. Now that he no longer worked for the railroad, they had moved from the company house into a rented house in town. Katie had rented the little upstairs apartment that Laura had rented when she lived in Summit City. She was planning to move in as soon as she finished her schooling.

One evening, Katie called Laura on the phone, "Laura, I am sorry to impose on you, but I need to move back to Summit City. Would it be possible for you to move me back to town? I have added a few small pieces of furniture, but I think they will all fit in a car. If not, I will let my roommate have them. I am graduating on the first, but I need to be out on the third of August."

Laura had to bite her tongue before she answered. "Why yes, I could do that, but if you might have more than I can haul in the car, I have one other thought. I would need to check with Tag's schedule, but occasionally he has meetings in Lincoln toward the end of the month. If so, he could bring your belongings in his truck. So, you would try to be out on the second, is that right? I will check with him and call you back.

Katie, I am sorry to hear about your father. I have heard that you will be helping your mother, but are you planning to work as well?"

"Yes, I have an interview with Dr. Jessup as soon as I get back to town. I would like to get on with the hospital. Let me know what Mr. Taggat has to say. Thank you, Laura. Goodbye."

Before the evening was over, Laura went to the living room where Tag was reading the newspaper. She sat down in a chair near his and said, "Tag, I had a call from Katie. She is graduating the first of August and needs to be out of her apartment on the third of August. I could go get her, but she may have more furniture than I could get in the car. I told her I would check with you to see if you had any meetings at that time. It would save us some gas and would certainly be a big help to me. I am not certain if I could find where she lives. Katie is the one that directed me there the first time. In fact, I can't even remember her street address."

Tag quickly spoke up. "1804 Walnut Street, Apartment 14." And then he blushed.

Laura spoke up just as quickly, "Of course, you remembered. It is the return address on each letter she sends us. How foolish of me and then how fortunate for me to have married a man that is so observant. I would have driven to Lincoln and my mind would have gone blank. Thank you, Tag. Oh, and as soon as you check your schedule, I will give her a call."

Laura returned to the kitchen to finish the last of the dishes. She stopped and poured herself a cup of coffee and leaned against the counter. She smiled to herself. She thought, *this is such great fun when you know things that other people don't think you know. He was certainly quick with his response to Katie's address.* Laura took a sip of her coffee. She thought. *I like manipulating people. It is fun to watch what they do when*

232

they think that they are manipulating you. It is like a chess match. I venture that before I finish this cup of coffee, Tag will come in here with the perfect schedule for the first of August. She took one more sip. She heard Tag crossing the living room floor.

He entered the kitchen and said, "Would you believe it! I do have a meeting on the second, and we can get loaded first thing the next morning and be in Summit City shortly after noon. It is a meeting of the Brand Board at the Capitol."

"Now, isn't that a coincidence. Now will you be going down on the first or the second?" Laura asked. "I thought if you were going down on the first, I could go along and perhaps take in her graduation."

"That would be nice," countered Tag, "but the meeting is in the afternoon and I had planned on leaving early in the morning. That way I could put in one more day of work. I'm sorry to disappoint you, but we are a bit behind with our haying."

"That's all right, Tag, it was just a thought." Laura turned out the light and said to Tag, "It is rather late, so I will call Katie tomorrow." Laura thought, *I like this game; 'maneuver and manipulate.' It is better than chess, as you don't have to set up a board each time.*

CHAPTER 16
THE GRADUATION!

Laura was curious about the relationship of Tylor and Katie. As of late, neither one had mentioned anything about the other in their letters to her. I rather doubt that Tylor is aware of the accident that her stepfather had incurred.

Dear Tylor,

Just a brief note to let you know what is happening here in Summit County. Please note that the news here at the ranch is so bland, that now I am reporting for the county as a whole.

Derk Donnelly was in a railroad accident the middle of the month. He is so disabled that he can no longer work. Katie is coming home after graduation to help care for him. She is also hoping to find work at the hospital. I feel sorry for her mother. She has those four boys and they have had to move out of the company house.

This morning I received a graduation announcement from Katie, which added to my sorrow. Katie has worked so hard to become a nurse and now she won't have anyone to see her graduate. Tag is going to Lincoln the day after her graduation for a meeting. He will bring her things back for her. I had wanted to go with him, but we would have to go a day early to attend the graduation. We are behind with our haying and he didn't want to lose an extra day.

I am glad that you enjoy your horse, Domino. You were always gentle with your horses. It is good that you can have one of your own to ride. I was thinking, perhaps when you have some time off, we could meet half way and spend a few days together. Is there anything between here and Kramer, other than wheat fields and feedlots, where we could spend some vacation time?

Think about getting together!

Love, Mother

The day that Ty received the letter from his mother, he also received what appeared to be a graduation announcement from Katie. He read his mother's letter. He then questioned if he should even open Katie's letter. He opened it and saw that the printed invitation contained the usual graduation information. Inside was a small sheet of paper folded in half. He opened it and read the contents of her note.

Dear Ty--I questioned if I should send this announcement and how you might receive it as well. However, I would be remiss if I failed to acknowledge how much you have helped me attain this goal in my life. Thank you very much for your support. I am saddened that our friendship has been severed as a result of my poor judgment. I certainly understand how you must feel.

Love, Katie

Ty thought, *Katie, Katie; always the one with poise and dignity despite the circumstances. I cannot abandon her now in this moment of exhilaration.* The next morning, Ty stopped at the office and asked to have the first two days of August off of work. He had decided if things didn't work out right, he could come back a day early. Already, he was planning what to get her for her graduation. He paused to ask himself; *why am I so excited about this trip?*

On the morning of the first day of August, Ty left Kramer at four in the morning. He wanted to take his time and possibly catch a nap in the event that the situation deemed that he drive back that night. He arrived in Lincoln at four that afternoon and decided that a bus station was a good place to nap. After an early supper, he was at the Memorial Annex in plenty of time to watch for the graduates when they arrived. Looking around, he saw Katie talking to another girl. Before approaching her, he looked over the crowd to see if Tag was anywhere around. Ty came up behind her and asked, "Pardon me, m-m-miss, but are you K-K-Katie O'Neal from S-S-

236

Summit City?"

Katie spun around and hugged Ty. "Oh, Ty, you came. You came." She took her handkerchief and was wiping her eyes and said, "Don't worry Ty, these are happy tears, these are happy tears. Now I have someone at my graduation!"

A lady nearby who had been watching the happy moment, said, "Make that two someones."

Ty and Katie turned around. Katie said, "Laura!" Ty tried to speak, but could say nothing as he held his mother. Laura saw the fear in Katie's eyes. She and Katie hugged one another and Laura whispered in her ear, "He is not here."

Ty said, "I don't know if this a-a-pro-pro--." Ty started over, "I don't know if this is p-p-proper, but I b-b-brought the graduate a c-c-corsage to wear tonight." He handed Katie an orchid corsage.

Katie handed it back to Ty. "Here, you are supposed to pin it on me."

Ty held up his stub hand and shook his head, so he handed the corsage to his mother to pin on Katie's dress.

It was an exciting evening for Katie. She was named the valedictorian of the class. At the reception that followed, she kept her hand on Ty's arm. They were having cake and punch at the reception and Laura asked, "Tylor, what are your plans for tonight and tomorrow?"

He said, "I had p-p-planned to drive b-b-back tonight, b-b-but I am having so much fun, maybe I will get a r-r-room and drive b-b-back tomorrow."

"That's a good idea," said Laura. "You can get a room where I am staying and we can eat breakfast together. Then we will load up Katie's things and we can each be on our way." As an afterthought, Laura turned to Katie. "My room has two beds in it. If you want, we can stop at your apartment and get your nightclothes. Then, you can stay with me in my room. We can eat at the motel and everyone can be on their way. This will let us visit as late as we wish."

Katie said, "I don't want this night to ever end. I am having so much fun. It has been over four years since we have all been together. I like the idea of us all staying at the motel. I'm ready when the rest of you are."

"If it is all right, Tylor, I will drive the truck to the motel and you can follow in your car. Then we will all go to Katie's and get her things."

Katie rode with Ty while they followed Laura to the motel. Katie said, "Ty, I was unsure about sending you an invitation to the graduation, but now I am glad that I did. Thank you so much for driving all this way." She didn't say anything about his last visit to Lincoln. The memory was best left untouched.

Ty looked over at her and said, "When M-M-Mama wrote me that no one w-w-would be at your graduation, I thought that you had w-w-worked hard to make a s-s-success of yourself. I thought that it was a shame that you h-h-had no one to share the m-m-moment with you. I d-d-didn't know that Mama would be h-h-here. She must have had the s-s-same idea."

When Laura and Tylor were waiting in the car for Katie to get her nightclothes, Tylor asked, "Where is F-F-Father?"

Laura was in the back seat and she reached forward to touch Tylor's shoulder. "Son, the Lord works in mysterious ways. Tag intended to leave me home, but I wanted to come to the graduation. He didn't think that I could drive by myself, especially the truck. Yesterday, the tamest horse on the ranch kicked him so hard that he can hardly walk. This morning, I left him on the couch and here I am. I'm happy for Katie. She has worked hard for all of this."

On the drive to the motel, Tylor asked, "What do you ladies think of my car?"

Katie said, "I like it. It is rather unique and would

certainly be easy to spot in a parking lot. But, if it were stolen, how would you describe it to the police?" They all laughed at the joke.

After returning to the motel, they had late coffee together. They reminisced of earlier times. Ty had a gift for Katie. Katie opened the small box and saw that it was a wristwatch. It was one used by nurses. Katie kissed his cheek and said, "Oh, Ty, I will think of your gracious spirit each time that I look at this marvelous gift."

A stab of jealousy struck Laura when she heard Katie's response. *How dare she act this way with my son, when I know good and well her relationship with Tag? I can tolerate her betrayal of our friendship, but I don't like what she is doing to Tylor.* Laura asked, "Katie, when did you start calling him Ty? He has always gone by Tylor!" *Laura thought that it sounded much too personal.*

Laura's tone of voice startled Katie. "I'm sorry," she said, "I thought that he told you."

Now Katie was starting to frighten Laura. She replied, "Told me what?"

Amidst all the exchange of words between the two women, Tylor was trying to explain to his mother why Katie called him Ty. Unfortunately, as he began to form the words that he wanted to say, one of them had already replied to the other. Finally, he was able to intervene. "Mama, my b-b-boss at the feedlot told me his son T-T-Tyler was killed in the war. He said it would b-b-bother him if he heard p-p-people call me T-T-Tylor, because the names s-s-sounded so similar. He asked if I w-w-would go by Ty while at the f-f-feedlot. I agreed, and I wrote K-K-Katie about our conversation. She l-l-liked the name and has been using it in our c-c-correspondence. With you I use Tylor, but with K-K-Katie, I prefer Ty."

Laura nodded her head. Now she understood.

The next morning, they had breakfast together. Ty

239

helped load Katie's furniture in the truck. He placed a tarp over the box of the truck and secured it with straps. Each of the women hugged Tylor, as they prepared to leave. Katie wanted to tell Ty that she loved him, but was reluctant to express her love for him. She was uncertain if Ty had any feelings for her, or if he was just being nice. Leaving the parking lot, he gave them a wave of the hand and started his journey back to Oklahoma.

CHAPTER 17
A SHOT IN THE DARK

Ty returned to the feedlot and he viewed his trip to Katie's graduation with mixed emotions. *She acted as if the scene with Tag on my previous visit to Lincoln had never happened. But why wouldn't she, as I acted like a moonstruck fool. Maybe I did get carried away with the corsage and the gift of the watch. I fear that I don't know much about women.*

While Ty pondered these things, Laura had her doubts as well. *Now that Katie is living in Summit City, how discreet will Katie and Tag be with their relationship? Above all, I don't want Tylor hurt. Perhaps it is just as well that he has two more years in Oklahoma.*

A week after the graduation, Laura wrote Tylor a letter.

Dear Tylor,

This is a note to let you know that we made it home without any problems. Katie drove most of the way. She said it has been such a long time since she has driven. I didn't mind it a bit. It gave me an opportunity to view the landscape. The trip from Lincoln is certainly relaxing after the traffic in the city.

Tag is better, but he has a terrible bruise on his upper leg.

Katie started working at the hospital the next day after we arrived home. She works from 3:30 in the afternoon until midnight. Incidentally, I learned this morning that her stepfather is back in the hospital.

We are having a difficult time with our haying. Tag is just now able to return to the hayfield. I have been going out each day to help where I can, checking the windmills and putting out the salt for the cattle.

Tylor, it certainly was good to see you after all this time. I had a call from Lionel the day after I got home. He wanted me to tell you that they are quite happy with your work at the feedlot. He is making it a point to report back to the Summit County Court.

Write when you can.

Love, Mother

Tylor was glad for his letter, but was disturbed that she had to work in the hayfield. Working around the machinery can be dangerous at times, but maybe she spends more time checking the cattle. If Father didn't spend so much time going to those meetings, he wouldn't be so far behind. Also, Ty knew that when Jim left the ranch, he left a big hole in the operation. As far as Ty knew, Tag hadn't been able to find a foreman with Jim's knowledge. I always wondered why Jim left. He would never say anything about the reason for leaving.

Before Tylor had an opportunity to write his mother, he received another letter from her.

Dear Tylor,

I am writing to let you know that Katie's stepfather died yesterday morning. He had been in the hospital about ten days when he died. He never fully recovered from his accident. I'm not sure what Darla will do, now that Derk is gone. The youngest of the four boys is nine, so I imagine she will look for some kind of work. I am unaware of what kind of settlement she might have received from the railroad, but it is unlikely that it is sufficient for a family of that size.

That is all the news for now.

Love, Mother

Meanwhile, Sheriff Morgan was dealing with his own problems. He liked Sundays. They were the quietest day of the week. The businesses were closed and he didn't have any patrols in town or throughout the county. But, as the week progressed, the problems seemed to escalate, until peaking on Saturday night. He could handle Saturday nights, but it was the presence of Tag Taggat in his town late at night during the week. He had no set schedule, but he was sure to be seen at

242

one of the bars at least once a week. More disturbing was when his truck was parked after midnight in front of the upstairs apartment at 127 River Street, most recently rented to Miss Katie O'Neal. How ironic; this was the same apartment that the then Laura Martin had rented when she moved in from the Good Hope School 25 years ago.

Sheriff Morgan never liked these love triangles. A barroom brawl he could handle, but a love triangle was usually nasty. Tag Taggat could be mean, having been raised in Barton County. But Laura, the prim lady of New England upbringing was another thing. He compared her to gasoline. Controlled in an engine, it could do mighty things, but ignite it on the ground, you better stand back. His first encounter with her was over two of the deputy's dogs. She almost beat them to death over a pan of cupcakes. At one time, she was sleeping with a revolver under her pillow. I imagine that she still is, but she also knows how to shoot it, and shoot it well.

Not only was the sheriff concerned, but also Dr. Jessup pondered over his latest hiring at the hospital. Katie O'Neal was an excellent nurse, but he was not immune to small town gossip reaching his ears. He met Katie in the hall one afternoon before she started her evening shift. "Katie," he said, "you have been with the hospital two months now. Usually I meet with our new employees after that period of time. What is a good time for us to go over your scheduling, and any concerns that you might have regarding your employment?" He paused a moment and then continued. "Would tomorrow afternoon be all right, say at one o'clock?"

Katie nodded and replied. "That will be fine. Then I will see you tomorrow at one." She left to begin her shift.

The next day at one, Katie stopped at Dr. Jessup's office. He motioned for her to sit down. He went to the door and closed it behind her. Katie thought that he was certainly being secretive about their meeting. The doctor began by asking, "Katie, I am going to get right to the point. This is a small community and no one blows their nose without the whole community knowing it. I'm concerned about your relationship with Tag Taggat. Are you having an affair with Tag?"

Katie answered him sharply. "What does your community say? Does it say that I am having an affair?"

"Katie, there is no need of getting angry. You have not answered my question. Are you and Tag having an affair?" Dr. Jessup folded his arms, awaiting Katie's response.

Katie folded her arms and angrily replied, "And, neither have you answered my question as to what your community says about us having an affair."

Dr. Jessup quietly responded. "Katie, we can go back and forth all afternoon, but I'm not going to play your game with you. I feel somewhat responsible for putting you in this situation. Your mother came to me with a concern of your stepfather being way too familiar with you. She asked counsel in regard to this matter. That is when I directed you to Laura Taggat. Not knowing that I have put you in a situation in which you are more vulnerable than you were originally. It is no secret that Tag Taggat and I have no love for one another. I consider him a bully. I see him as one to take advantage of others. Katie, you are no longer a child, but an adult that is certainly capable of making your own decisions. It doesn't look good on a person's resume to have only been employed at a hospital for two months. Therefore, unless you make an effort to sever your relationship with Tag within the next four months, I will dismiss you after being employed here for six months. Do you have any questions?"

"No sir. You have made yourself quite clear." Katie got up to leave.

"One more thing before you leave. Katie, you are a fine nurse. Don't spoil a future in nursing for the likes of a man that

can offer you nothing but heartache." Dr. Jessup took her hand
in the two of his and gently squeezed it.

Katie left the hospital in tears. She respected Dr. Jessup,
but she knew that she could not abandon Tag Taggat so easily.
She still had two hours before reporting for duty. She began
to walk aimlessly, unsure of where she wanted to go. She
continued walking and was astonished that she could go no
further! She had come to the Dismal River. Some years before,
someone had placed a bench on the bank of the river. Evidently
that person enjoyed coming here to watch the water flow by,
leaving the city on its journey to the Gulf of Mexico.

Katie knew that Laura often sat by the Dismal River
where it cut through the 99 Ranch. It was there that Katie
would see Laura, praying and weeping as she sought God's
will. Katie wanted to pray, but she was uncertain of what to
pray for at this time. She sensed that Laura knew about Tag and
her. It was at the graduation ceremony when they first hugged
and she said, 'he isn't here.' Tag was right when he had said
that Ty wouldn't hurt his mother in telling about seeing Tag at
Katie's apartment in Lincoln. But surely the town wags would
let Laura know that Tag had spent time at Katie's apartment
here in Summit City. If the town wags had informed Dr. Jessup,
surely they would not pass up the opportunity to inform Laura.

Katie remained at the Dismal River until it was time to
go to work. Still she had not prayed.

The late days of summer turned to the early days of fall.
Unknown to those at the 99 Ranch, today was the beginning
of events that would change the day to day history of the ranch
into something dramatic. It had started by Laura driving to
Madden to Harley the boot maker. He had made a pair of boots
for Tylor, which was to be his birthday present. She picked
them up, and returned to Summit City. It was there that she
mailed the boots to Tylor.

Arriving home, she began to prepare dinner for Tag and

herself. Tag had come into the house, and finished washing up when the phone rang. Laura said, "Tag, can you get the phone? I'm busy making gravy and can't leave the stove."

Usually Laura did what talking that needed to be done on the phone. Tag didn't like using it. He said, "Hello." After a pause, he said, "Yeah, this is Tag. What do you want?" Another pause, and finally he said, "I suppose we could be there at that time. You said tomorrow at ten o'clock. Goodbye."

"What was that all about?" asked Laura.

"That was Todd Holliday. He wants us to come to the bank at ten in the morning and bring our record books. Those people always have to snoop through your business, as if we weren't going to pay back the money that we borrow." Laura saw that Tag was not happy with the phone call. Laura had learned that if Tag was not happy, nobody was happy. She thought, *if I had only taken the phone call, I would have been able to present it to Tag a bit differently. I fear that he may go into the meeting tomorrow with a chip on his shoulder.*

The next day, as if an omen of the things to come, the morning dawned with a red sunrise. The day showed little of the sun, while a cold wind blew in from the north. Tag and Laura went to the bank. Mrs. Stahl ushered them promptly into Todd's office. Laura remembered it was different than the first time that she came to this bank. She was an eager schoolteacher, intent on borrowing $50.00. Now they were borrowing thousands of dollars.

Todd's father Ken, did his business in what might be called a cubbyhole with no door. Since that time, the bank had expanded and now Todd had his own office with a door.

Todd welcomed them. He got right down to business. "Tag and Laura, since the drought of a couple years ago, your operation has been falling behind further and further. The income of the ranch is unable to meet the demands of the annual real estate payment. It is now more dependent on the operation borrowing to meet that payment. You reduced the cow numbers to compensate for the drought, but now your income is insufficient to meet the loan obligations."

Todd paused. That was an opening for Tag to interrupt. "Are you trying to say that you want your money now? That you no longer intend to finance us if we don't come up with more money!"

"Basically, that is correct," replied Todd. "We cannot continue to finance an operation that is continually losing money. We have partnered with other financial institutions to provide funding for the real estate and the operations. Unless you come up with additional capital, we will no longer provide financing and will expect payment of your obligations."

Laura asked, "What time frame are you considering?"

Todd answered her, "We would prefer to have our money by December 31$^{s.t.}$. However, if it is necessary to liquidate the assets, we realize that more time would be needed. We will work with you, if that is the case."

Tag jumped up and started pounding on Todd's desk. "No banker is going to sell me out! I can remember when you worked on that ranch. You were no good then and you are still no good!"

Laura went to Tag's side. Grabbing him by the arm, she tried to pull him back. She pleaded with him, "Please Tag, please don't be angry. We can work it out." In order to break loose from her, he flung his arm back and she landed against the wall with a thump. She lay still, not saying anything.

Todd got up from his chair. In an even tone, he said, "Mr. Taggat, please leave my bank." At the same time he was getting up, he reached under the desk and pulled out a sawed off baseball bat. Once again he spoke. "Mr. Taggat, please leave my bank, now!"

Tag left, not waiting for Laura to join him. Todd heard the roar of a vehicle, which he presumed to be Tag in his truck.

He went to Laura. She was starting to moan. She said, "I'm sorry, Todd, I'm sorry." He helped her to her feet. Leaving the room, she spoke once again. "I will wait for him out front. Tag will be back for me. I'm sorry, Todd."

At noon, Todd left the bank and Laura was still waiting for Tag. When he came back at one, he stopped at Nick's Café. He purchased two sandwiches and brought them to Laura. He handed them to her and went to get her coffee. When Todd came back, he took her hands in his and said, "When Tag comes back, is it safe for you to go home with him? I have never seen a man so angry."

Laura nodded, "It will be all right. He will get over it and we will get through this money problem. You never said, but how much more money do we need to continue to operate?"

Todd didn't answer her. His thoughts were on something else. He remembered Laura when she lived in his parents' home when he was in high school. The things that he remembered and others spoke of were the softness of her hands. Today, her hands were as rough as the hands of a cowboy. He was amazed. Laura has been working hard to make the ranch a success. "Oh, excuse me, I was thinking of something else. I am thinking about $100,000 is needed."

Laura was silent. Todd observed her for a moment. He didn't wish to interrupt her thoughts. Others said that Laura always has a plan. Todd sensed that Laura was putting a plan together at this time. She looked up and said, "Thank you for the sandwiches, Todd. That was thoughtful of you. If you don't mind, I will stay here. Tag will soon come for me."

The bank employees were preparing to close the bank for the day. Todd came to Laura. "It is now four o'clock and we will be closing the bank in a few minutes. I have arranged for my wife Marilyn to meet us here at the bank and we will take you home. Is that all right with you?"

Laura nodded, but said nothing. She had shed a few tears and had been wringing her handkerchief in her hands for some time.

When Todd drove into the yard of the ranch, he was amazed at the shabbiness of the appearance of the ranch buildings. He hadn't been here since shortly after the death of TJ. At that time, the buildings were well painted and neat.

Laura got out of the car. Todd asked, "Will you be all right, or do you want us to stay with you for a while?"

"No, no," she replied. "I will be fine, and thank you for bringing me home. I'm sorry to be such a bother to you today."

"We were glad to do this for you. Give me a call when you can. We will see if we can work this out. None of us need to do anything rash at this time. Goodbye, Laura."

Laura had a light meal. She was exhausted, so she decided to go to bed early. She was preparing to go to bed, when the phone rang. When the caller identified himself as Sheriff Morgan, her heart skipped a bit. He said, "This is Sheriff Morgan. Is Tag there?"

"No, but I expect him soon. Is anything wrong? I could have him call you when he returns."

Sheriff Morgan replied, "I was hoping to catch him at home. I didn't want to alarm you, but I will give you the message. I spotted Charles Williams this evening. I thought that we had lost him forever. I will be patrolling in the Good Hope area tonight, but I wanted you to know. Be sure to lock your door. I will let you know if I learn anything more. Take care of yourself Laura."

Before Sheriff Morgan had finished his call, Laura was shaking. She relived Charles Williams' attack on her almost 25 years ago. *Oh, why isn't Tag here at this time?* Laura locked all the doors and checked the windows. She rechecked her revolver before she slid it under her pillow. Sleep did not come easy. She awakened at the slightest noise.

249

Laura would doze and then be awake, checking the alarm clock by her bed. She remembered back 25 years ago when her alarm clock was the only weapon that she had to ward off her intruder. She had struck him alongside of the head after biting him in the neck. Tonight, should Charles Williams come calling, she was prepared. She had slept with the revolver under her pillow for 25 years in anticipation of his return!

Suddenly, Laura was awakened. She looked at her clock and saw that it was 1:25 a.m. But, something was different. Car lights were shining in her bedroom window through the drapes. *Evidently, Tag has found his way home. But, these were different. These didn't display the same pattern that the lights of Tag's truck did when he came home after dark.* Laura got up and slipped on a robe. Sliding her hand under her pillow, she grasped her revolver. She flipped the safety in the off position and made her way to the living room.

Laura took a deep breath as she faced the front door. The lights of the vehicle no longer showed in the night. However, the yard light near the garage cast some light through the living room window. Laura could hear her heart pounding while she waited.

She heard the turning of the doorknob, but it did not click to indicate that it had been released. Suddenly, the door flew open as Laura heard the shattering of wood! The intruder had kicked the door in! It slammed against the wall! There he was, silhouetted in the frame of the doorway! He started forward! Laura yelled, "Stop! I will shoot! Stop! I have a gun!" The intruder continued to come forward in a lumbering manner. *Instantly, the thought flashed through her mind, 'Charles Williams, prepare to meet thy God.'* Laura didn't remember pulling the trigger, but she heard, bang, bang, bang! It was three quick shots! And then, the intruder was upon her, and the revolver slid from her hand. *She could only remember hearing herself scream!*

CHAPTER 18
THE CALL TO RETURN

Katie O'Neal had awakened earlier than usual this morning. It was the same morning of the events that the Taggat family was experiencing with Todd Holliday and the Cattleman's Bank. She had not slept well. She had a premonition that this was to be an unusual day. She looked out of her small second story apartment. The same morning dawned on Summit City that had dawned on the 99 Ranch. The sunrise was just as red. Katie shuddered when she heard the wind blowing in from the north. Last night, she had tossed and turned, while she pondered her relationship with Tag. It had been a month since Dr. Jessup had met with her and had basically given her an ultimatum. Either sever her relationship with Tag, or be terminated after six months of employment. She liked her job, but, she was unsure if she was able to convey to Tag what Dr. Jessup expected of her.

Katie dressed hurriedly and walked to Nick's Café to see her mother. Darla Donnelly had started working at Nick's shortly after Derk had died. It had provided her with some extra income and kept her busy as well. Occasionally, Katie would stop in and see her mother at work. Just being able to see her mother working was an encouragement. It provided the company of others, as well as preventing her mother from dwelling on the loss of her spouse.

When she entered the café, Darla had coffee waiting for Laura at a table. "Katie," she said, "I have good news. Nick has given Dan a job after school. He cleans up and helps with the dishes. Also, Nick is teaching him some cooking. It gives him some spending money, as well as prestige that he is helping with our finances."

"How are the boys adapting?" asked Katie.

"They are doing quite well, really. I am amazed at

251

how well they are doing." Darla reached across the table. She continued, "It is their sister that I am worried about. Katie, what is the matter? You don't appear to be eating very much. You seem a bit withdrawn. I hear things here at the café that people wouldn't say if they knew that I was your mother. Don't let Tag Taggat drag you down!"

Katie got up abruptly from the table. She slapped a dollar bill on the table. "That's for my coffee and the advice that you have given me. This town talks more about Tag Taggat and me than they do of the weather. I am fed up with this town and their gossip." Katie tugged on her coat and rushed out the door, running back to her apartment.

She managed to take a short nap before she had to be at work. Her work was the best part of her day. She could shut out the world on the other side of the front doors of the hospital. She could do what she was trained to do. If only she could monitor her personal life outside of the hospital as well.

Katie and one other nurse were on duty this night. Things went well, but they kept busy, so the time passed rather quickly. At 11:30 the night nurse came on duty and they exchanged information. That made it possible for the evening nurses to leave right at midnight.

Katie backed out of the parking lot. Immediately, she realized that she had made a mistake. She normally parked in one certain spot. Usually, in backing out she turned her wheel to the right and she would be on the street that would take her home. When she came to work in the afternoon, there was a vehicle parked where she normally parked, so she drove to another spot. Consequently, she left in her usual manner, but this time she came out of the lot that would put her on Main Street. This mental error would change her life completely. Had she gone home in her usual manner, she would have been in her apartment in less than five minutes. The wrong turn put Katie O'Neal on a life-changing path beyond her wildest dreams!

Katie came to The Corner Bar and she saw that Tag's truck was parked at the curb. Her first thought was, *would he come to see me tonight?* It was then that she saw Tag on his hands and knees, groping on the ground. Katie found a parking place nearby and went back to where Tag was, still on the ground. "Tag, what is the matter?"

Tag looked up. "Oh, Katie, I have lost my keys. I thought they might be on the ground."

Katie said, "Just a minute and I will get a flashlight. Did you see them fall to the ground?" Tag grunted, but he kept on scraping with his hands. Katie went to her car and retrieved her flashlight, shining it all around the truck. She looked in the ignition and on the seat. "Here, stand up, and we can look in your pockets." Though he stood, he could barely stand. It appeared that he had been drinking heavily. Katie searched all of his pockets. While she was searching him, he grabbed and kissed her. She hissed at him, "Stop it, Tag! I can't find your keys if you are trying to maul me!" She gave up and said, "Let's go inside and see if they are there."

Tag stumbled along with her and they entered the bar. Tag said, "Katie, let me buy you a drink. We will look for the keys tomorrow. Bartender, give us a drink." Tag pulled a roll of bills from his pocket and put a five-dollar bill on the bar.

Katie grabbed the bill and said, "No more to drink until we find your keys." She asked the others in the bar "Have any of you seen the keys to Tag's truck?" Everyone shook their head and continued with their drinking. Katie said, "I will look one more place. I will be right back." She went to the men's restroom. She looked around and spotted the keys under the sink. She put them in the pocket of her nurse's uniform and returned to the bar. Upon her return, she saw another drink in front of Tag. She grabbed the glass and poured it on the floor. "I said, nothing more to drink." She turned to the barkeeper.

"You heard me. Now give me back his money for that drink!" He sheepishly went to the cash register and returned with the money. "All right, Tag. I will take you home and you can come back tomorrow and look for the keys. Let's go." She started him toward the door. He shuffled along. After he went through the door, Katie turned and tossed the keys to the barkeeper. "Keep these until tomorrow."

When they got into her car, he asked, "Katie, are we going to your place?"

She lied to him. "No, it is late and as soon as I get you home, I have to go to work. You can come to my apartment another time." A ten minute drive brought them to the 99 Ranch. She saw that there were no lights burning in the ranch house. They neared the house and Katie said, "Now, Tag, let's be quiet so that we don't wake Laura."

Katie had to laugh. Tag tried to tiptoe along. He had his index finger to his lips and said, "Shh, we don't want to wake Laura. Shh, we don't want to wake Laura."

Katie went to the door and tried to open it, but it was locked. Tag had no keys, so she said, "The door is locked. I know where Laura hides the key to the front door. I will get a key." She remembered Laura showing her which rock she had hidden the key under.

She started around the corner of the house when she heard Tag mumble, "No one is going to lock me out of my house." That is when she heard the crashing of the door. Tag had put his foot into it, shattering the wood that held it. Katie heard Laura shouting and then the three shots being fired and the screaming of Laura.

Katie rushed to the house. She shouted, "Don't shoot! It's me, Katie! It's me, Katie!" Still remaining outside of the house, she reached around the corner of the doorway and turned on the light in the living room. Laura was still screaming. She saw Tag on the floor, but she could only see him, but not Laura. She spotted the gun along the wall, so the fear of being shot diminished. It was then that she observed Laura flailing her arms. Tag had fallen on her. Katie rushed inside and finding the gun, she put it in the sink in the kitchen. Going to Tag, Katie rolled him off of Laura. The flesh was torn where a bullet had pierced his shoulder near his neck. Blood was gushing out of the wound. Though three shots were fired, she didn't see any other wounds.

Once Laura was free of Tag, she looked down and saw all the blood that had spilled on her robe and nightgown. One more time she screamed and left the living room. Katie heard her in the bathroom, running the water.

Katie ran to the towel drawer. Grabbing towels she pressed them over the wound in Tag's shoulder, trying to slow the flow of blood. He was conscious. She told him, "Here, hold this tight to your shoulder. I need to call the rescue unit."

Katie started to dial the number. She experienced such shaking, that she tried to sit down to steady herself. She had worked some in the Emergency Room at Lincoln. Though she had helped treat gunshot wounds, it was nothing like this where she knew the individual. When she got through to the dispatcher, she said, "This is Katie O'Neal. I am at the 99 Ranch, the home of Tag Taggat. He has been shot in the area of the neck and shoulder. He is conscious, but he is intoxicated. I am a nurse and I will try to stop the bleeding. Also, notify the county sheriff. Is there anything else that you need to know?" There was a pause. "No, it was not self inflicted, but I do believe that it was accidental. The person that did the shooting is here. I am in no danger."

Katie returned to Tag. He was quite pale. He had lost a lot of blood. After a time, the Rescue Unit arrived. Right behind them was the sheriff. He came into the house and immediately asked, "Who is it? I was patrolling the area and saw the Rescue Unit with their flashing lights."

Katie said, "It is Tag. I need to go see about Laura." She went to the bathroom and tried the door, but it was locked. She could hear the water running. "Laura, open the door. It is Katie." Not getting any response, she used a device on her key chain for opening bathroom doors.

Laura was under the shower, running the water over herself and scrubbing away. Katie went to her. The water was ice cold. She had run all of the hot water out of the tank. Katie thought that Laura kept washing the blood from her skin, not being satisfied that she was clean. Katie shut the water off and dried Laura, trying to get her warm. Katie said, "Tag is going to be all right. Now I will find you some clothes and you can stay with me tonight. Stay here until I bring your clothes." By the time that she was dressed, the Rescue Unit had left with Tag.

Laura and Katie went to the living room. Katie said, "You are chilled. Let me fix you some tea, and then I will talk with the sheriff." A few minutes later, she had the tea ready for Laura. She sat at the kitchen table, staring into space.

Katie wrapped the gun in a cloth, taking it out to the sheriff. She handed the gun to Sheriff Morgan, saying, "Sheriff, knowing you, this is not as bad as you might think it to be. I want to take Laura home with me. She is in shock over this whole thing. She has not said a word since I last heard her scream. We will come to your office tomorrow morning. I think that perhaps she should have her attorney with her when she talks with you. I was outside when the shooting occurred. I do believe that she shot in fear, but at no time did she say his name. We will go now. Look around as much as you want, but turn the lights off when you leave."

The sheriff nodded and then added, "Miss O'Neal, you might want to have your attorney there as well. You and Laura Taggat are two of a kind. If this wasn't planned, then things fell into place quite smoothly. This could be the perfect murder, except for the fact that Laura missed her target by about six inches."

"Sheriff Morgan, Laura doesn't miss. She fired three shots. One hit him, where did the other two go? Instead of jumping to conclusions to solve this so-called perfect crime, you might want to do a little police work." Katie started to leave and then turned back. "Sheriff, feel free to use the phone in case you want to alert your deputy to watch my apartment, lest we skip the county. Goodnight, Sheriff."

Katie got Laura into the car. As soon as she could, she started the heater. Laura was still cold from her shower. When they arrived at her apartment, she had Laura undress. She found one of her own nightgowns for her to wear. Laura rubbed her hand over the fabric and as she looked up, she uttered her first words since the shooting. "This is pretty. Does Tag like to have you wear this when he stays with you? Katie, I know about you and Tag. You may not think that I do, but Katie O'Neal, I know. I followed him to Lincoln one time, so now I know that he is a drunk and an adulterer."

Ignoring Laura's remarks, Katie said, "Let's get you to bed, so you can warm up." Katie got her into the bed and covered her up. She was still cold, but Katie would come back later and try to warm her with her own body heat. She removed her uniform and put it to soak in the kitchen sink, hoping to get the blood out of the fabric. She called the hospital to see if there was any news regarding Tag's condition. The nurse did relate to Katie that he was still in surgery. It was now 4:00 a.m. when Katie slid under the covers to help provide some body heat to warm up Laura. Laura was asleep, but sleep would not come to Katie O'Neal!

After dozing briefly, Katie was awake at seven in the morning. She looked out. The morning promised a good day, a day of sunshine and warmth. Katie started the morning coffee before calling the B & B Feedlot. When she was connected with the receptionist in the office, she asked, "Is Ty Taggat available? This is Katie O'Neal in Summit City, Nebraska. I need to speak with Ty. This is an emergency." There was a pause, while the receptionist was talking. "Very well, I will wait a moment. Evidently I have caught him at the right time. Thank you for getting him."

Katie began, "Ty, this is Katie. Oh, Ty, can you come home? We need you here. Last night your mother shot Tag. It was an accident. However, it appears that he will recover. She thought him to be an intruder when he broke into the house. She is here with me, but she is still in shock. We will meet with the sheriff this morning. I will call her attorney to be present as well. Can you come?"

Ty responded, "I am sure that I c-c-can, but can you c-c-clear it up there for me to c-c-come? I am still on p-p-probation. Are you sure that I n-n-need to be there? It s-s-sounds like you have things under c-c-control. Tell me K-K-Katie, where were you when all this was t-t-taking place?"

"Ty, let's not get into all of this just now. I'm not happy that I was in the middle of all that took place, but I will explain when you come." Katie didn't want to upset Ty with all the details.

"All r-r-right," Ty said. "I will start to get things r-r-ready at this end. You m-m-make sure you get p-p-permission for my r-r-return. Goodbye, Katie."

"Goodbye, Ty." Katie hung up the phone, not looking forward to explaining to Ty her part in all that took place.

Katie had a cup of coffee. She was prepared to fix breakfast once Laura awakened. At eight o'clock she called Leon Kelly. "Mr. Kelly, this is Katie O'Neal. Have you heard the news of Tag Taggat being shot?" There was a pause as Leon indicated that he had heard the news. "Good," said Katie. "I was counting on the Summit City grapevine. Laura Taggat is asleep at my house. Can we meet with you at about nine this morning? I have called Tylor in Oklahoma. We really need him here. Laura is somewhat unnerved over the incident. Can you arrange for him to have clearance to enter the state? Preferably on a permanent basis, but at least temporarily until all of this is sorted out. Incidentally, I was at the ranch when Tag was shot, so the sheriff is interested in my story as well as Laura's. We will see you at nine, but the clearance of Tylor is top priority."

Katie went to see if Laura was awake. She found her awake, staring at the ceiling. Katie sat on the edge of the bed. Rubbing her arm, she smiled, and said, "Laura, I have some coffee and breakfast for you this morning. How are you feeling today?" Laura jerked her arm free and rolled on her side to face the wall away from Katie. Katie grabbed her by the shoulder and rolled her back so that she was facing Katie. "Not so fast! You shot Tag last night and now we need to face the music this morning! Get out of bed and get dressed. We have to be at Leon Kelly's office by nine this morning!" Katie turned and went to the kitchen to start breakfast.

The two ladies arrived at Leon Kelly's office at nine that morning. It took about all the patience that Katie could muster. Laura had been insolent toward Katie all morning and it continued, particularly while Katie was trying to tell Leon what happened last night. Finally, Leon said, "Mrs. Taggat, will you wait in the reception area while I cross exam Miss O'Neal." Laura went out and it was then that Leon said, "Miss O'Neal, Laura Taggat is my client. It might not be in the best interest that I represent the both of you. I am aware of your relationship with Mr. Taggat. From what I have heard, it is certainly not a healthy relationship. I suggest that you may want to find your own attorney to represent you. Incidentally, Judge Burns has signed a temporary hardship waiver for Tylor. He can be in the state for ten days, effective tomorrow morning. You may use my phone to give him a call. I'm sorry, but our interview is over."

Katie called the feedlot and left a message for Ty

259

that it was clear to come home for ten days. She then left the attorney's office and went to the hospital. Katie inquired at the front desk about Tag. Dr. Jessup came by and said, "Katie, come to the cafeteria and have a cup of coffee with me." Katie nodded and followed him to the cafeteria. They got their coffee and found a table that was rather secluded. Once they sat down, Katie began to weep. "Doctor, how is he? You were so right! Tag has brought me nothing but heartache, but I can't seem to help myself." She tried to wipe the tears from her eyes before she continued. "I want it to stop between us, but I don't know if I can with him hurt and everything."

Dr. Jessup said, "Katie, don't do anything just yet. Let him get better. Then he can't pull the old 'I am sick routine' on you. You can do it, now that you know it must be done. Sheriff Morgan has been asking a lot of questions. He did say that he was going to question you and Laura as soon as possible. You might want to see an attorney on this one."

The word attorney brought about more tears. Katie said, "I took Laura to see Leon Kelly. I thought that he could represent both of us, but he has refused. I was only trying to help Tag get home, but now people are thinking that I set him up for Laura to shoot. I wish Ty were here, he would understand. Why did I come back to this place anyway?"

"Katie, I will have our hospital attorney sit in with you. His name is Perry Anderson, and he represents about five hospitals around this area. He will see that you get a fair shake." The doctor paused, for he had another thought. "As to Tag, he is going to live, but he is going to lose a great deal of mobility in his right shoulder. What you thought was one bullet hole amounted to three entry wounds that you could have covered with a teacup. The three tore up a lot of muscle. At that range and with that accuracy, Laura could have directed those three shots anywhere she wanted. She wanted to stop him, not kill him. Your quick action saved his life. At least, he owes that much to you. Remind him of that when he starts to whine about your leaving him."

Katie said, "Thank you, Dr. Jessup. I need to go see the sheriff."

Dr. Jessup said, "Katie, if needed, I will be there for you to verify what your quick action did to save his life. One time, I told Tag that I hoped to see him on the operating table. At such time, I would search his body for a soul. Early this morning, I searched and found none. Perhaps another time I might find it if it is during the daylight hours. At three in the morning is not a good time to operate. Look after Laura, or at least until Tylor gets here."

The hearing went well, with all the attorneys and witnesses present. Sheriff Morgan understood the fear that Laura had exhibited when she shot her husband. She was presuming it to be Charles Williams that the sheriff had reported as being in the county. Charles Williams she feared. Tag Taggat she did not. After the hearing, Katie took her home with her and everything was fine with Laura. However, she wanted to go back to the ranch to get her clothes.

Katie convinced her to go to Nick's Café and spend some time with Darla Donnelly while Katie went for the clothes. She wanted Ty to oversee the cleaning up of the house before Laura returned. The huge splotch of blood on the living room carpet was a grim reminder of a fear filled night. Katie didn't go to work the night following the shooting. She didn't want to leave Laura alone, nor did she have any desire to be alone as well.

At six the next morning, Katie heard a knock on her door. There stood Ty. He asked, "Is coffee r-r-ready? I'm s-s-starved?"

CHAPTER 19
THE PLAN

Katie looked into Ty's eyes and reached out to hug him. "Oh, Ty, you are home, you are home. It was awful, just awful. Just hold me for a moment." Katie sobbed. The agony of the last 36 hours was being released. Ty held her, but rather awkwardly. Katie pulled from his arms and drying her eyes, she said, "Ty, give me a minute or two and I will fix you breakfast. Your mother is still sleeping." Katie began filling the coffeepot and pulling out items from the refrigerator. She turned to him and asked, "No eggs?"

He laughed and replied, "N-N-No eggs."

Katie asked, "Have you had any sleep at all?"

"I s-s-stopped at about two o'clock this m-m-morning and had a couple hours of r-r-rest. How is, Father?" Ty had taken a chair, while he waited for his breakfast.

"He will live, if that is what you are wondering. I talked with Dr. Jessup yesterday. He did indicate that he would lose some mobility in his right shoulder." Katie placed a mug of coffee in front of Ty.

He took a sip and asked, "What happened, K-K-Katie? What r-r-really happened? I need to know?"

Katie sat down near Ty. Taking his good hand, she held it and said, "Ty, I can't go through that again. Your mother and I told the sheriff everything. It would be best that you read the report to satisfy your curiosity. Right now, I don't think your mother or I can go through the horror of that night again, we just can't." She went back to the stove and started frying the bacon, while she put the first of the pancake batter on the grill.

Katie put the pancakes on Ty's plate. He asked, "When is M-M-Mama going home? She can't s-s-stay here until Father g-g-gets out of the hospital."

"Ty, the first thing that you need to do, now that you are

home, is to do something about the living room at the ranch. The front door needs to be repaired and the carpet replaced. There is a big splotch of Tag's blood in the middle. I don't want to seem bossy, but when your mother awakens and is fed, I have a plan for the day. Do you want to hear it?" asked Katie.

"Of course," said Ty. "I may v-v-veto it, but I will hear your p-p-plan."

"I don't think your mother should see the house in the state that it is in now. I propose that we leave her with one of the neighbors there at Good Hope so that you and I can get the house in order. I know that the bathroom is a mess besides those things that I mentioned. I was thinking that Cindy Holler might be good for Laura. What do you think?" asked Katie.

"No v-v-veto here," said Ty. "Get M-M-Mama up and let's get started."

Katie called Cindy Holler. She was glad to have Laura for the day. Katie had Ty stop at the Corner Bar to get the keys and retrieve Tag's truck. Katie drove her car back to her apartment. All of them went to the Holler Ranch to leave Laura for the day.

When Katie and Ty arrived at the 99 Ranch, Ty surveyed the damage to the front door. The door was okay, but the casing had been split out. Ty declared that he could repair it with some new boards, stain and varnish. The carpet was another matter. Ty asked, "K-K-Katie, do you have any suggestions r-r-regarding the c-c-carpet?" He was amazed at the size of the blood spot.

"The Mercantile in town handles carpet and they have their own installer. I think that it would be well to have the installer to measure the room. Then, we can go in and pick out what they have in stock. A situation like this, they might give it priority."

Ty nodded, "C-C-Call them." Ty went outside to look around. He observed that the ranch was in a state of deterioration. It had been almost three years since he had last seen the ranch. All he could do was to ask himself, *what has happened here?*

Katie came out. "They will send their installer out right away to measure the room. If we choose a pattern that they have in stock, it will be finished by tomorrow night. Otherwise, we will have to wait for them to have the carpet shipped in, and that would be about two weeks."

Ty said, "Let's get f-f-finished here. If we p-p-pick up Mama after d-d-dinner, we can look at carpet this afternoon. She needs to be in on the c-c-carpet choice." Katie nodded in agreement.

Katie cleaned the bathroom and gathered up the blood soaked garments of Laura's. She burned them in the trash barrel out near the garden plot. She looked over the fence, observing the cluster of weeds in the garden. Even though autumn was passing and frost had stopped the growing season, she saw that what had once been a flourishing garden spot, had produced nothing this year.

Katie had finished with her cleaning and had fixed dinner for the two of them. She had changed the bedding and washed what laundry that needed washing. She packed a small suitcase of Laura's things. Ty could come here to sleep, but Laura would stay with Katie until all evidence of the shooting was repaired. Katie went to the front door to call Ty for dinner. "My, you have made great progress. I never observed such skill when you lived here before. You have done so well, I will offer you dinner. However, I fear that the dinner does not measure up to your skill as a carpenter."

Ty smiled. He replied, "Katie, the f-f-feedlot has been a great l-l-learning experience. As far as your c-c-culinary ability, I have never had a b-b-bad meal from you. I take that b-b-back, your e-e-eggs are utterly inedible."

"I must agree," she said. "Even now, where you threw

those eggs in the backyard, nothing has grown to this day. Ty, what has happened to this ranch? I remember hoeing in the garden, but now, there is nothing but overgrown weeds. They are everywhere, even in the lawn."

Ty nodded. "I have n-n-noticed it too. The d-d-deterioration is unbelievable!" Tylor was silent; neither of them saying anything. "I have n-n-noticed the change in you as w-w-well. After this, how w-w-will it affect you?" Katie gasped! Ty quickly said, "I'm s-s-sorry. I should n-n-not have s-s-said that to you."

"No, that is fine." Katie continued, "I deserved that, and you are entitled to an answer as well. What I am about to tell you, I want you to hold me accountable. In the next few days, as soon as Tag is doing better, I intend to tell him that it is over between the two of us. I am finished! I have told Dr. Jessup as well that I am through with Tag. I am sorry of all the hurt that our relationship has caused. However, had I not been here the other night, Tag would have died."

Once again there was silence between them. It was then that Katie spoke, "I don't know what happened earlier in the day. Your mother said that Todd Holliday and his wife took her home after the bank closed. Maybe your mother will tell you. Evidently, Tag had been drinking all day. Why, I don't know, but something set him off. Come, let's eat before it turns into a bad meal."

They ate in silence, each pondering their earlier conversation. When finished, Katie did up the dishes and they went to get Laura at the Holler Ranch.

Arriving at the Mercantile, the three of them began to look at rolls of carpet. At each roll, Laura shook her head. Katie said, "Now, Laura, if we order from the samples, it will take two weeks before it can be installed. That is fine, because we want you to find a carpet that you will be happy with in the days to come." They continued to look, but none of the samples pleased Laura. Ty sat down on a roll of carpet in total disgust.

Katie said, "Laura, we have looked at every roll and sample of carpet in the store. What do you want?"

Laura pointed to a display of six-foot by eight-foot carpets. "I want one of those. We can lay it over the blood spot and that will be fine."

Ty jumped up, and asked, "Why, M-M-Mama, why?"

"The bank is going to foreclose on the ranch!" Then Laura clapped her hand over her mouth, as if she wasn't supposed to tell.

"Who said that M-M-Mama?" Ty demanded.

Laura looked ashamed for what she had said. She closed her eyes and shook her head.

Katie went to her. "Laura, Tylor needs to know. Was it Todd Holliday?" Laura nodded. She started to weep as Katie held her in her arms.

"That's all right. Tylor needed to know. He came here from Oklahoma to help you. Don't feel bad about telling us about the bank. Did Tag leave you at the bank and then Todd and his wife take you home?" Laura nodded again. Katie turned to Ty. "I think that we need to go to the bank. Do you agree?" He was stunned at the news. He could only nod at Katie's suggestion.

Going to the door of the Mercantile, Katie said to the sales clerk, "We will be back after we have made a decision. Thank you for your patience."

They walked to the bank and as they entered, Katie thought that Ty would ask to see Todd, but he was unable to speak. He nodded to Katie, as if to say 'you do the talking.' Katie asked, "Is Mr. Holliday available. Mrs. Taggat and her son Ty, have an urgent matter that they need to confer with him at this time." After Mrs. Stahl left, Katie said to Ty, "I will stay here while you do your business with Todd." Ty shook his head again.

Todd came out. He greeted the ladies and shook hands with Ty. "What can I do for you today? I'm glad to see you, Tylor. How is Tag doing?" Ty nodded to Katie.

Katie said, "Mr. Holliday, we were at the Mercantile looking to replace the carpet in the ranch house that had become soiled. Laura refused to have it replaced. She said that the bank was going to foreclose on the ranch. Is that true?"

Todd wondered why Katie was doing all the talking, but consented to answer her question. "Two days ago, I told Tag that we couldn't finance him another year. The operation was losing money each year. If that were the case, then it would be necessary for the Taggats to liquidate their holdings in order to pay the bank. Tag became quite upset and evidently spent the rest of the day drinking. Incidentally, the bank doesn't condone excessive drinking among our borrowers. I did indicate to Laura, at her request, that if $100,000 was injected into the operation, we would continue to serve them. However, because of Tag's belligerence, we no longer care to have him as a customer."

Katie then asked, "Even though $100,000 was brought into the ranch, you wouldn't work with the Taggats? Is there an alternative for them? Otherwise, they would have to find funding with a bank outside of Summit City."

It was then that Laura spoke up. Katie noted a certain gleam in her eye that had been absent the last two days. "Todd, would you do business with the 99 Ranch if we were to incorporate, provided that we were properly capitalized?"

"I would think so, but not if Tag was the operator of the corporation." Todd was emphatic that Tag was no longer welcome in his bank.

"How about if Tylor was the operator of the corporation?" questioned Laura. Immediately, Ty came to attention at what was going on in the office.

Before Ty could respond, Todd said, "We would gladly

268

welcome Tylor in that capacity. We are aware of his work record at the B & B Feedlot. One thing I failed to mention. No matter who you have running the operation, as long as we have one dollar loaned to the corporation, we want to have a member of the bank sitting on the corporation board. Think about this and get back to me. And Laura, I was out there yesterday afternoon. Replace the carpet. You don't want that reminder. Tell the carpet people that I will guarantee the payment." Todd stood up, as if to dismiss them. He shook everyone's hand and they left his office.

When they got out to the street, Laura said, "Let's go buy some carpet. I know just the one that I want. After that we will have pie and coffee at Nick's. Then it is time for Katie to go to work. Tylor and I will have one more stop to make before they shut this town down. After supper, Tylor and I will go see Tag."

After selecting the carpet, they drove to Nick's Café and had their pie and coffee. Laura said, "Tylor, you were awful quiet in Todd's office. What do you think about running the ranch? Are you up to the task?"

Tylor looked at his mother. "I want to thank you f-f-for the c-c-confidence. But, I would have to have free run of d-d-doing the hiring. My f-f-first and only choice for ranch f-f-foreman would be, Jim McCann. If I c-c-couldn't have Jim, then I w-w-wouldn't want the job."

"I'm glad you said that, Son," said Laura. "It is time that Jim returned to the ranch."

Laura went out to get in the truck. Katie was talking with her mother, while Ty was paying for the pie and coffee. She and Ty went out together. Katie said, "I'm thinking that the shock of the shooting has worn off. Laura Taggat is working out her plan. Now, someone needs to find the $100,000 to add to the pot." Ty laughed and nodded his head.

Katie said, "Drop me off at my apartment. I will go to

work tonight, but Ty, stay with your mother until I get off work. Help yourself with whatever is in the pantry."

Laura directed Tylor to Leon Kelly's law office. They entered the office. Looking around, Tylor noticed a ticker tape machine in the corner with the long ribbon of paper extending from the glass. Leon was reading the tape. Looking up he saw Tylor and Laura enter the office. Laura asked, "Are you going to abandon your law practice now that you are following the stock market?"

"No," he said, "but it certainly is beneficial in helping my clients with their estate planning. Hello Tylor, glad to see you back. What can I do for you folks today?"

"Well," said Laura, "there are a number of things. We want to incorporate the ranch. If we can get Tylor's probation revoked, we want him to run the ranch. It appears that Tag will not be able to handle it any longer. The other thing, as we incorporate, we need $100,000 to put into the corporation to appease the current creditors. This would probably be in the form of a personal note, independent of the corporation. Our stock would be collateral on the loan. I figure with your broad expanse of this estate planning, you might have someone looking for this type of investment."

Leon said, "Let's take this one step at a time. The incorporation, I would rather pass it on to another attorney. Karl Larson is a good attorney for setting up corporations. I see that my doing this and brokering the loan might cause some conflict, so I would say that you go with Karl."

Leon got up and went to the file cabinet. Pulling out a file, he brought it to the table where everyone was seated. "As far as the probation being revoked, we have three possible roadblocks. One is Karl Larson, the County Attorney. If we were to throw him the corporation bone, that would take care of him. The other two are Judge Burns and Sheriff Morgan. In all probability, Judge Burns will take Sheriff Morgan's recommendations. The sheriff has a tendency to get nervous. However, if I were to remind the sheriff that Tylor did find his grandson, and that you will have gainful employment, he might go along with the revocation. I am thinking that he has kept close tabs on your conduct in Oklahoma. Let me feel him out. We still have more than a week to work on him."

Leon got up and laid the file on his desk. He came back and sat down. "As to that much money that you need, it will be hard to come by. Unless of course, someone comes along that wants to invest in a loan at a little higher rate than the norm. Would you be willing to pay one point higher than what the bank would charge?"

Laura said, "I suppose, if that is the best that you can do. I know good and well that they can't get what the bank gives. I don't see that they would have that much risk, but see what you can do for us."

Leaving Leon Kelly's office, Tylor remarked to his mother, "You l-l-like what you have been doing. I have h-h-heard that Laura Taggat always has a p-p-plan. That is what you have been d-d-doing this afternoon. I am anxious to see your p-p-plan at work when we g-g-go see Father this evening."

Laura and Tylor opted to eat supper at Nick's Café that night. It was a pleasant fall evening, so they had walked to supper and then a short walk to the hospital. They had barely entered the hospital, when Katie came to them. "Tag is very upset that you have not come to see him. I told him that you have been in shock and just now recovering. I explained that you would probably come this evening. He is in a bit of pain, so please, please do not upset him. Keep in mind that I do have to stay here until midnight. I want it as calm as possible. If he gets too irritable, I will come to his room and take his temperature or do something to distract him."

Stepping into the room, they took note that Tag was

leaning back with his eyes closed. Laura whispered, "He is resting."

Tag opened his eyes and said, "I heard that."

Laura went to his side and grabbed his good hand with both of hers. She pulled it to her lips and kissed it. "Tag darling, I'm sorry for the hurt that I have caused you. Please forgive me. When you broke in, I thought that you was that awful Charles Williams. I was tempted to shoot point blank and have that dreadful man out of my life, but I just couldn't kill another human being. Tag, will you forgive me?"

Tag jerked his hand back. He said, "I will forgive you for not killing me. But with all this pain, I cannot forgive you for shooting me. You and that fool gun! How do I know you won't shoot me in the middle of the night?" He turned to Tylor. "And, what are you doing here? Did you think that I was going to die and you came for the funeral? Don't you wish! Get out of here, the whole lot of you! Can't you see that I'm in pain? Katie, Katie, get them out of here!"

Katie had been outside of the door, so she rushed to his side. "There, there, Mr. Taggat. Don't get so excited. Now calm down or I will have to have them leave. It is time for your pain medication, but if you take that, you won't be able to visit with them."

"I don't care," he bellowed. "I want them out of here."

Katie tried to reason with him. "But Mr.Taggat, they have just arrived. If they come back in the morning, will you feel like seeing them then?" He nodded and rolled to the side.

Katie went to Laura. She said, "I was afraid of this. He has been temperamental all evening. He will feel better in the morning. He is just in a lot of pain. I will give him his medication and it will put him out for a time." Katie then turned to Ty. "I sensed that Tag was not happy to see you. Perhaps it would be best at the next visit for Laura to come by herself. I will go for his medicine now." Leaving the room,

272

Katie saw that Tub Turner, the cattle buyer, had been outside of the room and probably heard Tag's outburst. She remembered that Tub Turner was the one that had spread so many stories about Ty in the days of him running the countryside.

Shortly after midnight, Katie returned from work. It had been a big day and she was glad to be home. Laura was already in bed. Ty left to go to the ranch as soon as she was home. Sleep came swiftly that night and when she awakened, she was startled at the time. The clock on her nightstand by the bed said five after nine. Laura was gone, but that was fine. Katie considered that now Laura had come to grips with the shooting. She had evidently made the coffee, but it was now lukewarm. Katie warmed it up and enjoyed the tranquility of the morning.

While Katie was sleeping, Laura had been busy. She had her coffee and then walked to the Dismal River. While sitting on the bench nearby, she planned her day. She asked God for direction for the day and that she could be at peace with Tag and he with her. After her time of prayer, she went to the hospital. She stepped into Tag's room and she saw that the nurse had brought his breakfast on a tray. Tag was struggling to eat with his left hand. She sensed his frustration in trying to keep the food on his fork.

"Good morning, Tag," she said and gave him a smile. "Here, let me give you a hand. First of all, let us straighten your covers and get you sitting up. Let's have you turn around and hang your feet over the side of the bed. That will make you more comfortable. I can feed you if you like, but let me try something different. I have trouble eating scrambled eggs with a fork on a good day. So, let me go to the kitchen and get you a tablespoon. Then, you can get a reasonable mouthful with the larger spoon. It isn't 'Emily Post,' but who cares." Laura left his room and returned with the tablespoon. "Here we are." After a time, Tag had his plate clear of food. "Now, wasn't that better?" She set the tray to the side, while Tag drank his coffee.

"As soon as you get the bandages off, you will be back to as good as new."

Tag looked at Laura. "Well, little Miss Sunshine, that isn't what that quack of a doctor tells me! He tells me that I will have very little mobility in that arm. You shot enough holes in that shoulder to throw a tomcat through it. I will be lucky enough to steady a fork so that I can cut my own meat. How are we going to live with the bank hot on our tail and me crippled up? You would have been better off if you had killed me."

"Tag, quit talking such nonsense!" Laura was infuriated. "The night of the shooting, I had no intention of killing anyone. When I aim a weapon at a target, I know where I will hit it. That night I knew where I was aiming. If you hadn't run into me, you would have had three more holes in that shoulder. You could have stopped the moment that I yelled, but you were so drunk you continued to blunder forward. As far as the bank being hot on our tail, I spent yesterday cutting some slack with the bank. If we can find someone to loan us $100,000, we can continue to operate and they won't sell us out. However, they do have some stipulations, which you might not like. With the added money, we will need to form a corporation and the bank will want to have one person on the corporate board. The bank will no longer work with you because of that ruckus with Todd the other day. We will have to hire a foreman or manager to run the ranch and answer to the corporate board. By way of the grapevine, I heard that when you left me sitting in the bank here at Summit City, you were trying to borrow money from the bank in Madden. What did they have to say?"

Tag looked sheepish. He said, "They turned me down. They said they had enough credit risks without taking on anymore." Tag looked down for a moment. He then looked up and asked, "Laura, who would loan us $100,000, and who could we get to manage the ranch? I can't work, but I can manage."

Laura answered, "Tag, I am working with Leon Kelly to raise the $100,000 at this time. The bank will not approve you as manager. You have a lot of contacts across the state and I know that there is something for you. You are not just sitting on the couch, but the bank will not permit you to manage. It is doubtful that we can find another bank to finance us. The bank said that they would accept Tylor as ranch manager."

Tag was furious! "I will not have that no-good kid running my ranch. Three years ago he was running with the dogs, and you want him to run the ranch! He isn't smart enough to open the gates for a ranch manager!"

"Stop it! Stop it right now! Since the day that I brought Tylor to the ranch, you have not shown an ounce of compassion toward that boy. He has loved you and honored you and tried to please you, but you gave him nothing! Absolutely nothing! Right now, he is the assistant manager of a custom feedlot with a 25,000-head capacity, and you call him no good! He may not talk very well, but he knows what he is talking about. Right now, if we can get his probation period revoked, he is the bank's choice as manager! Tag, I'm sorry to ruin your day, but I have work to do in order to get us solvent once again." Laura spun around and left Tag with his feet hanging over the edge of the bed.

Laura stopped at Leon Kelly's office to inquire about the loan and the revocation of Tylor's probation. Leon said, "I have an appointment later this morning with Sheriff Morgan and Judge Burns. I did have a brief conversation with Karl Larson about the corporation. He has no problem with shortening the probation. However, I am not having any luck on the loan."

Laura said, "I will leave now. I need to go to the bank and get money for the carpet. Keep working on the loan and I will see what I can do as well." Laura left and returned to

Katie's apartment. Katie was making up the bed when Laura came into the bedroom.

Laura started packing her clothes into the small suitcase that Katie had packed for her the day before. "What are you doing?" asked Katie.

"I'm going home, that is if you will take me." Laura snapped the lid shut on the suitcase. "I will make one stop at the bank to get money for the carpet and then if you will take me home, I will be out of your hair. I need to get my car and make a trip to Madden. Thank you for your hospitality, but I have things to do. Tag will be home in a few days. Seeing the pain that he is in, I will need to make him comfortable."

Katie said, "Let me change my clothes and comb my hair and I will take you to the bank."

Laura started for the door. "I don't have time to wait for you to do all that. I have things to do today. I will walk to the bank and you can pick me up at the Mercantile." Before Katie could respond, Laura was out the door and down the steps.

Laura knew exactly how much money she would need to pay for the carpet. She got the keys to her safety deposit boxes and counted out the cash, placing it in an envelope in her suitcase. She made the trip to the Mercantile and had completed her transaction for the carpet by the time Katie arrived.

On the way to the ranch, Laura was silent, impervious to any attempt of conversation that Katie tried to start. Before long, Katie gave up and she too remained silent. It was as if Laura was in another world. When they arrived at the ranch, Laura got out of the car. She went to her own car, placing her purse and suitcase in the backseat. She said, "Fix Tylor dinner. That is one of the things that I failed to teach him. I will be staying here tonight, and no, I don't want to see the carpet until this evening. Thanks for the ride." Laura left in a cloud of dust, headed toward the bridge that crossed the Dismal River.

Later that afternoon, Katie reported for work at her appointed time. She saw that Tag was to get out of bed and begin walking in the hall. She wanted to tell Tag that they would no longer be able to see one another, but was uncertain how to approach him. She decided it would be best if she conferred with Dr. Jessup in regard to the timing.

At about the same time that Katie was reporting for work, Laura entered the office of Leon Kelly. Leon greeted Laura in his outer office. "Laura, I have some reasonably good news. I have been meeting with Judge Burns and Sheriff Morgan. I didn't get everything that we had hoped for, but we did reach a compromise. I see it as a compromise that accomplishes what we intended and it also provides for the sheriff to save face. Tylor will still be on probation for the five-year period, but now he must reside in the State of Nebraska. Also, he will be prohibited from having any firearms. At any time he is to leave the state, he must have permission from the probationary officer. It still gives Sheriff Morgan the power that he desires, but will not use. He has no interest in staying up late at night to spy on Tylor." He asked, "Is that sufficient, Laura?" She nodded her head and smiled with satisfaction. She would have her son at home!

Laura reached into her purse and handed Leon a slip of paper. "Here is something I want you to put in your safe until we have the corporate papers. I had to personally guarantee the amount. I trust that it will be noted in the corporate minutes." It was a Cashier Check for $100,000 written on the Merchants Bank of Madden. "I trust that this check will assure me a seat as a director of the corporation."

Leon was shocked when he looked at the check. That certainly didn't take Laura long to raise the money. Who did Laura know in Barton County that would loan her that much money? Most of the people in Barton County that had that much money were other Taggats!

CHAPTER 20
A HEALING OF THE HEART

Tag was recovering from his wounds. Katie saw that he was to be dismissed tomorrow afternoon. Before she went on duty, she stopped in to see Dr. Jessup. He looked up from his desk when he saw that Katie was almost in tears when she approached. He spoke up, "Tell me Katie, what brings you to my office on the verge of tears? Or should I say, who?" He paused. "Let me guess, could it be, Tag Taggat?"

"Oh, Dr. Jessup, I promised you that I would tell Tag that we were through with one another. Now, I am not sure that I can do that, at least until he is well. I don't want to hurt his feelings."

Dr. Jessup turned red in the face with anger. "Katie, don't worry about his feelings, he has none. I have known him and done business with him for over 25 years, and he has no feelings! He will use you and abuse you until you are sucked dry. Tag will be leaving tomorrow afternoon, so I want you in here at nine in the morning to tell him it is over. You are not scheduled to work tomorrow evening, so you will not be around when he leaves."

"All right," Katie said, "but will you be there with me when I tell him?"

"Katie, I wasn't with you when all this began, and I won't be with you when it is over. However, I will be in the hall to assure you that he will not be abusive. That much I will do for you. Remember, nine o'clock tomorrow morning!"

After a sleepless night, Katie arrived at the hospital a little before nine. She entered Tag's room, prepared with a speech which she had rehearsed most of the night. She reached to close the door, but then she saw Laura by his bedside. Surprised, she said, "Oh, I didn't know that Laura was here. I will leave."

"No, no," Laura exclaimed. "They are letting Tag out early and I came to take him home. All of you have been so good to him. I fear that you may have spoiled him."

Katie was unsure of what to do now, but she determined that she had to act. Touching Laura's arm, she said, "Laura, if you will step outside for a moment, I have a few last minute instructions for Tag, now that he is going home. This may be the last opportunity to avail yourself of some of our fine hospital coffee." She moved Laura to the door and saw that she was going for coffee. She then closed the door.

Leaning against the door, she said, "Tag, it is over! It is over between the two of us. I don't want you to come to my apartment, nor do I want you to call me. It is over!"

Tag was getting angry. "Let me tell you something, you little tramp! It is never over until I say it is over! You will be back. You can't leave me alone. Just because Tylor has come back, you think you can dump me for him. Just don't you forget, he doesn't want you either! Why would he want you after you have been Tag Taggat's girlfriend? Go ahead and ask him, or better yet, ask his mother. Get out of here for now, but when I get well, I will be back at your door. Not only will I be there, but you will be glad when you hear me knocking!"

Katie ran from the room. Laura was not in the hallway and Katie ran for the front door. Blinded with tears, she failed to see the man coming in as she was going out. She bumped into him and he steadied her when she started to fall. He exclaimed, "Katie O'Neal, I wanted to see you, and here we are." It was then that he saw that she was crying. Taking her by the arm, he took her to a secluded area near the door. "Why are you crying? Has something terrible happened?" Then she realized whom she had bumped into. It was Pastor Roth of the Good Hope Community Church!

"I'm sorry," she said. "I wasn't watching where I was going. Please forgive me."

"That's fine, but you are obviously upset. Is something wrong? I was coming in to see Tag Taggat this morning. Is he all right?" Katie nodded. Pastor Roth continued, "I had heard that you were back in Summit City and I had hoped that I would see you in church. I remembered you coming with Laura some before you went off to school. Might we see you in church soon?"

Katie sharply answered back, "Why would you want to see a sinful person like me in your church? Surely you have heard of me and my reputation."

"Yes, Katie," Pastor Roth answered. "I have heard of your reputation. I have heard that you are an excellent nurse. I've also heard that through your nursing skills, you undoubtedly saved Mr. Taggat's life. As a pastor, I do not solicit gossip, but sometimes it hits me, a lot like slinging mud. If you are referring to your apparent illicit relationship with Mr. Taggat, yes, I am aware of that as well. Katie, I welcome all sinners in the church at Good Hope. Romans 3:23 'For all have sinned, and come short of the glory of God.' Some are saved by grace, while others choose not to be saved. But Katie, you have not told me why you are upset. Perhaps I can help you."

"It's Tag! I just came from his room and I told him it was over. I didn't want to see him again and to leave me alone. He laughed at me and said I would be back. I tried to live a good life when I was in Lincoln. I would go to church, but I come to Summit City and I fail. I have betrayed Laura's trust, but I can't help myself. I am a failure and I hate myself for it." Katie began to sob.

"Katie, let's go into this counseling room here to the side where we can be alone. Perhaps I can give you some hope." Pastor took Katie to the room, but he left the door open to avoid further gossip. "I have a few verses from the Bible that may explain what is happening. I can see that you are sincere in wanting to live a good life, but it doesn't last. Titus 3:5 'Not

281

by works of righteousness which we have done, but according to his mercy he saved us.' The 'he' here is Jesus Christ. He is the one to save Katie O'Neal, not Katie herself. Why do we feel bad about the sin in our lives? It is evident, as we read Romans 6:23 'For the wages of sin is death; but the gift of God is eternal life through Jesus Christ Our Lord.' Do you see this?"

"Will Jesus save me?" Katie asked. "Then, I can't save myself?"

"No, Katie, you can't, but someone else can." Pastor Roth continued. "Acts16:31 tells us, 'Believe on the Lord Jesus Christ, and thou shalt be saved.' He is the one to do the saving."

"I want to be saved, Pastor. I believe that Jesus has saved me." Katie paused, as if in thought. "But, what if I fail? Will I lose my salvation? Tag says that I will come back to him."

"Katie, you are still mortal and you will sin, but I John 1:9 reads, 'If we confess our sins, he is faithful and just to forgive us our sins, and to cleanse us from all unrighteousness.' Verse 10 continues, 'If we say that we have not sinned, we make him a liar, and his word is not in us.' Katie, Tag took advantage of you when he should have been protecting you. Tag is a domineering man. But keep in mind, I John 4:4 'Ye are of God, little children, and have overcome them: because greater is he that is in you, than he that is in the world.' Today you have made your first step toward a victorious life."

Katie dried her eyes and now had a smile on her face. "Thank you, Pastor. You have shown me how to have peace and confidence. I remember a song that you sang at your church when I went with Laura. It was called 'Burdens Are Lifted at Calvary.' How strange it is that it would come to mind just now."

Days are filled with sorrow and care,
Hearts are lonely and drear;

Burdens are lifted at Calvary--Jesus is very near.
Burdens are lifted at Calvary, Calvary, Calvary;
Burdens are lifted at Calvary--Jesus is very near.
(John M. Moore)

"I will leave you now to your thoughts," said Pastor Roth, getting up from his chair. "Should you have any questions, or if Tag insists on bothering you, please give me a call. I am happy for you. My wife and I have been praying for you, and we will continue to pray. I will go see Tag now. I have been praying that his heart might be softened to the things of God."

Katie continued to stay seated. "Pastor, I have the need to see Laura. Will you ask her to meet me here?"

"Certainly," he said, "but are you sure that you want to see her just now?" Katie nodded. She folded her hands and remained silent.

Pastor Roth left, and after a short time, Laura appeared at the door of the counseling room. Katie indicated for her to have a seat close by. Laura saw that she had been crying. She asked, "Katie, what is the matter? Pastor Roth said that you wanted to see me."

Katie fell to her knees and laid her head in Laura's lap and clasp Laura around the waist. "I'm sorry, Laura, I never meant to hurt you. I betrayed your trust, but you never brought me to account for the wrong I caused you. It was never meant to be this way, but it continued to escalate with Tag. I have told Tag that it is over, and I have asked God to forgive me. I have been assured by the words of the Bible that God has forgiven me, and now I am asking you to forgive me as well. My heart cannot bear the sorrow that I have caused you, when I came between you and Tag." Her tears continued to flow as she pleaded with Laura.

"Oh, Katie," sobbed Laura. She too had been brought to tears. "I fear that I didn't handle this very well myself. I didn't know how to stop Tag. I was at a loss as to how to deal with Tag's infidelity. Though I felt betrayed, I knew that you had not abandoned me, which has been evident since the shooting. I forgive you Katie. You have always been like a daughter to me. I am happy that you have found the 'peace' of God. This has given me the greatest joy!"

Katie said, "Thank you, Laura. Unfortunately, this has not been without consequences. I think it best that I not be in your home in the presence of Tag. I am determined to make a clean break. In fact, it might be best that I leave Summit City. There has been entirely too much heartache. I will miss you, Laura Taggat. You have been such an inspiration to me."

"I understand," said Laura, "and I shall miss you. Maybe it is for the best, I don't know, I just don't know."

Later, Laura brought Tag home. While he was resting, she went to the Dismal River to meditate about her time spent with Katie. She began to pray, "Father, I thank you for touching me today when Katie shared with me her new found faith. This is what I have been praying for since she first came into our home. I thank you that she has made the decision to remove herself from Tag and his dominion over her. It grieves me that apparently she will no longer be in my life as well. Help her in these days." Laura returned to the house to look after her husband.

CHAPTER 21
THE TWO-YEAR PLAN

Ty was busy, trying to get things organized, but he had two things that were heavy on his mind. Foremost was his need to call Bill Boyle to let him know of the situation that he was facing here at the 99 Ranch. If Bill would let him leave the feedlot to run the 99 Ranch, the second was to convince Uncle Jim to work as the foreman on the ranch once again. But, first things first.

Ty called Bill Boyle and explained the situation. Bill's response was, "Ty, you have been a good employee and I will miss you. I understand that you are needed there at home. Keep in mind, if you ever need a job, come on back. We have cattle in those new pens that you oversaw in the construction and everything is working perfect."

Ty replied, "Thanks for helping me l-l-learn about the feedlot b-b-business. I will be d-d-down to get my horse and g-g-gear within the n-n-next week. I will s-s-see you then. Thanks for everything. G-G-Goodbye."

Ty then drove out to the Bill Dolan Ranch to see Uncle Jim. When he drove in, he saw that Jim was riding into the corral astride his favorite horse. Ty walked to the corral where Dog greeted him. He was amazed at how happy Dog was to see him. Jim unsaddled his horse and after turning him loose in the corral, he came to greet Ty. They hugged one another and Jim asked, "How is Tag?"

Ty answered, "He is alive, b-b-but he won't get m-m-much use out of that r-r-right arm. Jim, I have c-c-come home to manage the 99 Ranch. The b-b-bank threatened to f-f-foreclose on the ranch. This is what t-t-triggered the events that ended in T-T-Tag being shot. I am sure you have heard the s-s-story by now. Mama has s-s-secured additional f-f-funding, but the bank won't w-w-work with Tag after he threatened T-T-

285

Todd. That is where I entered the p-p-picture. The r-r-ranch will be incorporated and I have agreed to b-b-be the m-m-manager, but only if you will c-c-come b-b-back as the foreman."

Jim took a while before answering. He scraped the edge of his boot in the powdery dirt of the corral. Finally, he looked up. "You say that Tag is out and has nothing to say about running the ranch?" Tylor nodded. "I will need to talk with Bill Dolan. He has been counting on me to take care of his cows. I will visit with him this afternoon and let you know." They began to walk toward the house, when Jim turned to Tylor and asked, "You are sure that Tag will not be running things?"

"Tag will be one of the d-d-directors on the board, as w-w-will Mama, Todd, Karl Larson and I. Each d-d-director will have one v-v-vote. Only Tag, Mama and I will own stock. Tag w-w-will have ninety shares, Mama eight shares and I w-w-will have one. Tag only wanted 99 shares issued instead of the usual 100, d-d-due to the f-f-fact of it b-b-being called the 99 Ranch. Mama got eight shares b-b-because she has b-b-brought in $100,000 of which she is liable. My one share will c-c-cost me $12,500, of which I will be w-w-working off to pay for at this t-t-time. Karl has indicated that it is a p-p-pretty tight document. The b-b-bank has had their attorney l-l-look it over as well."

Jim asked, "How is your mother doing with all this turmoil?"

Tylor replied, "She is d-d-doing well. She has worked hard to f-f-forestall this foreclosure in order to save the r-r-ranch."

Jim said, "I see Katie occasionally. I like Katie, but at times she remains a mystery to me, both good and bad. I understand that she is the one to save Tag from bleeding to death. If you see her, tell her hello for me. Tylor, I will check back with you after I talk with Bill Dolan."

Tylor didn't respond to Jim's comments about Katie. He

nodded his head and with a flip of his hand, he left the ranch.

Katie O'Neal left the hospital after she had made her peace with Laura. She was excited about her newfound faith. She wanted to share with her mother, so she stopped at Nick's Café. Katie saw that it was too early for the dinner crowd, but she was surprised that the café was empty. Nick was reading a paper at the counter. "Good morning, Nick. I stopped in to see Mother, is she here?"

"No," he said, "things were rather slow, so she went home for a few minutes. She is coming back at about eleven. Stick around if you like. I might even find you a cup of free coffee."

"Thank you, Nick, but I will be on my way. I may catch her at home. Otherwise, I will see her later." Katie left the café and continued to her mother's, which was close by. She stepped up on the porch and knocked once. She entered the house, calling out, "Mother, are you home?"

"Katie," Darla called out, "I am here in the laundry room, sorting clothes. I am glad you came. I have some good news. I will stop, so that we might visit. I just had a cup of coffee, but I will share another with you and tell you my news." She poured the coffee and brought out the cookie jar and set it in the middle of the table.

Katie asked, "What is the good news that you have for me? It must really be good to be so excited."

Darla said, "I'm getting married! Nick has asked me to marry him!"

Katie was shocked! "You mean, Nick at the café? He asked you to marry him? But, Mother, you haven't really known him that long. Are you sure that this is the right thing to do? Let me put it this way, do you love him?"

Darla laughed, "Katie, what does love have to do with it? I was madly in love with the first two men that I married and they made me miserable. Nick is kind and gentle and he

287

loves your brothers. Besides that, I like him. Maybe in time I will learn to love him."

"Mother, I am happy for you. I'm sorry that I questioned you. I'm sure that you and Nick will be happy. Have you set a date, or made any plans at this time?"

Darla replied, "No date, as of yet. We are just getting used to the idea. I realize that some people think that you should wait at least a year before you remarry, but I'm not really set on that notion. I know that you moved back to kind of help look out for the boys and me. So now, that will set you free to run off with that terrible Tag Taggat, if you so desire. Maybe you won't want him now that he has been crippled up from the shooting."

"Mother," said Katie. She paused before she continued. "This morning I told him that we are through and that I no longer wish to see him. In fact, now that you will soon be married, I may return to Lincoln or Omaha. I will try to start my life anew. Summit City seems to have a long memory when it comes to a person's past."

"I need to get back to the café," said Darla. "You never said why you stopped to see me, but I need to hurry. Sorry. Bye." Darla left, leaving Katie still sitting at the kitchen table. Katie had wanted to share with her mother how she had received Jesus Christ as her Savior. Also, that she and Laura had been reconciled. Perhaps she can share at another time, yes, perhaps at another time.

In another part of the county, Laura Taggat was trying to get Tag comfortable after the trip home from the hospital. Neither one had said anything about a visit from Katie O'Neal. However, Tag was confident that he had not seen the last of Katie. In retrospect, Laura was confident that Tag had indeed seen the last of Katie.

After dinner, Tag looked out the front window of the living room and saw a green truck drive through the yard and continue on to the barn. He thought that the truck looked familiar. After the occupant stepped out, it confirmed his first intuition. It was Jim McCann! He hollered at Laura, "Get me my boots. We have a trespasser on the ranch."

Laura brought him his boots and was helping him put them on, when she asked, "Who is trespassing, Tag?"

"It is Jim McCann, that's who! I told him to never come on this ranch again and here he is in broad daylight!"

It suddenly dawned upon Laura why Jim had left so suddenly at the time of TJ's death. It was Tag's doing. She got between Tag and the door. She said, "Tag, he will be working for Tylor here on the ranch. That was one of the stipulations Tylor requested, that Jim was to return as foreman."

"We'll see about that! Now get out of my way!" With his good hand, he backhanded her alongside of the head, knocking her to the floor. She lay there, stunned by the blow. He bellowed out, "Where's my hat?" He went out in the front yard, waiting for Laura to bring his hat.

Laura got up off the floor and yelled after him, "I'll get it for you." Going to the bedroom, she returned with his hat in her left hand. She opened the front door and flipped his hat into the air as if it was a pie tin. She said, "Here is your hat, go out and make a fool of yourself." Brandishing her handgun in her right hand, she fired three bullets into his hat before it fell to the ground. She said, "Tag, that is twice in the last two weeks that you have put me to the floor. Be careful, the next time you might be wearing that hat when I use it for target practice." Tag picked up his hat and stomped out of the yard. She heard his truck start up. Through the dust that he had stirred up, she saw the truck crossing the bridge of the Dismal River.

Jim was discussing with Tylor the conversation that he previously had with Bill Dolan, when they saw Tag leave the ranch. Jim explained that he was to receive a share of the current calf crop of the Dolan Ranch which they had initially agreed upon. Bill wanted to sell his cows and rent the ranch to the 99 Ranch, that is, exclusive of the buildings. Bill had plans to make the house a weekend retreat and hunting lodge during the fall hunting season.

Tylor said, "I n-n-need to come up with a b-b-budget for the ranch. Give m-m-me two weeks and have him c-c-come up with a figure for the annual use of the g-g-grass. I am p-p-presuming that we will have to f-f-fix the fence. Rather than him f-f-furnishing m-m-materials, we can furnish the m-m-materials as well. We are d-d-down in cow numbers here at the ranch. Suppose of his 75 cows, we t-t-take our choice of 50 head. Oh, and we g-g-get to keep Dog."

Meanwhile, Tag had arrived at Karl Larson's law office. Tag charged in and demanded, "I want to see Karl. This corporation thing is crazy."

Karl heard the commotion. "Come in, Tag. Is there a problem? I thought that we had covered about everything. The first notice of incorporation was printed in the paper this week."

"I won't live on the same ranch as Jim McCann. I didn't know he was part of the deal. Four years ago, I forbade him to step foot on my ranch and I see him there this afternoon." Tag slammed the desk with his good hand.

"Tylor was to have free rein in hiring the help and he chose Jim. Do you want to live somewhere else? You are receiving a monthly draw as it is now. I guess if you want to use that money for renting or buying a house, it is up to you. Your living in the present ranch house was part of your package. Tell me what you want and the board of directors will see how we can make you happy. Right now, you have kept your truck and Laura her car. Also, keep in mind, once the ranch becomes solvent, distributions will be made available to the stockholders, based upon the number of shares that are recorded on the books. Basically, that would be 90% for your share."

Two days later, the board of directors met and approved a $400 per month housing allowance for Tag and Laura, to run for a 10-year period. They would vacate the ranch house within a thirty-day period. Laura was saddened that she would be moving from the ranch. She and Tag would be looking for a house in Summit City. Now she was beginning to have second thoughts about the incorporation of the ranch. *Was this a ploy of Tag's to be closer to the liquor establishments, as well as Katie O'Neal?*

She could be at ease because of the latter. Tylor left for Oklahoma with the ranch truck and horse trailer to get his horse at the B & B Feedlot. That same day, Katie O'Neal loaded her belongings in her car and left town. She told only her mother and Dr. Jessup where she was going. She had made room in her car for the sewing machine that Laura had given her while she was still in high school. The only thing she left behind was the gossip and the sorrow of living in a small town in the Sandhills. However, the one intangible thing that she took with her was the love for the one man that she could not have. Would she ever find or care to find one to replace her love for Ty Taggat?

When Tylor returned with his belongings and his horse Domino from Oklahoma, he was excited to be back in the Sandhills of Nebraska. His mother greeted him when he unloaded Domino from the trailer. "Oh, Tylor, that is a beautiful animal, and so gentle! No wonder you returned to Oklahoma to reclaim him. Go ahead and put him away and I will fix you something to eat. I have been busy packing things. We did buy a house in Summit City. It is the one that Viola Teasdale lived in when I first met her. It is an older home, but has been well maintained."

Tylor said, "Domino has had a l-l-long trip, but when he has r-r-revived a bit, I w-w-will bring Katie out to l-l-look at him. She was excited when I tried to d-d-describe him to her."

291

"Oh," said Laura. "I guess you didn't know. Katie left town while you were in Oklahoma. Nobody seems to know where she went, or at least, no one is telling where she went. I'm sure that she told her mother, and possibly Dr. Jessup. She probably used him as a reference. Normally she would have told me, but for obvious reasons, she did not. I'm sorry that she felt the need to have left this way."

Laura witnessed the dejection on Tylor's face, but she also understood why Katie left. Towns like Summit City across America are units of caring and sharing, but they also know one another's secrets, that are remembered for years. *Perhaps in my own life, had I relocated to a larger city, it would have been different. In the city, people living next door have no idea of the makeup of your life, nor do they care. Had I left Summit City before Tylor was born, it would have certainly been easier for him. I could have passed myself off as a war-widow and possibly continued with my teaching. Choices, always life changing choices!*

While Laura was alone with her thoughts, Tylor had his own thoughts. He slowly led Domino to his new home. While Tylor made his way to the stable, he couldn't understand why Katie left. Before he was half way to the stable, it came to him why she left. *I had given her no reason to stay. My pride had prevented me from reaching out to her. But whenever I wanted to reach out, the image of my own father with his arm around Katie, still in her bathrobe, seemed to fill my head! There was Tag, standing bare footed at the door of her apartment, offering me a cup of coffee!*

Tylor jolted back to reality when his left hand gripped the doorknob of the door of the back porch. His thoughts of Katie and Tag had so engrossed him, that he was unaware of stabling his horse. He was not sure if he had fed and watered him. Tylor shook his head as if to clear away the cobwebs.

Laura had stopped to fix dinner for Tylor. He asked,

"M-M-Mama, what is Father d-d-doing these days?"

"He and Tub Turner seem to have a deal worked out at this time," she replied. "Tub will be buying fat cattle for the packing plants, so he will be working more to the southern part of the state. Tub wants Tag to be an order buyer for feeder cattle in the Sandhills. It will be good, and help him forget the ranch. Incidentally, I am leaving all of the furniture in the house for you and Jim. In all my married years, I have never had the opportunity to do much furniture shopping. Hannah Williams has some time off from Congress and is going to help me set up my house. She plans to have one bedroom as her home away from home. Leaving the ranch has been difficult for me, but this will give me a break. My milk cows were not a part of the corporation. Jim said that you were planning to have two family men to help on the ranch. Feel free to help yourself to the cows and chickens. I may ask for a little cream and eggs from time to time. I know some of the ranchers are no longer milking cows any more, but the fresh milk and cream were always so nice."

"Not to change the s-s-subject," Tylor said, "but, I have put t-t-together an operational packet for the n-n-next two years for the r-r-ranch. It includes our expenses and income, and j-j-just what we p-p-plan to do in the next 24 months. Can you c-c-call a meeting of the d-d-directors so that I can p-p-present this? Also, I want to make some p-p-purchases. I am planning to d-d-defer the sale of the calves. It will be t-t-tight for the cash f-f-flow, but it should c-c-come out all right as we get on schedule."

Laura commented, "It is good that you spent time at the feedlot. It certainly has prepared you for this responsibility. I don't expect that Tag will attend the director meetings unless he wants something. It is a matter of pride. Can you give me a clue of what you have in your plan?"

"Yes, yes I will," replied Tylor. "The c-c-calves this

year are not as h-h-heavy as they should be and the m-m-market is down. So, I plan to hold them over and f-f-feed them g-g-grain and hay. The hay crop is short, so I w-w-will save the hay for the c-c-calves. I have m-m-made a tentative deal with Carl Barnes' son-in-laws. You know the ones that m-m-married the t-t-twins. They farm a lot of c-c-corn and I will rent the c-c-cornstalks. If we run the c-c-cows there through the winter, it will s-s-save our hay. In the s-s-spring we will s-s-sell the calves that we winter over."

Laura said, "It sounds like a lot of work, but I guess that is why Todd and I had enough confidence in you to let you manage."

Tylor smiled at his mother's remark. "M-M-Mama, I don't like d-d-debt. I see the need for debt for major p-p-purchases, but I want to see this ranch d-d-debt free at some time d-d-during each year. You s-s-saw what excessive d-d-debt did to Father. I have h-h-heard from others how you struggled to k-k-keep the ranch solvent. I don't w-w-want it to happen again."

In the days that followed, and in the two years that followed the days, the 99 Ranch prospered. It prospered because the manager and those who worked with him saw that it did well because of their labors.

But Tylor also had a five-year plan. The plan was to start a feedlot. Tylor knew from his first day as manager where he would locate the feedlot. It was an area where the soil was firm; unlike much of the Sandhills with its porous soil. So, they built their first pen, with the intent to add more each year.

On a spring morning, Laura had the urge to go to the Dismal River in Summit City to pray. She sat on the bench and began to reflect of the events of the past. *I remember Galatians 5:22, 23 'But the fruit of the spirit is love, joy, peace, longsuffering, gentleness, goodness, faith, meekness, temperance.' In times of sorrow and despair, many people*

294

blame God for their woes, but fail to give Him the glory in the good times. Whether it be feast or famine; life or death; I see the goodness of God. Yes, I can now claim that I have witnessed God's goodness. I have found the 'Goodness, Goodness of God at the Dismal River.' It is my prayer that Tylor might find 'love' in his life, and that he might find a wife to cherish and to share his dreams. Just because the romances of Becca and Katie didn't materialize into matrimony, it doesn't mean that he should not marry. Lord, send him a wife to cherish and love, that I might say that he found 'Love, Love at the Dismal River.'

THE END